TO PAY A DEBT

The Teacher's Crooked Trail

BOOK 9
HOME ON THE RANGE SERIES

Rosie Bosse lives and writes on a ranch in northeast Kansas with her best friend and husband of many years. Her books intertwine history with fiction as she creates stories of the Old West. May you meet some new "friends" and revisit old ones in this ninth novel in her Home on the Range series.

TO PAY A DEBT

The Teacher's Crooked Trail

Rosie Bosse

Cover illustrated by Cynthia Martin

**POST ROCK
PUBLISHING**

POST ROCK
PUBLISHING

Post Rock Publishing
17055 Day Rd.
Onaga, KS 66521

www.rosiebosse.com

I dedicate this book to my spunky Irish grandmother, Catherine Feeney Gallagher. She left a comfortable life in Altoona, Pennsylvania to make a new home with my grandfather on the plains of Kansas.

The Little One-Room Schoolhouse

The little school is standing with its once busy door ajar,
  But no small feet rush up the steps for schooling anymore.
White or red, stone or wood, they all served their purpose well;
  And those who could afford it topped their school off with a bell.

So many kids from five on up to those in teenage years;
  They learned reading, writing, and 'rithmatic though some did it with tears.
The olders helped the youngers and their reading was aloud,
  And those who didn't want to learn would disrupt and clown around.

The bell would mark the start of school and it tolled again when class was out,
  And many feet rushed out the door to do chores at home, no doubt.
The teacher stayed to wipe the boards and scrub the daily dirt away,
  Then she'd close the door and hurry home to prepare another day.

Those schools were scattered everywhere, and the teachers did their best,
  To tend the fire, to sweep the floor, and to educate, no rest.
Through blizzards, rains, and scorching heat—the little schools stood proud.
  And even now some still remain, their old frames and walls to wow.

Some little schools outlived their time and are used as storage sheds.
They hold hay or fodder for the cows, where rodents make their beds.
A piece of scattered history, a few saved now and again—
Museums to show our children, how school was taught back then.

A treasured piece out of our past, a room with many scars
From heavy feet or pocketknives or the doodlings of art.
We pass them driving down the road and some we barely see,
While others beckon from their homes underneath the trees.

"Come back—come back and make me whole—fill up my walls again.
I still have use, I am still strong, open my door and do come in.
Let me tell you stories as I whisper through the wind
Come in, come in and stay awhile—let me be used again."

Rosie Bosse, 8/7/23

Prologue

One-Room Schoolhouses

The typical one-room schoolhouse is often depicted as a white or red wooden building. However, materials and color varied depending on the area and what was available. Sod, stone, and adobe were used where trees were scarce. If trees were available but a sawmill was not, the boards were hand-sawed.

Teachers in one-room schoolhouses had many expectations placed on them. They were required to arrive at the school early enough to start the wood or coal stove that kept the drafty building somewhat warm in the winter. They also pumped or drew the school's daily water from a well, a cistern, or even a creek. The cleanliness of the school was the responsibility of the teacher, and most took great pride in how their classrooms looked.

Because music was such an important part of society, the acquisition of a piano was an event to be celebrated. While not all schools could afford them, those that did used them with pride.

Running water and inside toilet facilities were not available in most schools in the early 1900s. Students and teachers used the outhouse placed on the school grounds.

It wasn't until the 1930s that inside plumbing became more common, and those were difficult years. Because of the terrible drought and the Great Depression, both water and money were in short supply nationwide. That in turn made inside toilets and running water a luxury that many could not afford until the 1940s and 1950s.

Still, the little schoolhouse was the pride of the community. It represented civilization and education. It also became the gathering place for the community. Dances and box suppers were held there. In some cases, church services even took place in the small building.

In the rural or isolated areas, the single teacher often boarded with a family. Depending on her contract, her room and board were paid by her or provided by the parents in the area. Either way, the family she stayed with was usually reimbursed, providing them with welcome income.

There were no set wages for rural teachers. They received pay based on what the community could support or was willing to pay. Teachers in the late 1800s were certainly not paid the $30 per month plus room and board that a cowhand received.

Most teachers in the late 1800s were single women. In fact, many teacher contracts dictated that once a woman married, she could no longer teach.

Many early teacher contracts did contain morality clauses. An example from an 1872 Illinois teacher contract for one-room schoolhouse teachers reads, "Women teachers who marry or engage in unseemly conduct will be dismissed." Of course, "unseemly conduct" was not defined. Instead it was left to the discretion of the rule-makers. Interestingly, the same set of rules states, "Men teachers may take one evening each week for courting purposes, or two evenings a week if they go to church regularly."

My maternal grandmother taught coalminers' children in the mountains around Altoona, Pennsylvania in the late 1800s. She was paid $7 per month. $2 of that amount was then paid to the family where she boarded.

History of the Chalkboard

The earliest chalkboards were rectangular, two-sided stone boards made from slate. The edges were often wrapped in leather or wood to protect the children's fingers from the sharpness of the stone. They were popular in early schools because slate was less expensive than pen or graphite and paper.

Slate is naturally available in most parts of the world including North America. The mining boom in the United States in the 1800s uncovered large amounts of this dark, metamorphic rock.

Intense heat and pressure inside the earth push tiny grains of clay and ash into the rock. When it is forced into layers, one side naturally becomes smoother.

Mining of this rock became more popular with the development and growth of the railroads. It was mined mostly in northeastern states and shipped by rail throughout the west to be used in the many schools that were opening there.

Penmanship was an important skill, and students were expected to master both printed and cursive writing. This was a challenge since light-colored slate pencils were used. Later, chalk was introduced. It was preferred over slate pencils because the writing was smoother. However, both smeared making it difficult to keep one's work neat. In addition, most schools provided students with one slate board to complete all their lessons. That meant their boards had to be checked and erased many times each day. This required much memorization, not only by the students, but also by the teacher.

Although many different mediums have been used as educational tools through the centuries, the first wall-mounted blackboard appeared in a geography classroom in Edinburgh, Scotland in 1801. The headmaster and geography teacher at the Old High School, James Pillans, is credited with this invention when he mounted a large piece of slate on his classroom wall. In September of that same year, a wall-mounted blackboard was first used by George Baron to teach mathematics at the United States Military Academy at West Point in New York. This was the first known use of a wall blackboard in the United States. Still, wall-mounted blackboards were considered a luxury. While they were popular with teachers, not all schools could afford them.

Blackboards changed little until the 1960s when the greenboard was introduced. It was comprised of a steel plate coated with a porcelain-based enamel. It was lighter and more durable than slate and was also thought to be easier on the eyes. In addition, the chalk powder showed less. Blackboards then became known as chalkboards.

While some chalkboards are giving way to whiteboards and more complex technologies, the invention of the early blackboard positively impacted classroom efficiency. Because of its cost and practicality, the chalkboard may never disappear completely.

Council Grove, Kansas

In 1825, a treaty was made with the Osage Indians to allow the Santa Fe Trail to go through their lands in the "Great American Desert." This important meeting took place in an area known as "The Grove" giving Council Grove, Kansas its first name. Grove was soon a gathering place for travelers and wagons trains as they moved West. It remained as such long before it ever became a town. Today, a portion of the Santa Fe Trail forms the main street in Council Grove.

The Post Office Oak tree was almost two hundred seventy years old when it died in 1990. The old tree was nearly eighty feet tall and was located in the campground used by those same emigrants. From 1825 through 1847 or even longer, a cavity at the base of the tree was used as a drop-off point for mail and letters. Messages were left for personal reasons, but the tree was also used to share general information regarding the conditions of the trail, Indian difficulties, and where to find the best water.

Council Grove's first postmaster was appointed in 1855. Because there was no post office, mail was handed out on the street or left on the floor of one of the stores for recipients to sort through.

The Last Chance Store was built on a corner lot in 1857. For a time, it was the "last chance" emigrants and freighters had to buy supplies in the six-hundred-mile stretch between Grove and Santa Fe in the Territory of New Mexico. Merchandise was purchased in Saint Louis and carried by boat to Westport Landing in present-day Kansas City. From there, mule teams pulled the heavy loads by wagon.

The settlement of Grove became a city of the third class (with class being determined by population) on April 30, 1869. In June of the following year, Council Grove held its first election.

As the traffic on the Santa Fe Trail slowed in the 1860s due to the wide reach of the railroads, cattle drives began, and Council Grove became known as a cowtown. By the early 1880s, Council Grove had nine grocery stores, two hardware stores, several dry goods stores, a bank, three livery stables, a lumber yard, four hotels, a steam-powered grist mill, and four churches. It also had three eating houses.

The Hays House, one of those restaurants, was built in 1857. It is the oldest continuously operating restaurant west of the Mississippi River.

Fort Laramie

Construction of the first Fort Laramie was begun on May 31, 1834. When it was completed, it was called Fort William after the three partners who built it. The fort was sold twice in its first two years. Jim Bridger and his partners first acquired it. He then sold it to the American Fur Company.

By 1841, the old logs had deteriorated. New walls were planned, this time from adobe. Limestone was collected from the nearby bluffs, broken, and calcined (cooked) in hot kilns. The extreme heat caused the limestone to chemically release carbon dioxide. The result was lime. The addition of sand, gravel, and water created a simple but hard concrete. The American Fur Company called the new post Fort John on the Laramie (River). However, the name was soon shortened to Fort Laramie.

From its early beginnings, Fort Laramie was a lightning rod of contact between the native and white populations, including emigrants headed further west. In 1849, Congress allotted $4000 to purchase the fort. This purchase coincided with the gold rush in California.

The traditional fort that military architect First Lieutenant Daniel P. Woodberry designed was never completed. This was due to cost and limited access to materials. Instead, the fort was enclosed on two sides instead of four. Houses filled the other two sides.

Lumber and firewood details traveled forty to fifty miles each way to acquire wood. Mule-drawn wagons hauled twenty-four logs at a time to the fort sawmill to supply the fort's wood needs. Five thousand cords of firewood alone were used each year. The task of sawing those logs into cords of wood was usually a job for prisoners. By 1876, the soldiers were cutting hay and hauling two tons of grain each day for the horses and mules housed at the post.

Fort Laramie was a vital outpost. Its military history spanned over forty-one years, and it became an important part of Western expansion. In its early years, the fort represented the last trace of civilization. Even in the 1860s, it was the last place on the edge of a wilderness to mail a letter, trade stock, and replenish supplies. It was also the location of what was said to be "the first skirmish of the Indian Wars." A young Lakota named Crazy Horse witnessed that skirmish. One wonders how that fight affected him.

When gold was discovered in 1862 in what would become the state of Montana, John M. Bozeman offered to lead gold seekers and emigrants on his new trail. It was three hundred fifty miles shorter than the Oregon Trail route. However, it cut through prime Lakota hunting ground. The United States Government not only ignored Bozeman's flagrant disregard for the First Treaty of Fort Laramie signed in 1851, it authorized the War Department to improve the trail. Three forts were then constructed on the Bozeman Trail for the travelers' protection. They were Fort Reno, Fort Phil Kearney, and Fort C. F. Smith. By 1866, the Bozeman Trail was known as "the Bloody Bozeman" due to the Indian depredations.

The Second Treaty of Fort Laramie was signed in 1868. It called for the withdrawal of all soldiers along the Bozeman Trail as well as the destruction of the three forts. It also stipulated the Lakota relinquish their territory along the Oregon Trail. That included all the land around Fort Laramie. The Lakota were to be confined to a reservation in the Black Hills, part of the Dakota Territory.

That same year, Lieutenant Colonel George A. Custer was ordered to investigate rumors of gold in the Black Hills, a complete violation of the new treaty. Gold was found and another gold rush was on. That led to more fighting including the Battle of the Rosebud. In 1877, the Lakota tribal leaders unwillingly surrendered their beloved Black Hills. They also relinquished their hunting rights outside their reservation in the Montana and Wyoming Territories.

The army abandoned Fort Laramie in 1890. The buildings and land were auctioned off to local citizens. More than fifty buildings were moved or torn down for wood. Today, Fort Laramie is a National Historic Site.

Concord Stagecoaches

Concord stagecoaches were built in Concord, New Hampshire. They were fitted with thorough brace springs. These leather straps supported the body of the coach and served as springs. The swinging of the straps followed the movement of the horses. While a spring suspension would jolt the coach up and down, the swinging motion made by the Concords caused them to be the most popular coaches on the Cheyenne to Deadwood line. In Mark Twain's 1861 book, *Roughing It*, he said the Concord Stagecoach was like "a cradle on wheels."

The crowded conditions inside the coaches caused Wells Fargo to post rules in each coach dictating passenger behavior. One of those rules read, "Gents guilty of unchivalrous behavior toward lady passengers will be put off the stage. It's a long walk back. A word to the wise is sufficient." Another read, "Forbidden topics of conversation are stagecoach robberies and Indian uprisings." Recommendations were even made regarding what to pack and carry. Passengers often rode with bags on their laps and mail pouches under their feet.

Stagecoaches were not as romantic as they are depicted in movies. They were rough, dirty, and loud. Horses were changed about every ten miles, but passengers were not encouraged to disembark except at scheduled stops. If he or she chose to get off and was left, the next stage might not be through again for up to a week—and the stranded passenger could catch that stage *only* if a seat was available.

The Deadwood Stage

The Cheyenne and Black Hills Stage and Express Line was better known as the Deadwood Stage. Its starting point was the Inter-Ocean Hotel in Cheyenne, Wyoming Territory. The route ended in Deadwood, Dakota Territory. An 1877 advertisement bragged of six-horse Concord coaches as well as the shortest, safest, and best route to Deadwood.

What it didn't tell you was all three seats inside the coaches were packed to capacity, with a minimum of three riders per seat. The passengers in the middle seats faced the front of the coach. Their knees interlocked with the front-seat passengers who faced toward the back.

The middle seats were the least comfortable as the only back support was a strap. The most desirable seats were in the back of the stage, facing forward. If one was lucky, he or she might even get a seat on the far side of the stage allowing support on two sides. In addition, at least two passengers rode on top behind the driver where they clung to the luggage and trunk railings. The ad also didn't mention the outlaws and thieves who wanted the riches the stage carried.

The Deadwood Stage Line was established in 1876 by Captain F. D. "Frank" Yates and his father-in-law, W. H. Brown. Prior attempts had been made to create a route from Cheyenne to Deadwood but failed due to the many Indian attacks. Even though the stage route violated the Fort Laramie Treaty, few white people cared. Most non-native residents believed the Indians had already negated the treaty with their attacks and killing of soldiers, settlers, and miners.

The stage line sold two times over the next four years. Its final owner was Russell Thorpe, Sr. who owned it until the last coach was driven over the route.

Daniel Boone May

Daniel Boone May was born in Missouri in 1852. He later moved with his family to Bourbon County in the Kansas Territory where he farmed for a time with his father. Around age twenty-four, Boone and two brothers headed west to work in the freight business in the Black Hills. The work was dangerous, but the pay was high.

The Cheyenne and Black Hills Stage and Express Company was always looking for shotgun riders (messengers) to guard their gold shipments. Boone was soon recruited to ride the rough line from Deadwood to Cheyenne. The trials of the outlaws he captured sometimes led to acquittals, and Boone decided it was better to kill the outlaws than capture them. He earned a reputation as a dangerous and tenacious man to have on your trail.

In mid-1878, Boone was appointed United States Deputy Marshal. This gave him more legal standing in the capture or killing of outlaws. After one controversial death, he and another federal agent were charged with murder. The mining agency Boone rode for wasn't pleased about having an accused murderer on their payroll. He and an employee who defended his actions were fired.

When the trial was finally held, the jury in Deadwood declared both lawmen "not guilty" without even leaving the jury box. The crowded courtroom cheered. Of course, this only made his death threats and attempted assassinations increase.

Shortly after the trial, Boone disappeared from the Black Hills never to return. He is said to have died of yellow fever in Rio de Janeiro, Brazil in 1910 at fifty-eight years of age. Lawman, gunman, sharpshooter, and feared adversary, Daniel Boone May left his mark in Black Hills' history.

George Lathrop, Bullwhacker, Muleskinner, and Stage Driver

George Lathrop made his living as a bullwhacker (driver of a freightwagon, usually with oxen), muleskinner (someone who drove mules—a muleskinner could outsmart or "skin" a mule and make it do as he wanted), and stage driver from Kansas to California and back to Wyoming. He survived several Indian attacks, including one where he was the only survivor. He was a driver on the Deadwood Stage from 1879 until the route ended in 1887. The route itself changed over the years to include additional towns including the new communities of Lusk, Douglas, and Buffalo.

There is a picture of Lathrop and the Deadwood Stage in "Wyoming Tales and Trails." It was taken in front of the Swan Land and Cattle Co., Ltd. in Chugwater in 1884. A sign on the porch indicates a public telephone is available. Swan spent $1000 to run a phone line from

Cheyenne to his ranch—the equivalent of $31,000 today. The first phone exchange in Cheyenne was installed in 1881.

By 1886, the railroad had spread through most of the area served by the stage line. Progress overrode necessity, and the eleven-year-old stage line was obsolete. George Lathrop drove the last coach away from the Inter-Ocean Hotel in Cheyenne on February 19, 1887.

Hole-in-the-Wall

Hole-in-the-Wall is a pass through an eroded portion of a tall, sandstone rock mesa to gain access to the valley inside. That valley is located between the Bighorn Mountains and the Red Wall about forty miles southwest of Kaycee, Wyoming.

The towering, red, sandstone bluffs called the Red Wall run twenty-five miles along the eastern flank of the Bighorns. At Willow Creek, the Red Wall turns west and follows the southern edge of the mountain range another twenty-five miles. The sheltered isolation of the Red Wall country was a haven for various Indian tribes long before the White Man appeared.

Hole-in-the-Wall was used as an outlaw hideout most frequently from the end of the Civil War in 1865 until around 1910. The Wild Bunch (Butch Cassidy, the Sundance Kid, and News Carver), Jesse James, the Logan Brothers, Jack Ketchum, and other outlaws all used it as a hideout. They were often inaccurately grouped together and called the Hole-in-the-Wall Gang. Even though they did have their own set of community rules and functioned in an agreed coalition, the gangs who used the hideout all operated separately.

The 1876 battle of United States troops with the Cheyenne in the Red Wall country led to the tribe's removal to the Southern Cheyenne Reservation in 1877 in what would become Oklahoma. It also opened the door to livestock production in the area. The Powder River and Red

Wall country became a cattleman's paradise. They grazed their cattle on the open range where the buffalo once roamed.

The little valley inside the high, rock walls had been a haven for outlaws seeking safety away from the prying eyes of the law for many years, and it remained so. Around forty outlaws kept a semi-permanent residence there year-round for another thirty to forty years.

In its early years, a nearby creek irrigated the valley floor, and the grassy plateau at the top of the three-hundred-fifty-foot bluff made it perfect for grazing personal livestock as well as stolen animals. The valleys and canyons to the west of the Red Wall provided additional hideouts and ample storage for loot. Hidden caves were also plentiful. The outlaw haven was about a day's ride by horseback to civilization and provided three-hundred-sixty-degree views from the top. In addition, the difficulty and narrowness of the main passage leading into the hideout made it easy to defend. The outlaws moved additional boulders to make the ascent slower, directing riders within easy firing range.

While there was never a set leader, the hideout had its own set of rules for survival. Each gang was bossed by the leader of that gang. Because of this, disputes between gangs were handled according to specific rules. Each gang also supplied its own food and livestock. Of course, stealing from each other was not acceptable. Each gang built their own cabins according to need. They also built a community stable and a corral for livestock as well as other facilities to make their lives there more pleasant. From the safety of this hideout, each gang could plan activities without interference from the other gangs.

During its more than fifty years of use, no lawman was ever able to successfully enter and capture outlaws in the hideout. Neither was any lawman able to infiltrate the gangs there—at least none who lived to tell about it.

Of course, all was not peace and tranquility. Those who were there stayed because they were killers and thieves, living outside the laws of the time.

I read nothing about women inside the high walls. However, with the amount of time and number of outlaws who lived there both full and part time, logic says some women were likely there.

By the early 1900s, trains and banks were more difficult to rob. In addition, the isolation of Hole-in-the-Wall lost its appeal. The old hideout was eventually abandoned by the last of the outlaws.

Today, Hole-in-the-Wall is still difficult to reach. It is on private property and is now a part of the Willow Creek Ranch, a working cattle and horse operation. Tours are available to ranch guests.

In this novel, I took some liberty with community rules as well as my depiction of women inside Hole-in-the-Wall. Of course, this is fiction, so I get to do that!

Register Cliff

Register Cliff is located south of Guernsey, Wyoming on the south bank of the North Platte River. Located about fifteen miles northwest of Fort Laramie, it was the first resting stop for travelers on the Oregon, California, and Mormon Trails after leaving the small fort.

It is a chalky, limestone cliff that rises over one hundred feet above the North Platte River valley. Its high walls provided not only a little reprieve from the wind and sun, but the softer surface of the rock also allowed travelers to carve their names, dates, and even messages into the rock. In addition, the river watered the grasses of the valley providing ample feed for livestock.

The ruts of the old Oregon Trail are visible just below the cliff. That trail was sometimes called, "The Longest Graveyard." Of the estimated fifty-five thousand immigrants who traveled the Oregon Trail in the peak years alone, around five thousand died.

While many of the carvings on Register Cliff are from the 1840s and 1850s, other dates before and after are also carved there. Unfortunately, the softness of the rock makes it prone to erosion. Some of the earliest names are now lost. In addition, modern graffiti is a problem.

Because Register Cliff was such a popular stopping point, a small trading post was once located there. It became a Pony Express stop in 1861 and later a stage station. Also known as Sand Point Station, the tall out-cropping was a stopping point for thousands of people.

Just a few miles to the west is another historic site, Deep Rut Hill. Those ruts in the Guernsey State Park are the deepest ruts on the old Oregon Trail.

Charles Guernsey, an early cattleman in Wyoming, began his ranch a short distance from Register Cliff in the 1890s. He ranched there until 1926 when he sold to the Henry Frederick family. Descendants of the Frederick family still ranch there today.

A cave was blasted at the base of the cliff to store potatoes and other produce produced on the Frederick Ranch in the late 1920s. The stone walls provided cool protection in the summer and prevented the produce from freezing in the winter. Later, the large cave was used for machine storage. Henry Frederick donated Register Cliff to the state of Wyoming in 1932.

The next time you pass through Guernsey, Wyoming, take time to visit Register Cliff. Just maybe you will recognize some of the names recorded there.

Kaycee, Wyoming and the Johnson County War

John Nolan started his KC ranch on the Powder River in the late 1800s. He was the first homesteader in the area. By the late 1890s, Nate Champion and Nick Ray were running the ranch and owned his KC brand.

The ranch was claimed by some to be the headquarters for rustlers who were stealing cattle and hiding them in Hole-in-the-Wall. On April 10, 1892, fifty men, including Texas gunfighters hired by local cattle barons and supported by the Wyoming Stockgrowers Association, surrounded the ranch. They captured two passersby and bushwacked Nick Ray when he stepped out of the house. Champion dragged his dying friend inside. He fought the invaders off for nearly a day until they set the house on fire. Champion fled outside where he was killed.

Were Champion and Ray really rustlers or was this a ploy to scare the smaller ranchers into giving up their land to the large cowmen? The two hundred cowboys and citizens who caught and surrounded the gunmen near Buffalo believed the latter. The killers were saved from death by soldiers from a nearby fort. Most were put on a train to Texas. No charges were ever filed against any of the attackers.

Ned Champion kept a record of events the day he died. He slipped the journal into his vest pocket when he fled the burning house. His last entry was, "The house is all fired. Goodbye boys, if I never seen you again."

Champion was said to be a top hand and was known for his honesty. A brass statue of him stands in Buffalo, Wyoming, a tribute to a man who died fighting for the small rancher.

In 1896, Jim and Jesse Potts built a blacksmith shop just east of the burned cabin where Champion died. This was the first building in what would become the town of Kaycee. The townspeople called their town KC after Champion's KC brand. However, when a post office was added in the late 1890s, the government would not accept initials for a post office. The town's name became Kaycee.

The Inter-Ocean Hotel and Barney Ford

The Inter-Ocean Hotel in Cheyenne was the second such hotel built and owned by Barney Ford, ex-slave and successful businessman. It was completed in September of 1875. (The first Inter-Ocean Hotel was in Denver and was completed in 1874.) The hotel was said by some to be the finest hotel between Saint Louis and San Francisco.

The new Cheyenne hotel advertised rooms for one hundred fifty guests and a dining room that seated one hundred eighty. It was known as the finest hotel in Cheyenne and even had an electric bell system that connected each room to the front desk. In addition, it offered a gentlemen's reading room, a ladies' dining room, a gentlemen's club or saloon, a billiard hall, and a barber shop. Its saloon was busy and was popular with miners returning from Deadwood with bags of gold dust.

Financial overextension and business losses combined with the Panic of 1873 caused Ford to face bankruptcy. He sold his Inter-Ocean Hotel in Cheyenne in May of 1878. As he prepared to leave Cheyenne a second time and move to San Francisco, the city of Cheyenne bid him farewell with a parade. A newspaper article praised him and said, "The good wishes of our citizens accompany himself and his family to their new home." Barney Ford was going to be missed.

Ford's tenacity and fortitude did not allow him to stay down long. By 1880, he was in Breckenridge, Colorado where he opened Ford's Restaurant and Chop House. There he restored his fortune. He sold his business ventures in Breckenridge in 1889 for $20,000—a value of over $575,000 today. In 1890, Ford and his wife returned to Denver where he lived out his life.

Barney Ford was a firm believer in equality and freedom for all. He worked tirelessly through his lifetime against slavery and for the rights of black men and women. He also believed the American West offered opportunities to all men, regardless of their skin color. Ford is quoted, "Here he stands for what he is worth. Here he can occupy any position for which nature and education have fitted him."

Thank you for choosing to read my novels. May this ninth novel in my Home on the Range series be one that draws you in, makes you think, and maybe even makes you laugh from time to time. And may you decide to read it more than once. After all, a "keeper" is a book that should be enjoyed multiple times.

Rosie Bosse, Author
Living and Writing on a Ranch in the Middle of Nowhere
rosiebosse.com

Altoona, Pennsylvania
Wednesday, May 28, 1879

CHAPTER 1

MISS WHITMAN

ANNA WHITMAN STOOD IN THE DOORWAY OF THE little schoolhouse and waved as her students raced down the rough lane that led away from the school. Family members and friends ran together before they split in various directions toward their homes.

A small boy stopped. He walked back and smiled shyly at his teacher. Tommy's face was often dirty, and his yellow hair was shaggy. However, his big, brown eyes were always sparkling. Anna's heart melted as she leaned over to hug the five-year-old boy.

"You know, Tommy. I wasn't hungry at dinner. I didn't even eat my sandwich. Would you like to take it home with you? I have some work to do here to clean up. By the time I finish, it will be time to fix supper."

Tommy was quiet as he looked at the sandwich his teacher held out to him. He slowly nodded.

"I reckon that will be all right, Miss Whitman."

He carefully reached for the sandwich. He stared at it almost reverently.

"I'll save it till I get home in case my little brother is hungry." He smiled at his teacher before he carefully slid the sandwich into his pocket. He took it out once to smell it, paused, and slipped it back in.

Miss Whitman handed Tommy an apple as well. She had been saving it for a snack after school, but she knew the little boy and his family never had enough to eat.

"You eat that on the way home, Tommy. I dropped it today and those bruises will go bad quickly if it isn't gobbled right up."

Tommy grinned and turned to race down the lane. He waved over his shoulder and shouted as he ran, "Thank you, Miss Whitman! You are the best teacher in the world!"

The small first grader traveled nearly five miles to school each way, and still had chores to do when he arrived home at night. His father usually met him partway after school with the wagon and team, but he still walked a long way for such a small boy.

Miss Whitman smiled and waved at Tommy as she turned around. The smile remained on her face as she looked around the now quiet room. The walls of the one-room schoolhouse were covered with pictures and writings her students had completed. The younger children, especially, were excited to show their parents all their creations. Today was the last day of school, but everyone would be back on Friday for their grade cards.

Everyone would bring a dish of some sort and that food would be set out for a picnic dinner.

She sighed as she looked around the room. Even though she was ready for summer break, the end of the school year was always bittersweet for Anna. *I love teaching* she thought as she straightened the desks and began to sweep the floor.

Anna was on a full-year contract. That meant she was expected to do family visits and tutoring as needed throughout the summer. She didn't mind. That was one of her favorite parts of teaching. She loved meeting the parents and working with the children one-on-one.

In addition, the school building was her responsibility to keep clean. That too was part of her contract and had been since she took the teaching job six years ago at eighteen years of age.

The first year had been particularly difficult. Not only did she have to learn all the ins and outs of teaching, but every young man and his mother thought she was looking for a husband.

Anna rolled her blue eyes. "A man is the last thing I need." She thought of Wilbur Jackson and she scowled. The man reminded her of a rat. His spectacles hung on the end of his beak-like nose, and he leaned forward to peer as he walked. Narrow shoulders, thinning hair, and a constant frown made him an unattractive man. Besides, he was old enough to be her father. The fact that he was the wealthiest man in their small town didn't impress Anna.

Wilbur, on the other hand, was hoping Anna's head would be turned by his money. He had been persistent that first year. After his romantic overtures had been refused multiple times, the vindictive little man became rude and overbearing.

Anna poured some of the water she had heating on the stove into a bucket. She didn't want her long skirt to get dirty, so she tied it up. She hummed as she began to mop the floor.

The large chalkboard at the front of the room was a new addition this year, and most of the students loved it. *Well, maybe not the older boys.* Anna sighed. Once it was time to plant, it was difficult to keep the big boys in school, let alone encourage them to write in front of the class.

Anna wiped the chalkboard down. She dumped the water and refilled her bucket. She hadn't made it far when feet stomped up the steps and Wilbur Jackson appeared.

Anna quickly loosened her skirts and dropped the bottom of her dress down. She was angry at the man for barging in without knocking, but she tried to hold her temper.

"It's about time you cleaned this building up. Mrs. Cash in town reported to me that the children were spending their days in a pigsty. I decided to come by today to see for myself."

Wilbur Jackson leaned forward as he stared around the room.

"Yes, she was correct. This room is quite filthy." He wiped his hand across one of the slate boards laying on the corner of a student's desk. "Quite filthy indeed."

Anna tried to control her temper. However, heat, exhaustion, and frustration overcame her good sense.

"Is there a reason you stopped by today, Mr. Jackson? If it is just to complain, I do have a second mop. I would be glad to loan it to you."

Wilbur Jackson glared at her. "That mouth of yours is going to get you fired. I have been keeping a record of your insolence, you know. I have it all written down, and I will be presenting it at the parents' meeting this evening."

When Anna looked startled, Wilbur gloated as he nodded his head vigorously. "Oh yes. Tonight is the fourth Wednesday of the month which is when the parent board meets. It is time for your evaluation, and I am planning to make this your last year. I have found a very suitable candidate who has much stronger credentials than you. I plan to have her start on June first. And you, Miss High and Mighty—you will be out of a job."

Anna slammed the mop into the bucket. The dirty water splashed on her dress, but it also splashed on Wilbur Jackson's shiny shoes. He jumped back with a startled cry and Anna followed him.

"You go ahead and fire me, but I have a twelve-month contract. That legal and binding document was crafted by you, and we both signed it. It says you will pay me to work with students and parents over the summer.

"You want your new teacher to make parent visits? Fine. You may pay me while I relax with a cold glass of lemonade."

Wilbur Jackson pulled himself straighter and tried to intimidate the angry woman in front of him. He finally sputtered, "That contract doesn't mean anything. I'm the one who pays your salary, and I say you are fired without pay."

Anna pulled the mop back out of the bucket. When she started toward him, Wilbur ran for the door.

"Oh, you just wait! I will be sharing this with the board tonight. I know they will all side with me." The frightened little man was almost running when he reached the doorway.

Anna grabbed the bucket and threw the dirty water out the door. It splashed in the powdery dirt and sprayed up on Wilbur Jackson as he ran down the lane.

Even though it was warm, she slammed the door shut. She walked slowly to the front of the room. She sat down at her desk and stared around the pleasant classroom.

Heat and humidity always made Anna's hair curl and now it was falling out of the tight bun she wore to school. Ringlets of bright red hair were trailing down her neck. Anna Whitman was a pretty woman, but right now, she was an angry one.

"What a despicable little worm of a man. I am sure I will be fired and then what will I do? He will have to pay me over the summer, but come September first, I will be unemployed. Flory barely makes enough money to cover her share of our rent let alone pay for any food. We will be kicked out of our small flat and will be living on the streets."

Anna slowly stood. She hung the bucket on its nail and hurried for the door. "I have cookies to make, and I need to be back here by six thirty tonight. Drat that man.

"I'm sure no parent wants to meet on the last day of school when they will all be in here on Friday. This was all old Rat Face's idea, and now the rest of us must oblige him."

CHAPTER 2

PREPARATIONS

F LORY WASN'T HOME BY THE TIME ANNA FINISHED THE cookies, so she left her sister a note. Where Anna was tall and slim, Flory was short and curvy. Her younger sister had more suiters than she had time for, and Anna found it all quite exhausting. Flory kept company with two or three men at a time, and each thought he was the love of her life.

Anna shook her head. "Flory just breaks their hearts and leaves them in piles on the floor. I have tried to talk to her, but she just giggles and tosses her blond curls." She looked up at the two smiling people in the picture frame on their wall. "Mother and Father, I wish you had lived longer. I'm afraid I did a terrible job raising Flora. She is wild, brash, and uninhibited. I am so afraid she is going to get into trouble."

Anna was five years older than Flora. While the two sisters were close, their personalities were very different. Anna was careful. She barely made a move without planning while Flora was impetuous and flighty.

Their parents had died in a buggy accident ten years earlier. Fourteen-year-old Anna took a job at the shoe factory to support the two of them. The foreman hadn't wanted to hire her, but Anna soon won him over with her willingness to work and her cheerful attitude.

It wasn't long before she was promoted to the front office where she greeted the customers and measured their feet.

In the summer, nine-year-old Flora stayed with a neighbor in the mornings. In the afternoons, she laced shoes. It was dull work, but it kept her out of trouble and brought in a little more money. During the school year, Flora, or Flory as Anna called her, attended school.

The teacher, Miss Geissler, knew Anna was bright. She sent home books and schoolwork for her to do so she could continue her schooling. It pained her to see a girl as bright as Anna working instead of attending classes. She also had been Anna's inspiration to teach.

When Miss Geissler married in 1873, she recommended that eighteen-year-old Anna take her place. Some of the parents were apprehensive, but Anna surprised everyone, including herself. Now six years later, she was being fired.

"But am I sure I will be fired? Oh yes. Wilbur Jackson gets whatever he wants because his money provides most of the funding for this school. I certainly will be fired even if the parent board doesn't agree."

Anna hurried to the school. Each girl had brought a scrap of fabric from home last week. Anna helped the girls to cross stitch their names into the small pieces of fabric.

The boys had cut and sanded thin slabs of a small tree. Each carved his name on the bottom of the smooth, curved disk. Those plates and cloths would be used this evening to serve the cookies.

The room was cheery, and the cookies smelled wonderful when the parents arrived.

CHAPTER 3

A Horrible Accusation

ANNA SERVED THE PARENTS AS THEY ARRIVED. WHILE she was up and moving around, Wilbur Jackson rushed in. He took his place at the front of the room—in Anna's chair.

Looking unperturbed, Anna took a seat to the side and remained calm as the excited little man called the meeting to order.

"As many of you know, we are here tonight to discuss the future of our little school, and to decide who we want to hire for next year. Miss Whitman does have a contract through August. However, in lieu of information shared with me, I am suggesting she not be rehired for next year."

There was a stunned silence as the parents looked at one another. They stared from Wilbur to Anna.

One mother stood tentatively and asked, "Can you tell us what this information is? Miss Whitman has been nothing but excellent in the three years our children have attended this school. In fact, in the six years she has taught here, I have heard *nothing* to make me want to seek another teacher."

Wilbur smirked at the mother before he turned to leer at Anna triumphantly.

"Two weeks ago, Miss Whitman and one of the older boys went into the trees. Miss Whitman came out shortly after that and sent all the children home—except the young man, of course.

"Now none of us knows what took place. However, we can all imagine. An old maid such as Miss Whitman and a strapping young man in the prime of his youth—"

Anna jumped to her feet and pointed her finger at Wilbur. Her voice was low and angry as she hissed the words at him.

"How dare you disparage my students, you miserable shell of a man. You have no idea what took place that day, nor will I share it with anyone in this room. Suffice it to say that I spoke in person that evening with the parents of the students involved. And let me be very clear—nothing shameful happened.

"I am exceptionally proud of the young man who was involved. He showed kindness and decency I have never seen from you."

Anna looked around the room at the shocked parents. "You are welcome to discuss my qualifications amongst yourselves, but I will not be party to this charade. If you want my resignation, please let me know tonight. It will be on my desk when I clear my personal items out of this classroom tomorrow."

As she started to leave, Wilbur stepped forward and tried to grab her arm. "You will take nothing from this room!"

Anna jerked her arm loose from him as she pointed around the room. Her eyes reflected the anger she felt even as she tried to keep her voice even.

"When I took this job, there was nothing in this room but the teacher's desk and stove. I used my own funds to purchase many of the items you see on these walls, *including* the bookcases and maps. I also purchased the slate boards each child uses every day.

"I won't take anything the children personally use because I care about these students, but I will take *all* of my own teaching items."

Anna marched toward the door with her head held high and walked quickly to the little grove of trees that Wilbur had spoken of. Tears filled her eyes at the insinuations the vicious little man had made.

"What a despicable man. How dare he accuse Harry of improper behavior." Anna kicked the rock in front of her. "Poor little Martha. Who would have guessed her loose dress would have snagged on a branch as she slid down that big tree? It slipped right over her head and stayed at the top of the tree as she cowered on a lower branch. Very embarrassing for a fourteen-year-old girl.

"Harry was there when it happened, and he immediately ran to get me. I sent all the children home. They were finished eating their dinner. I hoped if I released them, no one would realize who was missing in the chaos.

"I gave Harry my shawl and he handed it to Martha while he climbed to the top of the tree to retrieve her dress—and he left the woods so she would have privacy putting her dress back on. He was nothing but a gentleman. And I know he would have rather been *anywhere* but rescuing a young girl's dress.

"Martha was so humiliated. I offered to walk home with her but she refused. She was crying when she left here.

"I drove out that evening and talked to both sets of parents. Martha was still upset. She said she never wanted to go back to school. Only by convincing her that no one knew a thing about the incident did she finally agreed to return. And now this!

"How dare Wilbur Jackson drag these children through the mud to get back at me!

"Well, he won. I am done here. Perhaps if I leave, this will all blow over."

CHAPTER 4

Angry Parents

WILBUR JACKSON WAS DELIGHTED. ALL THE PARENTS were upset. No one knew what to believe and everyone was angry.

Tommy's mother was usually very quiet, but she rose to her feet. Her husband tried to pull her down, but she shrugged him off.

"What kind of parents are we to believe something so terrible when we don't have the facts? Has Miss Whitman given any of us reason to question her behavior, let alone her character?

"I for one will not vote to send away one of the best teachers I have ever had the pleasure of working with." She held up the small rag she was using as a napkin.

"Did any of you look at these? Our daughters made them, and our sons cut and sanded the small plates we are using. They aren't perfect but they were made with a perfect love—a gift from our children to us a result of a school project.

"Have any of you kept track of the number of times our children have come home with an extra sandwich or an apple? Or how many times they had no lunch, and Miss Whitman shared her food with them?

"We have been blessed to have her as a teacher. Shame on all of us. We don't deserve her." As she sat down, some of the parents smiled quietly in agreement.

Wilbur jumped to his feet and began to shout.

"It is right in her contract! Read the morality clause! If she is ever even *suspected* of improper behavior, we may fire her. We may break her contract as well as withhold her pay for any unfinished months."

Sampson Jones slowly stood. Everyone knew he was sweet on Anna. They also knew she had turned him away for over two years. He had come directly from the coal mine to attend this meeting. His hands, face, and clothes were black with coal dust. Wilbur Jackson was his boss, but Sampson had a strong feeling that Wilbur Jackson had planned this entire fiasco. The vicious little man was nearly dancing with excitement as he gloated.

"Jackson, how many times in the first two years after Miss Whitman started teaching here did you try to court her?"

Wilbur's face turned a mottled red and he shouted, "This is not about me! I am not the one whose character is in question!"

Sampson slowly walked to the front of the room. He stared at Wilbur Jackson for a moment before he turned to face the parents.

"It is no secret I have been taken with Anna Whitman since the first day I met her. And not once has she ever been anything but a friend to me. Nor has she ever given me any reason to believe she ever will be anything but a friend.

"Anna is one of the finest women I have ever met, and yes, it would pleasure me greatly if she allowed me to court her. I know that is not going to happen, but it gives me no cause to tear her down and or try to ruin her reputation." He looked over at Wilbur Jackson and glared at the angry little man.

"Wilbur Jackson, on the other hand, is a vindictive little man who cannot believe a woman as fine as Anna *would* turn him down." Sampson added sarcastically, "Why, besides his money, look at all he has to offer."

Sampson's gaze was hard as he stared at Wilbur disdainfully. "Nope, Jackson. Money is all you have. You are a vicious, narrow-minded, greedy little man who tries to control those around you with threats. You figure you can get Miss Whitman fired because so many of these folks depend on your mine to make their living." Sampson rolled up his sleeves and grinned at the room. He turned again toward Wilbur Jackson.

"I'm single, Jackson. I don't need your job or your money. It is going to give me great pleasure to give you the walloping you have deserved for longer than I've known you."

Sampson's first slap nearly knocked Wilbur out. He jerked the smaller man up and shook him.

"Now that was an easy one. I want you to feel at least part of this." With that, he slapped Jackson again. After three slaps, the smaller man was cowering on the floor. Sampson picked him up and slammed his fist into the sniveling man's long nose. Wilbur's glasses broke and Sampson shook his hand as he pulled the glass slivers out. He looked at the shocked parents and pointed toward the door.

"Go ahead and vote to terminate Miss Whitman, but you make sure your statement says she gets full pay through August as well as a bonus of one month severance." He laid $10 on the table.

"I don't know what she makes in a month, but there is my share of her severance pay.

"I'm headed west on the first train I find. There is nothing to hold me here, but I hope you folks pay some mind to what I've said." He looked around the room and shook his head.

"You just lost the best teacher this little school has ever known, but perhaps you've freed her. Now she has no reason to stay around here. Just maybe the next school will appreciate her."

Sampson walked out of the school. He felt free too. He had a little money saved. With that little nest egg, he'd work his way west. Hard work didn't bother him. "And with luck, my next job will be above ground," he growled as he strode toward his run-down shack about a mile away.

CHAPTER 5

A New Beginning

ANNA WALKED HOME BEFORE THE MEETING WAS finished. She could hear loud voices arguing in the school, and she decided not to return. The sadness inside her was trying to leak out, but she forced herself not to cry.

"We are done here," she whispered to herself. "Old Mr. Murphy will offer me my summer job helping in his store. Of course, he will lose customers because of that decision. No, I won't do that to him. Flory and I need to leave—and where to go? The only living relative we have lives in Kansas.

"Aunt Mae's first husband owned a little ranch there. She told us a long time ago to come any time we wanted. I guess this is the time. I will talk to my sister when she arrives home. And tomorrow, I will clean out the school."

Anna pulled the small book of German from her pocket and stared at it. She tossed it beside the bed as she sat down.

"I guess I don't have to learn German now. I didn't want to anyway—I was only trying to learn a few words so I could teach my German students. Besides, they are learning English. By next fall, they should be fine." She smiled as she untied her shoes.

"Maybe I will learn Spanish. It is a romance language and is certainly not as guttural as German. Besides, I like how the words feel when they cross my lips."

Anna was asleep when her sister arrived home. Flory stared down at her older sister a moment before she met one of her many suiters on the porch of the large house where they rented a room.

The lady of the house where Flory was employed had quietly let her go that evening after supper. She paid Flory in full but told her not to return to work—not tomorrow, not ever. When Flory asked her why, the woman's only response was a terse, "Ask your sister."

The young man who came to call seemed to have all the details. Evidentially, Anna had breached the morality section of her teacher contract and she was fired. Everyone was talking, and according to what he had heard, Anna certainly wouldn't be working in their small mining community—not in any type of job.

For once, Flory listened quietly. Soon, she excused herself and sent the young man on his way over his protestations. She rushed back into the house and woke her sister.

"Anna! Anna! Wake up! Do you want to hear the good news? Now we can leave this place! We can go wherever we want! I want to go West. I want to hold hands with a man who doesn't have coal dust under his fingernails!"

There was a stirring in the bed as Anna rolled over. "You do realize all working men have the grime of their occupation on their hands. What kind of man do you want to court you, Flora? Certainly not a man who works for a living!"

The two sisters talked until late in the night. They had much to plan and think about, especially since the end of the month was only three days away.

There was only one town of any size in Morris County, Kansas where their aunt's ranch was located. Neither girl had been to Kansas, but they quickly penned a letter to their aunt. Flory would post it the next day.

Flory offered to check into buying tickets to Kansas while Anna cleaned out the schoolhouse.

"Go ahead and look at the route. We will wait to buy tickets until after the meeting on Friday though. I hope to be paid for May.

"If I breach my contract and leave before the year is ended, I will forfeit my pay for the next three months. I just don't see what else we can do though since we don't have the money to stay here any longer." Anna frowned and straightened her shoulders. She was worried but her sister was excited.

Flory fell asleep around midnight and slept soundly while Anna tossed and turned. She was terrified at the prospect of being unemployed. She remembered the hard days after their parents died and how she had struggled to support her sister and herself. Still, there was a tiny spark of excitement at the thought of leaving Altoona.

"It's not so much that I love it here. I think I'm just comfortable and afraid to take a risk."

Both girls were up early. Flory decided to help Anna for a few hours until the train depot opened. Besides, they both needed to go to the bank to withdraw their savings.

Anna's stomach clutched at the thought of using her small amount of saved money to travel. She whispered a prayer.

"Lord, please help this to be the right decision. Help us not to make rash changes that will affect our ability to support ourselves."

There was a note on Anna's desk when the sisters arrived at the little schoolhouse.

Miss Whitman, we are still planning to have the End-of-the-Year Potluck on Friday at noon. Please invite your sister and be at the school by eleven-thirty. We understand you need to pack your personal items, but we still want to show you our appreciation for your six years here.

Mr. and Mrs. Leechey and Tommy

Anna stared at the note a moment. Finally, she laid it aside. She looked around the school and stated quietly, "I only have one small box with a cover. I don't see how I can possibly fit all my books in it, and I hate to leave them here."

A horse and buggy pulled up outside and Flory ran to the door. She looked over her shoulder as she exclaimed, "It's Sampson and he has a large trunk in the back. He is bringing it in here!"

Sampson appeared in the doorway with a smile on his face.

"I thought you ladies could maybe use another trunk. I am leaving town this afternoon and I plan to travel light. You are welcome to this if it will help you out any."

Anna was startled. "Where are you going? I thought you planned to make a home here."

Sampson set the heavy trunk down and leaned back against the teacher's desk as he grinned at her. "I never have liked Jackson. That pompous little rat has been begging for a beating for as long as I have known him. I took out a little of my anger on him last night. I'm moving on before he sics the law on me. I didn't have much when I came here, and I'm taking even less with me when I leave." He gestured toward the trunk. "It's yours if you want it. It was my mother's and it's too bulky for the kind of traveling I intend to do."

Anna stared at Sampson in surprise. Her eyes moved to his cut knuckles. Sampson flexed his fingers as his smile widened.

"It wasn't much of a fight. More of a spanking. Still, I'm leaving town on the next train west.

"I have a little time to help you pack this morning. Then I can take anything you have packed to the station. The ticket master will keep it in his office overnight. We've been friends for a time, and I asked him about it yesterday."

At Anna's look of surprise, he added, "Maybe fill this with your books and your heavy things. That way you won't have to deal with all that weight on your own."

Anna touched his arm. "You have always been a good friend, Sampson." She paused and her face colored a bit as she added, "I'm just sorry—"

Sampson waved his hand as he grinned wryly.

"You're a good friend, Anna. Now let's get this trunk filled. My train leaves at two this afternoon."

CHAPTER 6

Making Plans

THE TRUNK WAS COMPLETELY FULL WHEN ANNA AND Flory helped Sampson load it on the wagon. He stared at Anna a moment before he kissed her cheek.

"Be careful, ladies. And if either of you ever need to reach me, write to Charlie down at the train depot. He will know how to get hold of me." He tipped his hat and climbed into the wagon.

Both women watched him leave. Flory turned to Anna. She started to speak but Anna shook her head.

"Don't say it. I know I should love him, but I don't. Now let's get the rest of this school cleaned out so I can go to the bank with you."

"I was just going to say he was the only young man in this town who didn't try to court me." Flory giggled as she added, "Maybe *I'll* write to Sampson!"

Anna rolled her eyes and the two sisters quickly finished. In the end, Anna decided to leave the maps. They were too large and bulky to travel with. She did take the small square of cloth Martha had cross-stitched with her name as well as the plate Harry had made for her. Her heart was tight as she closed the door and walked down the worn lane toward town.

One of Flory's suiters, Richard Ramsey, worked for the railroad. Although he was sad to see her leave, he offered to help the two sisters plan their route when he came over Thursday evening. He marked on their map the towns they would pass through. He tapped the small star on a town called Kansas City.

"You will make connections there with another line that runs southwest.

"That's where you will pick up the Missouri-Kansas-Texas train. Its name was shortened to the MKT but folks are just calling it the Katy now.

"That leg will take you to Council Grove." Richard looked from one woman to the other before his eyes settled on Flory.

"I could take some time off, Miss Flora—to make sure you get there all right, I mean," Richard commented cautiously. He cleared his throat and added, "Or even meet you somewhere."

Flory laughed and shook her head. "No thank you, Mr. Ramsey. I'm sure we will be just fine." She batted her eyelashes and gazed up at him as she added softly, "I know how to reach you though—if I change my mind."

Richard's poor heart fluttered but it did him no good. Flory sent him on his way once he finished showing them the route.

Anna stared at her sister a moment. She frowned as she shook her head. "That man would walk on glass for you, and you have no more concern for his feelings than you do that bug crawling across the floor."

Flory jumped up and stomped the bug. "Well at least I didn't stomp on his heart. I let him go thinking there is hope." She giggled as she hugged her sister. "Don't be so serious, Anna. You are a free woman now. You don't have to be all stiff and restrained anymore.

"Now let's get some rest so we are fresh when we go to your farewell party tomorrow." She giggled and added, "At least you get one. No one at my work was sad to see me leave!"

"No one but all the young men you have wrapped around your fingers," Anna commented dryly.

======= CHAPTER 7 =======

A Farewell Party

WHEN THE SISTERS ARRIVED AT ELEVEN-THIRTY, THE little school was a flurry of activity. Anna was amazed at the number of people in attendance. In fact, only two families were missing out of thirteen.

Martha shyly greeted them and hugged Anna.

"Miss Whitman, I am so sorry. This is all my fault," she whispered.

Anna shook her head. "Nonsense. None of this was your fault. Now you go find your friends. I will write you when I am settled. I will want to know all about your family and how you are doing." She hugged the young girl again and smiled as Martha hurried away. Anna did notice the dress Martha wore was fitted at the waist and she smiled.

Harry was the next student to approach her. He shook her hand and nodded toward his parents.

"I'm leaving too. Ma's sister several counties south of here needs some farm help. I am going to help her through the summer. After that, I might head west. I have always wanted to see Wyoming."

Anna had tears in her eyes as she listened. "Your aunt is lucky to have such a hard worker for a nephew. I'm sure she will try to talk you into staying longer. You keep up your studies though. You told me many times you wanted to be a lawyer, and you can't do that with the education you have now."

"No, but I have a good start. You were a great teacher, Miss Whitman."

Anna was quiet as she watched Harry walk away. He was soon in the middle of his friends, and they were teasing the girls. Not Martha though. The young woman helped her mother set out the food instead of giggling with the girls. Anna shook her head. *Poor Martha. Teenage years are so hard anyway without that kind of embarrassment. Of course, Harry will never tell and now he's leaving. I hope all this blows over.*

Mrs. Leechey clapped her hands.

"Come everyone. It is time to eat. Pastor Jones will lead us in prayer and our guests of honor may start the food line." She smiled over at Anna and Flory as the pastor began.

Some of the little children brought their plates and sat beside Anna. Tommy looked up at her with big eyes.

"Ma says you won't be my teacher anymore. Is that true?"

Anna smiled at him and nodded. "That's true, Tommy, but I'm sure your next teacher will be wonderful. I know you will like her every bit as much as me."

Tommy was silent a moment. He studied his plate and asked softly, "Think she will share her food with me? Most grownups don't share their food like you do."

Anna smiled at Tommy and gave him a hug. "I don't know about that, Tommy, but if I ever see you again, I will be glad to share my food with you—no matter how old of a grandma I am."

Tommy's eyes lit up and he laughed. "You can't be a grandma, Miss Whitman. You don't have a husband or any kids of your own. My ma says you don't even have a beau, but I don't know what that is. What is a beau?"

Anna laughed. "I'm not sure what a beau is either, Tommy. I guess that means if I ever had one, I didn't know it. Now eat up your meat so you can have some of that apple pie. I know you like pie."

All the parents came by to visit. They wished the two sisters the best of luck. No one mentioned the meeting the night before and Anna didn't bring it up either.

Once the meal was over, Harry's father, Babe McFab, stood. He was a huge man and had a commanding presence. Babe's voice was loud, and people stopped visiting when he began to talk.

"Folks, as you know we decided to go ahead and have this party to show Miss Whitman our appreciation. Now I have a bank draft in my hands." Babe held up a paper. "Wilbur Jackson isn't here this afternoon, but he *willingly* offered it to me today along with a letter of recommendation for Miss Whitman." Babe's eyes twinkled and the little group laughed. He turned his eyes toward Anna.

"You have been released from your contract, Miss Whitman, with full pay for the next three months. In addition, we took up a collection. Everybody gave a little to show our appreciation." He handed her a can a child had painted. Each student had signed it. When Anna removed the cover, she saw it was full of dollar bills and change.

The tears Anna had been hiding spilled out, and she sobbed as she stared from the bank draft in her hand to the can. She sucked back her sobs as she looked around at the group of smiling people.

Babe patted her back awkwardly. "No need for tears, Miss Whitman. It was the least we could do. Even though we know you are going to leave, those of us here want you to know we don't agree with the decision that was made. You are a fine teacher. We all hope you will teach other kids with the same love and joy for learning you shared with ours."

Anna tried to wipe her tears away but as the throng of smiling kids and adults surged around her, the tears came back. This time, they were happy tears.

It was a smiling Anna who locked up the little school after two that afternoon. She paused on the steps as she looked around before she hurried to catch up with her sister. They rushed to the bank to redeem Anna's bank draft. Anna left the schoolhouse key there, and the sisters hurried toward the train station.

CHAPTER 8

WHAT WOMAN WOULD DO THAT?

ANNA, LET'S STOP IN AND SEE MARY SNYDER ON OUR way. She lives in Kansas City. It won't be out of our way since we are going through there anyway. You know we received a letter from her just last week begging us to visit."

"Are you sure it is Mary you want to see and not her handsome brother? What does he do for a living anyway? I know he is in the cattle business there." Anna's voice was dry as she studied her sister.

"He's a cattle buyer. Oh, it sounds so exciting. He travels all over looking at cattle and arranging purchases. To be able to travel like that!" Flora pulled the letter from her bag and handed it to Anna.

"And look." Flora opened the letter to show Anna a poster. "This family in Kansas City is advertising for a nanny to stay with their children eleven days while they travel." She smiled at her sister and her blue eyes sparkled. "They are asking for a teacher." Her smile became wider as she added, "I already wired Mary. She is the one who sent me the poster. I told her you would take the job."

Anna stared at her sister in shock.

Flora giggled and continued. "We should be in Kansas City by Tuesday morning. That is the third of June. The parents don't leave until the next day. They will be back on the fifteenth. They are paying $5 per day, and you will stay in their home. They even have a cook and a housekeeper, so you will only be responsible for their children."

"Flory! We don't know them! Why in the world would parents hire someone they don't even know—someone with no credentials to show them? And what makes you think I want to work for them? We don't know what kind of people they are or what their help is like! I absolutely won't do it."

Flory's chin jutted out. "Well, the couple knows Mary and she will vouch for you. Besides, you have your letter of recommendation from the school. You can show that to them.

"As far as what they are like, Mary said they are wonderful people. You work, I'll stay with Mary, and we will both be happy!" She giggled again and waved some money at Anna.

"Besides, I have money. Mr. Gorman down at the post office gave this letter to me this morning." She leaned toward Anna and whispered, "I am going to be a mail-order bride!"

Anna stopped and jerked Flory around to face her.

"You did *not* answer that ad in the paper you showed me!"

"I did. He sounds nice. He lives in the Wyoming Territory and has two small children. He is excited to have me come."

Anna pulled Flory around the corner of a building and pushed her against the wall. Her eyes were furious as she shook her sister's shoulders.

"Flory, this is not a game. That man is looking for a mother for his children, not a girl who is going to drop in for a visit and leave. He expects you to make a lifetime commitment, and you—you can't even commit to one man a week!" Anna took a deep breath and stepped back, still glaring at her sister.

"What did you tell him?"

"I said I would arrive sometime this summer. I am to send a wire to Cheyenne when I leave Denver. The telegraph operator there will send it with the stage to Fort Laramie.

"He said I should take the stagecoach from Cheyenne north, and he would be waiting for me at Fort Laramie. He lives about an hour by wagon from there." Flory paused and looked away before she added softly, "I didn't tell him about you. He did mention in his letter that teachers were hard to keep in their little country schools, so I'm sure you will be able to find a teaching job with no trouble."

Anna jerked the envelope from Flory's hand and looked inside. "And what is this money for? Your train ticket?

"Flory, I can't believe what you have done." Anna's face was pale as she struggled to keep from shouting at her younger sister. "Do you even intend to go to Fort Laramie or did you just make all these promises so he would send you money?" Anna's voice was barely above a whisper and Flory looked away without answering.

"You have done a terrible thing, Flory. That man may have sent you his last $200, and you plan to use it to go shopping in Kansas City?"

"Oh, for Pete's sake, Anna. He can't expect me to marry without ever meeting him. What woman would do that?"

Anna shook the money in front of Flory's face and whispered, "You just *stole* $200, Flory. We are taking it back and *you* are going to apologize." Anna dropped the money in her bag and walked toward the street. She looked back at Flory.

"Don't talk to me. Don't even look at me. I am on the verge of tears now, and if you talk, I am going to start bawling." Anna turned to face the street and choked back the sobs that were forming deep in her throat. "I guess I will take that job in Kansas City," she whispered. "I am going to have to buy train tickets I didn't budget for."

CHAPTER 9

A Friendly Stranger

ANNA LEANED BACK AGAINST THE SEAT AND LOOKED out the train window. There were quite a few young men on the train, and those in the car where the sisters were seated were maneuvering to sit by both women. Anna glanced their way and then looked back out the window. She ignored the efforts of the young men to speak to her. She was still angry and was in no mood to entertain flirtatious men who most certainly were younger than she was.

Flory of course was delighted with all the male attention. From time to time, she glanced toward her sister, but Anna refused to look at her.

Anna pulled the blanket she had brought along over herself. Despite the noise of the train and all the talking, she drifted off to sleep.

She didn't hear the woman at the end of the row speak quietly to the man who crept up and tried to slip into the open seat next to her.

"Mister, I have a gun pointed at you and when it goes off, your manhood is going to be gone. Now you turn around and go back to where you came from—unless you don't mind losing what you seem so eager to share."

The man peered through the evening shadows at the woman who was talking. He looked one more time at the two young women sleeping at the end of the row. He turned and almost ran out of the car, looking back one more time before he stepped onto the gangway.

The woman grinned to herself and slid the Deringer back under her skirt. She looked over at the two young women and shook her head.

"Such peaceful innocence. Well, they won't be bothered on this leg of their trip." She stared across the car and frowned as she reminisced. *Yes, there was a time when I was innocent as well, but it didn't last long. Hopefully, these young women won't have to learn all the lessons I did.*

When Anna awoke, it was nearly nine in the evening and the train was quiet. She looked around. *I have no idea how women relieve themselves on trains.* A woman older than her was seated in the same row and Anna leaned toward her.

"Excuse me? Are you familiar with this train?" When the woman nodded, Anna asked, "Would you be so kind as to tell me what facilities are available on this train for our relief?"

The woman smiled at Anna. "First time to ride this train?"

"It is my first time to ride any train. I'm afraid I don't know any of the standard protocols."

The woman laughed and nodded. "It can be a little confusing. However, you are in luck. When the train pulls into the next station, jump off and run straight ahead. There is only one privy, and it will be right in front of this car." Her blue eyes sparkled as she added, "That is why I make a point to be in this car during the last leg of my journey."

"Are you going far?"

"To Kansas and then on to the Wyoming Territory. My sister and I are traveling together. We have never been out of Pennsylvania."

The woman studied Anna's face. She commented quietly, "You have family in both places, I presume?"

Anna blushed before she answered.

"We do in Kansas. The Wyoming part of our trip was just added, so I am not sure what to expect there. Truth be told, not in Kansas either. We have an aunt who lives in Council Grove. We will be stopping for a few days in Kansas City as well. I hope to earn a little more traveling money." She paused and asked cautiously, "Is Kansas as rough as everyone says?"

The woman laughed and shrugged. "Honey, it is rough everywhere if you land in the wrong place. Council Grove is a cow town so there will be lots of cowboys full of piss and vinegar." At the shocked look on Anna's face, she laughed softly. "I mean it will be full of wild young men. Women are a bit of a novelty, especially young and pretty ones. I'm sure your sister and you will be very welcome."

Anna looked at the seat beside her where Flory was sleeping. She sighed. "Not me, but I'm sure my sister will be."

The woman cocked one eyebrow and chuckled. "I take it you are the older sister." Her eyes became somber as she studied Anna's face. "It is a difficult thing to be responsible for another person's life all the time. Your parents passed when you were young?"

Anna's surprise showed on her face. She studied the other woman for a moment and slowly nodded. "I was fourteen and Flory was nine. It was very difficult." She shuddered and added quietly, "I don't ever want to be that desperate again. I guess it made me overly cautious." She looked over at her sister and shook her head. "Flory, on the other hand, worries about nothing."

The woman laughed out loud and once again, her blue eyes sparkled. "Of course not. She has you to do all her worrying." She nodded toward the door.

"Be quick now. The train is slowing and soon will blow its whistle. Wake your sister and we will move to the door. The men will naturally let us off first, and we can be the first in line." She gestured toward the front of the train. "Those poor blokes in third class won't make it in time, and they will be scrambling for a place beside the tracks."

When Anna stared at her, the woman laughed. "Honey, you and I need to talk more. You have a lot to learn before you reach Kansas."

The woman showed the sisters where the water tank was, and the three quickly washed their hands and their faces.

"We have about eighteen more hours before we reach Kansas City, Missouri. It will be nearly midnight when we arrive. Will someone be waiting for you?" When neither Anna nor Flory answered, the woman shrugged. "You can spend the night with me. Tomorrow morning, my driver will take you to your friend's house." She paused and then asked carefully, "You do have her address, don't you?"

Anna looked toward her sister and Flory laughed. "I almost threw this envelope away. Yes, here it is on the outside."

The woman studied the address and cocked an eyebrow at the two young women again.

"Well, let's eat something and maybe the two of you can tell me all about yourselves. Come, my friend packed a lunch, and there is enough to feed five hungry men let alone three tired women."

Flory dozed off but Anna and the woman talked for several more hours. Suddenly, the friendly woman frowned.

"How rude of me. I didn't even introduce myself. "My name is Tillie, Tillie Maynard."

Anna reached out her hand. "Anna Whitman and my sister is Flory. It is nice to meet you, Mrs. Maynard."

Tillie nodded as she studied the simple band on her finger. She was smiling when she looked up.

"My husband is a lawyer, but he works in real estate as well." Her blue eyes sparkled with merriment as she added, "I was an entertainer when I met him. He swept me off my feet and carried me off to Kansas City. My life has never been the same." She stared out the window for a moment before she looked back at Anna. "I was headed down the wrong path when Oliver came along." She shook her head and corrected herself. "Actually, I was a ways down that path when we met." Her smile became soft, and she patted Anna's hand as the younger woman listened to her words.

"Don't be afraid of love, Anna. When you find it, you hang on. Don't give up and don't settle for comfortable. You look for the firecrackers and the bright lights. You want to feel that tingle in your heart when he smiles at you. There are many men out there—good men too—who will be willing to give you a comfortable home…but nothing can take the place of true love."

She looked directly at Anna and asked, "So which of you signed up to be a mail-order bride—or did both of you?"

Anna gasped and glanced quickly toward Flory. She could feel the red creep up her neck as she looked back at Tillie.

"Flory did. I only found out yesterday. She has no intention of marrying him though—she just did it to get money for her train fare." Anna's voice was determined as she added, "I told her we were going to return the money, and she was going to apologize." Her voice dropped to a whisper. "I am so ashamed, both of Flory and myself. I have so failed in all I tried to teach her.

"And I am terrified to travel into the wild unknown. We will know no one out there. We know nothing about this man either other than he lives an hour by wagon from Fort Laramie in the Wyoming Territory… wherever that is."

"Does he have children?"

"Yes, two of them. They are two and five. He lost his wife a year ago and his children need a mother." Anna's voice caught as she whispered, "I can't believe Flory was so callous—to pretend she would marry a man who just lost his wife, a man who only wants a mother for his little ones."

"And your sister told you since you cared so much, you could marry him."

Tears filled Anna's eyes and she nodded. "That is exactly what she said. I don't know what to do. I don't want to marry a stranger. I have never even been in love. I want that love you talked about, and I am afraid I will never experience it—partly because I won't take any chances and now because we owe this man. Flory gave her word, and it is my responsibility to fulfill that promise."

Tillie's eyes were soft as she watched Anna. She hugged the younger woman as she smiled at her.

"Any man would be lucky to marry you, Anna. You make that trip and give that cowboy his money. But you don't have to marry him. He may be regretting his desperate move by now anyway." Laughter bubbled out of her as she added, "Of course, if he is rich and handsome, maybe you should give it a shot!"

Anna laughed despite herself, and the two women settled back in their seats.

"My Ollie will be at the station to meet me. I always tell him he doesn't need to come. He could just send a carriage, but he never listens." She smiled at Anna and patted her hand again.

"Oliver is a good man. We'll get you girls a good night's rest, and things won't seem so difficult maybe."

Tillie studied Anna's face before she asked, "How long are you planning to stay in Kansas City?"

Anna's tenseness was evident in her voice. "Flory volunteered me as a nanny for a couple who will be out of town for eleven days. They are leaving on Wednesday. Our friend assured Flory acquiring the job would be no problem. I was going to say no, but since we are traveling to Fort Laramie, I need to make some extra money."

"Who is the couple?"

"John and Charlotte Campbell. Our friend, Mary, seems to know them. I'm not sure how many children they have, but they were hoping to hire a teacher. I taught in Altoona, Pennsylvania for the last six years. Hopefully, they will accept me."

Tillie laughed softly. "Well, you are in luck. I know Charlotte Campbell well. I will give you a recommendation. In fact, she is my neighbor. We will make a trip over there tomorrow to introduce you." She paused and then asked, "Is Mary's given name Snyder?"

Anna looked at Tillie in surprise. "Why yes. Do you know Mary or her husband? His name is Ralph. I'm not sure what he does there, but she has a brother who is a cattle buyer."

Anna sighed deeply and added, "I have a feeling Abram or Abe as Flory calls him is the real reason Flory wants to stop in Kansas City. She has always been taken with him…as much as Flory can be interested in one young man anyway."

Tillie winked at Anna. "Perhaps we need to find Flory a job as well. Something to keep her occupied during the day and a place to stay where she is supervised."

Anna laughed dryly. "I could only wish."

Tillie squeezed Anna's hand. "You leave that up to me. Now you get some rest. The Campbells have four children, and they are wild little things. Bright as buttons but difficult to make focus on the task at hand. You will have your hands full." Tillie leaned back with a smile on her face. When she next looked over at Anna again, the young girl was asleep.

"Ah, Anna. You are a strong young lady. Flory doesn't know how blessed she is to have an older sister like you. How different my young life might have been had someone tried to steer me away from the hurdy gurdy halls and the entertaining that followed those dances.

"Bless Ollie. He didn't see me as a tainted lady. He loved me for what I was inside, and he whisked me away.

"The man who ran that hall in Cheyenne discouraged me. He said south-of-the-track girls like me never fit in on the north side. He was wrong though. Ollie took me from that life to Kansas City, and we started fresh.

"It hasn't always been easy, but the Good Lord was watching over me when He sent Ollie. One dance with that man and I knew I was in love."

Soon Tillie was also asleep. Except for the snores of many men, the car was quiet.

CHAPTER 10

THE MAYNARDS

THREE TIRED WOMEN CLIMBED DOWN THE STEPS OF the train when it arrived at the Kansas City Station. A tall man with white hair was waiting with a team of glistening horses. He scanned the cars and his face lit up with a smile when he spied Tillie. He waved and Tillie grabbed the girls' arms. She pulled them toward the smiling man. She leaned up to kiss him before she pointed to her companions.

"Ollie, this is Anna and her sister, Flory. They will be spending the night with us." She smiled at Anna and laughed as she added, "And Anna brought an entire library with her, so she will need help loading her heavy trunk."

Several cowboys were unloading their horses, and Ollie asked them for help with the trunk. They helped with big smiles and no complaints. They seemed shy and didn't try to talk to any of the women.

Flory and Anna were quiet as Ollie drove the horses under the carriage porch, stopping in front of the door. Lamps spilled light from the windows, and the large front door quickly opened.

Tillie whisked the girls inside and up the curved stairs. She opened the door to a spacious bedroom and pointed at the bed.

"You girls make yourselves comfortable. Sleep as late as you want. When you come down in the morning, we will eat. We can even draw a bath if you'd like. Afterwards, we'll meet Anna's new employer."

As the door closed softly, Flory threw herself on the bed.

"Anna, I don't know what you did to make friends with Tillie, but I am liking this. I love Kansas City already." She smiled up at Anna and wrinkled her nose as she laughed.

"Don't frown at me so, Sister. I know you are enjoying this as much as me. I thought we would be sleeping in a dreary boarding house. I never dreamed I'd ever stay in such a fancy house as this. Why it is a mansion!"

Anna nodded as she sat down. "Tillie was very kind to open her home to us. We must think of something we can do to show her our appreciation.

"Right now though, I just want to sleep."

Flory was still chattering excitedly when she realized that Anna was not responding. She rolled up on her elbow and stared down at her sister. She watched Anna as she whispered, "You go on south to Council Grove and visit our aunt. I am staying in Kansas City. Aunt Mae always liked you better than me anyway. I want to experience the life and excitement of a city." Flory rolled over on her back. She stared up into the darkness of the ceiling. "And I can't wait to see Abe. He promised to show me around and I am so excited."

The sisters were up early and hurried downstairs. Both were used to rising early for work and were refreshed even with five hours of sleep.

Ollie and Tillie were in the large kitchen. Ollie had his arms around his wife, and they were laughing. Tillie's smile widened when she saw the young women.

"Good morning, ladies. Sit down here and I will cook you some breakfast. How do you like your eggs? Ollie and I both love eggs, so we have them every morning.

"Bacon? Ollie made some biscuits and there is gravy too. Make yourselves comfortable, and we will have breakfast ready in no time.

"Did you sleep well?"

Anna nodded. "We did. The bed felt wonderful. Thank you so much for opening your home to us. You certainly didn't have to."

Tillie waved her hands.

"Nonsense. We love guests and not many of our friends stay over. Most of our socializing is here in town, so folks stay in their own homes."

She pointed to a large, rambling mansion about a quarter of a mile away. The wide front porch looked out over the Missouri River. "The Campbells live right there. We will drive over as soon as you are both ready. That will give you a chance to look their property over.

"Charlotte's children all love to ride horses and would like to spend the entire day outside. They are quite fearless.

"She is a wonderful friend. I am blessed to have her so close." She patted her smiling husband's hand and added, "Ollie and I simply adore their children. We have no children of our own but the Campbell children call us Ollie and Auntie. We love it."

CHAPTER 11

CHARLOTTE CAMPBELL

FOUR CHILDREN RUSHED TO MEET THE BUGGY WHEN Tillie drove into their yard.

"Auntie! Did you bring us presents? Mother said you were seeing friends back East. We missed you!"

Tillie laughed as she jumped down from the buggy. "I do have presents but let me introduce my friends first. Misses Anna and Flory Whitman, these are the Campbell children. Gerald, George, Christina, and Amy.

"Now let's go see your mother. I have a surprise for her too."

Charlotte rushed outside when she heard the children's voices. She hugged her friend.

"Tillie, it is good to have you back. It is lonely around here with you gone—even with all the noise those four make!" She pointed at the children.

"Go tell Robert I said you could go riding today."

She looked from Anna to Flory and smiled. "You must be Mary's friends. She will be down in a moment. She is cleaning upstairs.

"Do come in. How was your trip and how, pray tell, did you come to meet Tillie? Strangers on a train perhaps?"

Mary rushed into the room as they were sitting down and hugged both of her friends.

"Flory and Anna! I am so excited you will be staying in Kansas City for a time!" She looked toward Charlotte as she pulled Anna forward.

"Mrs. Campbell, this is Anna. She is the teacher I was telling you about. She is excellent with children, and I know she will do a great job for you."

Flory laughed and added, "In fact, she is such a great teacher that she insisted on lugging an entire trunk of books and teaching supplies with us. Poor Oliver left it on the buggy last night. It is certainly too heavy for one man to carry."

Charlotte smiled as she looked from one sister to the other. "Yes, books are a wonderful treasure.

"Let me tell you a little about our children. Gerald is our oldest. He is ten. He reads but doesn't enjoy it as much as we would like. George, our eight-year-old, loves to read. Christina is six. She is dying to read. That is why I asked for a teacher in my ad." She scooped a toddler off the floor as she smiled. "This little one is Amy. She is just two years old, but she tries to keep up with the rest of the children. Of course, they leave her whenever they can." She smiled over at Mary.

"Mary, why don't you show Flory around while I talk to Anna." She waited until the two women left before she turned to Anna with a smile.

"Tell me, Anna. Why did you leave a teaching job in the East to travel west into the unknown? That is very brave. I'm not sure I would be so courageous."

Anna's face paled and her breath caught. She looked from one woman to the other and took a deep breath.

"Mrs. Campbell, I have a letter of recommendation from the school where I taught. However, I didn't leave voluntarily. I was fired for a breach of my morality clause."

Charlotte's breath caught in her throat and Tillie raised her eyebrows as she watched Anna carefully.

74

Anna shook her head. "I did nothing wrong. However, two of my students were involved, and to have told the truth would have caused the young lady unbearable embarrassment." She took another deep breath before she continued.

"At recess, one of the older girls was climbing a tree behind the school. An older boy was on the ground talking to her. As she slid down the tree, her loose dress caught on a branch and slipped over her head. The young man ran to get me.

"Poor Martha was hiding in the tree. I gave the young man my shawl and had him climb up to get her dress. When he climbed down, I sent him home.

"I went to see both sets of parents that afternoon and explained what had happened. The young man was nothing but a gentleman, and the entire matter was an accident. I thought that was the end of it.

"Somehow, the man who funded the school found out part of the story. He made it sound like I was in the woods with the older boy. I refused to explain since to do so would have involved two of my students." She looked from one to the other. Tears sparkled in her eyes, but her voice was calm as she finished. "I was terminated and here I am."

Charlotte stared at her a moment in shock and Tillie laughed.

"Anna, I knew I liked you. Guts and balls—that's what you have." She squeezed Charlotte's arm. "Hire her now, Charlotte, or I am going to recommend her to someone else. Any young woman who will risk her reputation to save a student gets high marks in my book."

Tillie hurried to the door and whistled sharply. A young man appeared, and she pointed toward the buggy.

"There is a trunk in the buggy that needs to be brought in. Get someone to help you carry it in here right away."

She turned around and walked back to where Charlotte was sitting silently.

"Relax, Charlotte. I know John well enough to know he would want you to hire Anna. After all, she has a letter of recommendation from that school. She didn't *have* to share that story with you."

Two young men appeared in the doorway.

"Here is the trunk, Mrs. Campbell. Where do you want us to take it?"

Charlotte started to answer but stopped as her breath caught in her throat. She walked slowly toward them and touched the old trunk.

"Just—just set it down. I'm not sure so here will be fine for now."

The two young men set the trunk down. They nodded at the women and disappeared.

Charlotte's face was pale, and her hands were shaking as she turned toward Anna.

"Tell me, Anna. How—how did you come to have this trunk?"

Anna's eyes were large as she looked from the trunk to the shaking woman.

"Sampson gave it to me. Sampson Jones. He was a friend of mine in Altoona. He said it belonged to his mother."

Charlotte dropped into a chair with a small sob. She leaned toward Anna as she asked, "Sampson? Is he a dark-haired young man? In his mid-twenties?"

Anna slowly nodded.

"Sampson worked in a mine that was owned by the same man who ran the school, Wilbur Jackson. He was in some kind of altercation with Mr. Jackson after I was fired.

"He didn't give me all the details. He just said he was leaving with less than he came with, and I could have the trunk. He planned to take the westbound train and was traveling light."

Charlotte dropped on her knees in front of Anna and sobbed as she looked up at her.

"Do you know how to get in touch with him? Sampson is my brother! We were born in New York City. We were separated when he was just a little over a year old. Mother was dying and Father had abandoned us. Sampson was staying with our grandparents, but I was in school. People from the Children's Aid Society put me on a Baby Train headed west and some good people here adopted me.

"I tried to write to our grandparents, but the letters came back as 'Undeliverable. Addressee moved.' My family was lost to me until you showed me this trunk. It belonged to our mother and I recognized it." She hugged Anna as she laughed through her tears.

"Sampson surely told you how to reach him. If he was willing to fight for your honor, you must be very special to him."

Anna's face turned a deep red and she stuttered a little before she answered. "Sampson is a dear friend and has been for several years. Yes, I do know how to reach him. I have his contact information in my bag. I will get it for you." She paused and pointed at the trunk.

"If you have some crates, I will unpack the trunk so you can keep it. What a treasure to have something from your mother."

Anna stood and hurried outside to grab her bag. She could hear Tillie laughing as she talked to her friend. She took a deep breath and walked back slowly toward the house.

CHAPTER 12

A New Job

FLORY CHATTERED NONSTOP ON THE WAY BACK TO Tillie's house but Anna was quiet. Tillie listened and then patted Anna's arm.

"We had better get you ready. Charlotte wants you there by seven tomorrow morning." Her eyes crinkled as she laughed. She added, "But then, it's not like you need to pack."

She turned to look at Flory.

"Flory, I have been thinking. I would like to give my house a good cleaning and go through some clothes I want to get rid of. I have quite a few dresses that are just begging to be worn. I will never get in them again. Besides, they are too young-looking for me now. How about I hire you to help me? You can work for me and stay here until Anna finishes her job. And maybe in the evenings, you and I can make those dresses over, update them so they will work for today's fashions. What do you think?"

Anna turned her head to keep from smiling. For once, Flory was speechless. Tillie had appealed to Flory's hunger for new clothes, clothes that would cost her nothing but a little work—plus the opportunity to live in a mansion for eleven days.

"I would love to do that, Tillie! Do you think I could maybe have one day off a week to see the city? Mary doesn't have to work on Sunday's, and I would love to spend that day with her if it's all right."

Tillie smiled and nodded.

"I don't want to work on Sundays either, but we will certainly need to work in the evenings if we are going to get those dresses finished before you head to Council Grove. Why even if we work on one every day, we will never get done. There are just too many."

Flory was bouncing with excitement and Tillie winked at Anna.

"It's settled then. I will pay you $1 each day to help me, and you may take any dress you finish with you when you leave. Of course, some of them will be for Anna so she may need to try one on from time to time. How does that sound, Anna?"

Anna laughed and hugged her sister. "One is enough for me. Flory is the one who loves pretty clothes, although I don't know where she plans to wear them." She smiled at Tillie and added, "Thank you, Tillie. That is very generous. And a simple thank you is certainly not enough for all you have done."

Tillie's eyes crinkled at the corners as she laughed. "Nonsense. I have enjoyed you girls' company. Besides, if I get those closets cleaned out, Ollie will be so pleased he just might go with me on my next trip. Perhaps to Cheyenne in the Wyoming Territory.

"Badger McCune up there has been pestering us to come and visit. Ollie has known him for years. I have too actually. I met him when he lived in Kansas City. In fact, Badger is the one who introduced Ollie and me. I was working in Cheyenne, and he was passing through.

"Later, I met his wife, Martha, in Manhattan, Kansas. Of course, that was before they married.

"Now let's hurry on back to my house. We can look at those dresses so Anna can pick hers. It's going to be a busy eleven days and we need to get some good rest tonight."

CHAPTER 13

So Many Dresses

ANNA COULD ONLY STARE WHEN TILLIE OPENED THE doors to the large closet. Dresses were packed in tightly. Dresses of all colors and fabrics. Most of the sleeves were short and the necklines were low. Still, they could be altered with a little fabric from the full petticoats underneath.

Tillie opened a second closet and pointed inside. "The first ones are party gowns, but these aren't as fancy. They are more dignified maybe."

Flory's face was excited as she touched each dress. She finally pulled one out.

"I am going to work on this one tonight. Oh, Anna! This is going to be so much fun!"

Anna lifted out a deep green skirt with a jacket over it. The fabric was soft but heavier—an appropriate dress to wear to meet Flory's cowboy.

Tillie's eyes were soft when she touched it.

"Ollie had that made for me in Cheyenne, and I was married in it." When Anna started to put it back, Tillie shook her head. "I can't wear it anymore and there is no need to just stare at it. You try it on. If you like it, I would love for you to have it. Maybe you will think of me when you wear it."

Anna slipped into the green suit and smoothed it over her hips. The bodice was loose, but the skirt fit perfectly.

"It is beautiful, Tillie. I'm sure you were stunning in this."

Tillie loosened the bun on Anna's head and dropped her red hair down. Her skin was a creamy white and she was lovely.

"*You* are stunning, Anna. You are a beautiful woman and don't you ever forget that."

Tillie looked at Flory's pile and began to laugh. Flory was already trying dresses on. She had three that she wanted for sure with four more laying on the bed.

"I declare, Flory, you might have to stay longer than eleven days to get all those altered. Pick two and let's take them to my sewing room. We just as well start now. We can talk while we sew."

Tillie's sewing room was bright and cheery. It was obvious she sewed often as partially completed projects were folded everywhere.

She moved some piles aside for the younger women to sit and pointed at a basket of fabric remnants in the corner.

"Dig through that basket. It is full of lace and scrap fabric. You can use anything you want out of it. You girls make yourselves at home. I am going to see what we are having for dinner.

"Our cook fixes dinner and supper five days a week. We are on our own most weekends although sometimes she prepares things ahead for me to warm up." She winked at Anna and laughed as she hurried out of the room. "I'm quite spoiled but I like it."

Flory looked over at Anna. Her face was in awe as she touched the dresses.

"Have you ever seen such beautiful gowns? Where in the world did she wear all these? And how lucky are we to have them *given* to us. I'm so excited!" Flory patted her chest. "I can barely breathe."

Anna nodded as she touched the green dress. "They are beautiful. Tillie is a very giving person. We are blessed to have met her." She turned around to face her sister.

"You make sure you work hard. $1 per day is over five times what you made in Altoona—and new clothes in addition to that. You make sure you work five times as hard."

Flory laughed and agreed. "You know I love to sew. It won't take me long to alter these. I'll see if there is anything else she needs me to work on. Besides, she is giving me Sundays off to spend with Mary. I wasn't sure what I was going to do for eleven days anyway."

Her eyes were somber as she looked at Anna. "I'm sorry I answered the ad for a bride, Anna. I really didn't intend to be mean or to steal that man's money. I just thought it sounded like a grand adventure. I'm sorry too that you are going to have to help me make things right." She hugged her sister.

"Thank you for always being there for me, Anna. I do appreciate you, even if I don't show it very often."

Anna laughed and hugged her sister back. "We will fix it. You work hard these next eleven days. Now we can both save a little money. And that is good since we plan to visit Aunt Mae before we head west."

CHAPTER 14

ELEVEN DAYS IN A NEW TOWN

THE ELEVEN DAYS WENT QUICKLY. ANNA DID schoolwork with the children for a couple of hours in the mornings. They rode horses or played outside before dinner. She let the older three choose books from her boxes to read, and she read aloud to all of them after dinner each day for twenty minutes. That seemed to make Amy sleepy. Once the little girl was down for her nap, Anna let the other children choose what they wanted to do.

The housekeeper kept an eye on Amy so Anna could spend time with the older children. Their activities ranged from digging in the mud by the river, playing ball with sticks and rocks, or going to visit Tillie.

Tillie always made a fuss over them when they visited. She made it a point to have some kind of treat when they appeared with smiles on their faces. Strawberries with whipped cream were their favorite.

Finally, it was Anna's last night there.

Christina's big eyes had tears in them.

"Who is going to play with us when you leave, Miss Anna? We don't want you to go."

Anna hugged the little girl and pointed toward the big clock. "By this time tomorrow morning, your parents should be arriving in Kansas

City on the train. They will be here in time for dinner. Now what do you think about fixing them something special to eat? Do you want to make them a cake or cookies?"

Gerald wasn't listening. He had found a book in Anna's box about the Wild West, and he was reading it slowly as he savored it.

Anna smiled at him as she touched his shoulder. "How about I give you that book, Gerald? You have been a great example to the younger children this week." She leaned over and whispered with a smile, "Even though you didn't want to study every day."

Gerald looked up with excitement on his face. "My own book? Thank you, Miss Whitman. I wish you were my teacher at school. She is old and grumpy. We don't get to do all the fun things you let us do."

Anna laughed. "Well, this was summer school, not real school. I wouldn't be able to let you do all these things in your real school either. But if I come back, I promise I will come to visit you."

Gerald looked at her with serious eyes as he shook his head.

"You won't be back, Miss Anna. At least not to stay. Auntie says you are a pioneer at heart, and you are looking for adventure. I think the West is exciting. I'd like to go there, and I don't think I would come back either. Maybe you can write us though."

Anna smiled at the serious young man.

"I will do that, Gerald, but I expect a letter from you as well—in cursive. I might even send you something from time to time. Maybe a new book or something the cowboys use—if I stay out there, of course. But then, even I don't know what is going to happen when I leave here."

Anna had a hard time getting to sleep that night. Her conversation with Gerald made her think.

"A pioneer? I don't think so. I am terrified to travel into the unknown. Flory is much more daring than me." Still, it was kind of exciting to think about a future she couldn't plan.

CHAPTER 15

A Surprise Guest

THE CHILDREN DECIDED THEY WANTED TO MAKE cookies. The cook wasn't excited, but she grudgingly turned the kitchen over to Anna.

"I promise to clean it when we are done," Anna stated with a laugh. However, she didn't imagine all the near disasters that could happen with four children in a hot kitchen.

The cookies were finally made. Many of them were burned or were too dark because of the variations in sizes, but the children were proud. They arranged a large plate of them and rushed outside to watch for their parents.

Anna sank down in a chair. The kitchen was a mess. Flour was splattered everywhere and dirty pans with burned cookie crumbs were piled in the wash area. The cook popped her head in the door with a frown on her face. It slowly changed to a glare when she saw the pile of scorched cookies. She sat down beside Anna. The young woman looked over at her with a tired smile.

"It seemed like such a great idea."

The cook burst out laughing. She pulled Anna to her feet. "I'll help you clean this up—but next time, I'm supervising!"

They were just finishing when the children started screaming, "Mother! Father! You're home!"

Anna hung up her apron and wiped the flour off her face. She smiled as the buggy swung up to the house. She stared at the young man riding with them.

"Sampson? They found Sampson?"

John lifted Charlotte down and Sampson began to unload the bags. When he saw Anna standing in the doorway, his grin became larger, and he strolled up to the house.

"I sure didn't think I'd see you again, and for sure not so soon."

"How did they find you?" Anna's face showed her surprise. "I—I only gave Charlotte your friend's name when she left!"

Sampson grinned. "Rails, telegraphs, and lots of contacts. I think John knows every railroad executive between here and New York. I was in Chicago when Charlotte's first message came. I had just taken a job working on the tracks there. Her second wire came shortly after I responded. She said they were on their way to see me." He chuckled and shook his head. "They changed their plans all around and headed for Chicago...and all because I gave my old trunk to a teacher who wouldn't leave her books behind." He studied Anna's face for a moment.

"You look happy, Anna. I think this change is going to be good for you."

"And you as well, Sampson." For the first time, Anna noticed that Sampson was quite good looking. His black hair was curly, his shoulders were wide, and his hands were strong. His smile was the same. Kind of a half-smile that grew slowly as it reached his eyes. His smile slowly faded as he watched her.

"When do you leave?"

"Tomorrow. Our train leaves at ten. We'll stop in Council Grove for a time before we leave for the Wyoming Territory. There are trains that reach all the way across Kansas now and into Colorado. From Council Grove to Cheyenne should take about two days.

"And then what?"

"I'm not sure. Flory won't marry the man whose ad she answered, and I have decided not to sacrifice myself for her mistake. I am thinking we may come back here. I might stay in Council Grove too. Flory likes the bustle of the city, but I am looking forward to open spaces.

"How about you, Sampson?"

"John has offered to take me on as an apprentice in his construction company. I didn't really have any plans, so I'll try this for a time. I prefer to work with my hands, and he has lots of building projects going on. I'll give it a year and go from there."

John called to him, and Sampson hurried to help his brother-in-law finish unloading the buggy. Anna stepped out of the way as they carried in a large, elaborate travel trunk. She bent to run her hand over the smooth wood before she hurried upstairs to finish packing her bag.

Dinner was loud and chaotic. The children were so excited to have everyone try their cookies they almost dropped the large plate as they carried it from person to person. Sampson caught it but the cookies fell all over the floor. He scooped them up and dropped them onto his plate. He bit into one of the many burnt ones.

"These are delicious, Anna. Just the kind of cookie I like." He grinned and winked when Anna blushed. Soon, the children were all over him, each telling stories as he or she remembered.

Only Gerald was quiet. He showed his father and Sampson the book he was reading.

"Miss Whitman is going to let me keep this book. I want her to come back and teach at our school, but Auntie says she won't be back."

Charlotte looked at Anna in surprise. She smiled. "Well, she is certainly welcome to come back. I'm sure we can find a teaching position for her. A new school is opening just a half mile away, so you will all be changing schools next year. That new school is in the process of hiring." She smiled at Anna and squeezed her hand, "And we will write you a letter of recommendation. A wonderful letter of recommendation.

"We all hope you come back, Anna.

"Once we are done eating, Sampson will take you over to Tillie's. She wants all of us to come over for supper tonight. She is having a farewell party for you and Flory." She smiled and pointed at the beautiful trunk.

"That trunk is yours, Anna. You need a strong trunk to pack your things west. It is a gift from all of us."

Anna stared at the trunk in surprise and shook her head. "It is truly beautiful, but I only returned what was yours already. I could never accept that. Thank you, but—"

Charlotte hugged Anna and whispered, "Nonsense. It's the least we could do. Thank you for helping me to find my brother."

Anna smiled as she returned Charlotte's hug. "You are welcome although I had little to do with that." She touched the trunk again as she looked over at Sampson. "Thank you again. I will treasure it always." She looked at the boxes of books and blushed slightly.

"I know it was silly of me to bring all my books. Still, I am pleased they will be able to make the trip safely."

CHAPTER 16

Sampson's Secret

WHEN THEY LEFT, SAMPSON TURNED THE BUGGY TO the left instead of toward Tillie's. Anna looked at him in surprise. He said nothing and Anna was quiet as she waited for him to speak.

Sampson drove to a little cove of trees. He pulled the horses to a stop before he turned to look at her.

"I have a confession to make, Anna. I have had a little time to think these last two weeks, and I learned something about myself.

"I have always been a little leery of women. Most females are unpredictable. They have always baffled me.

"You are different though. You don't play games. And even though we never courted, I convinced myself I was in love with you.

"Working with you and Flory as we packed the school, watching the two of you, made me realize I had mistaken friendship for love.

"You are a wonderful person, Anna. You are beautiful inside and out—a loving woman who will make a wonderful wife and mother. You are a woman a man can count on.

"But I realized you and I don't have the sparks some folks do. We don't light up at the thought of the other person. We are happy to see each other. We are comfortable around each other like a pair of old shoes—but we don't excite one another.

"You saw that right off, but it took me awhile. As I studied on that these last few weeks, I realized I wanted to court you because Flory had so many beaus. I was concerned she would never settle down to love one man.

"I convinced myself it was better to have a best friend waiting for me at home than to be heart-broken by a pretty little vixen who would toy with my heart." As Anna stared at Sampson in shock, he laughed and shook his head.

"Yeah, I know. Boring old Sampson could never slow Flory down long enough to even be noticed, but there it is. Good thing she's leaving. Now maybe my heart will give up on her, and I can move along without lying to myself."

Laughter began to bubble out of Anna. "I would never have dreamed you would fall for Flory's charms, Sampson. Oh my word. Men truly amaze me. *You* amaze me, Sampson."

Sampson grinned and his face turned red. "Yeah, me too." He clucked to start the horses and looked sideways at Anna again. "I just wanted you to know that before you left. You and I will always be friends though. You send word if you need help, and I will be there.

"You are a special gal, Anna. I want you to be happy. And may we both love with a passion someday."

Anna nodded and laughed softly. "Tillie and I had a conversation about love on the train. She has been a wonderful friend. I am going to miss her terribly when I leave."

Sampson turned the team toward Tillie's.

"Now keep my secret, Anna. Don't make me look like another one of Flory's love-sick puppies. "I'll just sit quiet tonight and let Flory do all the talking. Of course, if you want to pray a little, I am fine with that." He grinned over at Anna as his face turned red a second time.

Anna's laugh was longer as she agreed.

CHAPTER 17

FLORY'S ANNOUNCEMENT

SUPPER WAS LOUD WITH LOTS OF SPILLED DRINKS and dropped food by the children, but Tillie didn't seem to mind. Once it was over, she brought out wine for the adults. Charlotte talked about their trip and finding her brother. Tillie shared what wonderful help Flory had been, and Flory showed several of the dresses she had altered. The conversation was lively. Only Anna and Sampson were quiet.

Finally, Tillie turned to Anna. "Your train leaves at ten tomorrow. I think I will have Sampson drive you if John doesn't mind." John smiled in agreement, and Tillie talked more of what she would send along to make the trip easier.

Flory finally cleared her throat. She looked cautiously at Anna.

"Actually, I'm not leaving. Tillie and I visited several dress shops this past week and one of them offered me a job. I can work as a salesclerk during the day and do alterations on my own time. They will pay me for both." She looked down. Her breath caught as she looked back at Anna.

"I start tomorrow. Tillie said I can stay with her until I get on my feet. She will even help me find a place for us to live." Flory jumped out of her chair and dropped down in front of her sister.

"Please don't be angry, Anna. I love it here. My heart is happy, and I don't want to leave. Once you get back, we can move into a place of our own. Until then, I can stay with Tillie.

"I know you believe you have to go to Fort Laramie because of what I did and I'm sorry. I will even write Dan Morton a letter of apology if you want. I'm just not going to go."

Anna stared at her sister in shock. When her eyes met Sampson's, his smile was so delighted she almost laughed.

"Flory—I—"

"I know. I was very irresponsible and now I'm pushing this job off on you. Maybe we could just wire Mr. Morton the money. That way, neither of us would have to go."

Anna shook her head. "No, Mr. Morton deserves to be told in person. I will make sure he gets his money and your letter. I will return afterwards. Maybe I will check into that teaching job or maybe I will settle in Council Grove." She smiled as she looked around the room. "The idea of living in a small town appeals to me."

Her eyes settled on Sampson and she added, "I am counting on you to keep an eye on Flory, Sampson. You make sure she is safe."

Sampson's face was somber as he agreed. "I can do that. Maybe I can even pick her up in the evening some days if my work with John allows it."

Tillie looked from Anna to Sampson. She winked at him behind Flory's back. *This is going to work out splendidly, just splendidly.*

Charlotte clapped her hands and called to her children.

"This has been a very long day and we need to get you children to bed." She hugged Anna as she pressed an envelope into her hands. "I hope you come back. Thank you for all you did and for the book you gave Gerald. I have never seen him read with such intensity." She held Anna's shoulders and smiled at her again.

"You let us know if you need anything at all. Any school will be blessed to have you as a teacher, and I hope it is ours."

Anna and Flory followed the Campbells out of the house. Finally, the children had all hugged Anna multiple times, and John turned the buggy toward their home.

"I'll be by at nine tomorrow morning," called Sampson. He settled back in his seat and the buggy's gas lights bobbed as the carriage pulled away.

As the two sisters walked up the long stairs, Flory linked her arm through Anna's.

"I am going to miss you. This will be the first time we have ever been separated."

Anna laughed dryly. "Oh, I'm guessing you will be so busy with all your beaus you will barely think of me.

"Speaking of beaus, how is Abe?"

"I didn't even see him. He gave Mary a letter for me. He had to leave town unexpectedly. He is to be gone at least a month, maybe longer." Flory's mouth settled in a small pout before her face brightened again.

"These last eleven days have been just wonderful. Tillie is so wise. We talked about everything. I didn't realize how much I missed having someone older around to discuss things with." When her sister didn't respond, Flory whispered, "I have been so blessed to have you watching out for me, Anna. I do think sometimes though you were so busy parenting me that we didn't have time to really talk as sisters.

"I hope we can do more of that in the future." She jabbed Anna's side as she giggled and added, "And I promise to work hard to not be such a brat!"

Anna laughed. "That would be a great start. And be careful, Flory. Kansas City isn't Altoona. You don't know everyone here so don't be brash with who you walk out with."

Flory was quiet as the girls undressed for bed. She finally looked over at Anna.

"I can't believe Sampson is Charlotte's brother. Do you think he will stay here?"

Anna studied her sister. Finally, she shrugged. "If he likes what he's doing I would guess he will stay a while. I have never considered him much of a rambler. Still, he just arrived so I certainly don't know."

"Maybe I will flirt with him. I think I would like him to court me."

Anna stared hard at her sister. She finally turned her around to look her in the face.

"Sampson is not a boy, Flory. He's a man. Don't toy with his feelings because you will only break his heart one time. He won't stick around to give you a chance to make things right. Make sure you remember that if you choose to flirt with him." She added wryly, "Of course, there is always the possibility he will have no feelings for you at all, and your efforts at flirting will be wasted." Anna turned away.

She looked over at her sister one more time before she climbed into bed and commented quietly, "I kind of hope he doesn't notice you. It would be safer for his heart that way."

CHAPTER 18

A Talk With a Cowboy

TILLIE CHOSE NOT TO GO WITH THE YOUNG PEOPLE to the train station.

"I've never been so good with goodbyes. I'll just hug you here. And if you don't come back, I am coming to see you no matter where you are." She smiled at Anna and almost teared up as she hugged her.

Two of Tillie's stable workers helped Sampson load Anna's luggage. In addition to the large trunk with all her books, she also had a Saratoga trunk with her clothing and personal items. The tray on top allowed her to pack her smaller items separately, and the metal banding around the oak slats gave the large trunk extra protection. The trunk was Tillie's and the woman insisted Anna take it.

"You need something more than a handbag to carry your new clothes, and Heaven knows I have extra trunks. Take it, Anna. Consider it a gift and something to remember me by."

Flory was all dimples when Sampson helped her into the carriage and Anna rolled her eyes.

Sampson winked at Anna and grinned as he gave her a hand up. Anna almost laughed. *Maybe he will be able to hold his own with Flory. At least he seems to be enjoying himself so far.*

All three of them were quiet on the ride to the station. When they arrived, Anna couldn't believe the activity. Men, women, and children were hurrying in all different directions.

Groups of cowboys were loading their horses onto the train while others were leading their mounts down the gangplank. Several offered to help Sampson load the heavy trunks. They departed quickly with a grin and a hat tip to the women.

Anna could feel the tears welling up in her eyes, and she took a deep breath as she smiled at the two people in front of her. Flory began to cry, and Anna kissed her cheek.

"This will be good for both of us, Flory. Be smart and be safe. Listen to the people around you who love you." She hugged her sister hard and smiled at Sampson. He wrapped her up in a bear hug.

"Take care of my sister but don't let her break your heart," she whispered as she hugged him.

Sampson laughed and nodded his head. "I'll see if I can manage both of those things. It might be difficult."

Anna turned and quickly mounted the steps to the train. She waved at them from the doorway before she took a seat beside the window. Flory was still waving, and Sampson put his arm around her as they walked away. Anna took a shaky breath and leaned back in her seat.

Two cowboys climbed into the car. There were two seats to the left of Anna and the first cowboy pointed at them.

"Por favor, señorita. Would you share your seats with two tired vaqueros?"

Anna smiled up at them and nodded.

"Of course. Make yourselves comfortable."

The cowboys sat down. One immediately went to sleep with his hat over his face but the one beside Anna seemed inclined to talk.

"Your traveling trunk, señorita. It is very heavy. Perhaps you bring a dead man west with you. Your husband perhaps?"

Anna stared at the cowboy in shock. His face showed no emotion, but his eyes were laughing. When she realized he was teasing, she laughed.

"No, nothing so interesting. It is full of books. I am a teacher, and I couldn't bear to leave my small library back East." She stared at the trunk for a moment and added softly, "It seems quite silly now. I don't know exactly how I am going to move it."

"Ah, señorita. My brother and I will be happy to help you unload your trunk if you disembark before us. Unfortunately for me, we must go to Texas to shoot some banditos who have stolen our cattle. Otherwise, I would follow you to offer my services."

Anna's eyes opened wide, and she stared at the man beside her for a moment. When he flashed her an onery grin, she laughed again.

"I think you are a joker, sir, but I will accept your offer to unload my trunk when I arrive in Council Grove.

"Are you returning home?"

The man paused a bit before he answered. "Texas was our home. Now our patron is fallecido—now that he is gone—we must go back to sell his ranchero. Then we will return to our new home in Cheyenne.

"And you, señorita. Where do you go when you leave Council Grove?"

Anna was quiet a moment. When she looked at the cowboy beside her, his eyes were so friendly, so sincere that she answered him honestly.

"I am going to Fort Laramie in the Wyoming Territory. I go to return money to a man. My sister agreed to be his mail order bride but changed her mind. I believe he deserves to be told in person. I am going there to meet him." Her eyes were wide as she spoke. She paused a moment before she continued. "I know little about him. He lost his wife a year ago. He has two small children, and he wants a mother for them." Her voice dropped to a whisper as she added, "I am so ashamed of my sister for pretending."

The man smiled at her and leaned back in his seat. "Sí, I understand. You are the older sister and so you must fix this problem." He nodded at the young man beside him. "I have a younger brother who is a little salvaje—I believe you say wild." He rolled his dark eyes as he looked at her somberly. "Alas, he is not such an angel as I am."

Anna watched him for a moment. When the man winked, she laughed. "I think, sir, you are probably not such an angel yourself."

"But I am, señorita. My sainted mother gave me this name. Angel. Angel Montero." He pointed to the sleeping man beside him. "And that is my brother, Miguel. Our sisters are waiting for us to return to the North Country.

"The older one is not married. I think perhaps she will never marry. Maybe she will be with me forever. My sister is a difficult woman."

Angel's eyes were dancing with a secret joke and once again, Anna laughed.

"I think, Mr. Montero, you are not such an angel, and most likely your sister is not as difficult as you say. Perhaps you think all women are difficult."

Angel chuckled and waved his hands. "Perhaps you are right. And you, señorita. What is your name? Or do you not share your name with friendly vaqueros?"

Anna shook her head.

"I will talk to you, Mr. Montero, but I will not tell you my name." She turned her head to the window as she watched the tall grass rush by. It was waving in the wind for as far as Anna could see. "I am from Pennsylvania. This is the furthest west I have ever been." She looked out her window a moment longer before she looked back at Angel. "Everything is so vast—so spread out here. How does one find his way around?"

Angel shrugged. "It is not so difficult. You just ride a smart caballo. Caballos—horses as you say—never get lost. They always find their way back home. I just hang on and let my trusty caballo take me to where I need to go."

Anna studied Angel's face. She asked quietly, "And is your horse smart or do you ride in circles as it follows its tail?"

Angel's eyebrows lifted in surprise and he laughed. As he studied her face, his look became more serious.

"Tell me, señorita. Do you plan to marry the man when you give him back his dinero? That is a long trip for a woman alone to make with only a man waiting at the end."

Pink color traveled up Anna's neck. Her chin jutted out slightly. Her voice was quiet when she answered. "I considered it. I feel sorry for the man. How does one become so desperate to find a mother for his children that he advertises for a wife? But no. As one of my friends pointed out, he may have even changed his mind.

"So no, I go only to return his money and to apologize. My sister also wrote him a letter and I will give that to him. When I finish, I will return to Kansas City. It is possible a teaching job is opening there. Or I may return to Council Grove. My aunt lives there.

"My sister loves the hustle and bustle of the city, but I prefer it quieter."

"Perhaps the young man who bid you goodbye will be disappointed when you don't return, yes?"

Anna's eyes opened wide as she stared at Angel.

"I think, Mr. Montero, you are much too interested in other people's affairs."

Angel chuckled as he leaned back in his seat. "Only in the ways of the heart, señorita." He paused and added dramatically, "I know my heart will most certainly be sad when we part. Perhaps I shall have to search for you in Council Grove when I return from Texas."

"And I think, Mr. Montero, you are as windy as the breeze that blows the tall grass outside this window." Anna heard Angel laugh but she didn't look over at him.

"Señorita, may I suggest something to you?"

Anna looked carefully at Angel. She didn't agree but she waited for him to speak.

"May I suggest you leave your large traveling trunk of books in Cheyenne? The stagecoach north will most likely not allow you to take two such heavy trunks, and you for sure will have to pay much extra. Ask someone at the train station to have it delivered to señor Rooster at the livery." His dark eyes were sparkling as he added, "Besides, it will be easier for you to track down your man if you have less to carry."

"He's not my man."

"Of course, you could leave a little note for me at the big oak tree in Council Grove before you leave. They call it the Post Office Oak. There is a small hole at the base of the tree where friends leave messages for each other. You could tell me what you have decided to do. You could even ask me to visit you." Angel's grin was wide at the shock on Anna's face.

"Sweethearts leave messages there as well. I always stop there when I come through. But alas, no little messages for me."

Anna stared at the man beside her. His boldness shocked her, but she laughed despite herself.

"I guarantee you, Mr. Montero, there will be no note from me in your tree." Her face colored slightly, and she shook her head. "You are a bold man to suggest such a thing. And you probably read all the notes in that tree even though they are not addressed to you!"

Angel chuckled softly. His face became more serious when he spoke again.

"Make a point to talk to the people who run each stage stop. There will be no towns on your route, and it is important someone remembers you. And when you arrive in Fort Laramie, leave something of yours with a little note—to me perhaps. Put the date you leave on the note and where you go."

Anna was silent as she listened to Angel. She could feel her heart clutch in her chest, but she forced herself to breathe evenly.

"I think, señorita, it would be wise to leave a little trail behind you. That way, someone will know if you do not return. Then those who search for you will know where to look. Or they will learn you have married your man and decided to stay."

Anna's face became pale, and her eyes opened wide as she stared at Angel.

"Just to be safe, señorita. Fort Laramie is very far from Kansas City. If your el tronco—your trunk—is still at the livery in Cheyenne two weeks after you pass through, someone such as myself can search for you. He can read the message and know how long you have been gone."

Angel's voice was soft as he continued. "Only one man waits for you, señorita. You could disappear and who would know where you go? Your friends in Kansas City? They are too far away. No, I think you must leave a little trail."

"You do not know me, Mr. Montero. That is a lot to ask of someone I just met."

The sparkles were back in Angel's eyes when he answered. "I have a very large heart, señorita. One that is large enough to care about many women, especially beautiful women with hair the color of the sunset." He smiled at her and was quiet as he watched her face. His voice was soft when he spoke again.

"The stage to Fort Laramie is very wild, señorita. It would not be good for you to become lost."

"I will give it some thought, Mr. Montero. And thank you for your concern…even if it is only because you like to talk to women." Anna heard him chuckle again, but she kept her face to the window. *And I certainly will not leave my books or my beautiful trunk in Cheyenne. I know no one there and who knows what would happen to my trunk in a livery with all those animals.* Anna frowned as she thought about what Angel had said. *His advice was valid about leaving a trail. Something to ponder on.*

CHAPTER 19

AUNT MAE

A SHORT, OLDER WOMAN WITH A ROUND FACE AND large smile rushed to meet Anna as she stepped down from the train on Sunday afternoon.

"Anna! I received Florence's letter yesterday. She told me you were coming to visit!" She wrapped the younger woman up in a huge hug. She looked around her at the two young cowboys who were lugging a huge trunk down the steps and onto the train platform.

"You cowboys just bring that trunk right over here. And thank you so much for helping Anna with her traveling cases."

Angel and Miguel slid the heavy trunk of books into the back of the waiting wagon and Angel returned with Anna's second trunk. Miguel grabbed one end of it and the two men tossed it into the back of the wagon as well. Angel's face was serious as he nodded at the items in the wagon.

"I think, señorita, perhaps you should marry your man if he is large and strong. Your items are very heavy, almost more than a handsome vaquero such as myself can handle." He bowed deeply to her and jumped back onto the platform.

"Until we meet again, señorita!" Angel's smile was large and he winked at Anna as he tipped his hat. He was laughing as he ducked into the train.

Aunt Mae cocked an eyebrow and Anna rolled her eyes.

"Just a cowboy I met on the train. He was entertaining but was quite full of himself."

Her aunt laughed and hurried her to the wagon.

"You will most likely meet many young cowboys here, especially if you help me in our Last Chance Store while you are here.

"Now tell me all about this trip. What on earth made you come west? Not that I am complaining. I am delighted!" Her aunt talked excitedly, and Anna didn't have to answer even half of the questions she was asked.

Aunt Mae lived just outside of town on a small ranch. Uncle Chip had died ten years before. He had come once with Aunt Mae to visit them in Pennsylvania and Anna only vaguely remembered him. The ranch was tidy though with mended fences and a neat garden.

Anna looked at her aunt in surprise. "You run your ranch by yourself?"

Aunt Mae shook her head. She jumped down from the wagon and called, "I'm home, Herman. Now come up here and help us carry these trunks in."

An older man stepped out of the barn with a smile. A younger cowboy was closing the gate to a pasture. He mounted his horse and rode slowly toward the house.

"Anna, this is Herman Kelly. We married just last year. That young scamp is William Hanson. He has been helping me around here for the last six years." She waved her arm around the yard. "He's the one who really keeps things running. Herman and I mostly putter when we are not in the store.

"Herman owned the Last Chance Store with his wife. She passed about seven years ago." She looped her arm through Herman's and smiled up at him. "He has been pestering me to marry him for the last five years. I kept telling him we were too old, but he finally wore me down.

"Fellows, this is Anna Whitman, my niece. Her father was my baby brother."

The young cowboy dismounted with his hat in his hand. His voice was low, and he talked with a drawl.

"Pleasure, ma'am. Welcome to our part a Kansas. Y'all plan to stay long?"

Anna looked around at the three of them and stuttered a bit. "I—well—I'm not sure."

She looked toward Aunt Mae. "You mentioned you might need some help in the store. I'd be glad to help you out while I'm here. I don't want to be a burden since I invited myself."

Aunt Mae beamed as she grabbed Anna's arm. "Nonsense. You stay as long as you want. Herman and I love company. Neither of us have any children so we rarely have young folks around. It will be fun.

"Now you men bring those trunks in here. I am going to show Anna to her room in case she wants to rest a bit before supper."

The room that was to be Anna's was small but cozy. The bed was half the size of the one she slept in at Tillie's. Still, it was comfortable. Anna opened her chest and hung up her clothes.

Tillie had sent four dresses with her. Besides the green suit, there were two cotton dresses that would be appropriate to teach or work in, and one pale lavender party dress.

Anna shook her head as she looked at it. "I can't think of a place I would want to go where that would be appropriate." She touched the green suit and smiled. "What a wonderful gift Tillie has been to both Flory and me. A mother, a friend, and a big sister all tied up in one."

She loosened her corset and lay down on the bed. It was dark when she awakened. Her small watch locket showed eleven and it was dark outside. The house was quiet. Anna slipped out of her dress and climbed into bed.

CHAPTER 20

An Acquaintance in Common

LAUGHTER AND VOICES COULD BE HEARD FROM below when Anna awakened. She dressed quickly and rushed down the stairs.

"I'm so sorry. I didn't mean to fall asleep, nor to sleep so late this morning."

"Nonsense. You were tired.

"Now you sit down here and eat. You are just a little bit of nothing. I need to put some meat on those bones before you leave here."

Will tapped on the door before he walked in. He hung his hat on a nail and pulled up a chair.

"Thought I might ride around those cows in the south pasture. I heard a cat last night so there is probably some fence down if they spooked." He looked over at Anna.

"Want to ride along?"

Anna looked at him in surprise. "I—not today. I thought I would go into town with Aunt Mae."

"Y'all ever ride a hoss?"

"When I was younger, but it has been over ten years since I've ridden horseback. I don't even own any riding clothes."

"Britches work just fine. Mae can set y'all up if ya'd like to go sometime."

Will's intense blue eyes burned into Anna's and she looked away. *Britches! I don't think so! No lady would ever wear britches.* Her cheeks tinted pink at the thought.

Anna focused on her food and Mae laughed.

"We'll see if we can't fix you up with something." She waved her arm in a semi-circle. "They call the land around here the Flint Hills. Mornings are beautiful. You certainly need to go riding while you are here.

"Now eat your breakfast. We like to open the store by seven-thirty. I didn't do any restocking on Saturday, so I need to do that before we open this morning as well."

"Is your store open every day?"

"Every day but Sunday. Services are at nine. This next Sunday, we are having a potluck dinner afterwards.

"Herman and I take it easy on Sundays, but Will works hard every day." She smiled at the quiet cowboy. "We are blessed to have him around.

"Let me pack a quick lunch for us and we will take the wagon to town. Herman usually works around here for a time before he comes in." Mae jumped up and was rushing around the kitchen. She called over her shoulder, "No time for you to take a bath this morning. The men can bring water in tonight if you want one when we get home.

"Just use that basin if you want to freshen your face a little. We'll leave here in about five minutes."

Anna hurried upstairs and quickly twisted her hair into a bun. She touched the small cross around her neck that had belonged to her mother, slipped on her shoes, and hurried back downstairs.

Mae handed her a bag of produce and the two women were quickly on their way to Council Grove.

"Have you ever worked in a store, Anna?"

"I worked in the little store in our town every summer for six years after school let out in May. Old Mr. Murphy basically let me run it for him when I was there. I'm sure each store is a little different though, so just tell me what you want done."

Mae was quiet a moment. Her eyes were serious when she looked at Anna.

"Florence said you had been staying with a 'Tillie' while you were in Kansas City. I am guessing that was Tillie Maynard.

"Did she tell you what she did for a living before she married?"

Anna was quiet as she looked over at Mae. Her aunt almost looked angry.

"She said she was an entertainer."

"Ha! She entertained all right and most of it was without her clothes on. She was a no-good woman then, and I doubt she has changed much.

"Don't mention you know her while you are here. She broke up several marriages. Most of the women here will not look on you kindly if they know you befriended her."

Anna could feel anger pushing up inside her. She tried to pinch it off, but it leaked out in her voice.

"Aunt Mae, Tillie is my friend. I don't know what she was like when you knew her and quite frankly, I don't care. She is a good and kind woman now, generous with her home and her friendship.

"I won't mention her to your friends, but please don't disparage her in front of me. She has been nothing but a friend to Flory and me."

Aunt Mae scowled at Anna for a moment. Finally, she threw back her head and laughed.

"You sounded exactly like your mother just then. I always admired her spunk. She never took any sass off anyone. Came across as so quiet but she had whipcord for a backbone.

"I reckon that's fair. I won't talk badly of her, and you don't mention her at all.

"Now let's talk about what you would like to see or do while you are here.

"You know, if you would like to stay longer in Council Grove, I could certainly use your help. Herman froze his feet several winters ago and it pains him to stand for very long. In fact, if you could stay for the rest of the summer, that would be wonderful. I don't know what you have planned when you leave here but give that some thought. Summer and early fall are our busiest times, and September isn't that far away."

CHAPTER 21

ALL THIS FOR A WOMAN

ANNA HAD WORKED AT AUNT MAE'S STORE FOR LESS than two weeks when a voice she recognized spoke behind her.

"Ah, señorita, I see you found a job. Perhaps your man became tired of waiting and married someone else, yes?"

Anna turned around slowly as she blushed.

"I told you he is not my man, and yes, maybe he did. I wouldn't know."

"You don't go to Fort Laramie?"

"I am still going but not until later. Aunt Mae needs help here this summer and I am available. I will wire him when I leave Denver."

"Then perhaps I will see you when you pass through my town. There are not so many vaqueros in Cheyenne who can dance so well as me." Angel grabbed Anna's hand and twirled her around. He laughed when she almost dropped the britches she held in her hand.

"Señora Mae tells me there is a dance in town this evening. Perhaps you will do me the honor of attending it with me?"

Anna stared at Angel a moment and started to shake her head.

"Come, señorita. We may never see each other again. Don't break the heart of this tired vaquero so quickly. My brother and I must continue to Cheyenne tomorrow. A dance on a beautiful night with a handsome vaquero who can dance many dances without tiring. Say yes, señorita." His dark eyes sparkled as he held her hand.

Anna pulled her hand away and shook her head. "I have turned down several young men already, and I don't want to commit to going."

"Perhaps you don't like to dance?"

Anna looked away and took a quick breath before she looked back at him. Her voice was barely a whisper when she answered.

"I have never danced, Mr. Montero. I would only step on your toes, and we would both be very embarrassed."

Angel's laugh was light as he shook his head.

"My feet are very quick, señorita. I don't think you will be able to catch them—and if you do, it will be my fault. Now come. Say yes and I will bring la calesa—the—a buggy I think you say. And maybe a few flowers for a bella dama, a beautiful lady. I can teach you to dance. I think it will not be so difficult."

Anna wanted to say no but Angel's smile changed her mind.

"All right, but I don't want to stay late. I have to be at work by seven tomorrow morning."

Angel smiled and bowed deeply.

"I will see you at seven-thirty tonight, señorita. Until then." He backed out of the store with a smile and strolled jauntily up the street. When he was out of site, he almost ran to the livery to rent a buggy. He rushed back to the hotel where he was staying with Miguel and grabbed clean clothes before he headed to the bath area.

"So she said yes? All this for a woman? Never have I seen you work so hard to spend time with a woman. Perhaps I too will go to this dance to see what is so special about señorita Whitman." Miguel was laughing at his brother as he jabbed him. He grabbed clean clothes and followed Angel out of the room.

Angel slipped into a yard full of flowers and picked a few on his way back to the hotel. He dropped them in the water pitcher in his room and wandered down to the saloon. Miguel was in conversation with a cowboy at the bar. Angel laughed as he recognized the man.

The cowboy's face broke into a grin when he spotted Angel. He shoved his hand across the bar and gripped the rider's hand.

"Angel, ya durn cow dancer. Good to see ya. Are ya stayin' here or jist a passin' through?"

Angel shook his head. "No, señor Dink. We came through on the train. We are on our way back north. Señor Gabe bought a ranch and we work for him.

"Just an evening here and we catch the train tomorrow to Cheyenne."

Dink studied the two men and his eyes settled on Angel.

"Ya shore look all gussied up. Don't tell me y'all have a date tonight?" When Angel's smile became bigger, Dink snorted.

"Shoot. I cain't find a gal in all a Kansas who wants to walk out with me an' y'all jist waltz into town of an evenin' an' have some little gal ya don't even know agree to go to a dance.

"Durn women. They shore know how to break a feller's heart."

Angel chuckled.

"And you, señor Dink. You don't stay in Dodge for the winter? I thought you had a riding job there."

"Naa. I thought I was in love with a gal down there, but she shut me down. I quit my ridin' job an' helped trail this herd up here. A feller outside town is drivin' some cows north, an' he's lookin' fer a few riders. I figgered I'd join up with him. We leave at first light. I had a few hours off so I thought I'd grab a beer.

"Boss thought mebbie some of us would want to get a bath 'fore we left so I come in town with the other fellers.

"Don't know why some folks put such importance on takin' a bath. I figger once a month is more than enough. Jist took one Saturday night an' that'll do me till the end of the drive." He swirled his beer a moment before he took another drink.

"There's a weddin' dance tonight an' it should be a big one. I hate to miss all that good food but I ain't a goin'. I'd jist stay out too late, probably git in a fight, an' be hurtin' all over. 'Sides, I cain't dance anyway. The bride, she be from a ranch family south a town an' the feller she's a marryin'—his pappy owns a big ranch to the west. Shoot, twixt the two families, they'll have nigh on half the grass 'round here tied up.

"Must be nice to marry money."

Miguel laughed and raised his glass. "Here is to amor, señor Dink. May love catch you someday!"

Dink laughed and raised his glass. "Here's to beer, cows, and women—an' in that order too!" He drained his glass and slammed it down on the table.

"Sure is good to see ya boys. I should a gone north with Gabe. Durn women.

"Maybe I'll see y'all up there. Ya never know." Dink strolled out of the saloon. He turned in the doorway and waved his hat.

"So long, boys. Have a good trip an' tell the fellers howdy fer me."

CHAPTER 22

A Date with a Cowboy

ANNA STARED AT THE LAVENDER DRESS FOR A MOMENT. She touched the soft fabric and finally slipped it over her head.

She had protested when Flory had folded it into her trunk. "I don't need it. Where in the world am I going to wear something like that?"

Flory had laughed and Tillie had hugged her.

"Take the dress, Anna. It will be beautiful on you."

Anna stared at herself in the mirror. The dress fit perfectly. The neck was scooped but not too low. Flory wanted to make it lower, but Anna refused to wear it if she did. "And make the sleeves longer, Flory. There are barely any there. I am not wearing a dress that shows that much skin."

Somehow Flory had managed to make the sleeves reach almost to Anna's elbows. They had tiny purple flowers woven throughout the fabric. Flory had added a sash of the same fabric. The dress was simple but beautiful, and Anna had to admit she loved it.

Aunt Mae knocked on her door and stared at Anna in surprise.

"That is truly lovely, Anna!"

"You don't think it is too much? It is much fancier than anything I have ever worn."

Aunt Mae shook her head. "You look beautiful. I thought I would come and see if you wanted any help with your hair, but it looks like you are ready."

She touched the small cross around Anna's neck.

"Marlena wore that on her wedding. Your mother was a beautiful woman and Alfred adored her. He gave it to her as a wedding gift, and she rarely took it off after that." She kissed her niece and held her shoulders as she smiled up at her.

"You are every bit as lovely as your mother was—tall and slender. Florence has her blond hair, and you have your father's red curls.

"Ah, but your father was a handsome man.

"Of course, Florence acts more like our side of the family with all her chatter and smiles. You are more like your mother. Such a quiet elegance without even trying."

Aunt Mae studied Anna's dress. She asked softly, "Was your dress a gift from Tillie?"

A blush climbed up Anna's neck before she turned away from her aunt.

"It was. I didn't want to take it and I'm not sure I should even wear it. I think I'll wear something plainer. This is much too fancy and I—"

"Wear the dress, Anna. It is perfect. Who knows when you will have a chance to wear it again, especially if you stay up North."

Anna looked at her aunt in surprise.

"I'm not marrying him, Aunt Mae. I am going to give him his money back."

Mae studied her niece and sighed.

"He will be a fool if he doesn't try to make you stay. You will fall in love with those little children, and it will all be over."

"I doubt I will even meet them. I told him the entire truth in that letter I sent him. He should receive it long before I leave. He may even tell me not to come."

Aunt Mae's eyes were soft as she looked at Anna.

"No, Anna. Your letter is going to make him fall in love with you before you even meet. Mr. Dan Morton's heart will be all a flutter when you step out of that stage. He will have those two little ones with him, and his smile will be so big you will see only that beneath his hat.

"They are all going to be there to greet you, and it will be all over for both of you." Aunt Mae smiled and hugged her.

"So you go to this dance tonight. You have fun with that handsome cowboy who is already waiting downstairs—and with flowers too.

"And just so you know, I recognize those flowers. He took them out of Ruby Masters' yard. I was down there yesterday, and she was showing them to me. She counted the blossoms she had too so don't talk too much about them." Aunt Mae's eyes twinkled, and she laughed as she hurried out of Anna's room.

"Now come down quickly so I don't run out of things to say to your cowboy."

CHAPTER 23

ANGEL

ANGEL SMILED UP AT ANNA AS HE STEPPED TO THE foot of the stairs.

"Señorita, you are a vision for these tired eyes! Surely I am not the only angel in this room." His dark eyes were dancing as he spoke, and Anna laughed in spite of herself.

"I think, Mr. Montero, you have had much practice at being charming."

"Si, señorita, but not often do I have someone so lovely as you to practice my charms on."

He bowed dramatically to Aunt Mae and presented her with the flowers he had stolen.

"Beautiful flowers for a beautiful heart. For you, señora. I managed to find these on the prairie with great difficulty. It seems they only grow in one small place, a location I cannot share with you."

Aunt Mae accepted them as she laughed. "Yes, I think it is best you don't tell anyone where they came from—and I will not tell Ruby Masters I have some of her beautiful flowers in a vase on my table!"

Angel's grin was wide as he bowed again to her. He offered his arm to Anna.

"Shall we go? I think my feet are very excited to dance tonight. They are happy for me to hold a beautiful woman and spin her across the floor."

"Well, your feet may be disappointed. I wasn't joking about never having danced."

"And I was not joking about showing you." He lifted Anna easily into the buggy and jumped in beside her.

Angel clucked to the horses and commented softly, "It has been many years since I have taken a woman to a dance."

Anna looked at him in surprise. "But you said you liked to dance."

"Sí, this is true. Most often I go by myself. Then I try to pick the prettiest girl to dance with. This time, I asked the prettiest girl to go with me."

Anna was quiet and Angel lifted a blanket from behind the seat.

"I will lay this beside you, señorita Whitman. Sometimes these rides can be cool although tonight feels quite warm to me."

Anna was quiet. She glanced at Angel before she asked, "How did you find me? I didn't even tell you my name."

Angel chuckled as he smiled down at her. "I asked for the new woman in town who had hair the color of the sunset. I checked in every saloon and was finally told your name." His dark eyes danced as he added, "All the men in the saloons knew of you. I think perhaps you have spent a little time there."

Anna's face turned a deep red and she sputtered as she answered.

"I—why I—I would never—how dare you ask about me in the saloons!"

Angel laughed down at her. "Don't worry, señorita. I knew your aunt had a dry goods store Besides, she said your name the day you arrived here. I looked for you in the stores. This town doesn't have so many that I couldn't find you."

Anna draped the end of her blanket over her legs before she looked at Angel.

"Tell me about your family, Mr. Montero. I know you have two sisters and a brother. What about your parents? How did you come to move from Texas to Wyoming?"

"Señorita Anna, we must not be so formal. We are friends, yes? I am Angel and you are Anna. No more Mister, sí?"

"Only if you tell me about your family."

Angel laughed and nodded. "Sí. We grew up on the Brazos River in Texas outside a town called Buffalo Gap. I am the oldest, then Miguel, then Merina and finally, our baby sister, Emilia. She is four.

"Our papá died moving cattle across the Brazos. He drowned when the cattle milled. They began to pile up and jump on each other in the middle of the river. Papá tried to break the mill and his horse went down. More cattle ran over him, and we could not save him. After that, Miguel and I took jobs to support our family.

"Mamá died about two years ago. Señor Cole, our patron, tried to help her. He called in his big doctors, but nothing could be done. And so, Merina did Mamá's work and her own. She also cared for our little sister.

"Then señor Cole decided to drive some of his vacas north to Dodge City in Kansas. It was a bad drive. He did not hire vaqueros, just some chicos who needed jobs. Those boys knew little of vacas and even less about trailing them—cattle, I mean.

"That is where I met señor Gabe. He tried to convince our patron one night that he should turn back or sell the vacas to him." Angel shrugged. "Señor Cole refused, and he died in a stampede the next night.

"There was nothing for Merina in Texas, so both she and Miguel met me in Dodge City—with Emilia of course. That was to be the end of our drive. It wasn't though. We took some of the cattle further north.

"Now Gabe is my compadre. I work with him. Perhaps he will marry my sister and take both Merina and Emilia into his home. I do not know.

"And Miguel—well, Miguel does what Miguel wants. He doesn't work so much as he uses his guns.

"Our home is now in the Wyoming Territory. When we get back, I hope to buy a ranchero close to Gabe's. Our families will work together to grow our cattle." He looked at Anna.

"And you, Anna? You have one sister. No other family?"

Anna shook her head. "No, just Flory. Mother and Father died in a buggy accident when I was fourteen. I took a job and studied after work to complete my schooling. Flory and I managed to stay together. When I was eighteen, I was recommended for a teaching job in our little town in Pennsylvania. I taught there six years. There was a problem at school, and I was released from my contract. That was when we came west.

"I don't think Flory will ever leave Kansas City. She is happy there. And I might stay in Council Grove. I like it here. I miss teaching but—it was difficult when I left.

"I do have two letters of recommendation. One is from the school there and one is from a woman I worked for in Kansas City. Still, I'm not sure. I don't want to go through that again." Anna shivered and Angel draped the blanket across her shoulders.

He was quiet for a moment before he commented casually, "Our little school south of Cheyenne is looking for a teacher. It is on a ranch. Many of my friends have children. My sister was going to teach, but she would rather work outside." Angel grinned and added, "Merina would rather rope calves and fix fence than teach school. She is a difficult woman.

"I told Gabe she was difficult, but he does not listen. He is thinking now of courting her. If they marry, he will have to put up with her forever."

Anna laughed out loud, and Angel grinned at her. "She is not so much an angel as me."

"I don't know that I could ever take a teaching job where I was a complete stranger."

"You know me."

"Yes, but you have no wife or children." Her body went still for a moment. She almost held her breath as she asked carefully, "Do you?"

124

Angel laughed and shook his head. "No, Anna. There is only me. Many women think they love me, so I often run away." Once again, his eyes were dancing, and Anna laughed as she shook her head.

Angel pulled the horse to a stop and jumped out of the buggy. After he tied the horse, he lifted Anna down. He tucked her arm through his and led her into the dance.

CHAPTER 24

A WEDDING DANCE

ANNA PULLED BACK ON HIS ARM. "I DON'T THINK THIS is a good idea. What if I trip you? Or fall down?"

Angel patted her hand. "Then they will think that we drank too much whiskey, and we are both mucho borracho—I think you say drunk."

Anna stopped so suddenly that Angel almost tripped. When she stared up at him in horror he began to laugh.

"Don't worry, Anna. I won't let you fall."

Many of the young men were leaning against one of the walls, and they all stared as Anna and Angel walked in.

"This was a terrible idea. I had forgotten how many men I turned down when they asked me to go with them tonight."

Angel grinned down at her. "Of course, because only a handsome vaquero could take such a beautiful woman to a dance."

Anna looked at him sideways and asked sarcastically, "Do you always call yourself handsome?"

Angel appeared to be shocked.

"Sí, of course! My ego is very fragile. I cannot speak the truth to myself on all things. What man wants to hear himself called homely?"

Angel appeared to be sincere, but his eyes were laughing. Anna tried not to but she laughed with him.

"Come, let's dance. We can look for seats as I swing you around." He spun her onto the wooden dance floor, twirled her in a circle and then caught her as they continued to spin.

"I think perhaps, Anna, you did not tell me the truth. I believe you have danced before."

"Only with my father when I was a child—and he did not hold me this tightly. Please loosen your arm."

"I cannot do it. I'm afraid I will drop you and everyone will think we are drunk. No, I think I must hold you tightly, so you don't trip or fall."

The dance was finally over, and Angel laughed down at her.

"See, we did not trip, and I did not drop you. Now tell me, Anna, was that not fun?"

"It was fun but next time I am going to brace my elbow against you. I think you are a very smooth vaquero, and I am not going to make it so easy for you to hold me tightly."

Miguel waved at them from across the room, and Angel guided Anna to his table.

"Señorita Anna, this is Miguel, my brother."

Miguel stood and bowed to Anna. "Yes, I see why my brother was so eager to stop here for the night. It is nice to meet you, señorita Anna."

Anna looked from one brother to the other. The two men almost looked like twins. Both were slim with curly black hair. Both had mustaches. Miguel's was bushy while Angel's was trimmed. Angel was also a little taller than Miguel. However, their family resemblance was even stronger when they smiled.

"I see charm runs in your family," Anna replied with a laugh. She reached out her hand to Miguel. "And it is nice to meet you as well, Mr. Montero."

Several young men were headed their way and Angel grabbed Anna's hand.

"This one is a waltz. Just listen to the music and slide. I will guide you."

Angel spun her out onto the floor. Anna was so caught up in the smoothness of the dance that she forgot to block him with her elbow. They spun across the floor and only Angel noticed all the angry glances directed their way.

He looked toward Miguel. His brother was relaxed with his gun hand hanging loosely by his side. He was smiling but Angel knew his brother too well.

When the dance ended, Angel led Anna toward the young men.

"Hola! My sister-in-law was pointing out her friends and I wanted to introduce myself.

"Angel Montero. I am in town for the evening, and I thought I would spend it with Anna as I passed through your fine town.

"You have lived here many years, yes?"

The young men were expecting a fight with the outsider, and Angel's friendliness caught them off-guard.

"Your sister-in-law?"

"Sí. Anna's brother asked me to look in on her. He is a big rancher up in the Wyoming Territory. Very fast with his pistols. I do not want to make him angry, so I did as he asked." He reached toward each of the men and shook hands as they introduced themselves.

"Now if you don't mind, señors, I must dance a few more dances before I take Anna home. I promised her brother I would not keep her out late."

He quickly turned Anna away from the puzzled young men and guided her onto the dance floor.

As he spun her into another waltz, Anna looked up at him. "I don't have a brother and now I am going to have to lie."

"Sí, but the young men, they were looking for a fight. I do not like to fight. Now, we are friends and there is no fight."

"It is always better to part as friends. What is to be gained by fighting? I am not from here and your sheriff might not look at a strange vaquero as a friendly man. Besides, I must keep Miguel from using his guns. He is not so much an angel as I am.

"Now come. Let us talk of pleasant things." His dark eyes danced as he added, "Your brother insisted I not keep you out too late."

They danced until ten that night. When the slow dance ended, Angel led Anna toward the buggy.

"See, I will have you home by ten-thirty. Then, I will go back to my room and dream about tonight."

Anna laughed softly.

"You are an interesting man, Angel. I just knew there would be a fight. You are a very smooth talker."

"Sí, I tell Gabe often he must let me do the talking. My compadre doesn't like people so much as I do. Perhaps if my sister marries him, she will make him less cranky." He shrugged. "I do not know. She is a difficult woman."

Anna laughed and the two of them rode in silence until they arrived at Aunt Mae's house. Angel looked over at her.

"I hope, señorita Anna, that you do not marry that cowboy. I will look for your trunk in Cheyenne." Angel's dark eyes were serious as he looked into hers and Anna looked away.

"I told you I have no intention of marrying him. I even wrote him and told him the truth. He will probably tell me to stay here. I doubt he wants anything to do with Flory or me."

"No, he will want you to come. What a woman to do such for her sister. Yes, he will want you to come, and he will want to marry you." Angel turned her head toward him as he whispered, "And what will you say?"

Anna stared at Angel and her eyes opened wide. She whispered, "I will tell him no."

Angel kissed her. The first one was just a soft peck. The second one was longer.

Anna was a little breathless as she pulled away.

"You remember that kiss, Anna. You remember it when he asks you to marry him. You leave that little message, and I will come for you."

Angel jumped down from the wagon and put up his hands to lift Anna down. As he stood close to her, he lifted up a curl that was hanging on her neck and dropped it. When he leaned in to kiss her again, Anna stepped back.

She turned and hurried toward the house. She stopped in the doorway and called softly, "Perhaps I will see you in Cheyenne, Mr. Montero. Until then," and she was gone.

Angel's heart should have been light, but it was heavy. As he turned the horse toward town, he shook his head.

"I think, señorita, you will not come back to me. I think I will have to search for you, and I fear you will marry that cowboy."

CHAPTER 25

A Short Summer

THE SUMMER WENT BY QUICKLY. ANNA WENT TO several dances with girlfriends, but she always went home alone.

Will finally talked her into riding with him. At first, she wore a pair of Uncle Herman's britches. However, they were way too big. Besides, Anna hated wearing britches.

Aunt Mae offered to help her make a riding skirt. Anna wasn't as talented as Flory with her needles, and it took her nearly three weeks to finish it. Will asked her every day if it was completed and was delighted when she said yes.

They rode out after church services on a Sunday. Aunt Mae insisted they take a picnic lunch.

Will was a little more relaxed since they knew each other better, and Anna enjoyed their ride.

They leaned against a fallen tree and visited as they ate.

When they finished, Will helped Anna clean things up. His hand touched hers as she folded the blanket, and he kept it there.

"Is there a chance for me, Anna? I don't want to bother ya if there ain't."

Anna shook her head as she smiled at him.

"You are my friend, Will. I'm glad I met you, but…"

"But there ain't nothin' more." He was silent a moment. His dark blue eyes drilled into her as he spoke.

"Yore in love with that Angel feller, ain't ya? I saw how dreamy ya was after he left. An' now yore headed north to meet another feller. It just don't make no sense a'tall."

Anna blushed a deep red. "I'm not sure if I'm in love with Angel or not and as far as Mr. Morton—I am going there to give him his money back. That's all."

"I did receive a letter from him thanking me for making the trip. He sounds like a nice man. He doesn't seem upset that Flory is not coming or that she wanted to keep his money.

"Besides, I may be back. Who knows where I will end up? It has been a wonderful three months here.

"I bought my train ticket yesterday. I will be leaving on September twenty-ninth. The stage to Deadwood takes fifty hours on average to go the full length. I am only going about a third of the way so that part of my trip should take between sixteen and eighteen hours. The north and south coaches meet each other enroute so they run each way several days a week.

"If I planned my route correctly, I won't have to stay long in the towns I go through. I should be in Fort Laramie early morning on the second of October." Her face blushed slightly as she added, "My longest stop will be in Cheyenne and that will only be overnight."

"That Angel feller gonna meet ya there?"

"No, he doesn't even know my schedule. I hadn't made travel arrangements yet when he was here." Anna's face became a little redder when she added, "Besides, I don't know where he lives.

"If we meet, it will be by chance."

"Hard to believe ya can make it all the way up to the Wyomin' Territory an' further in four days. That's a passel a travelin'." He grinned at Anna as he helped her up.

134

"We best get on back. Now that I know there ain't no hope fer me, I reckon I can relax an' enjoy myself.

"Probably should take a few more rides 'fore ya head out. Who knows when y'all be back on a horse.

"An' if ya see a woman up there ya think might work fer me, send her on down."

Anna rolled her eyes.

"Will, you have to be blind if you haven't seen little Sissy Hammond making eyes at you."

When Will stared at her, Anna laughed.

"Good grief, Will! She makes it point to talk to you after church every Sunday. She turns all pink when you smile at her. Of course she's interested!"

"Why she's nothin' but a kid. She was barely out a pig tails when I come here."

"She *was* twelve. Now she's eighteen and you are twenty-four. That is only six years difference.

"There's a box supper after church on Sunday. Buy her box and eat with her."

Will grinned at her and Anna laughed again.

"Men! You are so blind! How did you not figure that out?"

"I like ya, Anna. I'm glad y'all come here. I ain't never had a friend before who was a woman. I didn't even know fellers had woman friends.

"Y'all are all right. That durn smooth-talkin' Angel may have won ya over but y'all will always be my best gal friend."

Both were laughing when they mounted their horses.

"Two more weeks. I have some more places I want to show ya. I'd best get my days planned out."

CHAPTER 26

Anna's Farewell Party

AUNT MAE WANTED TO THROW A FAREWELL PARTY FOR Anna. Even though Anna argued, her aunt insisted.

"Just a few friends. Nothing fancy, I promise."

"I will be back. There is no reason for all this fuss. Besides, I don't know many people anyway. I have only been here a little over three months."

Anna's protests were wasted. Aunt Mae was not to be persuaded and the party was planned. People drove out to the Kelly Ranch after church on Sunday, September twenty-eighth, and it wasn't long before the yard was full of running children. The men had set boards over barrels and those were now covered with food.

Potlucks had always amazed Anna. *How do all these people find out, let alone know what to make? There is always such a variety.*

Even the young men who had tried to court Anna came, and most of them arrived together. After the dance, they had been good-natured about her refusals of all of them. Of course, besides Angel, Anna hadn't let anyone take her places or walk out with her. She was friendly to all of them but showed no interest in their attentions.

Anna paused to look for Will as she carried more pans of food to the table. He was leaning against the fence watching a very animated Sissy Hammond. He smiled as she looked up at him and talked excitedly.

Will had bid on Sissy's basket at the box supper last week. He bid it up to $15 before he walked away. In fact, he didn't even stay for the picnic. He was irritated and a little angry with himself for making a spectacle. Sissy was delighted though.

The young man who won was able to eat her food but even he could tell Sissy wasn't overly delighted with how things had turned out. He thanked her and strolled off to join his buddies when he finished.

Sissy promptly refilled the basket from the kettles and bowls on the table and made a trip out to the Kelly Ranch to find Will. They had a wonderful afternoon as they sat and visited under the big oak tree in Aunt Mae's yard.

Laughter bubbled out of Anna as she set the pan she was carrying down on the table. Aunt Mae looked up in surprise and Anna nodded toward the smiling Will.

"It looks like you had better make plans for a married hired man. He finally noticed Sissy Hammond, and he seems to be enjoying himself."

Aunt Mae was quiet a moment as she studied her niece's face.

"I thought maybe you and Will had something in common as much time as you spent together this last month."

"Just friends, Aunt Mae. Will is a fine man and he will make a wonderful husband—for Sissy, not for me." She laughed as Aunt Mae watched Will.

"Smile, Aunt Mae! Sissy is a kind person, and she has loved Will since she was in pigtails. I know this because she told me. Besides, her pa loves him, and they often work together. You are just going to have to share your best hand."

"My only hand, and Sissy's father owns a lot of land."

Anna laughed again. She waved at Will and hurried back into the house. She visited with several of the older women and was soon outside with another heavy pan in her hands.

Will strolled over with a grin on his face as he took the pan from her hands and set it down on the table. Anna tried to keep from laughing and Will's grin became bigger.

"I reckon I am a little blind but things are lookin' up." His eyes followed Sissy as she hurried into the house. "How did I miss Sissy was all grown up?" Will's voice reflected his confusion.

Anna bumped him with her elbow as she laughed. "Come on. Someone brought an entire ham, and I would like some help carrying it. There had better not be much more food. These boards are already swaying. Before long, they will collapse."

Everyone there made it a point to talk to Anna. They all wanted to make sure she knew she was welcome to come back. Anna just laughed.

"I have no plans to stay up North. I have very much enjoyed my visit here. And thank you for coming."

By four that afternoon, the yard was once again empty. Someone had taken the boards and barrels apart, and nearly everything was back in place.

Aunt Mae sank down on her porch swing and patted the seat beside her.

"Come sit beside me and let's talk about your plans. Tell me again when your train leaves tomorrow morning."

"It should be here around eight-thirty. I want to be at the station by eight in case it is running early. Once I leave, it is only about seven hours or so until I reach Dodge City. That train runs on into Denver and it should take me thirteen hours, maybe less. The agent said that leg will be slower since we will be climbing and will need to go through some mountains. From Denver, it should be less than three hours to Cheyenne. So, if all goes as planned, I should arrive in Cheyenne between six-thirty and seven-thirty on Tuesday morning, September 30.

"My stage to Fort Laramie doesn't leave until October second. That means I have a little extra time if anything is delayed. The stages going north leave Cheyenne on Mondays and Thursdays. I think that means the stages running south leave Deadwood on Tuesdays and Saturdays. I'm not exactly sure when they will be coming through Fort Laramie but I would assume the same day." Anna patted her aunt's hand.

"Don't worry, Aunt Mae. I will be fine. Lots of women travel by themselves now. It is much safer than it was even ten years ago. I promise to spend the night in Cheyenne and be all refreshed for the rest of my trip."

"I will worry. You write me when you reach Cheyenne. I want to know you made it safely. Those trains get robbed you know, and stagecoaches are dangerous. Why the outlaws are rampant up there not to mention the early snows and terrible roads."

"Aunt Mae, the trains running north haul mostly beef and provisions. Of course, there will be some mail too but mostly cattle from what I have been told. I doubt outlaws would want to rob them. But I do promise I will write you when I arrive in Cheyenne."

"And you write me again if you decide to stay."

Anna sighed as she looked at her aunt's face.

"If I stay—which I won't."

Aunt Mae took Anna's hands in hers. Her face was worried as she squeezed her nieces' hands.

"I wish you wouldn't go. I am so afraid something will happen to you. My mother said I had 'the gift.' I can often tell when something bad is going to happen. I feel it now in my bones.

"Just mail him the money. This trip isn't necessary anymore."

Anna kissed her aunt's cheek. "It is for me," she whispered softly. "I believe Flory and I owe Mr. Morton this. I will make the trip and pay him in person. Then my obligation to him is done." She stood and pulled her aunt up.

"I am going to bed. I think I am all packed, but I want to double-check things. I may store my trunk of books in Cheyenne instead of taking it with me. The station agent here told me I was going to have too much weight for a stage when I told him what I was taking."

Anna smiled and hugged her aunt.

"Thank you for a wonderful summer. You helped heal my heart and restored some of my self-confidence." She kissed her aunt. "I love you, Aunt Mae," she whispered. Uncle Herman was standing in the doorway with a smile on his face. She pecked him on the cheek as she hurried toward the stairs. "And you too, Uncle Herman."

Once she shut the bedroom door, Anna put both hands over her chest. "I don't feel so brave. My heart is about to explode. Truth be told, I am terrified about making this trip. Still, I believe I need to do it."

CHAPTER 27

ON A TRAIN HEADED NORTH

ANNA SETTLED BACK IN HER SEAT. THIS LEG OF HER trip was two hundred twenty-six miles. Aunt Mae had sent some food and water with her. *I might save that. If I have time to get something to eat in Dodge, I can eat Aunt Mae's food on the next leg of my trip.*

The conductor moved through the cars taking tickets and sharing information.

"We have quite a bit of freight to offload and cattle to load, so our stop in Dodge will be about forty-five minutes.

"You ladies might want to check at the Dodge House for the available services. Food to go is available at Beatty's."

The man moved on and Anna settled back in her seat. She was just starting to doze off when a man dropped down beside her. His clothing and hair were greasy, and she could see his yellowed teeth were broken when he leered at her.

"Travelin' alone? I guess I'll jist keep ya company part a the way. Now ya lay yore head over on my shoulder an' I'll put my arm 'round ya."

"I will ask you nicely, sir, to keep your hands to yourself."

The man laughed and a Derringer appeared in Anna's hand.

"Please move. I would hate to fire this while we are moving, but at this distance, I can't miss." Anna's blue eyes were angry, and the man stared from the gun to her face in surprise.

"Up! There are plenty of open seats further down. Take one at least three away from me and stay there. I've shot men before and I will do it again."

The man lunged to his feet with a growl and moved away. He glared at Anna several times as he shifted his body in the seat.

Anna calmly dropped the gun into the pocket of her dress and looked straight ahead. Her hands were shaking, and she folded them tightly on her lap. *Why did I say that? I have only shot this gun at targets, and only then because Will insisted I learn to shoot. I have never shot at anyone let alone hit them!*

The rest of her trip to Dodge was uneventful, but the town itself was a mecca of activity. Anna pushed her way through the crowded train depot and hurried up the street. There were many more people than there had been in Council Grove, and she could feel the vitality of the busy town.

Cowboys were everywhere but they were courteous and friendly. The Dodge House was accommodating, and Anna was quickly back on the train with a sandwich and a bottle of root beer. She had never tasted it before but had heard some of the drovers in Council Grove talking about it.

A small man with bright blue eyes winked at her as she sat down.

"Headed north, are ya?"

Anna nodded. "Yes, to Fort Laramie."

"Well you'ins be goin' right through Cheyenne. That's my town. Ever been up that way 'fore?"

"No, this will be my first visit."

The man grinned at her and put out his hand.

"The name's Badger. Pleased ta meet ya, Miss—?"

Anna shook his hand. "Whitman. Anna Whitman."

Badger pointed toward the two trunks. "I reckon those be you'ins. Ya ain't a plannin' ta take both of 'em on the stage, is ya?"

"No, I plan to leave one in Cheyenne. The station agent in Council Grove advised me not to take both. A friend I met on the train from Kansas City suggested I ask Mr. Rooster in Cheyenne to store one in his livery."

"I reckon he'd be glad ta do that. 'Course, that be a mighty fancy trunk ta store in a livery. I'd be glad ta haul it ta my house in Cheyenne an' hold it fer ya."

Anna stared at him a moment. She slowly shook her head. "I can't ask you to do that, Mr. Badger. It is full of books and is very heavy.

"You see, I am a teacher, and I just couldn't bear to leave my small library behind when I left my last job." She stared at the trunk a moment and her face slowly blushed. "I am beginning to think that was a mistake. It is very heavy and difficult to move."

"You'ins a teacher, is ya? Why we'uns been a lookin' fer a teacher fer our little school out south a town."

"Surely your school year has already started. Don't most schools start in September?"

"Some do. Most a the older kids have ta help with roundup so it's usually easier if we's ta start later. Things is kinda mixed up this fall with some a the big boys on the cattle drive. It were finally decided that the younger kids start in September an' the older fellers in October. A couple a the mom's is fillin' in durin' roundup. Once Miss Merina quits, we'd shore hire ya—if you'ins is any good." Badger's bright blue eyes snapped as he grinned at her.

"If'n you'ins want the job, I cin even take yur trunk out fer ya. Livin' quarters is attached ta the school. Purty handy an' lots a folks 'round ta help ya out."

Anna stared at him in surprise but she shook her head.

"No, I think I will leave it with Mr. Rooster. Mr. Montero suggested—"

"Angel Montero? Ornery little cowpuncher jist plumb full a the devil? Why he be a friend a mine. I'll jist plan ta hold you'ins trunk ta my house. In fact, you'ins cin stay the night with us. My Martha would skin me alive if I left a young gal at the train station when we could a given 'er a bed fer the night."

CHAPTER 28

BADGER AND PAUL

ANNA STARED AT THE SMALL MAN BESIDE HER IN surprise. She started to say no when a young man dropped down in the seat beside Badger.

"Badger, here's the food you wanted. The lady gave me two bottles of root beer when I said to bill it to you. Said to tell you the root beer was on the house."

Badger grinned and pointed from the young man to Anna.

"Miss Whitman, this here fine young feller be Paul Rankin. He come along with me ta help. I'm a gittin' ta be an old feller, ya know."

"Paul, this here lady's a teacher. I'm a tryin' ta convince 'er ta come an' teach at our little school."

The young man studied Anna a moment before he stretched out his hand.

"Pleasure, Miss Whitman. Are you moving to Cheyenne?"

Anna laughed and shook her head. "No, I am just passing through. Mr. Badger is trying to talk me into staying, but that is not part of my plans."

"Miss Merina is our teacher right now, but she will be resigning as soon as the men get back from the drive they are on." When Anna stared at him, he added, "She married Gabe Hawkins this past summer. Him and some of his hands helped a fellow up in the Montana Territory move some black cows north. They should be getting back any time. When he gets back, Miss Merina is going to help Gabe on their ranch."

Anna smiled as she listened.

"Do you like school, Paul?"

"Oh yes, Miss Whitman. I especially like doing my sums. I think I'd like to be a banker one day." Paul's blue eyes were bright with excitement as he talked. He was a tall, slender boy with curly brown hair. His gaze was direct, and his face was open and friendly.

"My pa's not so sure. He said he hasn't met many bankers he likes."

Anna laughed and nodded. "Well, there is room for honest men in all professions. I'm sure your father will approve if that is what you decide to do.

"Do you have brothers and sisters?"

"Yea, Sam is older than me. He's fifteen. He hates school and only wants to be a cowboy. That's why he went on the drive with the men. Abigail is nine, Henry is seven, and Olivia is four.

"My Uncle Rowdy has six kids. Rudy is the oldest. He's been gone for two years but he is coming home next summer when his schooling is done. He went to St. Louis to study law. He wants to work with our lawyer in town when he gets back." He looked away before he added, "There are lots of little kids in school this year, so I reckon it will be noisy.

"Sam and Nate hired on to trail north with the riders on the cattle drive. Nate is Gabe's little brother, and Gabe is the trail boss.

"Pa wouldn't let me go. He said I was too young." Paul looked sideways at Badger and grinned.

"I sure was glad when Badger asked Pa if I could come with him on this trip. Roundup was finished early last week. Badger and me headed out as soon as it was over.

"We've had a lot of fun. Badger knows pertineer everybody, so I have met lots of folks. We rode the train south down here from Cheyenne.

He took me all over Denver and Dodge City too. We have eaten at lots of different eating houses and just had a grand time.

"We are headed home now. School for me will start next week.

"Some of our Arapahoe friends are sending their kids to school this year too. Pa says we'll probably have to help the teacher talk to them for a time until they learn English." He grinned and added, "Ma says they will all know enough to learn. She says Pa thinks he knows everything."

Badger grinned and winked at Anna, and she laughed. Before long, the conductor stopped by to check their tickets and stayed a while to visit. Badger seemed to know him well. The conductor nodded at the smiling young man.

"So, Paul, how would you like to come up front and ride in the engine for a time? Badger said you might be interested in seeing what makes this train roll down the tracks." The conductor's face was friendly as he spoke.

"Say, that would be just fine! Can I come now?"

The conductor nodded and an excited Paul followed him toward the front of the train, listening closely as the man talked to him and pointed out parts of the train.

Badger watched them go with a smile on his face. However, his eyes were serious when he looked over at Anna.

"You'ins don't talk like no gal from Kansas so I'm a figgerin' that you'ins is from back East. Now most little gals don't jist pack up an' move unless they's a reason, an' a powerful good one. You'ins in trouble, Miss Whitman? A runnin' away from somethin'?"

Anna's blue eyes opened wide as she listened to Badger. She was quiet a moment. She slowly shook her head before she answered.

"My sister and I both left. Our leaving was a combination of several things.

"However, the reason I am going to Fort Laramie is because of my little sister. Flory is nineteen and very impetuous. She answered an ad from a man by Fort Laramie who was looking for a wife." Anna looked away from Badger and her cheeks blushed.

"She had no intention of marrying him. She wanted the $200 he was offering in travel money so she could leave the little town we lived in. When I found out, I took the money and now I am going to Fort Laramie to return it." Anna took a shaky breath before she continued. "I know I could mail it, but I just feel like the man needs to receive it in person. I don't have any brothers to protect our family's honor, so it is up to me.

"I have never traveled before this trip and have always considered myself a little timid. Thank Heavens, everyone I've met has been very helpful."

Badger listened intently as he watched Anna. His blue eyes twinkled as he nodded.

Anna continued, "First we met a friendly woman named Tillie on our way to Kansas City and she invited us to stay with her. In fact, Flory is at her home now. Tillie helped her to find a job and has been a wonderful friend.

"When I left there, I stayed for several months with my aunt in Council Grove, Kansas. I had just intended to stop for a few days, but she needed help for the summer in her store. Her hired man became a good friend. He even taught me how to shoot. I didn't think I needed to learn but he insisted." Anna laughed and pointed to her handbag.

"Now I am traveling with a six shooter and a Derringer. My mother would be horrified."

Badger chuckled. "Miss Anna, I don't think fer nothin' that timid describes you'ins. You's a powerful determined woman. I think you'ins cin take care a yur own self on this here trip. An' don't be worrisome 'bout usin' them there guns. You'ins is a goin' into some unsettled country an' the Deadwood stage is fer shore a rough one too."

Badger's smile became bigger as he added, "I reckon that Tillie be Tillie Maynard."

Anna's eyes opened wide in surprise.

"You said your name was Badger—you must be Badger McCune! Tillie mentioned you."

"Shore now, I knowed Tillie 'fore she moved ta Cheyenne. I knowed her in Kansas City 'fore it become civilized.

"Oliver be a friend a mine an' I told 'im to dance with 'er when he passed through Cheyenne one time 'bout ten years ago. He warn't much fer hangin' out in dance halls or saloons, but I knowed Tillie needed 'er a good man. She warn't a bad gal. She jist got caught in a bad place. I knowed she were lookin' fer a way out.

"Them two be good fer each other. Oliver is 'er rock an' Tillie be his wings. They's a fine couple. Too bad they never had no kids. Those little ones would a been spitfires."

Anna stared at Badger for a moment and finally laughed.

"Mr. Badger, I believe I will take you up on your offer to store my trunk. I think you know people everywhere."

"Wahl, I been 'round fer some long time. I be an old feller, ya know." Badger grinned at Anna and she laughed again.

CHAPTER 29

Train Robbers!

THE TRAIN WAS DUE TO ARRIVE IN DENVER CITY between four and five that afternoon. As it climbed through the mountains south of the new town, it slowed to a crawl. The wheels squealed as the train stopped abruptly.

Badger stood and grabbed his gun. He pointed toward Anna.

"Git down on the floor. We don't have no cause ta stop here an' that means they's a problem. An' grab that six shooter out a yur handbag. You'ins jist might need it."

Paul appeared just then and Badger handed his revolver to him.

"Paul, ya take my handgun an' crawl up there beside Miss Anna. Ya stay low. Bullets cin whip right through these here cars an' I don't want neither of ya ta git hit."

As Anna dropped to the floor of the car, she heard shots outside. A man hollered and guns began to fire. Badger shoved the heavy trunk of books across the aisle.

"Ya two stay down 'hind that there trunk. Ain't no bullet a goin' ta get all the way through them thar books."

A man shouted outside and then attempted to open the door to their car. Badger's voice was soft as he called to the man jerking on the door.

"Mister, I be an old feller an' I ain't got much patience. Me an' Ol' Betsy here, we is jist a itchin' ta shoot somethin'. Now if'n you's ta open them there doors, I'm a gonna blow a hole through you'ins big 'nough ta see the sun shine through ya. Now ya think on that an' then ya back away.

"An' ya tell ol' Tom he better hightail it back up ta Canada. He thinks he got away scot-free on that there train robbery over ta Nebrasky, but I knowed Tommy Nixon fer more'n a few years. I knowed his voice, and I seen 'im when ya boys rode up. Now ya tell yur boss that. An you'ins tell 'im Badger's a waitin' on 'im in this here car an' we's all loaded fer bear."

The man outside was quiet. Before long, horses came racing alongside the train. They pulled up outside the train door and loud voices were arguing.

A man shouted, "McCune? We'll leave your car alone—not because we can't get in but because we know you'll take some of us with you.

"Now you take your old tail back to Cheyenne and keep it there."

"Keep talkin'. I'm a gonna count ta three an' then I'm a gonna start blastin'."

The horses started running and Badger hollered, "Three!" He jerked open the door and started firing at the fleeing men. One fell from his saddle, and another grabbed for the saddlehorn as he jerked sideways in the saddle. The rest of the outlaws didn't slow down and were soon out of sight.

Badger jumped down. Several men from the train joined him as they slowly walked toward the fallen man, guns ready.

The outlaw was dead. Two of the younger men lifted his body and carried him back to the train. Badger jumped into the car and pushed the heavy trunk back against the side of the car. He gave Anna a hand as she slowly sat up.

"Durn outlaws. Always a figgerin' they cin disguise their faces. Shoot, ever'body knows we all talk different, ride different, an' cuss different. They's always a hollerin' 'round an' then they think folks won't know who they is."

"That feller what died was a hangin' 'round Denver whilst we was there last week. Didn't recognize 'im, jist knowed he looked like trouble.

"But he ain't trouble no more.

"Now, Miss Anna, let me help ya back up ta yur seat. The excitement's all over. Jist as well catch ya a little rest whilst it's still night."

Anna's hand slowly relaxed on the six shooter. She eased the hammer off before she dropped it into her bag. Her hands were trembling, but she straightened her shoulders and sat back in her seat.

Badger grinned at her, and he patted Paul's back.

"You'ins done jist fine. Won't be no more trouble now, so git some sleep." He sat back in his seat and pulled his hat low. Soon soft snores were coming from under his hat.

Sleep didn't come as easy to Anna and when it did, it was full of nightmares. She awoke early and read for a time before the rest of the car began to stir. It seemed forever before the train reached the Denver station around four-thirty in the morning on September thirtieth.

CHAPTER 30

NORTH TO CHEYENNE

DENVER CITY WAS TEEMING WITH ACTIVITY AS THE train pulled into the station. The stop would be a short one, but Anna rushed with the rest of the woman toward the privies that lined the tracks. Even though the smell was unbearable, she was thankful she didn't have to travel far. She washed her hands and face in the water tank close by and hurried back to the train. She dug out the sandwich Aunt Mae had packed for her and opened her warm bottle of root beer. She ate quietly as she watched the crowds of people through the open door of the train.

People rushed back and forth as they conversed and called in their own languages. Some passengers were met by family, and the greetings were happy and excited. Others just stepped off the train and blended into the sea of human bodies that surged and pushed against each other.

Anna shivered and sunk deeper into her seat. She remembered what Angel had said about her just disappearing with no one to know. *It could happen so easily, and this is a city. What will it be like when I leave Cheyenne?*

She smiled as she watched Badger and young Paul climb back up the steps. Each carried a package of food and a bottle of root beer. Badger looked over at her and grinned as he sat down.

"Three more hours, Miss Anna, an' we'uns 'ill be in Cheyenne. Then you'ins cin relax an' even take a bath if'n ya want. My Martha 'ill fuss over ya like an ol' hen onc't she gits home from her little shop. I'll take you'ins by our house. If'n she ain't ta home, I'll wander on downtown ta tell 'er we'uns have us a guest.

"Young Paul here is ta head on home soon as we'uns git there. His pa has work fer 'im ta do an' it's been a pilin' up!"

The stop in Denver City was a short one and the train started the descent toward Cheyenne. Anna dozed and the three hours went by quickly.

She jumped when the conductor hollered, "Cheyenne is the next stop! Gather your bags and don't leave anything behind. Forgotten items are sold to the highest bidder at the end of the line!"

Badger stood quickly and reached a hand to Anna.

"We'uns be in Cheyenne, Miss Anna. Now you'ins let me help ya down these here steps an' then we'uns 'ill find us a wagon ta tote yur trunks." He whistled loudly and an old man with a feather in his top hat wheeled his wagon toward them with a grin.

"Rooster, this here be Miss Anna Whitman. She be stayin' with my Martha an' me till her stage leaves on Thursday. Pull that there wagon right on up here.

"Paul, find some riders ta unload these here trunks. Ol' Rooster an' me—we be too old ta be packin' heavy things like that."

Six smiling cowboys quickly surrounded Anna. They ducked inside the train, arguing with each other over who should carry the trunks since six was certainly too many. The two who were not carrying them jumped into the wagon bed and carefully lifted the heavy trunks in. All six were grinning as they removed their hats and nodded shyly at Anna.

"Boys, this here be Miss Anna Whitman. She be a passin' through but we's a tryin' ta talk her into ta stayin'. She be a school marm."

The smallest of the six men stepped forward. "Welcome to Cheyenne, Miss Whitman. We're riders fer Lance Rankin's Rocking R. He's young

158

Paul's pa. I'm Jonesy, that tall galoot is Stretch, next is Shorty, then Baker, Bell, an' Beans.

"We'd be happy to follow ya on over to Badger's house to help ya unload if you'd like."

The rest of the riders twisted their hats and nodded in agreement as they continued to grin.

Anna laughed and nodded.

"That would be just fine. I'm sure Mr. Badger would appreciate the assistance."

Bell stepped forward first to help her into the wagon. The six riders were quickly in their saddles and followed the wagon as it headed down the street.

The conductor yelled at them as they rode by.

"You fellows better be back here in two shakes to unload these bulls or I'll turn 'em out on the street."

Jonesy chuckled as he turned around. "Sure will be, Dick. An' by the time you get all those folks offloaded an' get those livestock cars lined up with the pens, we'll have us two or three hands of cards played to boot."

Dick growled again and Paul appeared.

"I can help, Mr. Devers. I'll have the pens all ready for you to unload as soon as the cars are close enough. I left the back gates open so they can get to the water tank if that's okay."

Dick Devers growled a little more. He finally grinned down at the sincere young man in front of him.

"That'll be just fine, Paul. You know, if your pop had about five more boys like you, he wouldn't even need those ornery cowhands.

"Now you come with me, and Jake will show you how he backs this train up."

CHAPTER 31

BADGER'S FAMILY

THE COWBOYS HAD THE TRUNKS UNLOADED QUICKLY and soon turned their horses back toward the train station.

"Now you'ins jist make yur own self ta home, Miss Anna. My Martha has done left fer work but she be home by noon. We'uns 'ill have us a little somethin' ta eat here afterwhile."

Anna sank down on the bed and loosened the pins that held her hat on. She set it on a little stand close by.

The small room was cozy and welcoming. A handmade quilt lay across the bottom of the bed and tintypes of smiling families lined the top of the heavy dresser that stood across the room. A tied rug was beside the bed.

Anna slipped off her shoes and lay back on the bed. "Just a quick nap. I'll just close my eyes for a moment…"

It was nearly six-thirty that evening when Anna awoke. She sat up with a start and slid her feet into her shoes. She hurried to the door. She could hear voices talking and laughing as she moved quickly toward the kitchen.

An older woman looked up with a smile and moved to greet her.

"Anna! It is so nice to meet you. I'm Martha and this is Sadie. She is one of the finest seamstresses I have ever met. She helps me in my little clothing shop.

"That sharp young man is Levi but we all call him Slim. And this is little Rose." She lifted a small girl of around three up to hold her.

"We waited supper for you. Sadie's husband is out of town, so I invited her to eat with us tonight. Now you sit down, and we will have food on the table in just a bit."

Martha began to bustle around, and Badger carried in a large jug of root beer.

"Any a you'ins want a glass a root beer with yur supper? I know those kids will. How 'bout ya ladies?"

Sadie smiled at Anna. She caught her breath and put her hand to her stomach. Anna could see her baby's movements as it shifted her dress.

"When is your little one supposed to arrive?"

"In about three weeks. Doc says a month but I am usually early." Sadie's smile was friendly as she looked at Anna.

"So Badger told us you are a teacher. Any possibility we can talk you into staying? Merina married in July and as soon as Gabe returns, she is going to resign." Sadie's brown eyes sparkled with merriment as she added softly, "I hear you've met Angel."

Anna's face blushed and she looked away for a moment before she responded. All three adults were watching her, and she laughed as she nodded.

"Yes, I met him on the train when he was headed south to Texas." Her blush became deeper when she added, "He surprised me by stopping in my aunt's store in Council Grove on his way back here. He took me to a wedding dance in town that night and we had a lovely time."

Sadie laughed and patted Anna's hand.

"The Monteros moved here with Gabe Hawkins this past summer and they are a delightful family. Merina is coming tomorrow after she finishes at school to pick up a shirt for Nate. He is her husband's younger brother." Sadie studied Anna's face and then stated, "I'm sure Merina would love a little help if you'd like to volunteer tomorrow. Perhaps you could tell them what life is like on the other side of our country. Many of these children have never been outside Laramie County."

Anna's eyes opened wide, and she looked over at Badger and Martha.

"I—well I—I wouldn't know how to get there. Besides, I'm sure she has her day all planned out."

"Merina is a new teacher. She is doing a wonderful job, but I know she would love some help. We opened the school this year to our Arapahoe friends and about ten of them are coming every day. Merina has her hands full, and I know she would appreciate a visit from an experienced teacher."

Badger winked at Anna.

"Shore now, I'd be pleased ta take ya on out there tomorrow. I need ta see Lance anyhow. He cin loan you'ins a hoss ta ride in or you'ins cin come in tomorrow after school with Miss Merina." His grin became bigger when he added, "Else you'ins cin hang out with me in the saloons. I be a beer-drinkin' man." He winked at Anna as he talked, and she laughed.

"I believe I would rather help at the school." She looked at Sadie and then Martha. "I was going to leave my heavy trunk with you but if the children need books, I can loan them to your school until my return."

Sadie leaned forward as she smiled and nodded her head in agreement. "That would be wonderful! Books are very hard to come by here. We try to order a few at a time but as the school grows, we never have enough.

"It's settled then. You can go out with Badger first thing tomorrow." She laughed as she added, "Badger was sure you would agree. He sent a message out with Lance's hands already. They will pass it on to Merina to let her know you will be helping tomorrow." Laughter bubbled out of Sadie at Anna's shocked face.

"Anna, when this family adopted me, I learned quickly to just roll with the surprises. Badger just makes things happen, and Martha is his co-conspirator.

"Just relax and enjoy all they have planned for you while you are here."

CHAPTER 32

A Rough Ride

ANNA LEANED FORWARD TO LOOK OUT THE WINDOW of the stage. She waved to Badger and Martha. The coach filled quickly. Badger had told her to choose a seat against the back of the coach since that was the most comfortable seat. She sighed quietly as she leaned back. She not only had support on the back, but she was also against the side panel. "Hopefully, I will be able to rest some on this trip," Anna whispered to herself.

The driver stuck his head inside the open door.

"We'll change horses 'bout every ten miles but ya won't get out that often. We have two scheduled stops 'fore we reach Fort Laramie—one at Horse Creek Station an' one at Chugwater Station. Chugwater is where we'll stop to eat." He looked at Anna as he added, "Things are a little primitive along this route. Just ask me or Boone here if ya need somethin'." His eyes settled on each man in the coach.

"Miss Whitman is a passenger on this coach an' that means she's in my care. If I hear one complaint from her regardin' poor behavior, I'll toss ya out regardless of where we are or how many wolves we hear a howlin'.

"Now hang on—it's a rough ride." The driver slammed the door shut, climbed on top of the coach, and snapped his whip. The half-wild horses exploded into a run and Anna grabbed for the edge of the seat to hang on.

The cowboy across the way from her grinned. He made a sign with his hands that followed the rolling of the coach.

"Roll with the rhythm of the hosses. A coach surges an' rocks accordin' to their movement. Just let that motion move ya. Then ya won't have so much trouble hangin' on."

Anna gave him a quick smile. His advice was sound, but she still hung on.

Conversation picked up in the coach and Anna listened quietly. Gold seemed to be on everyone's mind.

"Heard a young rancher up by Fort Laramie hit a vein of gold. Looks like a rich one too. Right smack in the middle of his ranch.

"Now ya talk about lucky. He owns all the land four miles out on each side. Nice ranch an' now gold to boot."

"Ain't he the one who lost his wife to the pox a year or so ago? Martin or something."

"Morton. Dan Morton. Yep, that's the one. Nice feller. His wife was a right pretty gal. Friendly too."

Anna tried not to show her interest as she sat up a little straighter. She turned her head toward the window and listened closely.

"Too bad about her dyin'. Two little kids an' now no momma. Maybe he's lucky in gold but I'm a guessin' Dan would a kept his wife an' let the gold go, given the choice."

A swarthy man facing the back of the coach narrowed his eyes down as he listened. They were almost slits as he studied each person on the coach.

Anna glanced up when she felt his eyes on her, and she almost shivered. She pulled her cloak closer around her shoulders and looked away.

I heard Morton sent off for a mail-order bride. I'm a bettin' that's who this gal is. Why else would a self-respectin' woman ride this stage north? The man's eyes slid off Anna and watched the barren landscape. *The second day of October. Sure hope we don't get caught in a snowstorm. That would make my plans a little difficult.*

Anna watched the landscape change. It almost looked like they were passing through mountains. The wind whipped through the coach, bringing in dirt and cold air. She unfolded the blanket Martha had sent with her and began to wrap it around her body.

The swarthy man leered at her. "If yore cold, come on over here. I'll keep ya warm."

Anna ignored him but the cowboy across from her did no such thing.

"There ain't goin' to be talk like that in here, Nealy. Old George up on top won't have to throw ya off—I'll do it my own self, an' I'm a guessin' I'll have volunteers to help me too."

Nealy man glared at the cowboy who spoke and almost replied. However, the looks on the faces of the other men inside the coach warned him away. He glared at the cowboy and sank back in his seat. *We'll see how big you talk when my boys stop this coach. Ya think yore a big man now but I'll trim yore sails.*

The stage let everyone off at Horse Creek Station. The friendly cowboy pointed toward a privy behind the station.

"Ma'am, if ya want, I'll stay a distance away an' make shore ya ain't bothered."

Anna nodded appreciatively and hurried that direction. As she shut the door, she heard the cowboy growl, "That's close enough. There's a lady in there. Git behind me 'cause I'm next."

She straightened her dress and took a deep breath before she opened the door. She smiled at the cowboy as she hurried toward him.

"Thank you, sir. That was very kind of you." The cowboy grinned and nodded as Anna rushed toward the station. She wanted to wash her hands and get a drink before she reboarded.

"Fresh water in here, ma'am. Just now drew it from the well. I'll even give ya yore own jar if ya want to take some along." The station keeper's face was friendly as he spoke.

Anna smiled and nodded. The man quickly filled a jar and Anna hurried back to the stage. She stopped when she saw Nealy sitting in her place. Once again, he leered at her and patted the seat beside him.

Anna's blue eyes snapped, and she bit off her words as she spoke. "Mr. Nealy, I am only going to ask you one time to move back to your own seat. Then I am going to shoot you…and I'm sure no one will fault me based on your previous behavior." Anna's hand was in her pocket and Nealy stared in shock from her face to the hard, round object protruding through her skirt. He started to speak, and Anna lifted the Derringer from her pocket. Her hand wanted to shake but she held the gun firmly.

"Now, Mr. Nealy."

Slade Nealy cursed as he slid across the seat to the other end. When the men began to climb inside, he sullenly moved back to his former position.

The friendly cowboy's eyes narrowed down when he looked at Anna's pale face. He grabbed Nealy by the collar and threw him out of the coach. As the man hit the ground, the cowboy followed him.

"If ya want to take this farther, let's do it now. Fists or guns but ya ain't gettin' back in that coach."

Slade Nealy was quick with a gun but the man challenging him was Daniel Boone May.

Boone was a known gunman. He had earned his name and the reputation that went with it. He didn't draw unless he intended to kill, and he was ready to draw now.

George Lathrop jumped up on the stage and grabbed the lines. "Boone, ya keep yore gun on Nealy till we are out of sight but git in if yore goin'. I ain't waitin' on ya."

Boone backed away and climbed quickly into the stage. He winked at Anna and grinned as he drawled, "I reckon we'll all have us a little more peace an' quiet now." He nodded toward the men beside him, "And a little more room too. Move on over, boys. We cin spread out some now."

Anna could feel the tension drain out of her as the stage pulled away from the station. "Thank Heavens that Nealy man is gone," she whispered to herself as she looked out the window.

Once again, conversation picked up. The cowboy named Boone was quiet for a time as he listened to the men around him talk. Finally, he asked Anna, "Ya have folks meetin' ya somewhere? This here's a rough stage line, an' the towns ain't much neither."

"Yes, in Fort Laramie. I am visiting a friend. I have family in Kansas and plan to return on the next stage south."

Boone listened to her and nodded. His eyes twinkled as he asked, "Ya ain't one a them mail-order brides, are ya? If ya are, I might have to run a ad my own self.

"I've read those ads before. I always wondered some on why a woman would answer one."

Anna's face turned a deep red, but she shook her head. "I would never promise to marry a man I didn't know. No, this is just a short visit and then I am returning to Kansas."

The passengers were all tired when the stage pulled into the Chugwater Station. The station keeper lived there with his family, and his wife had a meal prepared.

Anna washed her hands and her face before she entered the large kitchen. Boone had saved a place for her beside him, and she sat down quietly.

The steak was tough but tasty, and Anna ate hungrily. The woman had made bread and the passengers slathered it with the butter and jam the woman placed on the table. She stopped beside Anna.

"I do have one bed available if you'd like to overnight here. Of course, the next stage might be full."

Anna shook her head. "No, I am fine. I am only going to Fort Laramie, so I don't have much further to ride." She remembered her conversation with Angel, and she made a point to smile at the woman as she thanked her.

"Thank you so much for the delicious food. And please, tell me your name."

"Agnes Phillips and that is my husband, George. And you are?"

"Anna Whitman. It's a pleasure, Mrs. Phillips. I was warned the food might be less than desirable, but I will be sure to tell those who ask that yours was delicious."

Agnes beamed at the young woman and patted her arm. "I will watch for you on your return trip, Miss Whitman. Now you have a safe ride on into Fort Laramie.

"There is only one hotel there. You tell Randolph I said to give you his best room." She patted Anna's arm again and hurried to bring out more food. The smile remained on her face as the last of the passengers climbed into the coach. She waved to Anna as the coach pulled away.

"I hope that young woman will be all right. This stage line is a rough one to ride, and especially for a young woman by herself."

George gave his wife a squeeze as he watched the coach rock down the rough road.

"That cowboy who saved her a seat was Boone May. I'm not sure if he was paid to keep an eye on her or if he just happened to be on the same coach. Either way, Miss Whitman is in good hands. Now let's get this mess cleaned up so we can get those young ones to bed."

"I'll feed and water those horses, and then I'll be back in to help." George strolled outside, whistling as he headed for the barn.

CHAPTER 33

FORT LARAMIE

T WAS NEARLY MIDNIGHT WHEN THE STAGE ROLLED into the station at Fort Laramie. A buggy was waiting there, and an old man was standing beside it. In the moonlight, Anna could see his seamed face.

Boone jumped down and helped Anna from the stage. She thanked him and he grinned.

"It was my privilege, ma'am. Now ya have a safe time here, an' if ya see ol' Badger McCune when ya pass through Cheyenne, ya tell 'im I got his package delivered jist fine." He tipped his hat and was gone.

While the luggage and mail were being unloaded, the old man limped toward the stage.

"You must be Miss Whitman. Dan Morton asked me to pick you up and take you to the hotel. He said he'll be in at seven tomorrow morning to meet you for breakfast."

The relief Anna felt showed on her face.

"That would be wonderful. I am so relieved I don't have to find transportation and a hotel in the dark. Please tell me your name, sir."

"Just call me Mike, Miss Whitman. Dan is sure thankful you made this trip."

Mike gave her a hand up and turned the horses down a dark street. He whistled softly under his breath for a time. He finally cleared his throat and commented quietly, "I reckon you are the gal who answered Dan's ad for a wife." He turned to face her as he added, "Life out here ain't easy. Don't be thinking this here is a picnic you can take part in for a month or two before you waltz on back to wherever you came from. Dan's a fine man, and those two little ones are mighty close to my heart too.

"If you aim to marry Dan, you make sure it's forever."

It was too dark for Mike to see Anna's face turn crimson, but he heard her breath catch in her throat. When she spoke, her voice was soft but firm.

"Mr. Mike, I am not here to marry Mr. Morton. I am here to return the money he sent my sister. She answered his ad but had no intention of coming. When I found out, I wrote him and apologized. I only came to give him what is his. Once Mr. Morton has his money, I will be returning to Kansas."

Mike listened in surprise and then he grinned. "You are an honorable woman, Miss Whitman."

"I try to be. I have no brothers, so the honor of my family's name is on me. My sister wrote Mr. Morton a letter of apology, and I will be giving that to him as well."

Mike stopped in front of a run-down hotel and climbed down slowly. He limped to the other side and helped Anna down with a smile.

"You go on in and tell Randolph I said to give you that room that looks over the street. When he's done checking you in, he can get on out here and help me with this trunk."

Anna laughed softly and hurried into the hotel. She didn't ask Randolph for his best room but the one she received was clean and comfortable even if it was shabby.

"I'll bring some water up for you in the morning if you want to take a bath, Miss Whitman."

"That would be wonderful, Randolph. Perhaps around six? Thank you and good night."

Randolph waited until he heard Anna's door close before he hurried outside. The two old men drug her trunk up the stairs. Anna opened the door and showed them where to put it as she thanked them. They set it down and were quickly gone.

Anna sat down on the bed. She took off her shoes and rubbed her aching feet. She dropped her dress and corset to the floor before she crawled into bed. As she sank into the mattress, she smiled. *I made it! I traveled by train and stage by myself, and I arrived safely. Now to return Mr. Morton's money. Soon, my obligation to him will be ended and I can return to Kansas.*

CHAPTER 34

DAN MORTON

ANNA WAS IN THE LOBBY OF THE HOTEL FIFTEEN minutes before seven the next morning. She felt clean and refreshed, but her nervousness was causing her palms to sweat.

A little after seven, a nervous man appeared. He was tall with curly, black hair. His eyes were blue, and a smile seemed to linger around his mouth. He didn't see Anna as he hurried through the door.

"Is there a Miss Whitman here? I was to meet her at seven this morning."

Anna stood and Randolph pointed behind the man.

"Right there. She arrived last night. Mike brought her up."

The man turned slowly and stared for a moment at Anna. He walked toward her, smiling as he reached out his hands.

"Miss Whitman—I'm Dan Morton. I wasn't sure you would come!"

Anna laughed softly and nodded her head. "There were several times I would have turned around if I could have."

Dan laughed and agreed. "You came a long way. Let's eat. I brought the children with me, and they are always hungry." He tucked her hand under his arm and led her outside.

Two small children were standing in the back of a wagon. The little boy had black, curly hair like his father and bright blue eyes. He smiled shyly at Anna.

The little girl's hair was a mass of blond curls. The bonnet she wore was hanging down her back and her pinafore, which was probably clean before she left home, was dirty and wrinkled. She jumped up and down in the wagon excitedly.

"Let's eat, Papa. I'm hungry!" She stopped and stared at Anna for a moment. She tried to climb out of the wagon.

"Are you going to be our momma? Our momma died and I asked God to find us a new one." The little girl's blue eyes were serious as she spoke, and Anna's heart melted.

She smiled at the little girl and kissed her cheek. "I'm your papa's friend and my name is Anna.

"Now let me guess." She smiled as she looked from one to the other. "I'll bet you are Zach and you are Amanda." As the children bobbed their heads, Anna asked softly, "May I come and eat with you?"

Both children nodded again as they stared at her. Dan laughed as he gave Anna a hand up into the wagon.

"They are both quite excited to meet you. Of course, we don't get much company, so they are excited to come to town and meet just about anyone if you want to know the truth."

Anna laughed and Dan turned the wagon toward the only eating house in town.

"Fort Laramie isn't too fancy but it has what we need. Would you like to ride out to the ranch with me after breakfast? I know you want to catch the next stage south, but it won't be through here until early Monday morning."

Anna's eyes opened wide. "I thought it would be through here tomorrow morning. "

"No, it comes through Fort Laramie on Thursdays and Mondays. You probably met it in passing last night along the road somewhere."

His smile became larger as he continued, "That gives us a little time to get to know one another before we take care of the business you traveled here to complete." He paused for a moment before he added carefully, "If you want to, of course."

Anna thought hard before she answered. "I—I guess that would be fine. I didn't realize I would be here so long. I would like to leave a letter with the sheriff right away though. It is for a friend to let him know I have arrived."

CHAPTER 35

A Little Note

ANNA ALREADY HAD THE NOTE WRITTEN. SHE ADDED a few lines and reread the short note.

Friday, October 3rd

Angel, I arrived in Fort Laramie on Thursday, October 2nd. I am staying at the only hotel in town—I'm not sure if it even has a name. Randolph is the owner, and he is a very nice man.

I did leave my trunk of books in Cheyenne. Badger McCune and young Paul Rankin were on the same train as me from Dodge to Cheyenne. Badger insisted I spend the night with Martha and him. He offered to keep my books at his home. In the end, we left them at your little school. I am quite relieved they will not be stored in a livery with all the dust and animals.

I met Merina. I helped her teach on October 1st, the day before I left for Fort Laramie. Your sister is a delightful woman and a wonderful teacher. She is certainly not the difficult woman you told me she was!

Mr. Morton invited me to eat breakfast this morning with his children and him. They are precious little ones. We are going out to visit his ranch today.

The south stage from Deadwood only travels two days per week. It will be through Fort Laramie on Monday, October 6. I had no idea I would be in here for three days. I'm not sure what I will do during that time.

I am putting my mother's cross necklace in this envelope. I plan to pick it up on Monday before I leave. It is my greatest treasure, and I would never leave town without it.

Yours Truly, Anna Whitman

Anna kissed her necklace and dropped it into an envelope along with the note, took a deep breath, and sealed it.

On the outside she wrote: If not picked up by Monday, October 6, please send to: Mr. Angel Montero, Cheyenne, Wyoming Territory

"I have no doubt I will be back to pick this up. Still, precautions never hurt," she whispered as she hurried to the sheriff's office.

The sheriff was out but a young man was sweeping the floor.

"Excuse me, sir. I would like to leave this note for the sheriff. Would you make sure he receives it?"

The young man nodded and laid the envelope on the sheriff's desk with a smile. "Sure will. He went out to investigate a shooting west of town, but he should be back by dinnertime."

Anna thanked him and hurried outside where a smiling Dan Morton was waiting. He pointed at the basket beside him.

"Ruthie at the eating house packed us a picnic lunch, 'just in case you're not back by dinner,' she said." Dan's blue eyes were friendly as he smiled at her, and Anna nodded. By the time they reached the ranch, both children were in the front of the wagon and Amanda was on Anna's lap. Dan was easy to talk to and Anna enjoyed the ride.

Anna spent Friday and Saturday with Dan and his children. Dan didn't want to take the $200 back but Anna insisted.

"This is why I came. I am certainly not going to take it home with me."

They rode all over his ranch, went fishing, and watched the children play. Saturday afternoon, Dan worked with his horses and Anna read to the children until Mandie fell asleep. She leaned back against a tree and listened to the sounds of the birds. "What a relaxing two days. I almost feel like I have been on vacation." She laughed softly.

"Actually, this was a vacation. Never have I spent two days just reading and playing."

When Dan dropped her at the hotel on Saturday evening, he invited her to attend church with them on Sunday. Anna hesitated.

"I'm not sure if I should do that. Everyone will think we are courting."

Dan laughed. "That's true but they all think we are courting now. And what folks think doesn't matter so much, does it?"

"It does to me. No one here knows me, and I don't want anyone to get the wrong idea."

"How about I meet you at church? Howard Martinson has a place just south of mine. He's an older fellow. Lost his wife some time ago. I was to help him fix his wagon this morning but…" He grinned at Anna before he continued, "I was busy. We can ride over there Sunday afternoon—on horseback or take the wagon. It won't take long. He probably has everything done but mounting it. We usually eat dinner together once a week anyway.

"I'll have you back in town by late afternoon so you can be rested and ready for your trip south."

"Please, Miss Anna! Please? You promised to tell us a story about a canary that lived in a coal mine, and you haven't told us yet." Zach's face was happy and excited.

"Let's take the wagon, Pa. Then Miss Anna can sit in the back with us."

Anna nodded at the children as she laughed. "All right. I will meet you after church. And let's do take the wagon—on the condition you have me back in town by four tomorrow afternoon."

Dan grinned and nodded. "It's a deal.

The express office delivered a stack of wanted posters that Saturday evening to the sheriff's office. No one was there so the agent dropped them on the desk with a note to the sheriff. Anna's small envelope was soon on the bottom of many piles of papers on a very messy desk.

CHAPTER 36

A Friendly Pastor

NNA PACKED HER TRAVEL TRUNK THAT NIGHT AND
stood it in a corner of the room. She hung the dress she intended to
wear on the stage in the small closet. The room was tidy, and the bed
was made before she left for church on Sunday morning.

Services started at nine, but Anna was there before eight-thirty. No
one was inside yet so she wandered around the small building.

The little congregation was obviously proud of their church. It was
clean and neat. Most of the fixtures appeared to be handmade including
the altar and the large cross that hung above it.

The pastor, Reverend White, arrived shortly after Anna. He was a
round man with a big smile.

"You must be Miss Whitman. We all know when we have a guest
in our little town."

Anna laughed as she agreed. She pointed around the simple church.
"Your little church is beautiful. Did someone build your pews? The
workmanship is beautiful."

The pastor nodded. "Dan carved most of the wood items in here
including the altar. Several other men helped, but the items that required
craftsmanship were created by Dan.

"His wife was quite the artist. Mary painted the picture of the Resurrection there on the back wall.

"Did Dan tell you how Mary died?"

"He said she died of smallpox, but we didn't talk any more about it than that." Anna's voice was soft as she answered.

"Mary was a wonderful woman. She was loved by everyone. Several years ago, some of the girls south of the tracks became sick. They needed care and the doctor refused to go—so Mary went. Oh, I'm sure Dan was concerned, but Mary was a determined woman.

"Mary stayed there and treated them. Several died but most lived because of Mary's care. She never became sick either.

"About a month later, a traveling peddler came through town. He had some blankets he was going to sell to the Indians. Mary bought one of them. A day or two later, she contracted smallpox.

"Howard Martinson went to see Mary. He said that peddler intended to trade those blankets with the Indians in hopes of spreading the pox among them.

"He was furious. He had lived with the Indians at one time and had seen some buffalo hunters do the same thing. Dan was sick too but not so sick as Mary. Howard wanted to kill the man, but Mary begged him not to.

"Howard burned the blankets and ran that drummer out of town—after he tarred and feathered him.

"Some ladies in town kept the children so they wouldn't become sick. Those women south of the tracks came and cared for both of them. Dan got better but Mary died.

"Dan was devastated. He lost the love of his life and the mother to his children. They were so in love. Dan was twenty and Mary was nineteen when they married. Six years later, Mary was gone, and Dan was a young widower." The pastor was quiet a moment before he continued. His voice was soft as he stared at the cross.

"I advised Dan against advertising for a wife. I was afraid some woman would try to take advantage of him." He smiled at Anna. "He was so excited when your sister answered his ad."

Anna's face turned a deep red and the pastor laughed.

"Don't worry. Dan showed me your letter. I never told anyone.

"I have nothing but admiration for you, Anna. That was a difficult trip and a hard thing to do." He touched her arm before he looked away.

"I think Dan fell in love with you after that letter. I suggested he tell you to stay in Kansas but he refused. And now you must return home.

"Please don't think I am telling you this to make you feel guilty. I just haven't seen Dan this happy in some time."

Reverend White smiled at Anna again and patted her arm. "I need to greet my congregation, but just know, Anna—if you decide to stay, Dan won't be the only one who will be pleased."

========== CHAPTER 37 ==========

A Noisy Service

ANNA DROPPED DOWN ON HER KNEES IN THE PEW and stared up at the cross. Her eyes filled with tears.

"Poor Dan," she whispered. "He has been through so much. He barely mentioned Mary's death and he surely didn't tell me all of that. "Most of our conversation this week has been about land, cattle, mining, and his children. I didn't tell him why I left my teaching job, just that I had resigned. He never asked me any questions even though he could tell I wasn't sharing everything.

"And those precious children. What a difficult thing for them to endure."

Anna was sitting quietly when she heard the Mortons arrive. She recognized Mandie's voice as she whispered loudly, "But I want to sit up front. I can't see in the back. Besides, Mr. Pete's feet stink."

Dan's face turned red, and Pete Smith pretended he hadn't heard. Later, the old bachelor leaned over to smell his feet. *The kid was right. They do stink. Hmm. Guess I should wash 'em more than once every two weeks—should probably change my socks too. When was the last time I changed these socks? Cain't rightly remember. Probably the last time I washed my good overalls an' I don't remember when that was a'tall.*

Mandie skipped toward the front of the church. Dan pointed to a seat on the right but when Mandie saw Anna, she charged toward her.

"Can I sit with you, Miss Anna? I promise to be good, and I won't be noisy either."

The congregation tittered and Anna blushed. Still, she couldn't tell the little girl no. Dan followed his daughter and the three of them slid into the seat next to Anna.

During the service, Mandie fell off the seat twice. Both times, Dan lifted her up. The second time, he scolded her. Mandie rubbed her head and pointed at it. "Kiss it, Miss Anna. Kiss it and make it better," she whispered.

Anna lifted Mandie onto her lap and whispered to the little girl. Mandie smiled as she listened before she wiggled back to the floor. She was quiet until the next song. Then she stood on the seat and directed the congregation.

Sometimes, she sang loudly, making up words and music as she sang. Her version of "Shall We Gather at the River?" was "Let's go fishing at the river, the poopy, poopy, stinky river." The man behind them began to laugh and it was difficult for Anna not to join him.

The service was finally over, and Dan shook his head.

"I should have warned you last night to sit where Mandie couldn't see you. Of course, I'm probably too easy on her." For a moment, his eyes were watery as he added, "Mary loved to sing, and I see that love of music in Mandie." He rubbed his face and smiled as he watched his daughter. He looked at Anna and shook his head. "Sometimes it is just hard. I miss her so much."

Anna was quiet as she listened to Dan. Mandie was heading for the altar and Zach grabbed his little sister. She drug her feet and cried, but Zach pulled her toward the door of the church.

Dan stepped aside and let Anna out of the seat. They followed his children down the aisle and into the churchyard.

CHAPTER 38

ONE LAST DAY

MOST OF THE CONGREGATION MADE IT A POINT TO talk to Dan. He introduced Anna as a friend from Kansas who was visiting. She could tell from their faces that everyone knew Dan had advertised for a bride. Anna was quiet as they walked to Dan's wagon. Neither was talkative for the first few miles. When they were out of town about three miles, Anna turned toward Dan.

"Why did you advertise for a wife? Weren't you afraid of who would answer your ad?"

Dan was quiet for a time before he looked at Anna.

"A mother for the little ones was my main reason, but it was because of the loneliness too. I don't make it to town much and after the kids go to bed, I feel the emptiness of the house. It just settles on me." He was quiet for a time and his voice was soft when he continued, "Mary is everywhere. She is in me and around me. She is in the kids. I see her when Mandie sings and when Zach smiles." His eyes were sad when he looked at Anna. "I miss her," he stated simply. "I miss my wife."

Tears filled Anna's eyes and she whispered, "I'm sorry, Dan. If I could take some of your pain, I would."

Dan's eyes were clear when he looked at Anna.

"Stay. Stay for a time and let me court you. Let us see if there could be something between us.

"We talk easily and we make each other laugh. You like the children. Stay for a while and see if you can fall in love with me."

Anna looked away and the tears in her eyes threatened to leak out.

"Dan, I—" Her words were cut off as Dan slumped sideways on the seat. The report of a gun echoed away in the distance.

Anna stared at Dan in shock for a moment. He was trying to sit up. Anna grabbed him and pulled him up against her. She could feel the wetness of his blood on his back.

"Anna—take—take the lines. Whip the team and drive south. Zach—Zach knows were Howard lives. Go—Go—help. He'll help...." Dan struggled for his breath as he tried to hold himself upright. The lines slipped from his hands and Anna grabbed them.

"Zach! Zach! Climb up here and help me drive the team! Point them toward Howard's and make them run!"

Zach stared at his father and his lip began to quiver. Anna hugged him and whispered, "Make them run, Zach. We need to get help for your father."

The team raced into Howard's yard and the old man came out of the house pulling up his suspenders. When he saw Dan slumped in Anna's arms, he rushed toward the wagon.

"Whoa there. Whoa now." Howard was a huge man. He was old but he lifted Dan easily from the wagon seat and almost ran toward the house. He laid Dan on the kitchen table.

"You kids get inside. Shut those windows and lock the shutters. Put the bar over that door.

"Lady, get me some of that boiling water. If that bullet is still in there, it will need to come out."

He picked up Mandie and hugged her. "Now Mandie, I want you to crawl under my bed. You stay there until this nice lady comes to get you. Now go!

"Zach, you watch that window. Stand to the side. Keep away from the front of it. We don't need you getting shot too."

He looked at Anna. "What's your name?"

"Anna."

"You ever treat a gunshot wound, Anna?"

Anna's eyes were large as she shook her head.

"You just do what I tell you. Help me undo Dan's shirt. I need to see where that bullet came out or if it's still in there."

Anna's hands were shaking as she undid Dan's shirt. The hair on his chest was red with blood. It oozed from a large hole in his chest.

The old man rocked back on his heels with a curse. He walked across the room and slammed his hand into the door jamb. He slammed it three times, and each time it hit, Anna jumped.

Dan grabbed her hand.

"Not—not gonna make it. The kids—you take my kids. Please."

Anna began to cry. She held Dan's head and whispered to him. "Don't go. Your children need you. Please don't die."

For a moment, Dan's eyes were clear, and he tried to smile.

"Glad you came. You—you're a good woman, Anna. You take my kids." His body relaxed and Dan Morton was dead.

Zach slowly slid to the floor as he sobbed. Anna rushed over to him. She pulled the little boy to her and whispered as she comforted him.

"Shh, Zach. It will be all right. I'm right here. I won't leave you."

The little boy clung to her as he continued to suck his breath in violently.

Howard pushed his hands through his white hair. He looked down at the lifeless body of Dan Morton and a sob caught in his throat. He pulled the young man's body to his and held it while silent tears ran down his face. Finally, he wiped his eyes and looked hard at Anna.

"We need to assume that whoever shot Dan will be coming here. I don't know who it was. I'm guessing you don't either, but we need to be ready.

"Stay away from the windows and keep as close to the floor as you can. I'll need you to shoot so take this gun." He looked hard at Anna. "You can shoot, can't you?"

CHAPTER 39

THE STANDOFF

"SOMEBODY'S COMIN'!" ZACH'S VOICE WAS HIGH AS HE whispered.

Howard strode to the window and looked through the rifle hole. A man was riding toward the house carrying a white flag. Two more men were trying to slip into positions closer to the house.

The old man's first shot took the man carrying the white flag. His second shot caught the boot heel of one of the hiding men and the third shot missed.

"I don't parley with killers!" he shouted. "You shot without warning and for no reason. You'll get no quarter from me!"

"We want the map to Morton's mine. That and the deed. Give us that and you can all go free."

Howard fired toward the sound of the voice. "That deed is locked up in the bank in town, and you just killed the only man who had access. As far as the map goes, Dan was the only one who knew where that mine was.

"You boys are gonna get nothin' but lead, and that's a promise."

A voice sounded behind them. "That might be, old man, but you won't be around to know either way."

Howard started to turn and the man fired. The bullet entered under Howard's arm. He was dead when he slipped to the floor.

Mandie crawled out from under the bed and raced toward Anna screaming. Anna held both children tightly.

"You put that gun away. These children are already terrified. I am holding no weapon and both men are dead. Now put it down." Her voice was furious as she spat the words at the gunman.

He grinned at her as he lowered his gun. He strolled to the door and lifted the bar.

"Come on in," he called. "No one left in here to fight."

Slade Nealy was the first one through the door. He stared at Anna in surprise and began to chuckle.

"Well lookie who we have here. Miss High an' Mighty ain't so high an' mighty now. I knowed you was ridin' north to find a man. I reckon you was after Morton's gold too.

"Guess we'll have us some female entertainment while we comb those hills." He reached for Anna's arm, but she jerked it away from him.

"I haven't been in the West very long, Mr. Nealy, but I know bothering a woman is a hanging offence. I suggest you get on your horses and run while you can.

"No one here knows where that mine is. I didn't even know there was a mine until you men talked about it on the stage. And certainly, these children don't know. Now go and leave us alone."

Nealy leered at Anna. He turned his eyes toward the rest of the men.

"This here gal rode by herself up from Cheyenne. She didn't have nobody waitin' on her but Morton here. No one will even miss her. We can keep her out here as long as we want."

Several of the men looked uncomfortable. The last one through the door was a man Anna recognized. He had been in church that morning when Dan and she left. She looked away and hoped he didn't recognize her.

The man's voice was raspy as he spoke.

"You boys are forgetting one thing. I live in this town. If this woman gets traced back to me, I'm done here. I'll be hung right in front of my building." His hard eyes stared at Anna, and she could feel her skin crawl. "Ain't met a woman yet who was worth dying for."

Nealy cursed and kicked a chair. Anna jerked involuntarily.

"Ain't nobody here to tell an' we're a long way from Deadwood. I say we take our chances."

The man with the raspy voice turned toward Nealy.

"You want to fight me, Nealy? You think you're fast enough to pull leather before I shoot you? Let's try it, here and now."

Nealy's fingers twitched. He wanted to try. Maybe he could. Just maybe he was faster than Kadle. His hand hung there for a moment. Slowly he eased it away from his gun.

He pointed at the kids still clinging to Anna. "What about them? We need to git rid of them."

One of the younger cowboy's stepped forward. "I didn't sign onto this job to kill kids or abuse women.

"We have no map, no deed, and no one alive who can provide either one. This here deal went south before it started. I say we cut out while we can. Head on up to Deadwood like we planned. Maybe rob the stage and spend a little time at the Hole-in-the-Wall. That's what we originally talked about doing."

Kadle turned slowly toward the younger man. Before he could speak, the young man turned to face him. His voice was barely a whisper.

"Go ahead, Kadle. Pull leather on me, you sidewinder. You ain't seen the day you could beat me in a fair fight. The only way you can kill me is with a bullet to the back like you did Morton. But go ahead. I'd like to cut you down."

Kadle stared at the young cowboy for a moment. He finally shrugged. "All right. You take the kids. Make sure they never show up anywhere in the Wyoming Territory. Haul them out of here. Take them back East, adopt them out, or throw them off a train. I don't care as long as they never talk and never show up here again. You can take the woman too."

Two of the other men started to protest and Kadle swung his gun toward them. "I'm in charge here. We'll do this my way."

Zach's shoulders shook as he tried not to sob, and Anna hugged him.

"Don't worry, Zach. Don't you listen to those men. Let's say a prayer. We will pray that Jesus sends a friend to help us. Now close your eyes. And when we're done, I will hum a song.

"What song do you want me to hum?"

Mandie looked up. Her blue eyes were red from tears and her lips quivered as she spoke.

"Sing 'Jesus Loves Me.' Papa sings that to us every night."

Anna smiled at both children and began to hum. She hugged them tightly to her and prayed that Jesus *would* send someone to help them.

The young cowboy mounted his horse. "I am going to get us some meat. The old man has vittles but no fresh meat."

No one spoke but they all watched as he rode off.

Kadle nodded toward Nealy. "Slade, you follow him. Make sure he doesn't make it back." His eyes were hard as he added, "You'll only have one chance so make it count. And those kids aren't going anywhere. When we leave this country, we leave by ourselves." His eyes settled on Anna for a moment. He looked away as he kept his voice low.

"I thought there was something familiar about that woman and now I remember. She was in church this morning with Morton. She can identify me, so she is going with us."

He spoke softly but Anna heard enough to know what was being said. She pinched her eyes closed and forced herself not to cry out loud. Inside, she was sobbing in terror.

We have to get away. We must escape. It is our only hope.

CHAPTER 40

SNAKES IN A TUNNEL

"ZACH," ANNA WHISPERED, "HOW DID THAT MAN GET in the back of the house? Is there a door back there?"

The little boy nodded. "There are two tunnels. One is right behind the house. That is the one most folks know about. Grandpa Mortenson always keeps it barred from the inside. He must have forgotten, or those fellows would have never made it in here.

"The other one goes out through the root cellar. You push what looks like a box of junk over, and there is a hole under it."

"Do you think you can push that box by yourself?"

"I think so."

"I am going to offer to fix a meal. I am going to send you down to the root cellar for potatoes. When you get inside, bar the door if you can and get into that tunnel. Follow it all the way through and hide out there in the hills. Have you ever done that before?"

Zach nodded. "I know a couple of caves."

"Good. Crawl into one of those and stay there until it is almost dark. Don't light a fire and don't talk unless you hear my voice coming toward you. I will put some food outside the bedroom window. Once the sun sets, see if you can sneak close enough to get it. Don't make any noise and don't come until all the men are inside.

"Once you get the food, start walking. Don't walk home or toward town. Go to a neighbor's house and get help.

"And before you go into the root cellar, talk about snakes. That is important. Some men are terrified of snakes and maybe whoever follows you won't go inside." She smiled at the little boy and kissed his cheek.

"Do you know how to shoot a gun?"

Zach nodded as he looked up at her. Anna slipped her Derringer into his pocket.

"That little gun has two bullets, and it will only work on something close."

Several of the men were looking toward them and Anna squeezed the two children tighter. "Pinch your eyes shut and we'll say the Lord's Prayer in a whisper."

Kadle jerked Anna's shoulder back. "What are you whispering about?"

Anna looked up at the man as she recited, "and deliver us from evil for thine is the kingdom, the power and the glory forever and ever, Amen." Her eyes met his as she spoke. "We were praying. You are welcome to join us. I'm sure it would do you good."

Kadle jerked Anna's arm and pulled her to her feet.

"Don't you get smart with me, Missy, or I'll give you something you won't forget."

Anna stared at him for a moment. She was going to retort. Instead she spoke calmly.

"The children are hungry. If you will let me fix them something to eat, I will make enough for your men too."

Kadle let his eyes run down her body. He grabbed the sides of her dress where it flowed over her hips.

He leered at her as he felt with his hands. "Just making sure you don't carry one of those little two-bullet guns.

"I reckon that will be fine. You tell me what you need, and the boy can show me the way to the cellar."

"I ain't goin' in that cellar. There's snakes all over down there. Old Man Martinson liked 'em but I don't. I'm scared of 'em." Zach's eyes were wide, and he looked convincing. "He said they were only bull snakes, but I saw a rattler down there last time. I ain't goin' in there."

Kadle grabbed Zach by the collar. "I guess you will if I say." He laughed evilly. "Take your little sister. Let her go in first."

"I don't want to go! Don't let that mean man make me go, Miss Anna!" Mandie was beginning to cry again.

Anna leaned down in front of Mandie. "You take Zach's hand and stay right beside him. He will protect you. Now go. And Zach, bring me up potatoes and some carrots if you can find some."

Kadle shoved Anna toward the kitchen. "You get things ready and if I hear any noise up here, I'll shoot those kids."

Anna gripped the edge of the sideboard and breathed deeply. Her heart was beating furiously but she forced herself to be calm.

She lifted the bucket from the floor and handed it to the only man who hadn't yet spoken.

"Would you mind drawing some water? I will need to boil those potatoes and carrots." Her eyes went to Dan's body and she shuddered. "And please cover those bodies if you aren't going to bury them."

The man was quiet as he took the bucket.

"The name's Lep, Ma'am. Jimmy Lep. I'm sorry about this. I just wanted some gold. I didn't sign on to kill anyone, let alone women or children."

Anna turned toward him. Her blue eyes were bright and angry.

"That's the problem with being an outlaw, isn't it? One bad thing always leads to another. Shame on you. Your mother will be broken-hearted when she hears what you've done. And she will. You chose poor company to feed your thieving heart, and now you are as much a part of this as they all are."

There was a loud commotion from below. A door slammed and a gun went off. Anna could hear Kadle cursing and yelling.

"You open that door, you little heathen. Throw a snake at me, will you? I'll drown you in the well!

"Lep, get down here! Bring some kind of a bar to pry that door."

Jimmy grabbed a shovel from outside the door and ran toward the root cellar. As soon as he turned his back, Anna made a dash for the door. The man who had shot Howard Martinson blocked her way and shoved her back into the house.

"I knew you was cookin' somethin' up. Prayin' my eye."

"I was praying. And if the children are locked in the root cellar, at least they are safe."

The man studied her face for a time before he shook his head.

"Huh uh. You wouldn't leave here unless you was sure they was goin' to get out. You an' me will just wait at the back of that tunnel I used today. We'll wait for them to pop out. Kinda like little gophers. An' as soon as they do, I'm goin' to shoot 'em. Maybe you'll be a little easier to get along with if you don't have 'em around to protect."

He grabbed Anna's arm and jerked her around to the back of the house. They were above the creek when he turned her around and pointed toward a small hole in the side of the hill. It didn't look large enough for a man to crawl through.

"They should be comin' out of there any time." He cocked his gun and grinned at her as they waited.

The noise level in the house ramped up again. Gunfire along with crashing and banging was coming from the house. Before long, a furious Kadle appeared by the side of the house. He was gesturing and shouting.

"They went down a tunnel. I tried to follow them, but it was plumb full of snakes. I shot a few but they just dropped down from everywhere. We need to find where that tunnel comes out.

"Drag that woman up here, Meecher. I'll beat it out of her!"

Meecher jerked Anna around. "You knew there was a second tunnel. Where does it come out?"

Anna looked at him coolly.

"Mr. Meecher, I arrived in Fort Laramie on Thursday, and this is the first time I have been to Mr. Martinson's house. In fact, it's the first time I ever met Mr. Martinson. That's the name of the man you shot in the back in case you are curious.

"I had no idea there were any tunnels here until you came in through one. Perhaps the children know where they go. I'm not sure. Again, I only met the children three days ago.

"You can beat me if you want but I can't tell you what I don't know."

Meecher slapped Anna so hard he knocked her down. She stared up at him with fury in her eyes.

"You are a bully, Mr. Meecher. Maybe instead of beating me, you should just follow the tunnel. Surely you aren't afraid of a few snakes if two children can manage them."

Meecher backhanded Anna again. He grabbed her arm as he drug her up the hill.

Anna's lip was bleeding and her eye was starting to swell. Meecher threw her toward Kadle and growled, "I don't think she knows where that tunnel goes. I'm guessing those kids knew and she told them to take it. She's newer to the country than we are, and Dan didn't have time to show her much in three days."

Anna glared from one man to the other.

"You're right, I don't know anything about tunnels other than what you just said about the snakes. However, I would prefer the company of snakes to the likes of you. Go ahead and lock me in the tunnel."

Kadle stepped toward Anna with a growl. "I say she knows."

Jimmy stepped forward.

"Shoot, old Martinson probably has hundreds of tunnels up here in these hills if a feller knew where to look." He looked from one man to the other. "I don't mind roughin' her up but it ain't goin' to do no good.

She's too new 'round here. Even if those kids told her where it came out, do ya think a city gal like her could tell us? An' she sure couldn't show us."

Meecher looked over at Anna and nodded. "I'll agree with that. I say we have her fix somethin' to eat. Let that smell run up those hills. That little bitty girl will want to come out. She'll be powerful hungry by tonight. An' even if her brother don't let her come down, we might hear her a cryin'.

"Get to cookin'. An' it better taste good too."

Anna turned to face the men. Even though one eye was turning dark underneath, she smiled.

"I still need potatoes and carrots. Who is going to fetch those?" she asked sweetly.

The first cowboy stepped through the door just then. He dumped some onions and potatoes on the table along with a haunch of venison.

"Martinson has a garden out back. Looks like there might be some carrots and cabbage there. Want me to pick them too?" His eyes settled on Anna's face and his eyes were hard as they moved around the room. They settled on Meecher.

"Meecher, if you hit that woman again, I'll kill you in your sleep," he grated as he stared at the man. He looked over at Kadle. His grin was more of a smirk as he tried to egg the man on.

"And don't bother to wait on Nealy. He ran into something and he ain't comin' back." The cowboy glanced around the room and grinned again when he didn't see the children.

"Guess those little kids got loose. Well good for them. Those hills are a maze of caves and hideouts. Good luck finding them.

"Doolan's the name, Ma'am. You fix us some vittles and I'll make sure these men leave you alone."

CHAPTER 41

Mighty Spicy Vittles

ANNA OPENED HOWARD'S CUPBOARDS AND STUDIED his ingredients. She was hoping to find something she could add to the food to make the outlaws sick or sleepy. She didn't find what she wanted but decided to make the food very spicy. She smiled to herself as she set the seasonings she wanted to use on the table.

Jimmy and Doolan had carried the bodies of Dan and Howard outside. They buried them beside each other in the little cemetery on the hillside where Mary Morton lay.

Anna watched them as she cooked and several times she almost cried. *Dan, you were a fine man. Would I have stayed?* A sob escaped her. *What a shame these scoundrels ended your life so soon and left your children orphans.*

I will take care of them like you asked me. I will raise them as my own. A single tear slid down her face and almost dropped into the stew. Anna wiped it away irritably and pulled her shoulders back. *They will not break me. I won't give in to their terrors.*

Anna poured some of the stew into a jar before she added the extra seasonings. She screwed the lid down tight and set the jar aside under a tea towel.

She smelled the stew and nodded. "It will be tasty but it will burn coming out." Assuming one of the men would trade their bowl for hers, she added additional pepper on top of hers.

Meecher grabbed her bowl and slid his across the table. Anna said nothing. She lifted her spoon and took a bite. The inside of her mouth felt like it was on fire, and she smiled.

Doolan ate his food like nothing was unusual. Jimmy blew on his several times. Otherwise, he ate without complaining.

Kadle was sweating by the time he finished his first bowl. His face was red, and his eyes were watering. Anna picked up her bowl along with his.

"More stew, Mr. Kadle? There is plenty."

He nodded and Anna carried both of their bowls to the stove. She dumped the remnants of her bowl into his. She added more pepper and filled it to the top. She carried both bowls back to the table, setting Kadle's in front of him. She scraped the sides of her bowl while the rest of the men had seconds.

Meecher belched loudly and thumped his chest. He looked over at Anna suspiciously.

"Those were some fine vittles, but I don't think I've eaten anything quite so fiery. My stomach is talkin' back at me."

Anna smiled sweetly. "I have never had complaints about my cooking before, Mr. Meecher. Perhaps you aren't as tough as the coal miners in our little town in Pennsylvania. Spicy food is very popular there."

CHAPTER 42

Too Hot to Go Back

DOOLAN TOLD ANNA TO SLEEP IN THE BEDROOM AND no one argued with him. She was able to slip the jar of stew out of the kitchen. She opened the bedroom window and set the jar below the opening.

Before long, she heard stealthy footsteps, and she began to sing softly. The steps faded away while Anna sang a second verse. When she finished, all was quiet. There was nothing in the room to block the door, so she had to take Doolan at his word. Finally, she fell asleep.

The outlaws were slow getting up in the morning. Anna slipped outside to gather the eggs and feed the chickens. She was contemplating making a run for the hills when she looked toward the house. Meecher was standing in the doorway with a rifle.

She found some grain in the barn and hid a pitchfork while she was there. She scattered the grain to the chickens and gathered the eggs in an apron she had found in the kitchen.

Meecher blocked the doorway and Anna stopped in front of him.

"Mr. Meecher, I am losing my grip on these eggs. If I drop them, I don't think your friends will be very happy."

Meecher tried to rub against her as she passed him, and she rolled one of the eggs out of the apron. He cursed as it landed on his boot, and Anna walked quickly into the kitchen.

"You done that a purpose!" Meecher shouted. His boots were covered in yellow, slimy egg yolk.

Anna stared at Meecher a moment. She shrugged.

"What a waste of a good egg. And it will certainly smell bad by this afternoon. You might want to wash those boots off."

Meecher cursed again and stormed toward the horse tank. He wiped off what he could in the grass before he dipped his entire boot into the water.

Anna laughed softly. When she looked up, she looked into Doolan's eyes. He said nothing but he grinned as he turned away.

Martinson had a smokehouse and Anna grabbed a knife from the house as she walked toward it. She hid the knife in the folds of her apron.

A large ham was hanging on a hook, and she cut off portion for breakfast. She hid the knife under a shelf and returned to the house carrying the meat. Jimmy and Kadle were just sitting up when she walked back inside. No one seemed to notice she had taken a knife from the kitchen.

Kadle sat up and scratched his head. He looked around the room.

"Let's eat and pack up. We aren't staying here. Since those kids got loose, it is too hot for me to go back to Fort Laramie. There's a chance they might survive, and I can't afford to get caught if they do.

"I know some of the boys at Hole-in-the-Wall. We can hide out there for a time. I'd like to make forty to fifty miles a day. If we can do that, we'll be there in four or five days.

He looked from the men to Anna and added, "Once we get there, that woman can disappear, and no one will be the wiser. And if they do try to find her, they won't know where to look. Until then, I don't want a body or torn clothing left behind."

Anna felt a chill go through her. *Kadle is just cold. He has no feelings for anyone. Life or death—it doesn't matter to him. I need to play along. Maybe they will relax some when we are further away, and I can escape. Once we reach where they are headed, I am dead...or I will hope to be.*

"Take what you want out of the house but don't load your horses too heavy. We are going to be moving fast.

He looked over at Anna. "Get that meal ready. We leave in half an hour."

Anna prepared breakfast. She stared at her dress as she thought about the long ride. *I can't straddle a horse in this dress. It will ride up to my hips! Maybe I will cut the petticoat. If I slit it up the front and the back, it will stay down on either side of the horse. My dress will ride up and my petticoats will show. Still, it will be better than having everything around my waist.* She took a knife and walked back toward the bedroom.

Meecher grabbed her arm and Anna brought the knife up to his face. He bent her arm until she dropped it.

She looked over at Doolan. "I need to cut my skirts so I can straddle a horse. I have no riding skirt."

Meecher started to laugh. "Nope, ya cin jist ride with that dress up around yore neck. That will be mighty entertainin'.

Doolan handed her his pocketknife. "Use this and give it back to me when you're done." He looked over at Meecher.

"Leave her alone, Meecher. You aren't bothering her on this trip as long as I'm around." His smile was deadly as he grinned at the angry outlaw. "Of course, anytime you want to take me on, let's do it."

Kadle stared from Doolan to Anna for a moment. His eyes were cold when he walked to the kitchen. "You men had better eat up instead of standing around arguing. This grub is getting cold."

When the bedroom door closed, Kadle stared hard at Doolan. "You are pushing mighty hard for a new man. That woman is my property. Who I decide to share her with is up to me. Now you keep that in mind for the next four days."

Anna's hand shook as she opened the pocketknife. She stared at it for a moment and pulled the tiny, folded piece of paper out from beside the blade. Small writing covered it, and she squinted her eyes to read it.

Lay low and do as I say. Will try to get you out.

Anna covered her mouth with her hands. She heard the doorknob start to turn and she shoved the paper into her mouth, swallowing it quickly. When the door opened, she was trying to cut through three layers of petticoats. She dropped her dress and glared at Kadle.

"I can do this on my own. I certainly don't need any help from you."

Kadle stared a moment longer before he backed out and shut the door.

Anna stared at the mangled petticoat for a moment. She noticed a pair of britches hanging over the end of a chair. She walked quickly to the closet. Some of Mrs. Martinson's clothing still hung there. She grabbed a pair of britches along with a long shirt and quickly changed, pulling the britches on over her knickers.

She rolled her dress up in a blanket, folded the knife, and walked out of the bedroom. She tried to hand the knife to Doolan, but Kadle grabbed it. He opened it and inspected the blades. Anna's voice was sarcastic when she spoke.

"I was cutting cotton, not wire. I certainly didn't damage the blade."

Kadle didn't respond as he thrust the knife towards Doolan. He stared at Anna as if he was trying to see into her mind. She stared back at him. She despised the man and she let her disdain for him show. He shoved her toward the door. She grabbed a jacket from a hook as she walked by and walked toward the horses. She stared at them for a moment and looked back at the men.

Doolan grabbed the blanket bundle from her without speaking and tied it behind her saddle.

Anna grabbed the stirrup as she tried to pull herself up.

Meecher laughed. "Look at that. The little city girl don't even know how to ride. Here, I'll help you up."

Anna jerked away from him. "Don't touch me."

She tried to hold the stirrup with both hands as she lifted her left leg. The horse moved away and she almost fell down.

Jimmy grabbed her around her waist and almost tossed her onto the horse. Anna scrambled to hang onto the reins and maintain her seat. Her hands were shaking so bad that she didn't have to fake being afraid. Jimmy and Doolan adjusted her stirrups.

Anna looked at the horses. They were packed with items stolen from the house, but she didn't see any food or cooking utensils. She pointed at the smokehouse.

"Think we should take that ham in the smokehouse? Might be handy to have some meat with us."

Kadle glared at her. He barked some orders. The men tossed off some of the stolen items to make room for the ham and some cooking utensils. Soon, everything was repacked, and they were headed north.

Anna looked toward the hills. Her worry showed on her face. *Lord, please let the children make it to the closest house. Keep them safe.*

Meecher smirked at her. "Kadle decided to ride by Morton's house. We think those kids might have headed for home. We'll find them if they did, and we'll take care of them for good this time."

Anna tried to look unconcerned, but she was worried. She had told Zach not to go home but she knew Mandie would beg him. *I hope he holds strong.*

Kadle pushed his horse to a lope and the group was quiet as the horses' hooves thudded on the open prairie.

Tuesday, September 30, 1879
Bitter Root Valley,
Montana Territory

CHAPTER 43

Because of a Woman

ANGEL LOOKED BACK AT THE LITTLE CHURCH AND grinned. The wedding was over. Spur was now a married man. He'd be staying in the Montana Territory while the rest of the men headed back to Cheyenne.

Rock Beckler's dream to bring a herd of black cattle to his Slash B Ranch was fulfilled. He didn't get to see the end of that drive, but he would have been pleased.

Angel waved his hat as the riders loped their horses south down the valley. Spur was helping Clare into the wagon, and Angel chuckled as the kids all piled in. He could hear their voices and it made him miss his little sister.

Gabe's riders hoped to make thirty to fifty miles per day as they rode south to catch the train at Ogden in the Utah Territory. Their route through the mountains would slow them down some, but today, the riding was smooth. If all went well, they should be in Cheyenne by Saturday, October eleventh.

Angel frowned as he looked south. He urged his horse to go a little faster. Gabe looked over at him with a grin.

"Anxious to see someone, Angel? You probably have a woman waiting for you at home, just pining away. You must be missing her as quiet as you have been these last few days."

"Not waiting for me but I was thinking of a woman with hair the color of the sunset. Deep red with bursts of light. A beautiful woman who holds herself a distancia—I think you say aloof."

Gabe's grin became bigger and he shook his head. "You have always had a thing for red heads. And since when did a woman hold your attention for more than a day or two?"

Angel nodded somberly. "Sí, that is true. This woman I met on a train. She had traveled from the East to Kansas City with her sister. We talked for a time. Ah, what a woman." Angel smiled as he remembered Anna. His smiled died away and he frowned. "She was to travel to Fort Laramie to see a man.

"I think perhaps she is married by now. This man she went to see must have been very sad. He put a notice in the paper for a wife and mother for his children. What man would do that?

"Her sister pretended to agree so the man would send dinero. Señorita Anna, she planned to take the money back to the man. She was ashamed for her sister.

"I told her the journey would be dangerous. I did not think she should go but she insisted. I could not talk her out of it." Angel looked over at his friend and his dark eyes showed his concern. "Finally, I suggested she leave one of her trunks in Cheyenne. I told her it would be good for someone to know when she passed through. A woman by herself could be lost and who would know?" He shrugged his shoulders. "The trunk was not there when we left for this drive."

Gabe studied his brother-in-law in surprise for a moment before he answered.

"You met her on your way to Texas? Where was she traveling?"

"I met her on the Katy train. We had to go to Kansas City to catch it because of flooding to the south of Omaha in Nebraska.

"She was traveling to Council Grove to stay with her aunt. I do not know for how long. From there, she was continuing on to Fort Laramie."

Gabe's surprise showed on his face. "She'd have to go by stage from Cheyenne to get there, and that Deadwood route is a rough one."

"Sí, I told her this. I told her to just mail the dinero and to stay in Kansas, but she insisted she must go.

"She was much brave but I think it was a dangerous thing to do. For her, I think it was to restore her family's honor. She was ashamed of what her sister did."

Gabe was quiet a moment. Finally, he grinned at his friend.

"And now you know all about her. She is probably going to leave you love notes all along the way. Or maybe she didn't tell you her real name."

Angel grinned at his friend.

"Her name is Anna. Anna Whitman. I did stop in Council Grove on my return. That is why Miguel and I were a day late getting back to your ranch. I took her to a dance." Angel's dark eyes danced, and his grin became larger.

"I hoped dancing with a handsome vaquero such as myself would convince her to stay in Kansas or perhaps come and teach at our little school. She was much determined though. She was not so much charmed by me as I had hoped.

"I am afraid for her. If something should go wrong, she could just desaparecer—she would just be gone. Poof. And no one would know where she went.

"No, I do not think she will leave me a note. Perhaps she will marry the cowboy with the children. He will ask and it will be difficult for her to say no to the children.

"I think the señorita has a kind heart, and she will fall in love with the little ones. And the man, maybe she will come to love him as well." Angel was quiet as he looked over at Gabe.

"But who will know? He is the one she goes to meet and even he does not know her. What if the stagecoach is robbed? I have a bad feeling for the señorita. Something could go wrong."

Gabe listened to his friend. *Angel is right. The lady could just disappear.*

"When we get back, why don't you ride on up to Fort Laramie and check on her. Then you will know for sure." He paused as he looked over at Angel and grinned.

"Of course, there is always the possibility there will be a pile of love notes for you when we arrive. You will read them and head back to Kansas."

Angel shook his head. "This lady is not like that. She does not like to ask others for help, and she does not say unnecessary things. She is used to doing much for herself. No, I do not think there will be a note.

"I told her to talk to the station agents, to make many friends. Then maybe those friends will remember her. They can ask questions if she does not return when she is supposed to.

"Yes, I think I will travel to Fort Laramie, but I will not go to Cheyenne first. I will take the pass señor Spur used—Skalkaho Pass. I will take it east from this valley. I will follow the trail we used when we brought the cattle north. Señor Rock called it the Road to Montana but many call it the Bozeman Trail. I think I will stop at Hole-in-the-Wall just to be certain she is not there.

"When I find her, my heart will know if it needs to break or if I perhaps need to use my small knife." He smiled briefly at Gabe.

"I think I will take Miguel. He likes to fight, and it will be good to have my brother beside me."

The men parted ways about twenty-seven miles south of Stevensville. Angel and Miguel turned east to cross Skalkaho Pass while Gabe and the rest of his riders continued south.

All the men had two horses. Several offered to trade with the two brothers to make sure they had the strongest and the fastest. Angel hoped to cover fifty to sixty miles per day so they were going to be pushing.

CHAPTER 44

HONOR AMONG THIEVES

NGEL AND MIGUEL ARRIVED AT HOLE-IN-THE-WALL on the ninth of October. They had made the nearly six-hundred-mile journey in ten days and had averaged almost sixty miles per day. Even though they traded for extra horses three times, both the men and their horses were exhausted.

As they rode toward the hideout, a flash of light showed from the hill. Miguel stopped his horse. He looked around at his brother.

"Don't move. Just hold your horses quiet and wait for the signal."

Miguel faced the flash of light and put his hat over his heart. Then he spun his horse in a circle and waved his hat over his head.

"That signal is much like a dandy," Angel commented quietly.

Miguel grinned back at him. "The spinning and waving the hat is my signal. Now all who watch will know it is I, Miguel Montero, who is coming." Soon two flashes of light showed, and the two brothers continued toward the red bluff mountain.

"Many guns are following us as we ride. If we had not given the correct signal, we would have been cut down.

"Everything here is very secret. Never has a lawman made it through and lived to return.

"Hattie runs this place with an iron fist. Her name is Matilda Hatfield, but here she is known as Hattie. There are many gangs who hole up here, some for a few days and others for months. All do as Hattie tells them, and all her rules must be followed. Any man who dares to break one will be banished, never to return. If he breaks two, he will die.

"Hattie's husband was a bad bandito for many years. She helped him some and the rest of the time, she ruled her la fortaleza—this—this fortress, like a kingdom. Hattie is very tough, but she is my friend."

Angel was quiet as he listened to his brother. Finally, he commented, "I think you have spent too many years on the outlaw trail."

Miguel chuckled. "Sí, much time. Not so much anymore though. Now I prefer to stay closer to my family—and closer to the towns in the winter where the women are warm and friendly."

"I helped someone Hattie loved one time. We do not talk of it, but Hattie has not forgotten.

"We will go to her house first and tell her whom we search for. Hattie knows all that goes on. She has spies all over the Wyoming and Montana Territories, maybe even further. She will know if your woman is here."

Angel was silent. *Sí, I think she will be here. But how will we get her out with so many guns?*

Miguel led the way through a maze of box canyons to a well-fortified group of cabins. A solid house was built away from the rest and Miguel stopped his horse in front of it.

"I will go first. If Hattie wishes you to come in, I will call for you."

Miguel tapped lightly twice and firmly three times. He paused and tapped lightly one more time.

A tall old woman jerked the door open. She held a shotgun in her hands and her face looked fierce. It was drawn down in hard lines and her blue eyes were penetrating.

Angel could feel himself pull back, but Miguel's smile became larger.

"Hola, Hattie. I have ridden many miles to see your beautiful face. But I was not expecting such a poor welcome for a tired vaquero."

Hattie stared at Miguel for a moment. Her face slowly collapsed into piles of happy wrinkles.

"Miguel, you little sawed-off Mexican bandit! Come in here and give me a hug!" Hattie pulled Miguel through the door and closed it behind him.

She hugged him again. Slowly, her smile faded and disappeared.

"Miguel, I told you to go straight. I told you to never return to this place."

"Sí, I do it for my brother," Miguel explained as he shrugged. "He looks for his woman. We think she might be here."

Hattie's face became hard. "You know the rules, Miguel. When a woman comes here by her own choice, she doesn't leave unless her man leaves. And then she leaves only if he chooses to take her with him.

"Sometimes brothers or fathers come to find a sister or a daughter. Even then, there are rules."

"Sí, I know the rules, but this woman is a lady. She is a teacher. My brother believes she has been taken. She traveled to Fort Laramie to return money to a man. We do not know his name, but he advertised for a wife. The lady's sister told the man that she would marry so he would mail money. When the lady found out, she was very angry.

"She has no one to protect her name. There are no men. No one besides her and her sister." Miguel shrugged his shoulders again. "So, she traveled on her own to return the dinero and to preserve her family's name."

"Perhaps she married the man. We do not know, but my brother is convinced she is in trouble. He has the—what do you call it?—the sense? He can tell trouble sometimes before it happens, before things go badly. The feeling is very strong inside of him. He is much worried for the lady.

"We trailed cattle north to the Montana Territory. When they were delivered, we began to ride south. We came quickly. Now we are here." Miguel waited quietly when he finished. He knew Hattie didn't like women brought into her hideout against their will. She had the power to stop it and he hoped she would.

Hattie stared at Miguel for a moment. She nodded her head toward the door.

"Tell your brother to come in."

Miguel opened the door and a man stepped inside. He held his hat in his hands. Hattie stared from one man to the other. She thought maybe the two men were twins. They for sure were brothers. Miguel's brother's eyes had laugh wrinkles around them, but today he looked cold and dangerous.

"Why do you think the woman might be here?"

"There are few places where men can hide a woman if they wish to treat her badly. Señorita Anna is a lady. She would not come willingly, and if she was taken, there are children who are in danger as well." Angel's voice was soft as he continued.

"It has been nearly three months since I last saw her. I tried to talk her out of coming, but she was determined. She wanted to return the money her sister took.

"I think the cowboy she went to see would have asked her to stay. For many days, I thought she would marry him. But now, my heart tells me there is trouble." Angel's face was hard as he looked at Hattie.

"Anna is in trouble and there is no one to search for her but me."

Hattie stared at him and slowly nodded.

"She is not here. However, there is a woman who will be arriving tomorrow. She travels with four men. Perhaps it is your woman, perhaps it is not.

"The man this woman was visiting by Fort Laramie was killed. He was shot in the back. The children disappeared. I don't know what became of them, but the woman and the men who took her are on their way here.

"The man who leads them is cold, like a fish. His eyes are dead, and he feels nothing. His second in command is just as bad. He enjoys killing, but he prefers to kill slowly so he can enjoy the suffering.

"They do not come here often because they are not liked. The fact they are coming now tells me they are concerned of being caught by the law."

Hattie's eyes changed color as the light shined in them, and Angel watched her quietly.

Miguel did not look at Hattie. He watched his brother.

"When the woman comes, she will be given a chance to speak. If she wishes to stay, you must go. If she wishes to go with you, you may leave and take her with you." Her hard old eyes turned to bore into Miguel. "And you, Miguel—you must never return. Not as an outlaw, not to visit. Not ever."

"I plan to kill the men who took her. If they hurt her, I will do it slowly. I will split them open like one does a pig, and I will strangle them with what is inside their stomachs." Angel's voice was cold as he spoke to Hattie.

Hattie leaned toward him. Her old eyes glinted as she spoke.

"No one dies here unless I say. No one fights unless I give them permission. This is *my* mountain, *my* rules.

"If the woman has been hurt, you may challenge the lieutenant. You may not fight the boss. If you try to fight the boss, you will die. Nor can the boss fight you.

"If you challenge his lieutenant, that man may fight you if his boss gives him permission. If you challenge, you will fight to the death with whatever weapon he chooses. Fists, knives, and pistols are acceptable. So are machetes, swords, and shotguns. Only one weapon may be used.

"If your woman is not injured, you will take her and leave immediately. If she is injured..." Hattie shrugged. "Then we will tend to her. If she survives, you will leave when she can travel." Her hard eyes bored into him. "And if she dies, you will still leave and you will never return.

"What happens outside this place, I have no care of, but no revenge will be sought inside here."

Her face softened as she looked at Miguel.

"Show your brother to the cabin you will share. Then come back and drink whiskey with me. I have missed you, my little Mexican chico."

Angel went down to the creek and took a bath. He washed his clothes as well as Miguel's extra clothes. When he finished, he sat on the small porch in front of the cabin and smoked. *I only smoke when I am angry. This cigarillo does not even taste good, but it calms my nerves.*

The night was filled with the sounds of drinking and dancing from one of the buildings. From time to time, Angel heard a woman's shrill voice. "Perhaps that is a cry or maybe a laugh. I do not know." He finally ground the cigarette out and leaned back against the support post as he looked around.

"Evil lives here. This is not a good place to be. I will be glad when we are gone." Angel stood quietly and slipped into the cabin. There were no beds, so he rolled out his blankets on the floor, keeping his pistols and his knife close by.

It was late when Miguel came in. His brother tripped several times, but Angel said nothing. Once Miguel began to snore, Angel rose and blocked a chair under the doorknob. It was nearly morning when he finally fell asleep.

Angel was sitting outside when Miguel awoke. Once again, he was smoking a cigarette. His brother stared at him a moment. He waved down the hill.

"Come. We go to the chuck house. Throw down $20 and we can eat whenever we want." Miguel grinned at his brother. "I'm on your payroll, so you can cover my expenses too."

Angel laughed and the two brothers strolled down the hill. They laid around all morning. Finally, around two that afternoon, the sentry passed a message down.

"Riders comin' in! Four men, one woman, three packhorses."

Men came out of everywhere. Angel looked around in surprise. Over twenty men were gathered below Hattie's cabin. He heard stirring in the trees and knew there were additional men placed outside the clearing as well.

Angel identified the two men Hattie had described. The woman was slumped over her saddle. Only when one of the men lifted her head did he recognize Anna.

Her hands were tied to the saddlehorn, and her red hair was matted and dirty. When her head was turned his way, he could see her eyes were glassy. There were bruises under both eyes and her lip was swollen.

Angel stepped forward with a curse. Miguel shoved him back as he whispered, "Wait. Let Hattie handle this." He nodded toward the group of men.

"Kadle is the man leading Anna's horse and Meecher is his lieutenant. Kadle already broke Hattie's rules by bringing a woman here who cannot speak for herself. She won't tolerate this.

"Meecher thinks he's good with a gun, but I can take him. That means you for sure can. Kadle keeps a hideout gun up his sleeve so watch out for that."

Kadle looked around the men gathered there and gave them a big grin. "Look her over, boys. She goes up for auction tonight after supper. I know she looks a little tough now but wait till she's cleaned up.

"She's a feisty one so we slipped her some laudanum to make her more cooperative. It should wear off by morning." He leered at Anna and laughed. "I think she liked it by the time we gave her that third dose."

A low growl came out of Angel's chest and once again, Miguel shoved him. This time it was harder.

"Wait!" he hissed. "Don't test Hattie. Trust her on this."

Kadle was laughing as he dropped Anna's head.

"What we have here is a first-class city gal, a teacher from back East. Now dig deep, boys. I won't be letting her go for less than $1000. I can get that easy for her in Deadwood."

CHAPTER 45

An Iron Fist and a Kind Heart

HATTIE STEPPED OUT OF HER HOUSE AND STARED AT the cluster of men for a moment. She pushed her way through the crowd and stepped up beside Anna's horse. She lifted Anna's head carefully and stared at her before she turned her eyes on Kadle.

"She has been drugged."

"Now, Hattie, we only did that so we could travel. She was fighting us all the way and slowing us down. She'll be all right. We only gave her laudanum three times."

Meecher laughed wickedly. "I slipped her two more doses. I liked it when her eyes rolled back."

Hattie's body went still. She looked across the clearing at Angel before she turned to the man beside her.

"Cut her down. Miguel! Carry this woman into my house." She looked over the group of men. "One of you send Nettie up here."

Hattie stopped in front of Kadle and backhanded him.

"You knew the rules and you just broke them. Leave or fight. Make a decision." With that, she turned and stomped into the house.

Angel eased through the crowd of men. He pointed toward the house and back at Kadle.

"I think you are not so much of a man, señor. You must drug a woman to make her spend time with you."

The smile left Kadle's face and he tipped his shotgun forward.

"I could blow you in two. Who do you think you are to address me like that?"

"I think, señor, I am more of a man than you. If I traveled with such a woman, she would arrive with a smile on her face. She would not be beaten and forced to swallow drugs. I think you are not so much a man as you are a pig."

Kadle swung the gun toward Angel and pulled back both hammers. The sound of guns cocking came from all around them.

Meecher stepped forward. "I will fight him. Let me fight him, boss. I can squash him like a bug." He took Kadle's shotgun, released the hammers and dropped it to the ground.

Angel stared at Meecher and nodded. "Sí, I will fight you. Pick your weapon. I do not care what you choose. It makes little difference to me how you die."

Meecher adjusted his guns and grinned at Angel. "We'll do it with guns, and we'll see whose blood spills today."

Angel dropped his gun belt on the ground and opened his shirt to expose his knife.

"I do not think I will waste a bullet on someone such as you. I do not need a gun to kill a pig. But you, señor, go ahead and try to shoot me."

Angel looked at the men behind and around him.

"Perhaps you should move away. This bandito is not so fine a shot as he thinks. He will have difficulty hitting me."

The men spread out and Meecher cursed as he grabbed for his gun. Angel dodged sideways and ran towards him, throwing his knife as he ran. Meecher's first bullet barely missed. The rest of his shots hit the ground as he fell to his knees.

Angel kicked him over on his back and pulled the knife out. He held it over Meecher's stomach for a moment before he wiped it across the dying man's face.

"The señorita is a lady. I will not gut you out of respect for her. Still, you are a pig." Angel spat in Meecher's face. He stared hard at Kadle before he walked toward his cabin.

Kadle stared from Angel to Meecher. "He killed my lieutenant! That little Mex killed my lieutenant!" He pulled his six-gun, but Angel didn't turn around.

A voice sounded clearly through the trees. "Kadle, ya git on yore horse an' hightail it out a here. Miss Hattie done warned ya an' now yore out. This here place ain't open to ya no more."

Kadle stared around the group of men. He pulled himself straight and demanded, "How can I leave? My horse is worn down. I'll rest until morning and after that, I'll leave on my own time. I don't know why you so-called men take orders from a woman—"

Eight guns cut Kadle down.

No one said a word as a cowboy tied ropes around the chests of both men. He rode away, dragging their dead bodies behind him. The men who were standing there slowly started to walk away. Doolan and Jimmy followed them.

CHAPTER 46

I Prayed for an Angel

HATTIE OPENED THE DOOR AND HOLLERED, "GET some water in here. I need enough for a bath plus another bucket. And make it pronto."

Three men grabbed buckets. They filled them from the well and rushed toward the house. Once the buckets were set down, the men hurried out and all but one disappeared into the night.

Hattie's voice was hard as she pointed at the single man leaning by her porch.

"Send that little pig killer in here."

Angel straightened and waited for the man to approach him.

"Hattie wants you inside." He started to walk away but stopped as he looked over his shoulder. "Miguel your brother?"

"Sí. Our sainted mother called me Angel...but Miguel is not so much an angel as I."

The man chuckled. "Angel. That's a good one." His face became more serious as he added, "I'm glad you killed Meecher. He was a woman killer. And good riddance to Kadle too. This place ain't much to brag on, but it's better with them gone." He reached out his hand. "I'm Ned. I keep an eye on Hattie, kind of like her own special bodyguard. Hope your woman is all right." Ned nodded at him and disappeared into the night.

Angel stepped onto Hattie's porch. His step faltered as he walked inside. Hattie had placed Anna on a large table. Her head lolled to the side and Angel was afraid she was dead.

"Don't worry, she's not dead. We need to get these britches off her though. I think she has many sores from riding a horse for so long. I want you to lift her while I work her britches down."

Angel's face became even paler and he shook his head.

"I don't think the señorita would like me to see her without her britches, señora Hattie. I don't think this is such a good idea."

Hattie stared at Angel for a moment before she laughed. "I'll tell her I made you help me. Now lift her carefully. I'm guessing she has blisters that bled, and her bloomers will be stuck to them. If we tear them loose, she will hurt even worse and they will be harder to heal. I am going to try to soak them off in the tub."

The young woman called Nettie was pouring hot water into the tub and putting more into the large kettle to boil. She said nothing as Hattie talked and told Angel what to do.

Angel's heart squeezed as he looked at the bloody bloomers. He touched Anna's hand and whispered, "Ah, señorita. I should have found you sooner."

Anna stirred. Her eyes opened for a moment and she stared at Angel. A tear slid out of her eye, but she smiled. "I prayed for an angel, and you came. You are my Angel." Her eyes slowly closed and once again she went limp.

Angel's voice cracked as he kissed Anna's hand. "I will always come for you, señorita Anna. Wherever you are, that is where I want be."

Hattie grinned at him. "All right, lover boy. Grab her under her arms. We are going to sit her down in that tub. I think Nettie and I can get her out so once she is settled, you can go."

Angel supported Anna's head until Nettie knelt beside him. He kissed Anna's cheek and slipped out the door.

Hattie watched him go. She chuckled as she looked over at Nettie. "You and I could have done that by ourselves, but I knew that lovesick cowboy wanted to make sure his sweetheart was all right." She touched Nettie's black eye.

"Love doesn't do that, Nettie. You need to pick your men better."

Nettie was quiet as she looked up at Hattie. "I don't get to do the picking in here," she stated softly. The two women didn't speak after that as they worked to soak Anna's bloomers off her blistered legs.

CHAPTER 47

MIGUEL'S SECRET

MIGUEL SPENT TWO NIGHTS TALKING AND DRINKING with Hattie. Angel had not been allowed back inside Hattie's house and he grilled his brother each night when Miguel returned to their cabin. Angel wanted to see Anna, but Miguel just shrugged his shoulders.

He was always quiet when he came back so Angel knew their conversations were serious. The third night, Angel slipped close to the house and listened.

"I love her, Hattie."

"You can't love her. We had this conversation two years ago. Nettie made her decision when she came three years ago. I explained how things worked when she came with Dandy. She knew then if she didn't leave, she would never leave."

"She was young and she thought she was in love. Besides, where would she have gone? She knew no one outside her little part of Texas. It is not so easy for a woman on her own.

"I will challenge Luke."

"You can't. If you challenge Luke, you must stay. You promised me you would go straight, and I won't let you go back on your word.

"You are too quick with your pistols, Miguel. You would become a killer quickly. Then what good would you be to Nettie? You would be just another outlaw.

"There is no future here. This hideout has never been breached, but someday it will be. Someone will get lax, and the law will get in.

"Besides, I won't live forever. Someday, I will be challenged. Maybe even by some of my men. One day, there will be a fight and those on the other side will try to kill any who defend me.

"The world is changing, chico. Banks and trains are harder to rob, and the law has almost as many spies as I do. You have no future here. Leave. Leave and never look back. Nettie is dead to you."

Angel slipped around the corner of the house and moved close to the window where Anna lay. He hummed the tune to the "Red River Valley," and added a verse with words he had made up.

> I'm just a handsome vaquero
> I used to dance with girls by my side.
> My amor has stolen my heart now
> And this woman has filled up my mind.

Anna sat up with a start and she laughed softly.

"Go back to your cabin, Angel."

"Sí, I will but I must know you are all right. You were very sick."

"I am much better. The blisters on my legs are healing, but I don't think I can ride a horse yet.

"Then I will find a buggy to take you away. Goodnight, señorita. I hope you dream of me tonight."

Angel sang softly as he walked toward his cabin. A rough voice called for him to halt. He looked toward the voice and called, "I only walk in the moonlight to check on my amor. Now that I know she is well, I will go to my cabin." Angel continued to sing softly, and his singing changed to a soft whistle as he disappeared into the night.

CHAPTER 48

NETTIE

NETTIE APPLIED THE CREAM HATTIE HAD GIVEN HER to the sores on Anna's legs. Hattie didn't want them bandaged. She told Nettie they would heal faster if they were left unwrapped.

Anna leaned back on her hands and gritted her teeth as Nettie worked. She asked, "How can Angel get me out of here?"

Nettie looked at Anna in surprise. "He killed Meecher and Hattie's guards killed Kadle. Hattie has rules and Kadle broke them. You will be able to leave freely when you are able to walk."

A sob slipped out of Anna's chest and she took a deep breath. "I never thought I would be glad a man died. Now I am pleased two men are gone."

Nettie looked away. Her voice was soft as she spoke.

"I came here with a cowboy who worked on a ranch next to ours. He branded some mavericks and was accused of rustling. The rancher who accused him was powerful and everyone knew Dandy wouldn't get a fair trial." Nettie smiled briefly at Anna before she continued.

"When Dandy left, I ran away with him. We ended up here. I truly thought he was innocent." She shook her head. "I was a fool and now I am paying for it.

"Oh, Dandy was quick with a gun when he was sober. He made me all kinds of promises about how he would take care of me when we left here. The problem was, he couldn't handle whiskey. One of the men here got him drunk and challenged him for me.

"Dandy died a day after we arrived here, and I became that man's woman. When Luke came last year, he challenged and now I belong to him." Her voice was bitter as she added softly, "That was three years ago. I will never leave here.

"Most women only last five or six years in this place. They are either killed or they overdose on laudanum." Her eyes were sad as she looked at Anna.

"You are lucky you were drugged and couldn't speak. Kadle broke Hattie's rules by doing that. She won't allow women to be brought here against their will. Of course, some are threatened with death unless they say they want to stay."

There were tears in Nettie's eyes. "I was a foolish girl and now I am a slave to a cruel man who will someday kill me."

Anna stared at Nettie with wide eyes. "Perhaps you could leave with us. I will ask Angel."

Nettie shook her head quickly, "No, they would be killed. The only way a woman can be taken out of here is if a brother or a father comes. Even a husband cannot take his wife back. Hattie assumes if a wife is here, there is a reason.

"If a man comes claiming to be a brother or father, Hattie will ask him for a picture or something to prove who he is. In the three years I have been here, I have only seen two women leave—but I have seen many men killed who tried to rescue a wife or a sweetheart."

"But isn't your father searching for you? Or maybe a brother?"

"My father was angry when I ran away. I don't think he ever searched for me." Nettie smiled briefly. "My big brother was a wild cowboy. He was on a cattle drive to Dodge when I left. He might have searched for a time but where would he look?

"Dandy knew about this place, and we rode here as fast as we could. We avoided people and followed what some call 'the owlhoot trail.'

"It is not a real trail. More of a crooked route with select places to trade horses or stay overnight.

"We stopped only at ranches and farms which were friendly to outlaws. Those who lived and worked there would never share information about anyone who stopped." Nettie was quiet for a moment. Her voice was bitter when she continued.

"Looking back, Dandy knew too many outlaws to just be an innocent cowboy. I think he *was* a rustler. We traded horses at a hideout in The Strip before we headed north. Everyone there knew him.

"I was seventeen and thought it was a great adventure. I was a fool and I have paid dearly. In the end, I will pay with my life."

Anna was horrified as she listened to Nettie. The girl's life made hers look simple and easy.

Her breath caught in her throat. She touched Nettie's arm. "We just need to pray Hattie will break her rules for you or you can somehow escape."

Nettie laughed. "Prayers coming from here would be novel. Maybe the Good Lord would be so surprised He *would* listen." She squeezed Anna's hand.

"Thank you, Anna. This is very selfish of me to say, but I'm glad I was able to meet you. And I'm even happier you will not be staying."

Nettie stood and gave Anna a quick smile before she hurried out.

CHAPTER 49

A Brother's Love

OOLAN STOOD IN THE DARK BY THE CABIN HE AND Jimmy had been assigned and smoked a cigarette. His breath caught when the moonlight shined on Nettie's face as she hurried down the hill to the cabin Luke and she shared.

Doolan couldn't hear what was said when Nettie arrived, but he heard a crash. He guessed Luke grabbed her and threw her into the cabin. He cursed and threw down the cigarette. He turned up the hill and strode toward Hattie's cabin.

"Stop right there. One more step and you will be cut down." The sentry's voice was soft but clear.

"I need to see Hattie right away. I need to talk to her."

"Hattie don't meet with anyone but gang leaders. Tell your boss to set up a meeting."

"My boss is dead and so is his lieutenant. I guess that makes me the boss. Now tell me what to do to set up that meeting."

The sentry whistled shrilly and a man with a rifle appeared on Hattie's porch.

"This fellow wants a meeting with Hattie. He's one of them who came in four days ago with the woman."

The man on the porch waved and turned around. He rapped out a special knock on Hattie's door. When she opened it, he pointed behind him to Doolan and talked softly. Hattie listened quietly and finally nodded.

"Send him up."

Doolan walked slowly up to Hattie's house. The guard took his gun and pocketknife.

"Speak your piece and get back out here. Hattie don't normally see anyone of an evening."

Doolan nodded and entered when the guard opened the door.

He took off his hat and faced Hattie.

"Miss Hattie, my name is Tex Doolan. I want to talk to you about my sister."

Hattie stared hard at the man and laughed.

"Yeah, you and a dozen other men who come here looking for a lost love."

Doolan shook his head. He pulled a worn picture out of his pocket.

"Her name is Margaret. She left our ranch down south of the Brazos in Texas three years ago with a man. I tracked her north out of Oklahoma and into Nebraska. I lost her trail outside Cheyenne.

"How did you come to be here?"

"A fellow in Cheyenne remembered her. Said she was with a dandy-looking fellow. He gambled for a time at a saloon in Cheyenne before they headed north. A man at the livery there by the name of Rooster remembered her too. He said she was a real nice little gal and had a friendly smile. He could even describe her. He suggested I head this way.

"Rooster's the one who told me I needed to be part of a gang who knew this place to get in. I hooked up with Kadle and Meecher down by Fort Laramie.

"Miss Hattie, I've branded mavericks and eaten a few cattle that weren't mine, but I wouldn't call myself much of an outlaw. In fact, I was thinking on getting shut of Meecher and Kadle even before Kadle killed that fellow down by Fort Laramie. Shot him in the back real sudden like. I just about shot Kadle then, but another fellow had his gun on me.

"I was plumb worried when they took Miss Whitman. I knew she was in a heap of trouble so I stayed with them. I tried several times to get her away, but Kadle was suspicious. He kept her close to him." Doolan was quiet as he watched Hattie. He frowned and continued, "Margaret doesn't know I'm here.

"Shoot, I wasn't even sure she was here until I saw her tonight."

"I heard there were some kids with Miss Whitman. What happened to them?" Hattie's old eyes were bright and hard as she watched Doolan.

"I'm not sure. Kadle made them go with him to the root cellar in this house we followed them to. The boy didn't want to go and kept talking about snakes. I think maybe it was all an act because the kids somehow got away. They found a tunnel and went through it. Even though it was full of snakes, it didn't slow them down.

"Kadle was madder than hops. That's when he knew he couldn't go back to Fort Laramie so we headed up here."

Hattie stared at the picture Doolan had handed her.

"What makes you think she is here?"

"I saw her leave your house a little while ago. She went down the hill and into a cabin with some fellow. I think his name is Luke." Doolan's eyes were cold as he added, "He threw her into the cabin, and I heard a crash. I think he beats her. I could see a black eye when the moon caught her face.

"I've traveled a long way to find my sister. I want to know what I have to do to get her out."

Hattie stared at Doolan for a moment. She opened the door and hollered to the man standing guard.

"Send Miguel in here. And tell Nettie I need her."

CHAPTER 50

THE CHALLENGE

MIGUEL TAPPED LIGHTLY ON THE DOOR. HE WAITED for Hattie to answer before he stepped inside. He glanced from Hattie to the man in front of her but said nothing as he moved toward the side of the room.

"Miguel, this is Tex Doolan. He is here for his sister."

The two men stared at each other, and Miguel nodded. "Sí, I know this man. His sister is Nettie."

Miguel stepped toward Doolan with his hand outstretched.

"Señor Tex, I'd be proud to be your second if you need one."

"Oh, he'll need one and don't offer too fast. Luke is greased lightning with a gun or a knife, and the man he will bring with him is just as deadly."

She stared hard at Doolan. "You will challenge Luke to a fight. It will take place at noon tomorrow. The weapon will be of his choice." Her face was hard as she looked from him to Miguel.

"If Doolan wins, Luke's second has the option to challenge Miguel. If Miguel accepts, he will then choose the weapon."

Hattie's voice was soft as she looked from one to the other.

243

"There is only one chance. If Doolan is killed, the challenge ends. Either way, this place is closed to both of you." Her hard eyes moved to Doolan.

"You will ride out with your sister tomorrow or your body will be tossed to the wolves."

Hattie reached into a jar behind her and took out what looked like a coin. "Give this to the guard. He will deliver it to Luke."

There was a soft knock on the door.

"Miss Hattie?"

Hattie jerked the door open. When Nettie stepped inside, Hattie pointed toward Doolan.

"Your brother came for you. He is challenging Luke tomorrow."

Nettie's left eye was swollen shut and her lip was split open. She turned slowly toward Doolan and began to cry. He pulled her to him and held her as she sobbed.

"No! Go away. You can't beat Luke. He will kill you."

Miguel stepped forward and touched her cheek.

"Nettie, for you we will fight."

Hattie stared at the three of them and she almost smiled. Instead, she glared at Doolan.

"Now get. Be in front of my house at five minutes before noon and not one minute later. And Nettie, you will stay here tonight. You can sleep with Anna."

Hattie stood straight and tall until she was alone with Miguel. When the door closed, she slowly sank into a chair. Her hands were trembling, and Miguel poured her a whiskey.

She stared at the liquor a moment and smiled up at Miguel as she swirled it in her glass.

"Perhaps Doolan will win tomorrow, and maybe you as well. I hope so. I hope you can take Nettie out of here." A single tear leaked from her eye. "But if I have to watch you die, chico, it will break me."

Miguel took her old face in his hands and kissed both her cheeks. "Don't worry, Hattie," he whispered. "I have heard of this Doolan. He is very quick. Besides, Luke will be angry. He will drink tonight.

"And me? My heart is light because I will take Nettie out of this place tomorrow." He put his hand to her cheek and whispered softly, "But my heart is also sad because I will not see you again. I will miss you, Hattie. You will always be special to me."

Hattie stood and hugged Miguel as she cried silently. Her face hardened as she looked toward the door. She fiercely wiped her face and pointed.

"My buggy will be ready for you when the fight ends. Leave it at John Nolan's KC Ranch.

"Now go. And tomorrow, there will be no tears, no hugging. You will leave as no one of importance to me.

"Goodbye, my chico."

CHAPTER 51

A Bad Man

L UKE DICKSON HAD BEEN AN OUTLAW MOST OF HIS
life. Born into poverty in Missouri, he stole his father's best horse
and ran away from home at age fourteen. By fifteen, he had been jailed
twice for petty theft.

He signed on to fight for the South in the winter of 1864. He was
thrown in the brig for drinking and fighting with the other soldiers
before his first battle. He was also accused of killing a fellow soldier
during that battle although it was never proven.

Dickson was released to fight a month later. He deserted, stealing
horses and ammunition from fellow soldiers as he left. Once again, he
was accused of shooting a soldier he was fighting beside in the back.

He next turned up in New Mexico in 1876. By then, he was wanted
by the law in Texas, Kansas, and Missouri. He hung around with a young
man named Billy Bonney but left New Mexico in 1877 before the start
of the Lincoln County War there.

He ended up in No Man's Land where his gang preyed on the herds
headed north. In 1878, they killed some drovers and stole their entire
herd. His gang was able to sell the cattle before anyone realized they were

stolen. The gang left Dodge ahead of a posse and split as they headed north and west.

Dickson rode to Nebraska and joined a gang headed to the Hole-in-the-Wall. Before he arrived, he killed the second in command and took his place. The gang leader died mysteriously several days after they reached their destination and Dickson became the leader.

He challenged the man who was with Nettie shortly after that. Now, he was fully accepted as one of the deadliest men in their den of thieves.

Luke slammed his whiskey bottle down on the table in front of him. He stared around the dirty shack and cursed loudly.

"If Hattie hadn't called that wench up there, I'd have killed her.

"This will turn out jist fine. I'll kill Nettie's brother an' then I'll make 'er suffer ever' day till the end a her short, sorry life." He looked toward the door and yelled, "Sledge! Git in here!"

A slim cowboy with a smile that didn't reach his eyes slid through the door. "Yeah, boss?"

"You'll be my second tomorrow. Miguel is old Hattie's favorite, so we need to figure a way to swing this fight in our favor." His wicked face slowly broke into a smile. "Mebbie I'll make it a knife fight and put a little of that venom I collected on the tip. All I'd have to do is nick him."

Sledge slowly shook his head. "No one knows this man called Doolan. No one has even heard of 'im. He wears his guns tied down, but Shorty saw him practicin' today an' he was slow. Mighty slow. Some of the boys said he is from down south somewhere, but he ain't anyone they know.

"Naw, I think ya should just challenge 'im with guns." Sledge's icy smile became larger. "Even if ya drink all night, ya should still be able to beat 'im to the draw. No one here comes close to ya in a gun fight, let alone a wanna-be gunslinger."

Luke grunted and the two men proceeded to drink. They finished the first bottle and started the second before they called it a night.

CHAPTER 52

TO THE DEATH

A LARGE CROWD WAS GATHERED IN FRONT OF HATTIE'S house before noon. The old woman sat in a large chair on a platform her men had built. A rope fence separated the fighting area from the men who gathered there.

Nettie and Anna stood on Hattie's porch. Anna didn't want to attend but Hattie had insisted.

"When this fight is over, no matter how it turns out, you are leaving and leaving fast. I want you in that buggy and gone before the bodies are drug off." Her eyes moved to Nettie and she frowned before she added, "Nettie will only leave if her bother and Miguel win."

"Ned will lead you out. He is the man who guards my house. He is my most loyal man and he will make sure you get out safely." Hattie's old eyes looked tired as she continued. "I told him to just keep going no matter what happens behind him.

"This place is a powder keg. Too much greed and too many men who want me gone." She laughed harshly.

"Let them come for me. I'll take some of them with me when I go. They think I'm too old, but I still have some fight left in me.

"Ned's too good of a man to stay here though. He's tough in a fight and a good cowman to boot. He would die to keep me safe, and it wouldn't do a bit of good.

"You find a reason to keep him with you. And tell him not to come back."

Anna thought of that conversation as she looked over at Hattie. The old woman's eyes were once again fierce, and her face was set in harsh lines as she waited.

Luke climbed over the rope and strutted to the south end of the enclosure. Sledge followed him.

Doolan and Miguel were already waiting on the north end.

Sledge looked toward the two men. He cursed under his breath. Doolan didn't behave like a man who was concerned. For the first time, Sledge was afraid he had advised his boss wrong.

"Boss," he hissed, "that man's a gunslinger—I'm sure of it. His shootin' yesterday was all an act. Step to the side as ya fire.

"Better yet, use yore knife. This ain't his first picnic."

Luke stared at Doolan and cursed as he spat. "It ain't mine neither."

Hattie read the rules from a piece of paper. When she was done, she folded the paper and laid it on her lap.

"Luke, choose your weapon."

"Six-shooter." He slid his weapon out and twirled it around his finger before he slipped it back in his holster. He grinned at Doolan and laughed.

"Yore gonna die right here an' then I'm a gonna beat yore sister ever' day for the rest a her sorry life. I'll carve a little piece off 'er ever' night jist as a reminder of today."

Doolan stared at Luke in disdain and stated softly, "Dickson, you are a low-down, poor example of an outlaw an' even less of a man.

"I was at the Battle of Westport in '64. I was jist a kid, but we wore the same uniform. Uniforms didn't matter to you though. Y'all were a back-shootin', woman-beatin' coward then an' ya still are.

"Pull that gun, ya bloody traitor. Die today so my sister can leave free."

Some of the men watching had fought in that war. It wasn't discussed much inside Hole-in-the-Wall. However, one rule they all believed was a soldier defended the man next to him.

A slow murmur moved through the men and Luke grabbed for his gun. He tried to step sideways, but he tripped. His only bullet hit the ground in front of him because Luke Dickson, the bad man from Missouri, was already dead.

Doolan dropped his gun back in his holster. He looked around the group of men staring at him, and his eyes settled on Sledge.

"What will it be, Sledge? You want to take this fight on? How bad do you want Nettie to stay here?"

Miguel stepped forward with a smile on his face.

"I will let you choose, Sledge. Do you want to die by a gun or by a knife? Either is all right with me." He looked over at Angel and grinned. "But unlike my brother, I prefer not to throw my knives."

A knife appeared in Miguel's left hand. Most did not see it drawn nor did they know where it came from. He sliced through the air and the knife disappeared. Once again, a wave of muttering went through the group of men.

Sledge stared at Miguel, and he laughed sarcastically.

"Why would I fight for Nettie? Let's fight instead for yore life an' for old Hattie's as well. If I kill her little pet, she'll be a broken ol' hag, an' I'll be the one who runs this place."

He stepped back and held his hands loosely by his side.

"We'll use guns. I don't want to work up a sweat on such a fine day."

Miguel didn't answer. He almost looked like he was resting as he waited for Sledge to move. The man's eyes flickered, and Miguel pulled his gun.

Sledge staggered. He was weaving on his feet as he triggered his gun wildly three more times. He staggered again as he tried to spin. He pointed his gun toward Hattie. As he tried to fire again, Ned dove in front of her. The bullet caught him, and he fell to the ground. Sledge dropped to his knees as he stared at Miguel.

"Can't be. I'm the fastest man here. This can't be." He fell forward on his face and Hattie stood.

She leaned over Ned. He was trying to stand, and she pulled him up. She lifted his shirt to look at his wound before she turned around. Her finger quivered slightly as she pointed at the team one of her men was leading forward.

"Take that buggy and go. Put Ned up on his horse. He isn't hurt so bad he can't still lead you out." She spoke to the man behind her, and he tossed Angel a package.

"Don't stop until you reach the KC Ranch. You can bind Ned up there."

Hattie turned and strode toward her house. The men parted to allow her to walk through and she didn't pause or wait. She looked straight ahead as she entered her house and slammed the door.

CHAPTER 53

AN ANGRY WOMAN

NNA AND NETTIE WERE QUICKLY HELPED INTO THE buggy. Doolan jumped onto the seat beside them while Jimmy, Angel, and Miguel rode beside the buggy. Ned raised his arm stiffly and the little troupe left Hole-in-the-Wall quickly.

No one spoke for the hour it took them to wind through the canyons to the plains below. Only when they were out of rifle range did Ned slump sideways in his saddle. Angel caught him and the men lowered him to the ground.

Nettie jumped out of the wagon and quickly opened his shirt.

The bullet had cut across Ned's stomach and was deflected by his belt buckle. It tore a deep groove all the way to his ribs and broke his bottom rib as it passed on by.

Nettie stared at the wound a moment and laughed.

"Ned, we'll stop this bleeding and you'll be fine. That bullet didn't penetrate anything that mattered. We'll have the cook at the KC look at your rib. He might want to take the bottom part out. Take it out or not, you will be just fine."

The cowboy stared down at his stomach and passed out. Nettie's eyes sparkled as she laughed again.

"Ned can't stand the sight or smell of blood. He's a poor outlaw." Nettie applied some of the cream from the package Hattie had sent and wrapped a rag tightly around his stomach.

"That should hold him until we reach the KC Ranch. John Nolan's cook is an old sawbones. Hattie sends men to him if she can't treat them inside.

"He will let us spend the night. No outlaw is allowed to bother him. Hattie knows we need friendly faces on the outside too." Nettie's face colored and she laughed harshly. "We. I guess I have been a part of that group for too long."

She smiled shakily at Doolan. "Thank you," she whispered. She refused to look at Miguel.

Angel stared from Nettie to his brother, but Miguel kept his face still. When he did look at Angel, he shrugged. He helped load Ned in the back of the buggy but said nothing.

Anna looked at Nettie in surprise as she whispered, "Why have you not thanked Miguel? He risked his life to help you get out."

Nettie frowned at her. "I don't wish to talk about Miguel," she responded. "That part of my life is over."

Anna stared at her friend and shook her head. "You should still thank him. And if you don't want him around, you owe him an explanation."

Nettie's face was angry when she looked at Anna. "Like you and Angel? What does he expect from you? The two of you haven't discussed that either."

Anna's eyes opened wide, and she looked quickly toward Angel. He was looking ahead as he leaned down to talk to his horse and didn't seem to be listening to the women's conversation. She settled back in her seat and said nothing more.

CHAPTER 54

KC Ranch

JOHN NOLAN'S KC RANCH HEADQUARTERS WERE about twenty miles northeast of Hole-in-the-Wall. Both parties agreed to the unwritten laws of ranch etiquette. While John didn't condone the outlaws' actions, he also never refused a tired man a meal or medical attention. Horses were sometimes sold to the outlaw visitors as well, but the old rancher was too wise to buy or accept any animal in exchange.

Mary Nolan stood beside her husband and watched the buggy come up the lane. They both recognized it as Hattie's, but the two women in it were young.

John nodded behind him. "Tell Cookie to dig up some vittles." He squeezed his wife's arm. "We'd best make sure those women have a bed for the night too."

Mary hurried inside and John walked out to greet the newcomers.

"Howdy. Step on down. I reckon you folks must be hungry. My cook can fix you something pronto." He nodded at the buggy. "That's Hattie's rig. She all right?"

Doolan jumped out of the buggy with a smile as he stretched out his hand.

"Tex Doolan. You must be John Nolan.

"Hattie is as strong as ever. She said to leave the rig with you. We'd like to buy a couple of horses though if you have some, and a pack animal as well." He pointed his thumb to the back of the buggy.

"We have an injured man back there. Nothing too serious but we'd like your cook to look at him. We hear he's a sawbones."

John didn't say anything as he followed Doolan around the buggy. He recognized Ned though. *Ned is Hattie's most trusted man. I'm not so sure things are as good as this fellow says.*

Ned looked up and grinned at John.

"Hello, John. It ain't so bad but you know me. I can't look at it."

John laughed. He knew Ned would fill him in later and since the man was smiling, he felt a little better.

"Let's get you into the house. I'll have Cookie work on you there." He looked up at the women.

"You ladies come on in. The missus is getting a room ready for you. Shoot, by the time we get inside, she'll probably have hot water going for your baths."

Doolan helped both women down. John noticed how stiff the tallest woman was as well as the bruises on both of them. They looked like they would appreciate a warm bath and a soft bed as well.

He looked around at the three men on horseback.

"You boys come on in too. Some of my hands are gone for the night so you can sleep in the bunkhouse. There are some oats and hay for your horses in the barn." He started to walk away but turned and added, "Park Hattie's buggy in that small shed over there. All the horses can go in the corral."

Angel and Miguel pulled the saddles off their horses and unhooked the buggy. They found an old blanket along with a currycomb in the barn and began to rub their animals down. Jimmy just turned his horse loose and headed for the house.

Angel watched him go and commented softly, "A man who doesn't care for his horse is not so much of a man."

Miguel said nothing. Angel worked a while longer in silence. He finally turned to his brother.

"You were willing to die for señorita Nettie and still she refuses to look at you. Why is this?"

Miguel shrugged his shoulders.

Angel turned his younger brother around and stared at him for a moment before he returned to rubbing his horse down.

"I know you are in love with her. I heard you and señorita Hattie talking. It was good you helped to get her out, but I don't think she likes you so much."

Miguel cursed as he grabbed a currycomb.

"Do you have to listen to everyone's conversations? Why don't you just keep your nose out of my business."

Angel chuckled softly. "No, Miguel. I am your brother. Your business is my business." He smiled over his shoulder at his brother as he added, "But I think señorita Nettie does not hate you so much as she is afraid to like you. I think maybe you should take a walk with the small señorita."

"She won't walk out with me and with her brother around, I will never be able to speak to her alone."

Angel chuckled and winked at Miguel. "You leave the brother to me, and you take the small señorita for a walk. Perhaps when you return, both will wear smiles."

Miguel laughed and the brothers quickly finished rubbing their horses down. They did the same with Hattie's horses before they turned them into the corral.

The women were not in the kitchen, but the cook was cleaning Ned's wound.

Miguel grinned down at him. "I think it was good you were a hero but not so good for your rib. Now you will be missing one like a woman, yes?"

Ned started to laugh but groaned instead.

The cook glared at Miguel. "You get out of here. I want him to hold still so I can make sure there are no small pieces of bone in there."

John waved toward the men. "Come on over here and get something to eat. Cookie doesn't like anyone looking over his shoulder so we'll just leave him alone."

As the men sat down and started to eat, John looked across at them. "So where are you boys headed? Back down south?"

Doolan nodded. "I am. I have been looking for my sister for nigh on three years and finally tracked her to the Hole-in-the-Wall.

"My folks have a little ranch down south of the Brazos. Margaret and I will be headed there. The folks will be plumb tickled to see her. Ma has been worried sick."

"And the other woman?"

The men all looked at Angel. He paused before he answered, "The señorita is a schoolteacher. She was taken by some bad gringos about ten days ago. We found her and kindly asked them to return her." He grinned at John but added seriously, "I am not sure what the señorita will do. Her only family is in Kansas. Perhaps she will go there." He nodded toward Miguel and added, "My brother and I go to Cheyenne. We will help my sister and her husband on their ranch. Perhaps we will buy one of our own." He shrugged.

"We helped take a herd of black cows north into the Bitter Root Valley and are just returning. We have not talked much of what is to come."

John noticed neither the fourth man nor Ned said what they were doing. Still, he didn't ask. Obviously, these people were traveling together for convenience.

CHAPTER 55

PUSHING AWAY THE PAST

THE MEN VISITED FOR ANOTHER HOUR AS THEY ATE. John wiped his face and stood.

"Enough of this sitting around. I have some cattle I need to move.

"I'll see you fellas for supper. I try to keep a closer eye on my Herefords than you cowboys down south do with your longhorns."

Angel laughed and somberly commented, "Sí, those longhorns, they drop their calves as they walk, and the babies, they just jump right up and chase their mommas.

"You said your hands are not all here. Perhaps some of us can help you, yes? Jimmy and Doolan along with myself will come with you." He grinned at Miguel and winked, "Miguel is better with the ladies than he is with the cattle. We will leave him here to keep an eye on the women."

John laughed and the four men headed for the corral.

Miguel wandered around outside. When he heard women's voices, he walked back into the house.

Mary looked around in surprise. "Your friends are all gone?"

Miguel grinned, "Sí, they went to help your husband with the cows. They left me here to watch over you ladies." His eyes settled on Nettie.

"Perhaps Señorita Nettie will take a walk with me?"

Nettie started to shake her head, but Mary laughed.

"Go ahead, Nettie. Anna and I will start on supper. You can help when you get back. That kitchen is almost too small for three women anyway."

Nettie frowned as she walked slowly toward the door. Miguel stood back to let her walk through and she whispered, "I do not want to walk with you, Miguel. Do not take my arm—do not even touch me."

Miguel said nothing as he followed her toward the barn. Finally, he turned her around. The confusion on his face was easy to see.

"Nettie, why are you angry with me? I wanted to take you away last year, but Hattie sent me away. Now you are free and I am here. Why do you act like you despise me?"

Nettie's eyes filled with tears as she pulled away from him.

"Miguel, you represent everything I shouldn't have done. When I look at you, I see the mistakes I have made.

"I should never have run away with Dandy. I shouldn't have come here with him and I should never have agreed to stay." Tears leaked from her eyes as she continued.

"I only took up with him because you left. You went away. You left and never said goodbye. I thought you would come back but you didn't.

"Dandy convinced me to run away with him when he was accused of rustling. He was friendly and fun. I didn't think he had stolen those cattle and I agreed. Then things just spiraled out of control.

"He knew outlaws everywhere we stopped and everyone at Hole-in-the-Wall. That was when I realized I had made a bad mistake. Still, I was young, and I thought I could get out.

"I didn't though. When you showed up, you with your beautiful smile and your sparkling eyes. I just knew you were there to save me, to take me away. Instead, Luke challenged the man I was with, and I became his.

"I made myself hate you after that. And when you left again, something inside me died."

Miguel pulled Nettie to him as she cried.

"Nettie, please don't cry. I tried to get you. I told Hattie I would become part of a gang so I could challenge for you but she sent me away. She said I would become a killer. She said then I would be no good for you. She said you needed a good man, not a killer.

"There was nothing I could do. I couldn't sneak you out, and I couldn't challenge for you. I could do nothing and so I left. I didn't forget you though. I am here now."

Nettie pulled away from Miguel and stared up at him.

"Now you are here? Where exactly are you, Miguel? How many whore houses have you been in since you last saw me? You didn't try hard enough. You gave up.

"Go away, Miguel. I don't want to love you. I will marry a settled man, perhaps even one who is boring. But I will never have to wonder if he will come home at night or who he has been chasing in the saloons."

A tear ran down Nettie's face as she stepped further from him. "I am going to Texas, and you are staying here in the Wyoming Territory. That is best for both of us. You will never settle down, Miguel, and I don't want to live that kind of life.

"Now walk with me back to the house and don't speak to me of this again. You and I—we are finished. I beat out the fire I felt for you a long time ago. And the tiny spark that is left, I will put it out as well.

"I am thankful you helped my brother but being thankful is not the same thing as love."

Miguel said nothing as he followed Nettie. When Nettie reached the door, she looked back at him. "And my name is Margaret. Nettie stayed and Margaret was rescued."

Nettie didn't eat supper. She went to her room and stayed there for the rest of the evening. When Anna retired that evening, Nettie was asleep and tear stains showed on her face.

CHAPTER 56

Good News

NGEL HAD A LARGE SMILE ON HIS FACE WHEN THE
men returned. He looked at Anna as he spoke.

"The children have been found. They are staying with a family in Fort Laramie. That family wanted to adopt them, but the little ones, they say they wait for Miss Anna to return. She is to be their new mother."

Anna's face lit with excitement as she laughed. "When can we get them?" she asked breathlessly. "They must have been so afraid."

Angel's face was concerned as he answered, "The only way there is by horseback. We might be able to find a stage about halfway, but it is not so regular. Sometimes it runs, sometimes it does not.

"Do you think you can ride, señorita? Fort Laramie is over two hundred miles away. If we could go slowly, maybe twenty or thirty miles per day, it would be over seven days. If we travel fifty miles per day, we will make it in about four."

Anna smiled and nodded. "Let's try to go a little faster. My blisters are much better. I am anxious to find the children and get back to Kansas."

Angel watched her a moment and slowly nodded. "I will see about purchasing some supplies. Perhaps señora Nolan has some britches she will let you wear as well."

The little group split. Doolan and Margaret were headed straight south. Ned asked to go with them. Angel's party was headed southeast toward Fort Laramie. Jimmy decided to head south with Doolan, and Angel wasn't sorry. *A man who doesn't take care of his horse will shirk other duties as well.*

Anna hugged Margaret and whispered, "I hope we see each other again. I will miss you."

Margaret looked at Anna in surprise. She glanced toward Miguel and shrugged.

"Perhaps, although I have no plans to ever leave Texas again."

Angel had made a point to talk to Doolan about Anna's hard ride to the Hole-in-the-Wall. Their conversation had been long and detailed.

They had known each other growing up, but Angel decided he liked the man even better now.

"Perhaps, señor Doolan, one day you will decide to ride north again. You can come and work for me on my ranch." Angel's dark eyes were dancing and Doolan laughed.

"Maybe. I don't have plans to leave but ya never know." He nodded toward Miguel. "Miguel, I appreciate what y'all did for us. If ya make it south, stop in."

Miguel's dark eyes rested on Margaret, but she wouldn't look at him.

"Perhaps one day. Adios, señors. And you too, señorita Margaret." The men waved but Margaret ignored him.

"Perhaps I will make a trip in the spring," he added softly as they rode away.

Angel had laid a blanket over Anna's saddle, and he helped her onto her horse. Miguel grabbed the rope to their pack horse, and they turned their horses down the grassy lane.

They had already thanked the Nolans and said their goodbyes, but Angel turned around and waved his hat.

"If you come to Cheyenne, ask for me, señor Nolan. I will show you and your wife the same hospitality you have shown us." He tipped his hat to Mary Nolan and led off at a cantor.

Mary had found britches for both women, and even though Anna disliked wearing pants, they were more comfortable than the dress she had been wearing with all the layers under it. "Goodness, if I'm not careful, before long I will prefer britches to dresses," she muttered to herself.

Angel looked back at her and laughed. Anna frowned. *He can't have heard me. I was muttering and could barely hear myself. Still, he acted like he heard me.*

CHAPTER 57

REGISTER CLIFF

THE FIRST COUPLE OF DAYS WERE EASY RIDING, BUT the further they went, the quieter Anna became. The stage was not running when they reached the stage station, so they continued on.

Miguel shot a couple of rabbits, and with the supplies they had packed, their food was adequate.

They were about fifty miles from Fort Laramie when Anna developed a cough. Angel wanted to stop at a ranch and rest for several days, but Anna insisted they continue. Angel watched her with concern.

"I think, señorita Anna, you have been too much outside. I think sleeping on the ground is making you sick."

Anna glared at him. "It is just a cough. I'm sure it is mostly from the dust. Perhaps we can ride faster today. Then we will sleep in a hotel tonight."

It was early evening when Angel turned their horses toward a towering cliff in the distance.

"We will rest there tonight. You can sleep while the horses graze.

Anna started to argue but Angel shook his head.

"That tall rock is called Register Cliff. It is the only shelter between here and Fort Laramie. When we leave there, we will only be about fifteen miles from the fort." He added softly, "You are tired, Anna, and your cough is getting worse. I think a rest would be good. Besides, we have been pushing the horses. They could use a rest as well, and the grass is good in front of the cliff."

Anna said nothing. She slumped a little in her saddle and Angel slowed his horse to ride beside her.

When they reached the tall cliff, Angel lifted Anna down. She staggered a step before she stared up at the rock in surprise.

"It is so tall. It just seems to rise out of the prairie!"

"Sí. I do not know how it came to be here, but it is very old. Many have signed their names here. Some even leave little messages for those who follow." He took Anna's arm and led her toward the towering rock.

She walked beside it and read some of the names aloud.

"Some of these are so sad." She pointed at some words scratched into the rock. "This one says, 'Our baby died last night. We buried him here. There was no wood for a marker so this rock will be his stone.' How hard that would have been."

Angel nodded. "Some are sad but there are those which are happy as well. Look, there is a heart. Some lonesome cowboy professed his love to strangers."

Anna looked where Angel was pointing. It was a heart with two names inside. "John loves Sarah, April 1855." Her eyes moved a little further. A small heart close to the ground had a crooked line drawn through it. On one side of the line, "Anna" was written. The other side said "Angel."

Anna looked quickly at Angel, but he wasn't paying any attention. *Surely Angel didn't write that. There must be hundreds of Angels out there... there are certainly many Annas.*

"Have you been here before?" she asked carefully.

"Sí, when we took señor Rock's vacas north. We stopped here for a night."

Anna was quiet. She frowned and looked down at the heart again before she asked, "Did you carve your name here?"

"But of course, señorita Anna! I always carve little messages into the rocks. Sometimes, I pretend to be someone else. This time though, I was myself." His dark eyes were sparkling as he added, "I think it is much too high for you to see though. Only strong vaqueros such as myself can climb to the top of this tall cliff.

"Now come. You must rest. Even if we leave late in the morning, we will still be at Fort Laramie before dark."

Angel quickly unloaded the blankets and made Anna a bed. He covered her with another blanket and she was soon asleep. He watched her quietly for a moment before he leaned to lift a strand of hair off her cheek.

Miguel sauntered up to stand beside him.

"I think you have it bad, Brother. Never have I see you look at a woman so." His grin turned to a laugh and he added, "A little heart scratched in the rock? Yes, you have let your love show and she saw it."

Angel growled and he shoved Miguel.

"Go water the horses and stay out of my degocios. You have enough women difficulties of your own."

Miguel laughed as he led the horses toward the river. He took a bath while he was there. Angel said nothing when he returned. He grabbed his clothes and headed for the river. He called over his shoulder, "If señorita Anna awakes, try to get her to eat some of the food I cooked."

Anna didn't wake though. She slept through the night although she tossed and coughed often.

It was nearly five o'clock on Saturday afternoon, October 11, when they rode into Fort Laramie. They had taken the last fifteen miles slowly, but Anna was still pale and tired. Angel asked for directions to the hotel while Miguel took the pack horse to the livery.

Anna almost fell off her horse when Angel reached to lift her down. He wanted to take her to the doctor, but she refused.

"I'm just tired, Angel. Just let me go to bed."

Randolph was at his desk when they entered the lobby and he rushed to meet them with a smile on his face.

"Miss Whitman! We have been very concerned about you. Just follow me. Your traveling trunk is still in your room.

"Agnes Phillips was in last week to pick up supplies and she has been raising Cain about you. The sheriff finally sent out a search party. They found Howard Martinson and Dan Morton's graves. Horse tracks were all around Howard's house. Someone had run some cattle through the yard, and they wiped out all the tracks leading away from there. We just didn't know what had happened to you.

"Shortly after that, a ranch family several hours west of here showed up with Dan Morton's two little ones.

"Darn shame about Dan." His eyes were friendly as he added, "He was mighty excited about you coming. We were all hoping you would decide to marry and stay here."

Anna blushed and smiled as the man continued to talk. She coughed several times and Randolph looked over at Angel with concern. He was quiet as he unlocked the door.

"There you are, Miss Whitman. Everything is as you left it." He looked at Anna closely again. "Would you like me to call the doctor? You look a little pekid."

"I'm just tired, Randolph. I'm sure I'll be fine. Thank you though. I would love a bath if you would send up some water in the morning." She smiled at both men, coughing as she closed the door.

Randolph frowned as he looked at Angel.

"Miss Whitman doesn't look so good. She was healthy as a horse when she left. She's just plumb puny now."

"Sí, it has been a difficult few weeks. I will take some water up for her in the morning if you can tell me where the buckets are.

"I also need a room for my brother and myself."

Angel took both of their horses to the livery. When he finished rubbing them down, he wandered over to the saloon to see if he could get something to eat.

Miguel was sitting at a table and Angel joined him. He laughed softly as he watched his brother.

"I put a little note in señorita Margaret's saddle bag. I professed my love and promised to see her in Texas in the spring. I signed it 'Miguel' of course."

Miguel stared at Angel and laughed wryly. "I thought of writing a note, but I wasn't sure she would read it. I have been thinking about heading that way next spring. I am drinking this beer as I contemplate what I need to do to make her love me. Perhaps if I spend less time in the saloons."

Angel looked over at his somber brother. "Starting tomorrow?"

"Sí, tomorrow." Miguel grinned at him.

The brothers ordered food and were back in the hotel by nine-thirty that night.

CHAPTER 58

Dan Morton's Children

NGEL KNOCKED ON ANNA'S DOOR WITH HOT WATER at eight the next morning. He had been up since daylight, but he thought Anna might need more sleep.

She had a blanket wrapped around herself when she opened the door. Angel dumped the water in the tub and smiled at her.

"You look better this morning, señorita Whitman."

"The next stage will be through here on Monday morning. Should I buy three tickets? The children will be coming with you, yes?"

Anna paused as she listened. "Let's wait until after church. I hope to see the children there. I can talk to them and see what they want to do.

"I promised Dan I would take care of them, but they may not want to come with me. They may have already settled in with another family."

"They are very small?"

"Yes, Zach is six and Amanda is three." She rubbed her eyes and shook her head. "Much too young to lose both mother and father.

"I am so relieved they are safe. After we were taken, Zach led his little sister across the prairie to a ranch some distance away. I have no idea where it was, but Zach said he knew. He was such a brave little fellow.

"I gave him my Derringer and sent him to the root cellar for potatoes. He crawled through a tunnel full of snakes to escape. Terrifying." She shivered and smiled again at Angel.

"Thank you, Angel, for all you have done for me. I was so afraid.

"I thought I saw you shortly after we arrived at that terrible place. I wasn't sure if you were real though or if it was a dream until I heard you singing outside my window." She laughed as she closed the door.

"I'll see you after church."

Angel wandered down to the express office to check for passage on the stage. The ticketing agent recommended he buy the tickets now.

"I only have four seats left and those are middle seats. 'Course some feller will probably offer his seat to your wife and kids. Still, I'd buy them now."

Angel bought the tickets and went to find Miguel. He was in the only eating house in town.

Miguel listened as Angel told him his plans. He nodded and then gestured with his head toward the livery.

"I think I will leave today. I can take the extra horses with me. That way, we don't have to sell them. It is not so far, a hundred miles—perhaps a little more. I can be in Cheyenne a day or two after you if I leave this morning. I will take some oats with me since I will have more animals to care for."

The two ate quickly and hurried to the livery. Angel was thankful Gabe had paid him before they parted ways. His friend had insisted Angel also take an additional $100.

"You have a lot of miles to cover. You can repay me when you get home." Gabe had squeezed Angel's arm and said, "Be careful, brother."

Angel grinned. He was pleased Gabe had married his sister. He was looking forward to getting back to Cheyenne. *I had hoped Anna would stay in Cheyenne, but she has shown no sign of that. No, I think she will go back to Council Grove or maybe on to Kansas City. Doc can listen to her cough when we get back. Perhaps I can convince her to stay a few days in Cheyenne to rest before she travels again. And next spring, maybe I will make a trip south with Miguel.*

Angel waved as Miguel rode out of town. Both men were excellent horsemen and Miguel handled the lead ropes to the three horses easily. Miguel waved his hat and called, "Adios!" He turned a corner and was gone in a flurry of hooves.

Anna was just coming out of the hotel when Angel walked back up the street. He stepped up beside her with a smile.

"Perhaps Señorita Whitman would like me to walk her to church? I have heard this is a very wild town. It would be best for a lovely lady to have a strong vaquero beside her, yes?"

Anna laughed and took his arm. She coughed several times and Angel stopped her.

"When we reach Cheyenne, I will take you to the doctor. He is a fine doctor. Perhaps he can listen to your cough. There are many ways to get sick here, especially for one who is not used to riding all day and sleeping outside."

Anna stared up at Angel briefly before she looked away.

"Fine, but only when we reach Cheyenne. Not today."

A wagon was pulling up as they arrived at the church. The two small children riding in the back spotted Anna, and they began to shout.

"Miss Anna! You are back! We are going to live with you!" Two little bodies bounded out of the wagon and raced toward Anna. She knelt on the ground and wrapped them up in her arms.

"Zach and Amanda—I am so happy you are safe." She kissed each one before she stood. She turned them to face Angel.

"This is my friend, Angel. He found me and brought me back here."

Amanda stared up at the smiling cowboy.

"Are you going to marry Miss Anna? She is going to be our momma. Our first momma and papa are dead.

"If you marry her, we will have a new momma *and* a new papa."

Angel smiled at them, and his dark eyes danced.

"Sí, that is a fine idea. I wish I had thought of it myself. Perhaps I will talk to Miss Anna about it this evening." He looked over at Anna and winked while she turned a deep red. Amanda smiled up at him as she hung on tightly to Anna's hand.

"Come children. Please introduce me to the kind people you have been staying with." Anna hurried the children away and Angel chuckled as he watched them go.

CHAPTER 59

THE WISDOM OF A CHILD

IF ANNA HAD DOUBTS BEFORE CHURCH ABOUT WHAT the little ones wanted, it was clear by dinner time. They wouldn't let her out of their sight.

She sat them down after dinner and looked at each one seriously.

"Zach, Amanda, we will be leaving here. I am a teacher, and I will need to find a job so we can pay our bills.

"How would you like to live in Kansas?"

Amanda was chasing a frog. Kansas meant nothing to her, but Zach frowned.

"We won't live in our old house? Where will we live?"

"We can't live in your old house, Zach. I don't know how to run a ranch. I must make a living for us, and that means I need to find a teaching job."

Anna hugged him as she whispered, "I'm sorry your life is all mixed up, Zach. I will do the best I can. Maybe someday we will be able to live on a ranch again, but for now, we will have to live close to where I can find a teaching position."

She looked from one child to the other. "Do you need to go out to your house to get anything? We will be leaving on the stage tomorrow morning, so we will have to do that today."

"No, Mrs. Ault took us over there a couple of days ago. She packed up our clothes and even some pictures of Ma and Pa. She said she would bring them to town this evening."

Anna studied the little boy's face.

"Mr. and Mrs. Ault would love for you to live with them. Then you could stay here at Fort Laramie. Would you rather do that? Your father asked me to take care of you, but I know he would want you to be happy."

Zach was quiet as he thought about what Anna had said.

"No, I reckon we need to go with you since that is what Pa wanted." He smiled at Anna and his eyes became watery.

"Pa liked you a lot. He was going to ask you to marry him. He asked us how we would like to have you as our new mother."

Anna hugged the little boy. Her voice was trembling when she spoke.

"Oh, Zach. Your father was a fine man. He was kind and thoughtful. He worked hard, and he wanted the best for you and Mandie. You were blessed to have such a wonderful father."

Zach nodded and looked into Anna's eyes.

"Miss Anna, do you think you will marry someday? I'd sure like to have a pa."

Anna smiled and hugged him again. "I don't know, Zach. Marrying someone is a very big step. You must fall in love first like your mother and father. Sometimes it is hard to find someone you love."

"Well, maybe. I think Angel might love you. He looks at you like my pa used to look at my ma. Pa's eyes would be all smiley and he would hug my ma really hard. She liked it too because I asked her if she did."

Anna blushed. She almost looked around for Angel. He always managed to be where he shouldn't be, but she resisted the urge.

"We'll see. Angel is a nice man, but we don't know each other very well. Now let's get you something to eat. After that, I think we will all lie down for a while this afternoon."

Zach frowned. "I'm too big to take naps. I want to go fishing. Mandie needs to take a nap, but I don't."

Anna smiled at him. "I will see if Angel will take you fishing. How would that be?"

Zach grinned and nodded excitedly.

"Now come. Let's get something to eat."

THE BANKER'S SURPRISE

A MAN CALLED OUT AS HE HURRIED TOWARD ANNA, "Miss Whitman! Excuse me. My name is John C. Reynolds. I handle Mr. Morton's finances. I was wondering if you could meet with me this afternoon or evening. I understand you are leaving on the stage tomorrow."

Anna looked at the man in surprise. "Yes, that is correct. Mr. Morton and I never married though. I don't have any claim to his property."

"Mr. Morton had a will. He was very specific that his property go to his children and to the family who took them in should something happen to him. I need to talk to you about his property and assets."

Anna slowly nodded. "How about five this afternoon? I need to put Mandie down for a nap, but I should be able to meet with you then.

"Perhaps I will bring Mr. Montero with me. Where would you like to meet?"

"Just come by my house. I am the first one on the left side just past the livery. The big, white two-story house."

"Very well, Mr. Reynolds. I will see you at five. Good day until then."

She was hurrying the children back to the eating house when Angel appeared. He was carrying two fishing poles in his hand.

He pointed at Zach and back to himself.

"How would you like to go fishing with me this afternoon, chico? I think perhaps I know where the biggest fish are. We can eat dinner first. When we are finished, we can catch some fat grasshoppers.

"Perhaps I will show Miss Anna how to bake them in mud. We will have a fine supper."

Anna looked at Angel suspiciously but nodded.

"I will eat a big dinner in case you don't catch anything," Anna commented dryly. She smiled at Zach and added, "I think perhaps señor Angel is a very poor fisherman. That is why he wants to take you with him." Anna's face was serious, but her blue eyes reflected her teasing.

Angel nodded sorrowfully.

"Sí, this is true. It is difficult for me to catch a fish or a woman. Both avoid my lines."

Anna blushed and Angel grinned as he guided the little family into the eating house.

"I hear this place makes helado—I think you say ice cream. Maybe we will have some tarta—some pie and ice cream for dessert. I'm not sure Señorita Anna knows how to cook at all, so you had better eat much before she takes you home with her."

Mandie looked up at Anna with big eyes.

"You don't know how to cook? Who will feed us?"

"Angel is just teasing. I am an excellent cook. I can promise, you will never go hungry."

Mandie stared up at Angel. She finally asked, "Why do you say your words funny?"

Angel grinned at the little girl, "Why our Dios, He made me special. My head is full of special words, and sometimes they just fall out." He pointed up and around as he talked.

Mandie laughed. "You are a funny man, Mr. Angel."

"Sí, I must be funny and charming so the ladies will talk to me. Now come, let us be on our best behavior while we eat."

CHAPTER 61

FISHING IN THE LARAMIE RIVER

WHEN DINNER WAS OVER, ANGEL WALKED ANNA AND Mandie back to the hotel. Once they were inside, Zach and he hurried to the creek.

"Do you like to fish, Mr. Angel? My pa liked to fish. We went fishing every Sunday afternoon with Old Man Martinson." The little boy's lip trembled as he looked up at Angel.

"Those bad men who took Miss Anna shot him. They shot my pa too." His eyes were serious when he looked up at Angel.

"When I get big, I am going to find them. I will shoot them for killing my pa."

Angel stopped and knelt in front of the little boy. He spoke softly as he pointed upwards.

"Our Dios, He does not like it so much when small boys say things such as that. You see, Miss Anna prayed and our Dios, he listened. He asked me to help you and Miss Anna.

"My brother and I rode very far and very fast. We found her and we took her away from those bad men. So you see, you don't have to think about them anymore. They have already had their meeting with our Dios. He is the one who will decide what to do with them.

"Besides, one of those men helped Miss Anna. He was a good man, and he kept her safe when they rode far away." Angel smiled at the little boy and squeezed his shoulders.

"Now come. Let us think happy thoughts. Let us dream of fish so big they will break our poles. Let us smell them as they bake over hot coals." Angel took a deep breath and let it out slowly.

Zach looked up at Angel and smiled. As he took the cowboy's hand he said softly, "I like you, Mr. Angel. You are a nice man even if you do talk funny."

Angel's heart was a little tight as he looked down at the small boy.

"Sí, I like you too, Zach. Now be very quiet, very silencioso, so we can sneak up on those large fish."

Within a couple of hours, the two had caught three fish. One was small. They threw it back but the other two were large brown trout. Angel was almost as excited as Zach.

The two had their heads close together as they cleaned the fish. Angel pointed out each part of the trout as he disposed of it. He also helped Zach to rig a line to carry them.

"I think Miss Anna will be pleased with these fine fish." He paused as he looked at Zach.

"Perhaps we should cook them now. I will wrap them in some leaves and they will still be a little warm when Miss Anna finishes her meeting."

Zach looked at Angel seriously.

"That man she is meeting with was my pa's friend. Pa said he liked Mr. Reynolds because he was honest." Zach was quiet a moment before he added, "Miss Anna said she might ask you to go with her."

"Sí, I heard. That is why I think we should cook these fish early. Now quickly, find some dead branches and we will start our fire."

It was nearly four-thirty by the time the fish were baked. Angel slid them out of the fire and carefully wrapped them in leaves. He laid them on a flat rock to carry them back to town.

"We don't want the outside to break open. We will carry them carefully on this rock and our supper will be ready when the meeting is finished.

"We will take them to the livery. Old Mike will be there. He is the hostler. He will help you hide these fish so the dogs don't eat them.

"You be sure to invite Mike to eat with us. He was kind to Miss Anna, and he was a friend of your father's. He probably knows a nice little spot for a picnic."

"Do you know everybody's name here, Angel? You haven't been in Fort Laramie for long, but you sure seem to know a lot of folks."

Angel's eyes twinkled but he nodded somberly.

"Sí, it is important to me to know people. Their names, what they think, what makes them happy. Sometimes, if one knows what makes someone happy, he will also know what makes them sad.

"All of us want to feel that we matter. To make someone feel such a way is not so hard. It is a little thing for me to do, but sometimes, it is important to the other person."

Zach listened quietly. He said nothing when Angel finished but he thought hard about what the man had said.

Anna was waiting at the hotel when they returned. She looked anxiously at Angel as she spoke.

"A Mr. Reynolds asked me to come by and visit with him. I was wondering...."

"Sí, I will be glad to go with you. Old Mike at the livery will watch the little ones and we will all have some supper when the meeting is completed."

Anna stared at Angel. She looked away as her face turned a light pink.

"I think you just lurk around and listen to people."

Zach smiled excitedly at Anna as he pulled on her hand. "We caught some fish, and Angel and me cleaned them. He showed me their guts too when we pulled them out. They didn't smell so good, but I liked looking at them." His face was sincere when he continued, "And I can show them to you the next time we all go fishing."

Anna stared at the small boy and her face became pale.

"Then we baked them, and Old Mike showed me where to stash them away from the critters. We can play with him until you get back. And we are going to have a picnic!

"I think Angel knows pertineer everyone in this town, and he ain't been here long."

Anna looked from the excited little boy to the grinning Angel.

"I'm sure he does," she commented dryly. "And he knows them even better because he listens to everyone's conversations.

"Now come. Let's hurry so we won't be late."

CHAPTER 62

For Love of the Land

JOHN REYNOLDS OPENED THE DOOR QUICKLY WHEN they knocked.

"Mr. Reynolds, this is a friend of mine, Mr. Angel Montero. I asked him to come with me. I am not familiar with the way business is done out here, so I am hoping he will be able to guide me some if I need to make decisions."

Reynolds looked closely at Angel. He slowly nodded. He cleared his throat as he looked at Anna.

"What I am going to show you is very important. Unless you can trust Mr. Montero...."

Anna's chin jutted out slightly and her voice was tight when she responded.

"I have trusted him with my life. I can certainly trust him with some property."

Reynolds nodded and stepped aside.

"Please come into the kitchen. I have all the papers on the table so you can see them. My wife won't return until after seven this evening."

John Reynold's voice was serious as he began.

"Miss Whitman, about three years ago, Dan Morton discovered gold on his property. It was not a huge strike, but it was a rich vein." He had a map on the table and Angel pulled it toward him.

"It looks like señor Morton owned all the land around the dot you have marked, perhaps for five or six miles on all sides?"

Reynold's face showed his surprise. He nodded.

"Yes, he does. He is surrounded by three ranches, and two of those are very large. Dan has been getting squeezed for several years. As word of his gold strike leaked out, the threats have been getting worse. I am guessing the gold might be part of the reason he was killed."

Anna's face was pale. "Yes, it was. The outlaws wanted to know where the mine was. Of course, I didn't know. I didn't even know Dan had a mine until they mentioned it.

"I was afraid they were going to torture the children for that information. Zach barely mentioned the mine. I don't believe he knows where it is either."

When Anna finished, Reynolds leaned forward as he looked at the couple in front of him.

"Here's the problem. All three of the surrounding ranches want Dan's land. All of them have land that touches his. He has good water, and they want it.

"Outlaws and even some of the local people want his gold." His eyes were concerned as he looked from one to the other.

"It is going to take a lot of fortitude and gunpower to hold off those forces. With Dan gone, it is going to be even more difficult."

Angel was watching Reynolds closely. "You think señorita Whitman should sell the land. Let the big men use their own guns and men to hold it, yes?"

Reynolds nodded. "That is exactly what I think. All three of the cattlemen would buy today. If there is some kind of bidding competition, none will try to steal it.

"They all know about the gold so all of them will be forced to figure that into their bidding process.

"Dan didn't think there was much more gold beyond what he had already taken out. If he was right, the vein is done and the mine is worthless. I'm not a mining man but Dan was. I would be inclined to trust his intuition.

"The ore he mined that was not sold was shipped by stage to Cheyenne last month." He grinned as he added, "I put it in an old trunk and addressed it to the Cheyenne Public Library. Of course, Cheyenne doesn't have a library, but the shadier element of our society doesn't know that." Reynolds' smile became larger. "The sheriff was there to collect it.

"The top half was full of books. The ore was wrapped and stored in the bottom.

"The sheriff arranged for the ore to be sold. The money was deposited in an account under Dan's name and mine. I can send a letter with you so you can access that account. I have the claim ticket here.

"All three of the neighboring cattlemen are in town right now. They each approached me after Dan's death about buying his land. They all know I handled his finances.

"I told each of them I would talk to you. All three wanted to make an offer.

"Each put his offer in a sealed envelope." Reynold's held up three envelopes. "Here are those offers."

John Reynold's eyes were concerned as he handed Anna the envelopes.

"If you want to open these now, we can finish your business here today.

"I'm sure all three offers are fair since they all want Dan's land. I suggest you accept the largest one and leave town. I can wire you the money." He held out a legal document.

"This is the deed to Dan's ranch. I can sign it over to whomever you sell to should that be your decision.

"Quite frankly, Miss Whitman, your life is in jeopardy here. I see the beginnings of a range war and Dan's ranch—your ranch—will be right smack in the middle. Throw in a gold mine that has somehow become much larger than it is, and you are sitting on a powder keg."

Anna's breath caught and her hands shook as she took the envelopes. Each cattleman had written his name on the outside of the envelope.

She stared at the envelopes before she looked up at Reynolds.

"Mr. Reynolds, are these three ranchers from this area or all of them investors?"

Reynolds pointed at the two envelopes in her left hand. "Those two are local men."

Anna laid the third envelope on the table. She studied the two she still held.

"Do both of these men have children?"

Reynolds nodded. He pointed at her hands. "That one has three and the one in your right hand has ten."

Anna handed the last envelope to Reynolds. "Let this man buy the ranch for the amount he has listed inside."

Reynolds stared at her in shock. "Aren't you going to compare their offers? I can tell you the one you eliminated on the first round would most certainly have been the largest."

"Mr. Reynolds, I am not from around here, but I have seen what greed can do to a community. I recognized the name of the man on the first envelope. He is a man who invests in many ventures, a man who lives far away. He is not a man who will move to your community to build churches and schools. No, he is a man who is always looking for new ways to make money.

"Making lots of money is not a bad thing. However, I want Dan's ranch to go to someone who loves the land as much as he did.

"That land is not mine. It belonged to a man who worked hard to make a living. That man is gone. Yes, I am responsible for his children, but I took on that responsibility before I knew there was land involved." Anna pointed at the envelope Reynolds held.

"That man has ten children. I'm sure he offered what he felt he could afford, and with his family, he will stay here. He will try to succeed in this area. Perhaps some of his children will decide to continue his operation after he passes.

"You tell Mr. Ford the land is his. And you tell him every town should have a library." Anna's hand shook a little as she signed the deed.

She smiled as she stood shakily. Angel took her arm as she started to turn. "Please wire the money to the same account you opened in Cheyenne. I will be in there for several days before I return to Kansas." She smiled at Reynolds.

"Thank you for being Dan's friend and someone he could count on, Mr. Reynolds. Dan Morton was a fine man and chose his friends well.

"Please take your fee out of the total amount and send an accounting to the bank. Good day, sir."

Angel was almost laughing as he led Anna out of John Reynolds' house. He looked down at Anna and pulled her arm closer to his side.

"You are an interesting woman, Anna Whitman. I am thinking señor Reynolds is opening each letter to see how badly you handled that transaction."

Anna laughed shakily. "Well, I knew I couldn't stay here and run a ranch, let alone fight for it. The selling was easy. Deciding who to sell to was a little more difficult.

"Your Wyoming Territory is beautiful, but if it is to be settled, you need families. I'm a teacher, Angel. We need children to fill our schools, and we need involved parents to make them successful. With their large family, the Fords are invested here."

CHAPTER 63

A Sick Woman

ANNA WAS STRUGGLING TO CATCH HER BREATH AND Angel stopped. His eyes were worried as he looked at her.

"You are sick, Anna. Perhaps we should wait to take the stage another day."

"Angel, you said there is an excellent doctor in Cheyenne. Let's go to Cheyenne and I will let your doctor check me over.

"I really think I am more tired than anything else. All this traveling and jostling around is exhausting."

Angel said nothing but he was worried. *Tiredness and fatigue does not make a woman cough or lose her breath. I hope it is not something worse.* He nodded as he continued to watch her.

"Let's go to the livery and collect your children. Soon we will eat, and you can go to bed early. I will stay up with the little ones."

Anna barely ate anything. She excused herself and Angel hurriedly walked her back to the hotel.

"You should have stayed with the children," Anna said softly as Angel took her arm.

"I think señor Mike is enjoying himself. Besides, he has them busy making the ice cream."

Anna turned to face him. "Thank you for all you have done for me, Angel. For us." She smiled up at him and walked slowly into the hotel.

Angel frowned as he watched her. His concern showed as he walked back to the livery. However, when he walked into the barn, a smile was once again on his face and neither of the children knew he was worried about Anna.

Mike was panting as he strained to turn the handle of the ice cream maker. Angel grabbed the handle and talked to the children as he turned it easily. The ice cream still took longer than it should have because they checked it often to see if it was done.

It was a happy crew who headed back to the hotel at eight-thirty that night. Zach looked up at the smiling cowboy.

"I want to sleep in your room, Angel, and Mandie wants to sleep there too. We can sleep on the floor."

"Sí, you can sleep in my room. You can even have the bed. I am a strong vaquero, and I am used to sleeping on the floor...but you had better not snore." He swung Mandie around, shaking her as he talked. "If you do, I will *shake* the bed until you roll out."

Both kids were laughing and Angel was smiling as he tucked them in. He could hear Anna coughing in the room next to him. He shook his head as he listened.

"You sound like a man I once knew who had a sickness in his chest. I hope it is not the same for you. I will pray it is just the dust," he whispered. "Soon we will be in Cheyenne and Doc Williams will know what to do for you."

Angel made his bed on the floor and ran the route they needed to cover through his mind.

He shook his head. "It is a very long and hard stage ride. Perhaps I will ride on top to give Anna more room inside the stage. The men will allow her to board first, so she will be able to have a more comfortable seat."

CHAPTER 64

An Ornery Vaquero

THE STAGE WAS TO ARRIVE IN FORT LARAMIE AT EIGHT-thirty the next morning. However, it was an hour late due to a broken wheel. They changed horses at Six Mile Ranch and again at Eagle's Nest Station. At Eagle's Nest, the passengers were allowed to rest for about fifteen minutes and eat a little before reboarding.

Chugwater Station was the scheduled stop for dinner, and Agnes Phillips was delighted to see Anna.

"I pestered that sheriff in Fort Laramie until he went to look for you." She hugged Anna and patted the children on their heads.

"These must be the little ones who were lost. I am so pleased you were able to find them." Her face became serious as she whispered, "And I am so sorry about Dan Morton. I didn't know he was the man you were going to see. He was a wonderful father and a fine man." Tears filled her eyes as she hugged Anna again. "It is so wonderful you are taking his children in."

Agnes noticed Angel for the first time. He tipped his hat as he smiled at her.

Anna pulled him forward. "This is Angel Montero. He and his brother found me." She smiled at Angel as she added, "Angel has been a wonderful friend. I am going to miss him when I return to Kansas."

Agnes cocked an eyebrow as she looked at Angel. She pinched Anna's cheek and hurried back to her kitchen muttering to herself, "Back to Kansas? And you think you are going to leave that handsome cowboy here?" Agnes snorted. "Fat chance. If he found you in Hole-in-the-Wall, I'm guessing he is not going to let you go back to Kansas without him.

"Young women these days. I just don't know."

Agnes looked up when she heard Anna start coughing. She hurried to her cabinet and grabbed a bottle of cough syrup. She thrust it at Angel.

"Give Anna some of this. It will help with her cough."

Angel studied the bottle. He shook his head as he handed it back.

"I thank you, señora, but the men who took señorita Anna gave her many opio pills. They made her very sick. I do not think I will give her this."

Agnes listened closely and nodded. "You make sure she sees a doctor in Cheyenne. That cough is deep in her chest. It can change to pneumonia very quickly." She handed him another jar.

"This is a paste for her to put on. It will help loosen the heaviness in her chest. Have her use it now. I will slow the meal down so she has time."

Angel smiled as he took the jar. "I thank you, señora. You have a kind heart."

Agnes watched as Angel talked to Anna. At first the young woman shook her head but after he talked longer and gestured back toward the house, she slowly nodded. Anna hurried to the outhouse, and Angel knelt by the small children. Agnes couldn't hear what he was saying but the children smiled and took his hands as he led them toward the station house.

Anna's face was red when she returned. She whispered to Angel, "That paste smells terrible. I didn't put much on and still it fills my nose. I can't even smell this food, and now it is all over my hands."

Angel leaned toward her and sniffed. His dark eyes were dancing as he agreed.

"Sí, it is very strong. You will not want to get close to any men for some time. I think that is good for me. I, of course, like the smell of horse ointment. You may sit as close to me as you please." He winked at her and took the bottle of paste. He put some on his neck as he whispered, "Now everyone will think it is me who smells so badly."

Anna stared at Angel for a moment. Surprise and something else washed quickly over her face. She turned away from him without speaking. She finally laughed as she picked up her fork.

"You are an interesting man, Angel Montero. You are full of foolishness, but inside, you are very thoughtful." She picked at her food and looked up at him as she whispered, "And I am going to miss you when you are no longer around."

Angel leaned toward her. "But señorita Anna, I can always be around. Perhaps I will be able to convince you to stay in Cheyenne. Then my heart will not be broken, and you will not have to miss me."

Anna's body went still. She stared at her food. Finally, she looked at Angel to see if he was teasing.

Angel's face was serious, and Anna dropped her head.

"Shush. Don't talk like that. Someone will hear you."

Zach looked up from his food with a frown as he looked from one to the other. "Adults always whisper when they don't want us to hear what they say."

He pointed toward Agnes. "That lady in the kitchen said we were lost. We weren't lost. I knew where I was going.

"It was kind of scary when it started to get dark, but I had Miss Anna's gun. I knew I could shoot an old coyote if one came too close to us.

"I sure was happy to see Fords' house though. We stayed there for three days. They had so many kids around there. We never did run out of kids to play with. They offered to take us in too. I think it would have been fun to live there.

297

"Then Mr. and Mrs. Ault came out and talked to them. The adults sent all the kids outside, but Johnny—he's my age—he showed me where to hide so we could listen to their conversation.

"Mrs. Ault said they didn't have any kids and she sure would like to have us come live with them.

"I wasn't so sure. They lived in town, and I didn't want to live in town. I wanted to live on a ranch." He was quiet as he picked at his food. He finally looked up at Anna and smiled.

"We decided to live with you, Miss Anna, even if you don't live on a ranch. I sure hope you move to one someday though. I don't want to live in no town forever."

Angel grinned at the two children and nodded, "Sí, that is just what I was talking to Miss Anna about. I…"

Anna kicked his leg and Angel began laughing.

"I think Miss Anna will find a handsome vaquero someday, perhaps one as handsome as me." Angel rolled his eyes and put his hand over his heart. "Perhaps she will fall madly in love and that vaquero, he will whisk her off to his fine ranch. And there they will live. Happily. Not forever but for many years until Anna is an old grandmother with many wrinkles." Angel's face was serious, but his dark eyes were dancing as he spoke.

Anna's face turned a dark red and Zach grinned.

"I like that idea, Angel, and I hope that handsome vaquero is you."

Mandie was fidgeting on her chair and Zach grabbed her hand. "Come on, Mandie. I'll go with you to the outhouse. Hurry up though or we are going to miss our dinner."

Anna smiled as she watched the two little ones run across the dusty yard to the outhouse. Zach waited for his little sister. He made her wash her hands in the horse tank as they hurried by.

Angel nodded toward them. "I think your señor Dan was a good father. I think he loved his children very much."

Anna frowned at him. "He was *not* my man.

"He was a kind man though. His children were the most important thing in the world to him." She looked away and a sob caught in her throat. "I was beside him on the wagon when he was shot in the back. Zach drove the wagon and we managed to get to Howard Martinson's house. Howard loved Dan like a son. He cried when Dan died. Those outlaws knew about a tunnel that led into the back of the house. One came in through there while Howard was shooting at the outlaws in the front. That outlaw shot Howard."

Anna took a deep breath. She looked over at Angel and continued quietly, "That was when I knew we were in trouble. Kadle and Meecher were talking about killing the children. Doolan and Jimmy weren't in favor of it. Kadle was…Kadle was an evil man.

"Zach knew of the second tunnel that led away from the root cellar. He was able to get Mandie and him into it. The outlaws didn't follow because snakes fell on them." Anna's eyes were wet as she smiled at the two children climbing back onto the bench.

"You are a wonderful big brother, Zach. Now you be sure and thank him, Mandie."

The little girl smiled and planted a slobbery kiss on Zach's cheek before she began to eat. Zach rubbed it off, but he didn't complain.

Anna watched the children. She smiled and asked, "Does Mr. Ford's land connect with your ranch, Zach?"

He nodded as he shoveled his food in.

"Yea, it touches ours on the south side between us and Old Man Mortenson. They have ten kids, and we like to visit them. There is always someone to play with.

"That's why me and Mandie walked there. That and they were the closest."

"They sound like a wonderful family," Anna replied as she wiped Mandie's face.

Angel stood and pointed at the stage.

"Let's go. The horses are ready and we need to load." He grabbed Mandie's sandwich and wrapped it in his bandana. He lifted her up and took Anna's arm as they hurried to the stage. Zach shoved the rest of his food into his mouth and ran after them.

A burly man pushed by Angel and tried to climb in first.

Angel jerked him back and threw him to the side. He set the small girl inside the stage and gave Anna a hand up. Zach climbed in behind them. When the burly man tried to get in, Angel shook his head and pointed to the top of the stage.

"No, señor. You will ride on the top. Perhaps a little cold air will improve your manners, yes?" Angel was smiling but the smile didn't reach his eyes.

The man stared at Angel, but didn't like what he saw. He cursed once before he climbed on top of the stage.

Angel followed him. He had barely squeezed in between the luggage when the horses took off. The half-wild animals reared and lunged in their harnesses as the stage rocked down the bumpy road.

CHAPTER 65

CHEYENNE'S FINEST

IT WAS NEARLY TEN THAT NIGHT WHEN THE STAGE rolled into Cheyenne. The Wells Fargo Office still had a light on, and an old man in a top hat sat in a wagon in front of the building.

He jumped out of the wagon and hollered, "Any a ya folks need a ride? This here buggy's available fer jist a short time 'fore I go to bed." He was muttering as he walked toward the stage and jerked the door open. "Durn stages. Cain't never be on time. I'm always a waitin'…" When he spied Anna, he swept off his hat.

"Evenin', Miss. Rooster at yur service." He grinned as Angel dropped down beside him.

"Howdy, Angel. I wondered when ya'd show up. Gabe an' his boys rode in last week. Ol' Gabe said ya had some woman business." He grinned at Anna as Angel helped her out. "Reckon ya did at that.

"Now Badger done told me when a Miss Anna Whitman showed up, I was s'posed to bring 'er right over no matter how late. An' seein' as how Angel here is a smilin' so big, I'm a guessin' ya must be her." Rooster bowed deeply.

"Welcome to Cheyenne, Miss Whitman." He stared a moment at the two children who were sleeping on the seat. He grabbed the little boy.

"I wasn't expectin' no little ones but they's no problem. I'll jist lay this young feller in the back an' ya cin hold that there little gurl."

Rooster panted as he helped Angel lower Anna's traveling trunk.

"Durn, Miss Anna. Ya need to take ya some lessons from this here dandy vaquero beside ya on how to travel light. I be an old feller an' that there case is 'most more'n I cin handle."

Anna didn't answer. She held her chest as she began to cough.

"Señor Rooster, perhaps you can drive Miss Anna to Doc Williams? I don't think she feels so well. I will stay with her.

"And take the children to Badger's after that, yes?"

Rooster nodded and jumped into the wagon. He whipped his team, and they raced up the street to Doc's big two-story house. He pulled them to a halt and rushed up the walk to beat on the door.

Angel laid Mandie by her brother and lifted Anna out of the wagon. He was almost running as he carried her up the walk.

Doc jerked open the door. He waved at Angel to follow him and hurried down the hall to a clean room. He pointed at an exam table.

"Lay her on there. Josie will be here in a moment. She will help me get her out of her clothes.

"Now tell me, how long has she been struggling to breathe?"

Rooster backed out the door and hurried back to the wagon while Doc Williams fired questions at Angel. He listened to Anna's breathing and shook his head.

"Her breathing is rough, and I don't like how her lungs sound. I'll do a more thorough exam later though." He patted Angel's shoulder and pointed toward his waiting room.

"You wait there on those chairs. You can even pull a few together and sleep if you want. This will take me a little time."

Angel sat down shakily. He put his head between his hands. He said a prayer before he stood. He began to pace around as he tried to listen. Mostly, all he could hear were the mutterings of soft voices. In between, he could hear Anna cough.

Angel had been pacing for about a half hour when Badger appeared in the doorway.

"Doc still checkin' 'er?"

Angel nodded. He looked toward the exam room and shook his head. "Señorita Anna has had a difficult time. I think she spent too many days outside for one who was not used to sleeping on the ground. She was very sore from riding a horse as well." His dark eyes showed his concern. "The men who took her were cruel. It was good Miguel and I arrived quickly. Perhaps it was not soon enough."

Badger looked toward the sound of Doc's voice and nodded.

"I rode the train with Miss Anna from Denver up to Cheyenne. She be a fine woman. An' when she's ready ta leave here, we'll take her on back ta our place. My Martha 'ill fuss over 'er like an old hen, an' we'll have her back ta feelin' fine."

"And if it is pneumonia? There are not so many treatments for that, I think."

Badger grinned and patted the jar he was carrying. "We'll slip 'er some a this once Doc leaves.

"Ol' Doc, he's a good one, but he ain't so fond a my remedies. He's a willin' ta try new surgeries, but medicines he be more careful of.

"If it's the pneumony, Doc'll know shortly. He studies up on what ails folks all the time, so he'll have 'im some ideas. He ain't so sure of my potion though. That be why we'uns 'ill give it ta 'er when he ain't 'round."

Badger clapped Angel on the back. "Don't ya worry none. That there little gal be a whole lot tougher than most city folks. She has 'er a good heart too. Ya should prob'ly go 'head an' marry 'er." He paused and grinned at Angel. "But I reckon ya done thought on that a'ready."

Badger pointed at a chair. "Now ya sit yur own self down. Take ya a little nap. Doc'll let ya sit with 'er when he's done an' ya need ta be wakeful."

Doc finally came out of the examination room. His eyes were friendly when he motioned for Angel to sit down with him.

"I don't think Anna has pneumonia. However, she does have some congestion in her chest and she is exhausted. I would like to give her some laudanum to make her sleep and..."

"No laudanum, Doc. The men who took Anna gave her many pills. She was very sick. I don't want her to have laudanum."

Doc was quiet as he nodded.

"She needs to get some sleep though. She is struggling to breathe but I believe part of that is from anxiety and fear." He frowned as he thought. "I'm not sure what to give her that doesn't have opiates in it."

Badger held up his jar and shook it as he winked at Doc. "I have jist the thing here. Now ya go on ta bed, Doc. Angel here 'ill help me ta dose 'er. I guarandangtee she be sleepin' jist fine real soon an' most likely till mornin'. Angel cin stay. He cin call if 'n he needs ya."

Doc's frown turned to a scowl. "Badger, you know I don't believe in your potion."

"Don't rightly care if'n ya don't believe. The question you'ins has ta ask yur own self is, do it hurt ta try it? You'ins done run out a options, an' I'm a givin' ya one right here. If'n it don't work, it still won't hurt 'er none."

Doc stared from Badger to Angel. The younger man shrugged.

"It worked on Gabe. Perhaps we should try it."

"All right but not too much. I want her to be coherent in the morning.

"And don't you be spreading this around. I don't want to be known as the 'Quack' doctor from Cheyenne." Doc glared at both men one more time and almost stomped down the hall. Both men could hear him talking to Josie and his voice sounded angry.

Badger stood and pointed toward Anna's room. "Jist as well git this done. I ain't a stayin' here all night when I have a nice warm wife ta home."

CHAPTER 66

BADGER'S POTION

ANNA'S EYES WERE OPEN, AND ANGEL COULD SEE THE fear in them. He patted her hand and smiled at her.

"You remember Badger? He brought you some medicine." When Anna started to protest, Angel raised his hand.

"Anna, it does not contain opium. I told Doc Williams you were not to have any of that."

Anna's eyes were bloodshot as she stared from one man to the other. "What is it?"

"Somethin' I concocted my own self, Missy. It's done been used on most a the folks in my family includin' ol' Gabe. He be Angel's brother-in-law."

Angel's dark eyes glinted as he rolled them.

"Sí. Gabe, he was very excited to get home and most certainly, Merina was waiting for him at the train station." He looked over at Anna and added mournfully, "Ah, to have a woman waiting for you. What a joy that would be. And if she could cook and work hard, if she would pull off my boots and rub my feet, why I would be in Heaven."

Anna stared at Angel for a moment and then commented sarcastically, "Finding a woman to do that wouldn't be so hard. Many would do it for money."

Badger started laughing. He had a cup half full of his potion and he passed the cup to Angel.

"We'uns 'ill start with a half cup. She be plenty potent. That's what it takes ta dose most little gals."

Angel handed Anna the cup and she smelled it.

"I still can't smell anything but that paste on me. Does it smell bad?"

Badger's chuckle turned to a laugh and Angel shrugged.

"I think the medicine is not so bad." He leaned toward her and sniffed. "It does not smell so bad as your chest does right now."

Anna's face turned a dark red. She glared at Angel and drank the potion down.

"That wasn't bad and it went down easy too." Her face didn't change expression as she stared at them.

"So am I supposed to go right to sleep? I feel the same as I did before."

Badger stared at Anna a moment. He chuckled as he filled the cup a second time, this time two thirds full.

"That jist be the first dose. Sometimes we break it up some. Now drink this part down."

Anna drank it quickly. Slowly, her eyes began to glass over.

Badger grinned and thumped Angel on the back. "I reckon you'ins cin take it from here." He hurried toward the door, singing to himself as he rushed outside.

Angel watched Anna for a moment. She was humming to herself, but she was not going to sleep.

She looked up at him and smiled. Her smile was a little crooked, but her eyes were no longer glassy.

"Are you staying here all night? That doesn't seem so appropriate, does it?" She looked over his shoulder. She seemed to listen to someone.

"Mother, I don't know why he is here. No, we are not courting. We barely know each other." She looked around the room in confusion.

"No, this is not my bedroom. I don't know where I am." She stared at the wall before she looked at Angel in shock.

"I am in *your* bedroom? Why would you take me to your bedroom? I am not that kind of woman." She swung her feet to the floor.

"I am not spending the night with you. I am going home with my mother right now."

Angel put his hand on her arm. "Anna, please get back in bed. Tell your mother she can spend the night too if she wants."

Anna staggered and Angel helped her back in bed. She glared at him.

"Mother is not happy about this. She is going to get my father, and you don't want to be here when he comes." She looked around the room and saw the jar of Badger's potion beside her bed. Before Angel could stop her, she took three long swigs. He grabbed the jar as she started to drop it.

Anna's smile was loose when she looked up at Angel. She leaned forward and whispered loudly, "Maybe I will send my mother home. You are a very handsome vaquero." Her face became puzzled. She frowned and asked, "What is a vaquero? I have only met one man who told me he was a vaquero." She lay back in bed and closed her eyes.

"He was very handsome. I liked it when he kissed me. In fact, I liked it so much I ran away." She giggled as she stared at Angel. "Why would I run away if I liked it?"

Her eyes became large and she winked awkwardly at him. "I have an idea. Why don't *you* kiss me while my mother is gone? She would never allow it and I want you to kiss me."

Angel stared down at her and shook his head.

"I don't think that is such a good idea, Miss Anna. You only have your bedclothes on. It would not be appropriate."

Anna threw the covers off and looked down at herself. She had on knickers with a band a lace around the bottom and her bodice barely reached the top of the knickers.

"Why do women wear knickers? I wear them all the time. I even had them on under my britches when those outlaws took me. They bunched all up and gave me blisters. I don't know who took them off me. When I awoke, they were gone. My legs were a mess." She pulled her knickers up and stretched her leg as she lifted it. "Look. Those are the scars. They don't hurt so much anymore but I can still see them."

Angel looked down at Anna's long leg and looked away. He tried to bring the blanket up but she kicked it off. "Stop. I'm hot. I don't want any covers on." She looked up at Angel and smiled.

"Nettie is my friend. She told me to leave my knickers off when we rode together from that ranch." Anna leaned forward and giggled as she whispered to him, "It was very freeing to ride with nothing on under my britches."

Angel looked away, and for possibly the first time in his life, he blushed.

"Miss Anna, perhaps you should close your eyes. I think you should get some rest."

"But I'm not tired. In fact, I feel great." She smiled up at him. "I want to talk. I want to talk to you."

Her brow furrowed together. "I don't remember where those outlaws took me, but Angel found me." Her eyes were wide as she looked up at Angel. "He saved me. I was so afraid and then I heard him singing. My heart just jumped in my chest. I knew he had come to rescue me." She started to close her eyes, but they popped back open as she looked up at him.

"Have you ever kissed a woman? I mean *really* kissed a woman? The kind of kiss where you see stars in your head and your chest feels like it is going to explode. Have you ever had that kind of a kiss?"

Angel smiled down at her. He nodded.

"Sí. One woman. Only one woman did I feel like that when I kissed her."

Anna stared at him. She raised her eyebrows and mimicked his accent perfectly as she asked, "But you have kissed many women, yes?"

Angel stuttered. He slowly nodded. "Sí, but I have also kissed many horses. I think perhaps I have loved my horses more than I have loved the women until a very special woman came along."

Anna sat up and clapped her hands. "Tell me about her. Tell me about your special woman."

Angel sat down by the bed and took Anna's hand. He kissed it and smiled at her.

"She is a very beautiful woman. She is a lady in every way, a woman who holds herself apart from me. She is like the willow tree. A lady who is tall and slender with hair the color of the sunset. Her lips beg to be kissed, and when I did kiss them, they tasted like honey."

Anna's eyes were wide as she listened to him. "That was beautiful. No man has ever said anything like that to me." Her blue eyes were unblinking as she asked, "You love this woman, don't you?"

"Sí, very much."

Anna stared at him a moment. "What do you think my lips would taste like? I can't smell or taste anything but this terrible paste on my chest."

Angel laughed and pointed at the jar in his hands. "I think they would taste like this perhaps. I don't know. I am not going to kiss you because you don't have all your clothes on."

Anna lay back and pulled the covers over herself as she stared at Angel.

"I think you are a gentleman. Your lady is very lucky." Once again, Anna sat up and leaned forward. She whispered loudly, "I like Angel but I can't tell him. He is very conceited. If I tell him I like him, he will tease me."

She lay back in her bed and smiled. "Sometimes, I dream about him. He is a handsome cowboy, but I think he is very wild. He pretends to be a gentleman. I am not so sure he is though."

Angel laughed and leaned back in his chair. "Why do you think he is wild? And what is wild? Wild like a bird flying in the sky? Wild like a horse running in the wind?"

Anna shook her head. "No, wild like a panther that stalks its prey stealthily through the trees. Wild like a wolf that stands alone and calls to his mate. Wild like a cowboy." Her eyes were beginning to close.

She forced her eyes open and smiled at Angel. "You are my wild cowboy. I'm glad you found me."

Anna's eyes closed and she relaxed as sleep finally came to her.

Angel leaned over and kissed her gently on her lips. "You taste like honey still." He pulled the blankets over her and leaned back in his chair. His sleep was peaceful because he knew Anna was going to be all right.

CHAPTER 67

ANGEL'S FAMILY

DOC WILLIAMS WAS UP EARLY TO CHECK ON ANNA. HE frowned when he saw she was still asleep, but he nodded when he listened to her chest.

"That sounds better." He looked over at Angel and asked, "How much of Badger's potion did you give her?"

"We gave her a little over a cup, but she grabbed the jar and drank more on her own." His dark eyes twinkled as he added, "I think it was just the right amount. She slept well. Soon she will wake, and she will feel much better. A little headache perhaps but not so much of a cough."

Doc felt Anna's head. He opened the jar of badger's potion and gagged as he smelled the contents.

He was muttering to himself as he hurried out of the room. "I just don't understand. It makes no sense. She is resting easily. No opiates at all and still she sleeps peacefully. I don't understand."

Anna awoke about an hour later. She smiled at Angel. Her brow creased and she put her hand to her head as she frowned.

"Oh my goodness, does my head ever ache."

Angel grinned at her. "Good morning, Miss Anna. You look rested. Badger's medicine worked well, yes? You slept all night."

Anna stared at him for a moment. She looked down and pulled the cover up over her shoulders. She frowned as she looked around the room. She looked down at herself again before she looked again at Angel.

"You were here all night?"

"Sí, all night."

"No one else was here?"

"Just you."

Anna's face began to color. "That was not proper. What if someone finds out?"

"I wouldn't worry so much about that. But I think I would worry if someone heard how you were talking last night. You even made me blush…and Miss Anna, I *never* blush."

Anna's face changed from embarrassed to horrified. Angel chuckled and pointed outside.

"You might want to put some clothes on. My family is here. They will be in soon."

Angel grinned and stepped out, closing the door as he left. He heard Anna's feet hit the floor and a rush of activity as she hurried to get dressed. He began to laugh as he strolled outside to greet Gabe and his little family.

"Hola, señor! You are smiling! It is good to be home, yes? I see my sister has not run you off yet."

Emilia squealed as she slipped off her horse and ran toward Angel. He scooped her up, laughing as he hugged her.

"Hello, little sister. I think you missed me. Were you good for Nina while I was gone?"

"Yes, and I have a brother now! His name is Rollie, but he said I can call him Rabbit if I want to. He is so much fun…and here he is!"

Merina and Gabe were hurrying up the walkway with Rollie between them. Angel strolled toward them with his hand outstretched.

Gabe pushed his hand aside and wrapped the smaller man up.

"Hello, Brother. About time you made it home. We thought we had better come to town and meet this woman you rode over five hundred miles to save." Gabe was grinning and he stepped out of the way so Merina could hug her brother.

"Miguel is not with you?"

"No, Anna and I took the stage. Miguel is bringing the horses. He should be here today or tomorrow." He smiled down at his sister.

"You look very happy, Merina. I think you missed this big hombre, yes?"

Merina laughed as she looked from Angel to Gabe. "Sí, and I missed you too. It is good to have you home."

"And Anna? She will be all right?"

"Sí, Badger brought some of his potion by last night." Angel's grin became wider as he looked at Gabe.

"It took even more than you had to put her to sleep. I fear it would take much whiskey to make her drunk if she was a drinking woman." Angel turned back toward Doc's house as he waved his hand.

"Come. I will introduce you."

He smiled over his shoulder at Rollie and turned to squat in front of him.

"Hello, Rollie. Why you are just like talking to a miniature of your big brothers. How are you liking it here?"

"I like it just fine but next time, I don't want to stay home with the women. If you fellows go somewhere, I want to go along." Rollie's dark blue eyes were serious as he spoke.

Angel chuckled and he ruffled Rollie's hair.

"I think that would be fine. Still, we did need a man here to keep an eye on the women. I think it was good you stayed."

Angel laughed again and looked behind Gabe. "Where is Nate?"

"I left him at home to work. He was gone Saturday night as well as all day Sunday with Sam. He doesn't get another day off for a while. I swear, that boy would fish every day if I let him, and I don't think the fish even bite this time of year."

Angel grinned as he stood. "Perhaps it is better he chases the fish than the women. Be thankful, my friend."

Doc Williams stuck his head outside the door and waved at them. He was smiling as he greeted them.

"Come on in here. Good thing I don't have any sick patients today with the amount of noise you all make." He nodded toward the room where Anna was.

"You may take Miss Whitman to Badger's today. She should take it easy for a few days, but she seems to be much better. Even her cough sounds better.

"I believe that cough was from the dust so keep an eye on her. If it gets worse, bring her back." He started to add something but turned around instead.

"Knock first but I'm sure she will be happy to leave," Doc said as he hurried toward his office.

The noisy group traipsed through Doc's waiting room and waited while Angel knocked on the door. Anna didn't answer. Angel knocked a second time and poked his head into the room.

Anna was pressed against the wall. Her breath was coming almost in gasps.

Angel slid through the door and took her hand. Her eyes were wide and he pulled her up against him.

"They will all love you," he whispered, "Just like me." His dark eyes were intense as he smiled at her. "Besides, you already met Merina." He could still feel Anna shaking. "We will talk outside. It will not be so tight as in here." Angel opened the door. He kept his hand on Anna's waist as he followed her out.

"Perhaps we should go outside. You are all very noisy."

Merina stepped forward and hugged Anna. "It is so nice to see you again, Anna. You are feeling better?"

Anna nodded and Merina took her hand.

"Come with me. These man are very loud and it is almost stuffy in here."

Anna took a deep breath when they were outside. She pressed her fingers against her head and shakily released her breath.

"Your headache is from Badger's potion. It will go away after you eat. I'm sure you are very hungry.

"Badger will be here in a bit with his buggy. We are all to go over there for breakfast." Merina's eyes were friendly as she talked.

"How—how did you know Angel was back? We just arrived last night."

Merina laughed and her dark eyes danced. "One of Lance Rankin's hands was in town. Lance's ranch is next to ours. He rode over early this morning with a message from Badger.

"There are no secrets around here, Anna. Someone always knows what is going on, especially when Badger is involved.

"Isn't Martha wonderful? And Badger's an old softie when you get to know him." Merina's voice became softer as she added, "They took me in like their own daughter when I came here. They will you as well.

"Martha and Badger are like parents to everyone in our little community. They are the grandparents too."

A buggy rattled up the street and Badger hollered as he stood and waved.

"Now you'ins come on down here. I'm too old a feller ta be doin' any more walkin' than I have ta.

"Merina, ya ride with Miss Anna an' me. Let those there loud fellers come by their own selves."

Emilia wanted to stay with Angel, so Merina led Anna down to the buggy. Badger grinned at her.

"Ya shore look better this mornin', Miss Anna. Reckon that there medicine worked jist fine."

"I feel much better except for a terrible headache." Anna touched her head again and grimaced.

"That be from the wacky weed. It kinda loosens the tongue up some too so I reckon ya entertained Angel some 'fore ya went ta sleep." He grinned at Merina as he helped both women into the buggy.

"Merina here got ta listen some ta ol' Gabe. He blabbered all over hisself. Done poured out his love an' ever'thing.

"Worked out though, didn't it, Miss Merina? They's a happy couple now."

Anna stared from Badger to Merina. When the young woman blushed, Anna's face lost its color.

"It makes you talk? But I don't remember anything!"

Merina laughed and shook her head. "And you probably never will. It is almost like a truth serum. If you have ever thought it, you probably said it. And even if you didn't think it before but thought it last night, you said that too.

"Don't worry. Angel will tease you, but he won't tell anyone else what you said.

"Now tell us about your family."

CHAPTER 68

A WARM WELCOME

MARTHA OPENED THE DOOR WITH A BIG SMILE WHEN Anna arrived. Zach and Mandie rushed to meet her. They told her all about how much fun they had that morning. Martha was already Granny Martha to them. Zach was excited to meet Rollie and the little girls were soon busy playing with the new dolls Martha had made. Anna slowly relaxed.

Martha gave her a cup of hot tea and a biscuit. "It will help your headache," she whispered. She patted the younger woman on the back and hurried to finish breakfast.

"I have it nearly ready," she replied when Merina offered to help, "but you ladies can help me with the dishes when we're done."

Breakfast was a noisy affair. Anna watched the interactions between all the people. It made her realize how much she had missed having a family.

Angel and Merina both had dark eyes that danced and laughed. Little Emilia looked exactly like her older sister. Everyone, adults and children, considered Badger and Martha family.

When breakfast was over, Badger announced there would be a party at their house on Saturday.

"We'll have all the kids in an' have us a little get together 'fore the cold weather sets in." He winked as he looked at Angel. "That work fer ya, Angel? I reckon you'ins 'ill be in here most ever' day anyhow, won't ya?"

Angel's face showed no expression, but Gabe laughed out loud. Anna didn't know what it all meant. However, since it seemed to involve Angel and her, she blushed.

Once the meal was over, the men moved outside and the women began cleaning up. Anna was washing dishes and she could see the men through the window above the wash basin.

She smiled as she watched Angel and Gabe. It was obvious the two men enjoyed each other. *They really are more like brothers than friends.* She was brought back to the kitchen when she realized that Martha's question was directed at her.

"How did you meet Angel?"

Anna smiled as she looked over at Martha.

"We were on the same train. Angel and Miguel were headed to Texas, and I was going to Council Grove in Kansas to spend some time with my aunt." She laughed as she added, "I didn't even tell Angel my name, but two weeks later, he showed up in my aunt's store. He wanted to take me to a dance in town that night. I told him no, but he was very persuasive."

Martha was smiling and Merina laughed as she nodded.

"Yes, Angel has always been persuasive. And he loves to dance. Did you go to many dances back East, Anna?"

"No, I hadn't danced since I was small, and that was dancing with my father. I was worried I would trip but Angel didn't seem concerned." Her cheeks turned pink and she laughed softly.

"He told me if I tripped, he might fall down and then people would think we were drunk. I was a little horrified, but it wasn't a problem. He spun me so fast my feet barely touched the floor."

Anna's voice was soft as she looked at Merina.

"Your brothers saved my life. I'm not sure what would have happened to me if they hadn't found me at Hole-in-the-Wall.

"Miguel helped rescue another girl too. Her name was Margaret Doolan. She had been there for three years before I arrived. She was known there as Nettie. Her brother came for her, and Miguel helped him get her out."

Merina's eyes opened in wide in surprise. "I know this Margaret. The Doolans didn't live far from us in Texas, just a little further west on the Brazos. Margaret was sweet on Miguel for a time, but he was never a man for a woman to trust with her future." Merina frowned.

"I remember when she ran away. I didn't realize she had been held anywhere though."

Anna listened closely to Merina as she talked. *Perhaps that was why Nettie was so angry with Miguel.*

"The Doolans returned to Texas along with two other men. Margaret didn't think they would be up this way again." Anna paused before she continued.

"Zach and Mandie's father was the man whom I went to Fort Laramie to see. I returned the money he had given my sister. When he died, he asked me to take his children in. Of course, I agreed." Her smile was soft as she looked out the window. "Angel tried to convince me not to go. He said it would be a difficult journey and a dangerous one too. So no, I shouldn't have gone but I'm glad I did."

The women were quiet when Anna finished. Martha was dabbing her eyes and she hugged Anna.

"Well, I for one am glad you made that trip. You stay here as long as you want. And I know Merina would love to have you help at the school again as well."

CHAPTER 69

Taking Care of Business

ANNA AWOKE EARLY ON OCTOBER TWENTY-SECOND. She wanted to meet with the lawyer in town and talk to him about the account which had been opened for Dan's children. Zach and Mandie wanted to go with her so the three of them followed Badger's directions to the lawyer's office.

Martha frowned as they hurried out the door.

"Doc Williams told her to take it easy. I'm not sure she should be running around Cheyenne, taking care of business on foot."

Badger pinched Martha's cheek. "They be fine. I'm a guessin' Miss Anna be ready ta stretch 'er legs after bein' locked up fer so long." His grin became bigger and he chuckled.

"Ain't never seen ol' Angel so taken with a woman. He jist always skates 'round on the outside an' leaves 'em a wishin' he were still there. Miss Anna caught that boy up an' he don't know which a way ta turn.

"Yep, we be havin' us a party on Saturday."

Martha was quiet as she listened. Concern showed on her face when she spoke.

"Maybe we should wait on that party. Anna seems quite determined to leave. All her plans have centered around that. I'm not sure there has even been talk between them of marriage."

Badger shrugged. "We'll see. I'll tell 'em it's my durn birthday if she not be up fer it." He winked at his wife. "Ain't never had me a birthday party. Don't even know when I were borned. Jist knowed that I be older than my baby brother, Darby."

Martha smiled at Badger and laughed as he swung her around. "Don't care much 'bout when I were borned. My best day be the day I met you'ins." He swung Martha around the kitchen and bowed deeply before he let go of her hand.

"Mebbie when we'uns drop ya off ta yur shop, I'll jist wander 'round town some. Mebbie I'll run into Miss Anna an' I cin give 'er a ride back ta here.

"I'll talk ta her some an' see if'n I cin figger out what's a goin' on."

Badger hitched the buggy he kept in the barn behind his house as he talked to the horse. The mare was a Morgan, and she was anxious to run.

"Now simmer down there, Matilda. We ain't got far ta go. Still, I jist might take ya on out ta Lance an' Molly's. I ain't been out that way fer some time. 'Sides, ya ain't had ya a good run fer a time, an' it be a nice, cool mornin'."

Badger hurried into the house and was back quickly with Martha. He lifted her into the wagon as he laughed.

"Little Merina done bought a ranch whilst those boys was gone.

"That little ol' gal don't let no grass grow under her boots. That piece north a Endicotts come up an' she jist rode on over there. Surprised ol' Wilson but he sold it to 'er. Didn't make 'im no never mind who bought his grass long as they intended ta stick 'round Cheyenne.

"Wonder if'n she told Angel yet. Gabe, he were surprised but he jist laughed. He said Merina done took care a the books an' she knowed what they could afford.

322

"Gabe's boys be runnin' cows on Endicott's place too now. Margaret Endicott married Cappy an' they done moved ta Cheyenne. She sold that place ta Gabe right 'fore he left." Badger chuckled. "Lance better be careful or ol' Gabe 'ill own more land than him 'fore too long."

Martha listened quietly as her husband talked. Badger made it a point to know all that was going on in "his" growing family. He loved all the young couples as well. She scooted closer to him and smiled. Badger patted her hand and pecked her cheek before he continued.

"I think mebbie Merina done bought that ranch with Montero money though. That 'heritance from Cole come through whilst the boys was gone trailin' those cows. Ol' Cole were like a pappy ta those kids. He left 'em his ranch down ta Texas. 'Course the rest a that property he left 'em were a surprise." Badger thought for a moment and nodded his head.

"That Merina's a sharp one. Yep, I think she done bought it fer her brothers."

Badger dropped Martha off at her shop. He drove around town until he spotted Anna leaving the bank. Levi was beside her and he waved at Badger before he turned back inside. Badger pulled the buggy to a stop.

"Give you'ins a ride somewhere, Miss Anna? My hoss needs some runnin', so I thought we might take us a drive."

Anna paused as she looked down at the two children. She really wanted to walk but Mandie was complaining about her legs being tired.

Zach wasn't tired but the prospect of a buggy ride sounded much more fun than walking around town.

"Please, Miss Anna? I'd rather ride in a buggy and talk to Badger than do any more boring meetings."

Anna laughed and nodded. "All right. We'll go for a ride. When we get back though, we are going to get each of you some clothes. I'm not that handy with a needle, and Granny Martha said Sadie would help us out."

Badger lifted the little ones up and helped Anna into the buggy. He waved his whip toward the lawyer's office.

"That seamstress lady be ol' Levi's wife. She were a widow when he wandered into town. He was smitten right off but Sadie, it tooked her some time 'fore she falled in love." He grinned over at Anna and commented casually, "Love be a funny thing. It smacks ya out a nowhere. Ain't no logic or sense 'bout how it works.

"But it do work. Most a our kids is married an' happy married at that."

"I don't have time for love. I am trying to tie up business here so I can move back to Kansas. It will be too late for me to find a teaching job, so I will have to work at something else to support these children.

"Love and marriage would only complicate my life." Anna looked straight ahead. Her cheeks were pink as she talked, and her chin was set stubbornly.

Badger turned to look at her. His old eyes were serious as he studied the side of her face.

"Yur shore 'nough right. Love cin be mighty messy. Cain't keep it in tidy little piles. 'Course raisin' two little ones ain't a gonin' ta be easy neither." He grinned at her as he chuckled.

"Ya done complicated yur borin' life when ya made a trip west. Now ya have two little ones ta care fer, an ornery cowboy who pertineer laid down his life fer ya, an' yur runnin' from love 'cause you'ins is scared." Badger watched Anna as he waited for her response.

"That 'bout cover it?"

Anna looked over at Badger quickly. She started to speak but sat back in her seat. Her voice was nearly a whisper when she spoke.

"I'm terrified, Badger. Since we were young, my sister and I have scraped to get by. We didn't go hungry but it was because we both worked.

"I am terrified to depend on anyone let alone a wild cowboy. I don't even know if he has a job. If he was working for someone, how could he have taken time away to come look for me?"

Badger pulled his team to a stop. He reached down to set the buggy brake. He wrapped the lines around the brake handle and faced Anna. His voice was hard when he spoke.

"Let me tell ya a little 'bout Angel's family.

"He were raised on the back of a hoss, same as Gabe an' lots a other fellers 'round here. None a those Monteros had much growin' up. They scrapped and digged fer ever' meal.

"A wealthy man from Chicago by the name a Charlie Cole bought a ranch by their pappy's little spread down on the Brazos River in Texas. He hired their ma an' Merina ta work fer 'im. Their pa were a'ready gone.

"Angel hired on too. He could a took 'im a job anywhere, but he sticked close ta keep an eye on the womenfolk.

"Life were a little easier fer 'em after that. Then their ma died an' Merina tooked on her ma's work inside along with 'er own. She was a'ready a keepin' the books an' breakin' hosses. After that, she cleaned and cooked too. 'Course she had little Emilia ta care fer on top a her work.

"Cole, he decided ta take a herd up ta Dodge. Now Cole were a nice feller, but he didn't know nothin' 'bout cows or trailin' 'em. He'd never even been ta Dodge.

"Angel, he tried ta talk Cole out a that idea. Told 'im it were a bad one. But Cole, he be a stubborn feller, an' he was shore it would work.

"It didn't. Cole died down ta the Territory, runned over in a stampede. He musta had some misgivin's though 'cause 'fore he left on that drive, he willed his business dealins' an' ranch over ta the Monteros, ta be theirs when he passed on.

"See, ya met Angel an' Miguel when they was goin' ta Texas to sell that ranch. They had done decided ta make their home here. Angel prob'ly jist found out 'bout the rest a that deal last night 'cause he's been gone on that trail drive and lookin' fer you'ins up north fer most a three months now.

"Now my reason fer tellin' ya this ain't ta make ya marry a man ya don't love, but if'n you'ins has cold feet 'cause Angel ain't never gonin' ta be more than a cowboy…well, he a'ready is. An' 'sides, there's a powerful lot a women who'd be proud ta marry 'im as a cowboy, 'fore he even owned his own ranch. Angel be a fine man.

"An' as far as 'im a takin' time off ta come fer ya—Angel would a quit any job he had ta help those he loves. That's the kind a man he be. An' if'n ya ain't a willin' ta return that kind a love, why I reckon ya need ta git on back ta Kansas. You'ins cin find ya a fancy feller in Kansas City who cin support ya in the way you'ins wants ta live…if livin' be more important to ya than love."

Badger's blue eyes were like ice chips when he finished, and Anna turned a deep red.

"I—I—don't know what I want, Mr. Badger. I just know I'm afraid. Perhaps I will never be brave enough to live out here."

"Oh, you'ins is brave 'nough. You'ins is jist bein' a coward 'bout yur feelin's is all. You'ins is so fearful a love that you's a gonna run as hard an' as fast a ya cin…away from the one man who showed ya what love feeled like.

"Ya do that, Miss Anna, an' you'ins 'ill build a hard ol' shell 'round yur heart. There'll always be a reason not ta love someone." Badger's face softened a little as he watched the young woman beside him. Finally, he shrugged.

"It be yur life. Ain't none a my business, but I done told ya anyhow.

"An' if'n you'ins is a thinkin' on cuttin' out a here without tellin' that feller goodbye, then ya do it today. Ain't no reason ta waste 'round."

Anna's blue eyes were wide and tears filled the corners of them. She was quiet as the horse clattered down the road. At last, she looked over at Badger.

"Please take us back to town. I have already purchased our tickets. I will change them from Thursday to today. If you don't want to give us a ride to the train station, perhaps we can stop by the livery so I can ask Rooster."

Badger said nothing as he wheeled the buggy around. When they arrived at his house, he drug Anna's heavy trunks outside and used a board to lever them into the back of the buggy.

Rooster had caught his best top hat on a nail and tore a hole in it. He brought Martha home to get the needed supplies to fix it. She was just rushing out the door when Badger and Anna arrived.

Martha's face was pale as she watched her husband's angry movements. She said nothing. She could tell Anna was on the verge of tears as she quickly packed her belongings and the few things the children owned.

Anna paused in the kitchen. "I—I'm sorry Martha. We are leaving today. Please forgive me for being so rude."

Martha held Anna by the shoulders as she looked into her face. She hugged her tightly.

"You come back and visit any time. And if you change your mind before you get to Kansas, you jump right back on another train and come back here.

"And don't you worry a bit about Badger. His family and the love he has for them are the most important things in this world to him. He just can't understand why anyone would, in his mind, throw that away."

She kissed Anna's cheek. She put her hand over her heart as the young woman hurried to the buggy. Both children had fallen asleep and were still asleep when Badger cracked his whip over Matilda's back. The shiny buggy moved quickly down the dusty street toward the train station.

CHAPTER 70

Anna's Goodbye

ANGEL GRINNED AS HE WATCHED THE TRAIN CHUG south down the tracks toward him. The rails cut through Gabe's property, and sometimes, Angel raced the train.

The horse he was riding today was a long-legged bay. The gelding loved to run, and Angel held him in place until the engine passed. The passenger cars were scattered out after the engine based on the class of tickets.

The third-class tickets were the cheapest. Those seats were the least comfortable and the cars were closer to the front of the train. Usually, they were full of families, so he started his horse there, leaning low over the saddle as the gelding raced beside the train. It was a great sport, and he always waved his hat as they passed him by.

Today, he let the gelding run. He backed it off a little to run beside each car. The train was almost by him when he saw two small children waving excitedly. He pushed the horse closer to the train and raced alongside it as he grinned and waved his hat. When it started to pass him, he recognized Zach and Mandie.

Angel leaned forward and urged the horse to run faster as he looked into the car. Anna's face was pale when she looked out the window, and

Angel's shock showed on his face. He pulled his horse to a stop and watched silently as the train rumbled on into the distance. He sat on his horse and continued to watch until the train was just a speck on the rails that crossed the prairie. He turned his horse and rode slowly back toward Gabe's Diamond H Ranch.

Gabe met him with a grin. He enjoyed Angel's zest for life. The man worked hard but he always made time for a little fun too. His smiled faded as he looked at Angel's face.

"Everything all right?"

"Anna and the kids were on that train. She is gone."

Angel's voice cracked as he spoke. He turned his horse away from Gabe and rode back toward the house. He called over his shoulder, "I think I will ride over to the Wilson Ranch. I want to work on a few things there, maybe even get them done before the first snow."

Merina watched Angel from the window as he roped a second horse. He put a packsaddle on it and added some oats. He looked toward the house but didn't stop as he turned his horses to the northwest. Merina ran to the kitchen door.

"Angel! Where do you go? Gabe thinks it will snow tonight. If you are going far, at least take some food with you." She hurried back inside and grabbed a packet of food from the table. She had packed it for lunch at school the next day, but she could pack more. She ran after Angel and handed it up to him as she looked into his eyes.

"Anna was on the train?"

Angel gave her a twisted smile that didn't reach his eyes. "You are the lucky one, Merina. You found a fine man who loves you. I think I will not be so lucky. Nor will Miguel. Perhaps we are destined to be alone with our broken hearts."

Angel continued up the road and cut northeast through the pasture to the Wilson Ranch. The wind picked up and the temperature dropped. By the time Angel reached the ranch, snow was beginning to fall. He brushed his horses and put them into stalls in the tight barn. He forked them some hay and gave each a few oats. He watched them eat contentedly and laughed.

"You caballos have no concerns. Always, there is another meal, another trip to take. You carry us where we want to go with no worry of what is in front of you. Me, I am not so lucky." He turned to look out the door of the barn and watched the snow come down in large flakes.

"Miss Anna, you have broken my heart. I should have continued to love only the horses. I should never have kissed you."

Angel walked slowly up to the house and opened the door. He smiled as he stepped inside. Merina had negotiated the purchase of this ranch while they were on the drive north and Angel was pleased.

"I thought perhaps I would one day share this house with Anna. Now I know that is not to be."

He laid the packet of food on the old table and stared at the stone fireplace. It was already getting dark. He sat down in the kitchen and stared out the window. When he could no longer see, he went to bed in the cold house while the wind howled outside.

CHAPTER 71

A COLD NIGHT

A NNA SAT BACK IN HER SEAT. SHE TURNED HER FACE away so the children couldn't see her wipe her eyes. They were still talking excitedly about how Angel chased the train and how fast his horse could run.

She pinched her eyes shut but still the tears came. The look of shock on Angel's face cut deeply into her heart.

"I hurt him. He was kind and thoughtful of both the children and me, and he asked for nothing in return. He thought of us first and I hurt him. I did not even have the fortitude to tell him I was leaving.

"How could I have been so cruel to not even say goodbye?"

She thought about her conversation with Badger and a sob caught in her throat. *What if he's right? What if I am so afraid of love that I am pushing Angel away out of fear?*

The children were already hungry. Even though it was in the middle of the afternoon, she fed them their supper from the bundle of food Martha had slipped her. She wrapped them up in blankets and they were soon asleep, one on the floor and one curled up in the seat beside her.

And now what? I have no job in Council Grove except maybe at the store. I know Aunt Mae will take me in, but winter is coming and business

slows down. I doubt she needs help over the winter. Besides, now I have two
children. I most certainly will need to get a house of my own and that is
another expense.

"That lawyer I met with—I believe Mr. Parker is his name—is going to
make sure all the property transfers and payments were done correctly. Right
now, I don't even know how much money is in the account John Reynolds
opened for me. We may be destitute in just a matter of months.

Maybe I should just go on to Kansas City. Tillie would be delighted to
have us back, little ones and all. And just maybe that teaching position will
still be available.

Yes, I think that is what I will do. I will change our tickets and go on
to Kansas City. We might have to spend the night in Denver. Maybe we will
take a day and walk around. Who knows when we will have an opportunity
to go there again?"

Anna finally dozed off. She was awakened by a crash and a shudder
that reverberated throughout the train. They had begun to wind through
the foothills north of Denver and the train was stopped on a steep incline.
Anna looked out her window, but the snow was coming down so hard
that she could see nothing.

She tapped the shoulder of the man in front of her.

"Excuse me. Can you tell me what is going on?"

The man leaned out the window to look up and down the track.
He pointed in front of them. "There is a tree down. The crew is trying
to clear it off the track.

"I'm more worried about the tracks themselves though. This snow
came on fast. Those tracks were warm when the snow started. If the tracks
freeze up and ice over, we are stuck out here…at least until someone
comes to get us or until it warms up enough for the ice to melt."

Anna felt a chill go through her as she looked outside. The windows
were now covered in snow, and she could see nothing through them.

The man turned around again and pointed toward the children.

"You might want to do the same as them. We aren't going anywhere tonight so you just as well hunker down and get a little sleep. Hope you brought plenty of blankets and coats."

"We are not prepared," Anna whispered to herself. "I brought blankets but all we have are jackets. We cannot stay warm in a cold rail car for long."

Anna pulled the blanket tighter around Zach. She covered Mandie and herself with another larger one. Her feet were already cold. She pulled them up and tried to tuck them under her.

CHAPTER 72

STRANDED ON A TRAIN

ANGEL SCOOPED A PATH TO THE BARN THE NEXT morning. He fed the horses and saddled them.

"I just as well make a trip to Cheyenne and pick up supplies since I am this close.

"I can either come back here or head to Gabe's. I think I will go to Gabe's. That sky looks like we could get more snow, and I don't want to get stuck here for a week by myself. I would be a lonely vaquero."

Angel cut across country heading for the tall windmill. Wilbur Wilson had been one of the first in the area to put up a windmill. Angel rode around it as he studied it.

The windmill worked well when the water didn't freeze. Once everything froze though, the blades quit turning. Now the tank was frozen solid. Snow had covered the ice and the tank was full.

"Not much good in the winter. Good thing we have a creek."

Angel arrived in Cheyenne around eleven that morning. He purchased his supplies and took the horses to the livery. He was headed to the Tin House to eat breakfast when Rooster caught him.

"Did ya hear about the train?"

Angel shook his head. "What train? I just arrived in town. Is one late?"

"Naw, the one that left yesterday. Train is stuck somewhere south a Denver in the foothills. Somebody managed to git word to Denver but the mountains ain't passable 'round there a'tall. Denver wired Cheyenne to see if we cin send out a rescue party.

"Quite a few women an' kids on that train. It be mighty cold to be stuck out in the middle a nowhere."

Angel listened closely. Rooster had barely finished when the younger man raced out of the livery.

"The sheriff is in charge. Git on down to his office if ya want to help," Rooster hollered after him.

Rooster looked back at the livery. "Jist as well start puttin' runners on these here carriages. We's a gonna need 'em to haul those folks out."

Angel was back shortly.

"Sheriff Boswell wants to know how many sleighs you can have ready to go in an hour."

"I got two of 'em done. If ya cin help me, we should be able to have three more ready 'fore too long.

"Ain't gonna be enough though. They was probably a couple a hundred folks on that train. Each a these carriages only holds eight on a good day, maybe ten or fifteen if they's stacked in there. Could mebbie get twenty on if a bunch was little kids, but some would be a standin' an' that wouldn't be very safe. 'Sides, that'd be too heavy to pull."

Angel nodded and the two men began to change the carriages to sleighs. They caught a man who was walking by and asked him to deliver a message to the sheriff.

"Tell the sheriff Rooster has five sleighs. Tell him they will be ready in forty-five minutes."

Angel slid his pack off his second horse and threw a saddle on him. He raced over to the mercantile store. Isaac Herman handed him all the blankets he had in stock along with some jerky and crackers without Angel asking.

Some of the townspeople had changed their buggies over as well, and twenty sleighs were lined up on the street. Badger was the second in line with his. Angel jumped into the front sleigh and waved his arm. The caravan moved out, briskly at first. They slowed as the snow became deeper. Men on horseback led extra horses. A rider appeared and grabbed the reins of the two horses Angel had tied to the sled.

Angel shook his head. *We aren't able to move fast enough. If it starts to snow again, we are going to be in trouble. At a trot, we are only going to make ten to fifteen miles in an hour. We are going to run out of daylight. Besides, if we hit deep snow, that is going to slow us down.*

The good news is the wind will blow the snow across the grass. We should be able to cross the flat more easily. Once we hit the hills, it's going to be harder.

He kept the pace up until the horses started showing a little fatigue. He slowed the group to a walk to rest them a little. They were entering the foothills by sunset. The horses were stopped and rested about thirty minutes. One of the sleighs carried oats and all the men had buckets to melt snow. Each animal was fed and watered before they continued.

It was nearly ten that night when they reached the stalled train. Passengers jumped out and cheered when they saw the sleighs. As they gathered around, Angel pointed.

"The women and children will come first. We cannot get all of you in one trip so please help us get as many possible."

He jumped down and ran up to the train car he had seen Anna in earlier. Three bundles were huddled on the floor and Angel jumped into the car. Neither child moved when Angel touched them, but they were warm. He shouted for help as he lifted Anna up. Her face was pale, and her feet were stiff.

She opened her eyes briefly and smiled. "You found us again. I—I'm sorry, Angel." As he carried her, she wrapped her arms around his neck. "I'm so—so c—cold."

"Your feet are freezing, Anna. You didn't have more blankets?"

"I wanted the children to be warm. Are they warm? Amanda was cold earlier so I gave her my blanket." Anna's voice caught in a sob. "I wasn't prepared. I didn't take warm enough clothing or enough blankets."

Angel lifted her into the sleigh. Two more men handed him the children and he slid them in the front seat as well. He pointed to a young woman who was shivering but was still able to walk.

"Get up in this seat. I need you to sit next to this woman. Use each other to stay warm." He wrapped a blanket around Anna and the young woman. He tucked Zach between Anna and him. He placed Mandie on the young woman's lap and laid another blanket over them. His back seat was full, and Angel swung the sleigh around. He had the lanterns lit on the sides and he waved at four other sleighs that were also full.

"Follow me. We need to move out to make room for the rest. Sheriff, don't let anyone leave alone. We must stay in groups of five at least. Make sure the leader is familiar with the area."

Badger followed Angel down through the hills and five more sleighs were behind him. Once again, Angel rotated between trotting and walking. It was early morning when they arrived in Cheyenne. Three of the sleighs stopped at Doc's house and two went to the Rollins' House. Angel followed Badger to his house.

He carried Anna inside and Martha immediately took over. "Don't rub her legs. Bring me in a bucket of snow. I need to thaw her out slowly. Lay those little ones in there on that bed."

The house was a flurry of activity and Angel slowly backed out the door. He drove the team down to the livery. Rooster hitched two more horses and Angel headed south for a second trip.

Gabe jumped in beside him as they passed the ranch. "You sit back and get some rest. I can guide this team just by following the marks of the runners in the snow." As Angel leaned back in the seat, Gabe looked over at him.

"Anna and the kids okay?"

"I think Anna might have some frostbite. Her feet and legs were cold and stiff. The little ones were fine." He added softly, "She wrapped them in her blanket. She only had a cloak to cover herself."

Gabe was quiet. He didn't know what to say so he said nothing. Angel closed his eyes, and the two men rode in silence most of the way.

It took nearly twenty-two hours to make the trip to the stalled train and back to Cheyenne. Residents of the town had opened their homes to the stranded travelers and the ten sleighs that followed Gabe back into Cheyenne carried the last of the passengers. Gabe left those riding with him at Dyers Hotel.

He looked over at his friend. "Angel, you don't have that much meat on you and you are all gaunted down. You need something to eat and about ten hours of sleep."

"Sí, I am not so handsome now, but I don't want to stop for food. Just leave me at Badger's. I want to check on Anna."

Gabe nodded and turned the team toward Badger's house. Angel jumped down and Gabe headed the weary team back to the livery.

Rooster met Gabe at the livery and led the team inside. The two men worked to rub them down and Rooster commented, "Two hundred an' forty-two folks pulled off that there train includin' the crew. An' that don't count the hosses. That be a fair amount a folks to haul through the snow in two days."

Gabe nodded. "I'd like to get home before another storm blows in. It started to spit about an hour ago. You have a fresh horse anywhere?"

Rooster pointed at his personal horse in the back stall. "Take ol' Fred. He don't look like much but he's solid. An' git to movin'. That snow be kickin' up soon."

Gabe was quickly in the saddle. He rode out of town at a trot. The road south was packed with all the traffic and was slick in spots. Fred plodded along at the same pace. The snow and ice didn't seem to bother him.

Merina was watching for Gabe. She handed his horse's reins to Nate and led her husband into the house.

"Anna is all right? And Angel?"

"Angel's worn out but he's fine. I'm not sure about Anna. Angel thought she might have some frostbite." He looked at her and grinned. "You didn't ask about me. I kind of expected a more welcoming reception." Merina rolled her eyes, but she stretched up to kiss him as she laughed. Gabe's grin was wider as he hugged his wife. "I could sure use something to eat though."

CHAPTER 73

SNOWED IN

THE SNOW BEGAN AGAIN AND CONTINUED ALL NIGHT. Martha had people sleeping everywhere. Anna was one of the few who had a bed. Her face was still pale, but she was asleep.

Angel knocked on the open bedroom door. Martha was pulling Anna's blanket up and had a small frown on her face.

"Her legs and feet will be fine, yes?"

Martha frowned and slowly nodded. "She has some patches of skin on the ends of her toes that might come off, but they don't seem to be too deep. Her toes are warm though. I was worried she might lose one when she first arrived.

"I think it is good you got her out of there when you did. She has a few white spots on her face too. It could have been bad if she hadn't been warmed up.

"You can go on in and sit with her if you want. I'll bring some food in for you. I have enough food stock for about three more meals before we start running out of things."

Angel stood in the doorway and watched Anna for a moment. Finally, he slipped through the door and eased up beside the bed. Anna opened her eyes as he sat down. She stared up at him without speaking and a tear leaked down her cheek."

"Angel—"

"Shh. Don't talk. Just try to sleep. Soon the track will be cleared and you will be able to leave."

Anna turned her head and silent sobs shook her body. Slowly, she relaxed and went to sleep.

Angel kissed her hand and touched her cheek.

"My beautiful Anna. I will let you go. Your heart is free to fly to where it wants to go. I will not try to keep you here."

He backed away from her bed. There were people sleeping all over the house, so Angel rolled up in a blanket in the corner of Anna's bedroom. When Martha brought in the food, she could not even wake him to eat.

Sometime later, the two little ones came in and curled up beside Angel. He pulled them up next to him and wrapped his blanket around them without opening his eyes.

It was afternoon when Angel finally awoke. He slipped out of the bedroom and closed the door softly.

The house was busy as the women helped Martha prepare the evening meal. Badger had found a jug of root beer and was passing out drinks to any who wanted some.

He raised his glass to Angel and hollered, "There be the man a the day. This here be the feller what organized that there rescue." He winked at Angel as he added, "An' out a the jist plumb goodness a his heart."

Angel chuckled. "Sí, my heart is very big but now it is small compared to my stomach."

Several of the men laughed as they shook his hand. The women brought him a large plate of food and insisted he sit down at the table.

"We are eating in shifts but you may go ahead and eat first.

"Badger told us you made two trips. Thank you for working so hard to rescue all of us."

Angel ate quietly as he listened to everyone talk about the weather. The men said it wasn't unusual to get snow in October, but this snow was a particularly heavy one.

One man was visiting from Louisiana and had never seen snow before. "Lucky for me my friend sent a coat with me. All I brought along was a light jacket. I won't be traveling this far north or west in the fall again without a coat *and* a blanket!"

Someone banged on the door. When it opened, Miguel stood there with a smile on his face. He looked around the room in surprise.

"Did I miss a party? Rarely am I the last to know of such an event." He winked at Martha as he stepped inside.

"I was looking for a warm place to stay tonight. I was about forty miles out when that snow blew in. It has been a difficult day." He smiled at Angel as he strolled over to the table.

"Hello, Brother. I see you have just been sitting around and eating while I was gone, yes?"

The conversation picked up again and Miguel dropped down beside Angel.

"You are late. Was there trouble?" Angel watched his brother as he spoke.

"No trouble on the trail. A rider I camped with the first night said there had been trouble inside Hole-in-the-Wall. Hattie was injured. I turned around. By the time I made it back to Fort Laramie, I was told she had died.

"John Nolan had buried her on his ranch before I even reached Fort Laramie."

Angel was quiet as he listened. He spoke softly, "I am sorry, my brother."

"Hattie was tough but she had a kind heart." Miguel looked away and added softly, "I met her about four years ago. We became close. Now she is gone and my heart is sad.

"She tried to make me go straight. She didn't want me to become an outlaw or a killer." Miguel's voice cracked as he spoke. "I loved her almost as much as our own mother."

One of the women handed Miguel a plate and the two brothers ate in silence.

CHAPTER 74

LETTING GO

THE SNOW STOPPED DURING THE NIGHT AND THE morning broke bright and sunny.

Angel and Miguel were the first ones up. Martha served them breakfast. She looked at Angel several times and acted like she was going to speak. Instead, she just refilled his plate and began to wash dishes.

The two men thanked her and were gone before most of the guests awoke. Badger followed them out the door.

"I'm a guessin' they be gittin' that there train digged out today. An' they better. Folks an' livestock is a goin' ta start pilin' up." He looked from Miguel to Angel.

"Ya boys headed back home?"

"Sí, we have been gone too long. I think perhaps Gabe doesn't like the winter so much. He might make Merina work outside while he sits by the fire."

Angel's eyes were dancing as he spoke and Badger laughed.

"I doubt that but ya fellers have a nice trip back home. Mebbie one a you'ins cin pull the other so's ya cin pertend you's a skiin'."

Both brothers laughed. They headed down to the livery to get their horses. Miguel looked over at Angel several times and finally asked, "Miss Anna did not stay?"

Angel shrugged. "She is leaving. Her heart is not happy with mine. Perhaps she will find love somewhere else."

Miguel nodded. "Sí, I had this same conversation with my horse on the way back here.

"My horse, he told me I worry too much. I should just eat as often as possible, kick people I don't like, drool in the horse tanks, and buck a vaquero from time to time. He said there was little else in the world to worry about if that is done well."

Angel laughed and the two men waded through the deep drifts to the livery.

Rooster was just pulling his suspenders up when they walked into the barn.

Angel looked at his pack of supplies and at the ornery hostler.

"Any word on the train? I'm wondering if I should leave my provisions with Martha. She is feeding many people."

"Naw. They's a sendin' a couple a engines down this way to push that train. They'll probably hook onto it an' pull it a ways 'fore they reverse an' push it. Should be another train in here to pick up all those folks by one er so.

"Folks shore come together an' helped out these last two days. Makes me mighty proud a our little town."

He slapped his leg as he looked at Angel.

"I 'most fergot to give ya a letter. It come in the day after ya brung Miss Anna in."

Angel looked at Rooster in surprise as he took the letter. Scrawled on the outside of the envelope was a note from the sheriff in Fort Laramie.

"Sorry this is late. It slipped inside a stack of wanted posters and I just found it. Hope it ain't important. It was dropped off here on the fifth of October."

Angel studied the handwriting before he opened the letter. A woman's cross necklace fell out. He held it as he read the letter. He stared at the cross quietly before he dropped it inside the envelope. He handed the letter back to Rooster.

"Give that to Miss Anna before she leaves town. It's her mother's necklace. I know she will want it back."

Angel saddled his horse quickly, and without waiting for Miguel, he headed south out of town.

CHAPTER 75

A New Schoolmarm

CARE OF THE LIVESTOCK KEPT ALL THE RANCHES around Cheyenne busy, including Gabe's Diamond H riders. Angel seemed to be back to his normal self as he kept the bunkhouse in an uproar with his practical jokes and stories.

Merina was working with the older school-age boys at her house in the mornings and helping Gabe in the afternoons. No one mentioned why she wasn't teaching at the little school every day and Angel didn't ask.

When the men came in for breakfast on Friday, November twenty-first, Merina announced, "Badger is talking about throwing a birthday party next week sometime. He said there hasn't been a party around here for a while, and we need to have one before the winter settles in." She smiled at her brothers. "There might be a dance contest and I want one of you to do the Hat Dance with me."

Miguel shook his head. "I haven't danced that for nearly a year. Have old twinkle toes here dance it with you." He pointed at his brother. His smile was slow as he added, "I prefer more to watch than to dance. I am still looking for my next novia. I haven't had a steady la chica in some time."

Merina stared at him and muttered, "More like never."

She poked Angel. "You will dance it with me, yes? Gabe will have to play his harmonica since not everyone knows it."

Angel stared at his sister. His eyes settled on her stomach before he looked up at her face. His eyes were dancing and his grin was big when he answered.

"Sí, I will dance it with you, but I think you are going to be harder to hold. Your stomach is getting bigger every day. Perhaps you are growing old and fat. I think maybe you won't be able to move so fast. I might have to dance like an old man so you can keep up."

Merina glared at her brother. She started to respond but Gabe chuckled and put his arm around his wife.

"Merina and I thought maybe the noise level in this house wasn't high enough. We are adding another little Hawkins.

"Doc thinks it will come in April." He grinned down at Merina and started to say something. She shook her finger and rattled a torrent of words in Spanish as she pulled away.

Gabe chuckled as he watched his sassy wife.

"You forget, Merina. Everyone in this room speaks Spanish. No more cussing me and thinking I won't know." His grin became bigger as he looked at his friends.

"Must have happened the night before we left on the drive. Merina is worried what folks will think since I was gone for nearly three months after we married."

Angel and Miguel began laughing. Just then Nate walked into the room.

"Nate, you might as well know too. Merina is springing. We have a baby coming, probably during calving time." Gabe's voice was proud as he put his arm around his brother's shoulders.

Nate grinned and blushed as he looked at his sister-in-law. "Yeah, I know. She has been throwing up every morning before we start our studies.

"I asked Lance if he thought I should call the doctor. He told me not to worry. He said women do that sometimes when they're pregnant. He was laughing when he told Molly and she told Beth. They are all excited."

Merina stared at Nate in surprise and the men broke out laughing.

"Secret's out, sweetheart. You won't have to tell a soul. They will all be congratulating you the next time we see them. We'd better make that dance soon." Gabe kissed his wife and pointed at the bedroom.

"You go get the little ones up and I will fry these eggs."

As Merina hurried to the bedroom, Gabe nodded his head behind her. "It's the eggs. For some reason, she throws up every time she cracks one open. Doc says that's usually temporary.

"I hope so or I will be making my own breakfast for the rest of my life." He was still muttering as he cracked eggs into the skillet. "So much for marrying so I don't have to cook for myself. Durn females." He grinned over his shoulder as the men laughed.

"So this party. Is it Badger's birthday?" Angel's question was overly casual as he looked around the room.

"No, it's Miss Anna's birthday. She had some frostbite on her feet and couldn't get around well for a time after that train deal." Nate leaned forward excitedly as he spoke.

"While she was at Badger's, Gabe and Merina went in to see her. They wanted to talk her into staying through the spring to teach. I think she was a little scared of taking the train again this winter, so it wasn't so hard. Anyway, she agreed.

"She moved into the schoolhouse about a week later. She's been teaching there a month now." Nate was pleased to share what seemed to be new information with Angel. It was rare anyone heard news before the ornery cowboy.

Gabe didn't turn around as he commented, "Wasn't too hard. She seems to be an easy woman to get along with. I thought maybe she'd act like a pinched up old school marm. Not so much.

"She's darn popular with the fellows too. There's been a steady stream of cowboys by that schoolhouse ever since she moved in. Some of them are even wanting to go back to school."

He turned around to grin at Angel.

"Word is she might do a little tutoring this summer—you know, like working one on one with fellas who want to learn to read a little better." The devils danced in his eyes as he added innocently, "Say, you might want to sign up for one of those lessons, Angel. I hear she won't turn down anyone who wants to learn.

"'Course you'd have to get on her list. It's probably longer than a woman's dance card at a fancy ball."

Angel threw the metal plate in front of him at his friend. Gabe ducked and Nate caught it. He grinned at the two men as he set it down on the table.

He grabbed for a piece of bacon and rubbed his knuckles when Gabe whacked them with the egg turner. He dodged a second whack and sat down at the table with his bacon strip.

"Badger told me he was going to invite Miss Whitman's little sister out for a visit. She's living in Kansas City with an old friend of his. He said she's quite the looker and younger than Miss Anna." Nate grinned at the men and added casually, "Sam and me are going to be there to meet the train this afternoon. We'll give her a ride to Badger's house. Miss Anna is letting school out at noon today so she can be there too."

Gabe turned around with a frown on his face and Angel laughed out loud.

"Sí, I have heard señorita Florence is a niña hermosa, a beautiful girl as you gringos say. Yes, you should meet the train." He was grinning as he looked at Gabe. "You remember, my friend, when I said you should be pleased young Nate just wanted to fish. I think those days are coming to an end."

CHAPTER 76

A Friendly Visit

IT WAS A BUSY MORNING AND ANGEL PUSHED EVERYONE to finish. When he wasn't giving orders, he was restless and distracted. A little after nine, he saddled a fresh horse and rode north. Gabe grinned as he watched his friend disappear.

"About time he took a ride over to the neighbors."

Molly made it a point to be outside when she saw Angel riding up the lane.

"Good morning, Angel. Are you wanting to see Lance?" Molly's blue eyes were innocent as she looked up at him, but she couldn't keep the laugh out of her voice.

Angel removed his hat and grinned at her.

"I think, señora, there is little that happens which you do not know of. And perhaps even less you don't have a hand in.

"I just heard the new teacher may be going to Cheyenne to meet her sister this afternoon. I thought perhaps I should ride along to keep her safe." His voice was nonchalant as he added, "This teacher, she seems to get herself into difficulties."

Molly laughed and nodded. "I think that would be a great idea.

"You can borrow our buggy. Lance put the sleigh runners on it. Hitch the two big blacks to it. They need some exercise anyway." She started to turn away and added seriously, "Anna is a wonderful teacher, Angel. She has a kind heart and is generous with her time when it comes to the children."

Angel nodded and held his hat across his chest with a flourish.

"I thank you for the use of your sleigh, señora. Until I see you again. Perhaps at the dance my sister has been speaking of."

Molly smiled as she watched him go. "I hope you win her over, Angel. She has turned every other young man down who offered to drive her to town, and there have been quite a few of them."

Angel polished the sleigh until it shined and rubbed the horses down.

"Today we will pick up a special lady. You must be on your best behavior. This lady's experience with our Wyoming Territory has not been so good. We must make it better so she will want to stay." He tied his horse to the back of the sleigh and drove the blacks toward the little school.

Anna looked out her window and gasped. "Angel! I didn't know he was coming." She turned to the children behind her.

"Mandie and Zach—grab your blankets and your coats. Angel is here to take us into town. It is not polite to make someone wait so please hurry."

Anna bit her lips to give them color and tried to tuck a red curl back into the bun on her head. She took a deep breath and pulled the door open before Angel could knock.

When Angel smiled at her, Anna could feel her heart beating wildly in her chest. She forced herself to talk calmly.

"Good afternoon, Angel. What a surprise to see you. What are you doing here in the middle of the afternoon?"

Angel grinned at her as Mandie and Zach rushed around her. They both wore heavy coats and were carrying blankets. He bent down to hug each of them and lifted Mandie up.

"I was going to ask you if you needed a ride to Cheyenne, but I see you were expecting me." His dark eyes danced as he spoke. He smiled down at her and bowed. "But of course, many women wait for me by their doors, just hoping I will come by."

Anna stared at him and her cheeks slowly turned pink.

"I declare, Angel. You make me sound so desperate."

When Angel winked at her, Anna laughed. She pulled on his arm.

"Come in. It will only take me a moment to gather my things. I am spending the weekend with Martha and Badger. They invited my sister to stay as well.

"I can't wait to see Flory. We had never been apart until I took the train to Council Grove."

Anna grabbed her coat. Angel helped her put it on. He took the small satchel from her hands, and she grabbed a heavy blanket. Her smile was bright as she looked up at him.

"I'm ready." She paused and added softly, "I'm so glad you came by. I was afraid I would never see you again."

Angel smiled down at her as he took her arm.

"Miss Anna, I always know where the beautiful women are, and where they are, I try to be." His eyes sparkled as he studied her face. "You are staying through the winter, yes? It is very exhausting for this tired vaquero to keep rescuing you. Somehow you have managed to almost die twice, and you have only been in the Wyoming Territory for a short time.

"And what of me? Not so much as a kiss to show your gratitude."

Anna was quiet as she looked up at Angel. She stood on her tiptoes and kissed him quickly on the cheek. Angel pointed to his mouth, and she blushed.

"I will not. Kissing your cheek was much more forward than I usually am. That is enough.

"Come, children. Stop giggling and climb up in this sleigh." She was still talking when Angel grabbed her by the waist and swung her around. She almost screamed as he set her up on the seat and climbed in beside her. He was grinning and Anna laughed.

Angel looked back at the children and winked.

"Now you kids hang on. This road may be slick and I don't want you to fall out. You either, Miss Anna. You'd better hang onto my strong arm. I will even flex my muscles if it will make you smile."

Anna took Angel's arm and he stiffened it. He was looking straight ahead, and she pinched him.

"Stop it," she whispered. "These children will repeat all you say. And trust me, what they retell will sound much worse."

Angel chuckled and urged the horses to a trot.

The children became quiet after about a half hour. Angel stopped the sleigh and covered them with their blankets. When they started again, he looked over at Anna. His face was serious when he spoke.

"Why did you run away? You shattered my heart when I saw your face on the train. Why did you leave without talking to me?"

Anna was quiet. She finally took a shaky breath.

"You scare me. You make me feel things I have never felt before. I panicked that week. Badger could tell I was going to leave. He was angry with me for running. He said if I was going, then I shouldn't wait. I should go right away.

"I knew an hour after I left that I was wrong. I was trying so hard not to cry in front of the children. I couldn't believe it was you when you raced your horse beside the train. And when I saw your face and how hurt you were, my heart broke too." Anna's eyes filled with tears as she spoke.

"I hoped we would be able to talk when I saw you beside my bed in Martha's bedroom, but you were gone when I awakened." Anna was crying when she looked up at Angel.

"I'm sorry, Angel. I didn't mean to hurt you. I'm sorry I ran away and I'm sorry I broke your heart. The idea of loving someone and sharing my deepest thoughts with them terrifies me." Her eyes were wide as she whispered, "I'm afraid I will love you and you will leave me. Someday, you will just be gone, and I will be alone with a heart that won't heal."

Angel stopped the horses and pulled Anna close to him.

"My beautiful Anna. I will never leave you. I will always be beside you. And when I am not beside you, I will linger in your mind." He frowned and then added, "Unless our Dios takes me away—but even then, I will try to talk him out of it."

Anna sobbed softly and Angel pulled her closer.

"Sí, my heart has a very large scar on it. I think it will take many years of you kissing me to make it disappear. We should start now." He looked around and nodded, "Sí, the children are asleep and there is no one around to see. I think we should begin many years of kissing now."

The buggy stayed where it was for a time and only moved when the children started to stir. Anna was short on breath and trying to pin up the hair that had fallen out of her bun when Zach popped his head over the seat.

"Are we about there? This trip is too long." He scowled as he added, "I'm hungry. Don't you know I'm hungry?"

Anna's eyes were bright and happy when she handed him a sandwich.

"We don't have much further to go. You sit back and eat that. We will be at Granny Martha's before long."

CHAPTER 77

Many Years of Kissing

ANGEL WAS ALL SMILES WHEN THEY ARRIVED AT Badger and Martha's house. Anna was a little breathless and kept blushing.

Badger studied the two of them and nodded.

"'Bout durn time. I was thinkin' all my plans an' plottin' were ta be fer nothin'.

"Now how 'bout you'ins git yurselves on down ta the church. Talk ta that there padre an' see if'n he cin squeeze a weddin' in whilst Miss Anna's family's all here. Tomorrow'd be a fine day."

When Anna stared at him in shock, Badger shrugged. "Monday be good too. Yur sis leaves on Tuesday so it cain't be no later than that."

Angel grinned and nodded somberly.

"Perhaps we can talk to the padre this morning. You will watch the children, yes? Then we can have it decided when Miss Flory arrives."

He led a protesting Anna toward the door.

"That is too soon! What will people think? They will surely believe that I—I did something I should not have." Anna was whispering loudly as she pulled back.

Angel grinned down at her and shook his head.

"Most weddings out here are quick ones. Folks don't have the time or the care to mess around. Two weeks is about the longest anyone waits. Besides, if we get married by Monday, your sister can come."

Anna stared up at Angel. Her chin was set and determined.

"You haven't even asked me to marry. Badger *told* us to!"

Angel dropped down on one knee. He took off his hat and held it over his heart as he smiled up at her.

"Miss Anna, will you marry me? Will you give me many years of kissing you? Will you greet me with a smile in the mornings?" Angel's voice was soft as he added, "Will you let me love you always and never send me away again?

"Marry me, Anna. Make me the happiest vaquero in Cheyenne."

Anna put her hands over her mouth and laughed softly.

"Yes. Yes, I will marry you. I will love you forever even when you embarrass me. And I will kiss away that scar in your heart."

Angel stood and wrapped her up. He kissed her soundly. He bent her over backwards before lifting her into the sleigh.

They were both laughing when Angel drove away. He didn't turn toward the church though. They drove through town and down the rough road that led south out of town. When they were about three miles south of Cheyenne, Angel turned to the left down a narrow road that was more like a trail. The rough road wound around and stopped just above a small ranch. He turned the team down the lane and pointed at the house.

"This is where we will live. Merina bought it while we were on the drive. I have been working on it ever since you came back." He lifted her out of the buggy as he grinned at her.

"When a man has a broken heart, either he drinks or he gets much work done.

"I am usually a man of peace, but when I drink, sometimes I am not so friendly. I decided I would work."

He opened the door and let Anna walk in first.

The house smelled of fresh wood. A polished table stood in the middle of the kitchen. Four chairs were around it and what looked like a bird track was carved into the center.

"Is that a chicken foot?"

"No, it is a turkey track. That is what I call this place. The Turkey Track Ranch. I have trouble with reading. The words look like many turkey tracks to me." His face was still as he added, "That is why I have wanted to marry a schoolteacher. Perhaps she will do my reading for me and help me to get along in this difficult world."

Anna looked over at him quickly and Angel winked at her. "Alas, I was only able to find one teacher who would let me kiss her passionately. That is the teacher I decided to marry."

Anna blushed. "Those are things you cannot say in public, Angel."

He walked toward her slowly, "But here we are alone. Here no one will be around to see us when we kiss."

Anna backed away from him and shook her finger.

"You are a very bold man, and behavior like this is why I will agree to marry you quickly." She let him kiss her once before she pushed him away. "No more. Now show me the rest of our ranch."

CHAPTER 78

Anna's Family

MARTHA SMILED WHEN SHE HEARD THE TRAIN whistle blow.

"I am so pleased it worked out between Anna and Angel. Thank Heavens Doc Williams cooperated with us and told Anna she needed to stay off her feet for two weeks. Even though she was up in less time, she had calmed down some by then." She smiled at her husband and laughed softly, "I guess your scolding did her some good."

Badger grinned and winked at his wife as he hurried her to the sleigh he had waiting.

"Anna don't know yet but Tillie's a comin' with Flory. I done told 'er in my wire that if'n she wanted ta see that girl, she needed ta make a trip on north.

"I didn't tell 'er Anna was a marryin' 'cause I warn't so sure 'bout the timin', but Tillie, she be a sharp one. She'll know if Anna ain't a comin' back ta Kansas that a man be the reason.

"Now we need ta talk 'bout this here weddin'. Anna don't have no folks ta help other than her little sis so that makes us her closest kin. Us an' Tillie. I'm a thinkin' we need ta skip that there birthday party an' jist plan a weddin' party. We cain't be havin' us two big parties close-like, but we cin sure make the one that's comin' up a humdinger."

Badger craned his neck as people began to climb off the train.

"I ain't shore what Flory looks like, but I know Tillie. I reckon the two of 'em 'ill be together.

"An' where is that durn Angel? It didn't take him no four hours ta talk to that sky pilot."

They both turned around as a sleigh raced up the street. People scattered as Angel swung the sleigh around. He jumped down and lifted Anna to the ground. She ran toward the train while he held the team. When he spotted Martha and Badger, he led the team toward them with a grin.

"I took Anna to see where she will be living." His smile became larger as he added. "She is a distracting woman and I lost track of time." He winked at Martha before he continued.

"Father Cummiskey was at the church. He will be busy with confessions on Saturday but Monday at one in the afternoon will work." Angel tied the team and strolled up where Anna was waiting excitedly. Zach and Mandie pushed through the crowd to join them.

A small blond woman stepped off the train. Badger could see her dimples from where he stood, and he snorted. "More trouble. Should a knowed the little sister would be good lookin' too. These durn cowboys won't git no work done a'tall 'fore she leaves."

Sam and Nate pushed through the crowd. They reached Flory before Anna did.

"Miss Whitman? I'm Sam and this is Nate. We were sent to offer you a ride to wherever you'd like to go. Of course, we'd be happy to give you a tour of Cheyenne if you would like to see our town before you settle in for the afternoon."

The older woman behind Flory laughed. She reached out her hand and shook Sam's. She reached for Nate's and paused a moment before she took it.

"That would be just fine. Sam and Nate, I'm Tillie and this young lady is Florence. Now...."

Flory squealed and rushed through the crowd.

"Anna! Oh, Anna! I have missed you so much. And look, Tillie came with me! We can stay until Tuesday morning and not a day longer.

"Just look at you! Why you look like a real pioneer woman!" Flory hugged her sister again.

Anna laughed and looked over her shoulder for Angel. He stepped up beside her and bowed deeply with a flourish as he held his hat over his chest.

"Miss Whitman. It is my pleasure. And señora Tillie, it is nice to meet you.

"My sainted mother called me Angel. Angel Montero." He winked at Sam and Nate shuffling behind the women.

He pointed at the two small children beside Anna. "Zach and Mandie—say hello to your auntie."

Flory looked at the children in surprise, but Anna said nothing as she smiled down at the children.

Tillie was standing to the side. She smiled as she watched the two sisters. Anna was much more reserved than Flory, and the younger sister was even more animated when she was excited. She glanced again at the two young men and frowned slightly. Her smile was back in place when she walked up to them.

"It was so nice of you to offer to give Flory a ride. And what ranches do you work for?"

Sam pointed to himself. "My pa owns the Rocking R south of town. He bought it from Old Man McNary shortly after he married my ma." He jabbed his thumb toward Nate. "This is Nate Hawkins. He moved up here with his big brother this summer. They bought Badger McCune's place so we're neighbors."

Nate grinned and nodded.

Tillie laughed. "Neighbors, friends, and fishing buddies I'm guessing."

"Sure are. We both like to fish."

Tillie laughed again. Nate's eyes were a dark blue—*just like his father's. He seems to be more grounded though. I hope so. His father wasn't much of a man.*

Angel stepped forward.

"I think perhaps you are hungry? These two young men will be happy to drive you to one of our finest eating houses in Cheyenne.

"Sam and Nate—please escort these three ladies to your sleigh. We will meet you at the Tin House."

When Anna started to protest, Angel whispered, "Let the boys act as gentlemen. This will be their only chance to talk to your sister. The men will soon push them aside." He winked at her. "Memories, Miss Anna. Memories and stories are important."

He lifted the children up into Lance's sleigh and waved at Martha and Badger.

"Would you like to join us at the Tin House? I think perhaps it will be entertaining."

CHAPTER 79

OLD FRIENDS

IT WAS NEARLY THREE-THIRTY AND THE CROWD OF working cowboys who frequented the Tin House was mostly gone. Those who were still there perked up when Anna entered. They sat up in their chairs when Flory appeared. Most recognized the two young men who followed the women inside, and greetings were called.

Tillie's reception was mixed. Some of the men grinned and hollered at her while others pretended not to know who she was. One woman stood and flounced out of the eating house, leaving her food on the table.

Anna paid them no mind. Tillie was her friend, and she was delighted to see her.

"When did you decide to come? I had no idea although I am pleased. And even happier you were able to travel with Flory."

Tillie laughed and nodded. "Flory needs an escort. The men surround her constantly and she enjoys their attention.

"Now tell me about this man who won your heart. If you aren't coming back to Kansas, he has to be special."

Angel was talking to some of the cowboys at a back table and Anna smiled as she watched him.

"Yes, he is. I met him on the train from Kansas City to Council Grove. Since then, he has saved my life twice. I tried to run away but he…He is—oh Tillie, we are going to marry!"

Tillie looked at Anna in surprise and again at the smiling Angel.

"That is quite sudden. What kind of man is he, other than a cowboy?"

"He is bold and ornery and funny, all the things I am not. Yet he is kind and gentle. He loves his family, and he loves me." Anna smiled softly as she leaned forward to whisper, "He makes my heart beat quickly, and when he kisses me, I see sparks and stars.

"I found it, Tillie! I found the love you spoke of. It was terrifying at first, but I am so happy."

Tillie studied Anna's face and slowly smiled. She hugged the younger woman. "Good for you, Anna. Every woman deserves to find that kind of love.

"And the wedding? When will that be? How I wish I could be there."

Anna laughed softly. "You will be. It is going to be Monday at one. I want you and Flory to stand up with me." Anna smiled and added softly, "I am going to wear your wedding suit."

Tillie's eyes opened wide in surprise. She hugged Anna again.

"Now look at me. I never cry but I have tears now. What will I be doing at your wedding?" She dabbed at her eyes and looked up with a smile when Badger appeared. She stood and Badger hurried over to her.

"Tillie, it's plumb good ta see ya. This here pretty woman on my arm is my Martha. Martha meet Tillie. She be an old friend from Kansas City."

"Please sit down, Martha." Tillie leaned forward and took Martha's hand as she smiled at her.

"I believe we met one time in Manhattan, Kansas some years back. If my memory serves me, we were both helping take care of some men who had been injured fighting a bad fire."

Martha nodded as she remembered, and the two women began to visit.

Tillie smiled wistfully as she watched Anna.

"I am so happy Anna found a new life out here, but I am going to miss her. She is a special young lady.

"And tell me about those children. Who do they belong to?"

Martha and Tillie visited like old friends and were soon making wedding plans. Tillie wanted Anna to have a full reception with a meal and cake. She insisted it be provided by one of the hotels or eating houses.

"The women out here put in long hours. I can afford the meal and I want to do it. You take care of the location since I don't know what's available here anymore. And you invite whoever you want. Anna probably won't want to invite many, but you know who their friends are."

Around five, the party finally broke up and everyone loaded into the sleighs. Flory rode with Angel and Anna while Tillie rode with Martha and Badger.

Tillie had decided to stay at the Inter-Ocean Hotel. It had opened not long before and was considered the finest hotel in the West.

"I like my space. I can come over later this evening if that is all right with you, Martha. Besides, those two sisters need some time of their own." She smiled as she watched them. *Such a contrast.*

CHAPTER 80

Angel's Secrets

FLORY WAS BUBBLING WITH EXCITEMENT AS THEY rode in the buggy back to Martha's house. She leaned toward Anna and whispered, "I can't believe you are marrying! You barely looked at men in Altoona. So tell me all about Angel. Why is he so special?"

Anna looked over at Angel and laughed softly. "He is listening to everything we say. I know he can hear every word."

"He's not paying attention. Now tell me."

"Well mostly, it's because I like his sister."

Angel looked at Anna in surprise, and she jabbed him with her elbow.

"See! I told you he was listening. Angel hears everything. He remembers it too and uses it later to his advantage."

Angel chuckled as he winked at Flory. "Sí, Anna is correct. I like to listen. But it is because I have a very large heart. I care much about other people."

Anna laughed. "Some people but mostly it's because you are snoopy. You listen and adjust your behavior to make it work with what was said."

"I think listening is not such a bad thing. Perhaps because you are a teacher, you talk more than you listen." He winked at Anna. Before she could answer, he added, "But I like a woman who talks."

Flory laughed as she watched the two of them.

"Then you tell me, Angel. What was it about my sister that made you want to know her better?"

Angel looked over at Anna and smiled. "Ah, señorita, I like to look at beautiful women, but I like even more to talk to them. And if they have hair the color of the sunset, then I must know them.

"Besides, Anna was very friendly. Of course, she talked to all the men, not just me."

Anna sputtered, "I most certainly did not. I don't even know why I talked to you, and I certainly didn't tell you my name."

"Still, I found you when I came back through Council Grove. And you went to the dance with me even though I was a stranger. Yes, I think you are a very friendly woman."

Anna blushed. "I didn't know then why I agreed to go, and I still don't know.

"At the dance, he told some of the young men he was my brother-in-law. For the rest of the time I lived in Council Grove, I had to pretend I had a brother in Cheyenne.

"Angel is trouble." Anna looked over at him and laughed. "I guess I just like trouble.

"But enough about us. Tell me about your job. Are you still working at the dress shop?"

"Oh yes. I love it. I have met so many wonderful women. I think Tillie knows nearly every moneyed woman in the city. Of course, many of her friends purchased dresses at that shop before I went to work there. It is called Bella Robe which is French for beautiful gown. I nearly swooned at the prices the first day I was there." Her face showed her excitement.

"Tillie said there is a woman here who is making dresses in the latest fashions. Her name is Sadie. Tillie pointed out some of Sadie's dresses to me in Kansas City. She has seen them in St. Louis as well. Several of her friends have ordered them. Her label is 'Prairie Flower Creations.'

"Do you know her? I would love to meet her."

Anna laughed as she agreed. "We can go to her workplace tomorrow. Martha owns the shop and Sadie has a room in the back she works from.

"I have never ordered a dress from her for myself, but I bought one for Mandie and a shirt for Zach. I know I could make them, but I am so slow. You enjoy making garments. I don't.

"How is Sampson? You haven't even mentioned him. Is he still working for his brother-in-law?"

Flory looked at Anna and looked away quickly. She tried to sound nonchalant, but Anna caught the change in her voice.

"He's fine. He picks me up at work sometimes. Not as often as I would like him to. Sometimes he comes over and visits with Tillie. I think he actually likes her better than me.

"And he never asks me to go anywhere with him. Not on a walk, a picnic, or anything.

"One night after work, he came to pick me up. I had to stay late, and he waited for nearly an hour. When I came out of the shop, he stared at me. I thought for a moment something was wrong, but he was smiling.

"I don't understand him at all. He won't stay at Tillie's if other young men come to visit, and he laughs when I flirt with him.

"I have tried all of my charms on him and nothing works." Flory pouted a little as she talked, and Anna laughed.

"I told you not to play games with him. Just have a conversation, Flory, and stop flirting." She looked at her sister and added softly, "I doubt he knows you love to fish. Ask him to go fishing with you.

"I'm sure he would be surprised to see you in your overalls with the pant legs rolled up."

"Sí, I too would like to see that. Perhaps Anna will roll up her britches so I can see her legs," Angel stated with a laugh.

Anna rolled her eyes. "I don't like to wear britches, and once again, you just listened to everything. And you certainly are not going to see my legs."

Angel looked down at Anna's determined face. Suddenly, he leaned over and whispered softly, "I already have."

Anna stared at him in surprise but before she could respond, Flory sighed. She was quiet for a moment as she looked around.

"I don't see many ponds, Anna. Do they go ice skating here? Oh, remember when we went ice skating in Altoona. The pond in the middle of town would freeze and when the ice was twelve inches deep, the *Skaters Welcome* sign would be put up. I do love ice skating."

"Yes, I miss the skating too." Anna looked over the town of Cheyenne and added, "I always enjoyed those evenings on the ice.

"So does Sampson. He rarely was able to go with the rest of us because of his long shifts in the mine. He was an excellent skater though."

When they arrived at Martha's house, Flory jumped down. Zach was playing in the yard, and she ran over to play Smack Stick with him. Flory had quite a swing and the two enjoyed themselves.

Anna glared at Angel. He was grinning and ready for her denial.

"I have never shown you my legs, nor would I. Don't say things like that, even in fun."

"Ah, but it was not in fun, Anna. When you were sick and we gave you Badger's concoction, it took over a cup to make you sleep. You were quite talkative before it knocked you out." Angel's eyes were dancing and he whispered, "You told me many things, things that were not so appropriate for an unmarried woman to tell a lonely cowboy. We talked much that night. We even talked about why women wear knickers. And then you showed me your legs. They are very long."

Anna stared at Angel in horror. Her face blanched white before it turned red.

"I would *never* discuss that with a man and certainly not with you. I refuse to believe you." Once more, her chin was jutting out and sparks showed in her blue eyes.

Angel pulled her close as he laughed.

"Don't worry, señorita Anna. It will be our secret. Now come. I must get back home. I have played all day and Gabe will be concerned because I am not working hard enough at the ranch."

He lifted her down and tucked her arm into his as he guided her up the boardwalk to Badger and Martha's house.

"Perhaps you would like to go to Mass with me on Sunday? I will plan to come by at nine-thirty. Maybe we can even show your family our new home. Maybe you can cook for me, yes?"

He whispered in her ear, "Goodbye, my beautiful Anna. I think I will spin you often at our wedding dance so your dress flies up just a little and shows your legs."

Angel pecked Anna's cheek and strolled back to the sleigh, singing softly to himself. He looked back once and winked at her before he jumped up into the sleigh and turned it down the street.

Anna stared after him and a laugh bubbled out of her. Angel often shocked her with the things he said. *And I laugh. Shame on me. I am only encouraging his bold behavior.* She hurried toward the house and was smiling when she came through the kitchen door.

CHAPTER 81

How Could She Say No?

WHEN ANGEL ARRIVED AT LANCE'S RANCH, HE rubbed down the horses and polished the sleigh. He pointed his horse east. Lance waved to him as he rode by.

Angel turned his horse toward his friend.

"Hola, señor. Gracias for letting me use your sleigh today. Miss Anna let me take her to town. She also agreed to marry me."

Angel was grinning and Lance's eyes opened wide as he listened. He reached for Angel's hand and pumped it as he laughed.

"Well, it's about time. For a man with a reputation of being quick on his feet and so gifted with the ladies, it certainly took you long enough."

Angel nodded and answered almost mournfully, "Sí, the lady was not so taken by my charm. It was a difficult journey."

Lance nodded and laughed as he commented dryly, "I think you might find you have a few difficulties yet to come.

"And we'd better tell Mollie. She will never forgive me if she hears it from someone else." He turned toward the house and hollered loudly, "Mollie! Get on out here. Angel wants to talk to you."

Mollie appeared quickly in the doorway. When she saw Angel, she hurried toward him with a smile.

"Did the sleigh ride give you some time to talk, Angel?"

Angel's smile was large as he nodded.

Molly squealed in excitement. "She said yes! Oh, I prayed this would happen." She was laughing as she added, "I was a little worried. You seemed to keep tangling up your spurs.

"When is the wedding?"

"Monday at one and I hope your family can come. I think perhaps it will be large because Martha and Anna's friend, Tillie, made plans all afternoon." He chuckled as he continued, "I think perhaps we will have a dance. Merina was hoping to have one before winter shuts things down."

They visited more before Angel turned toward home and urged his horse to a lope.

He was singing when he rode up to the Diamond H Ranch.

Gabe and Nate were dismounting in front of the barn and Gabe looked up. He began to grin as Angel rode toward them.

"She finally said yes?"

"But of course. Why would she not? A handsome vaquero such as myself has swept many women off their feet. Miss Anna was much more difficult, but even she could not hold out forever against my charms."

Angel dropped to the ground laughing and Nate grinned at him.

"Congratulations, Angel. I like Miss Anna. I'm glad she will be staying around."

Emilia rushed out of the house followed by Rollie. She launched herself at Angel.

"You need to stay home, Angel. You have been gone too much and I have missed you."

Angel laughed as he hugged his little sister.

"How would you like to carry a basket of flowers at my wedding and toss them on the floor in church?"

Emilia shook her head somberly.

"I don't think Father Cummiskey would like that, and I don't want him to yell at me. He is very big, and his voice is very loud."

Angel set her down on the ground as he looked from Emilia to Rollie.

"Have you ever been to a wedding, Rollie?"

The little boy shook his head as he frowned.

"Well, Miss Anna and I are marrying on Monday. I need one of you to toss flowers and one to help me by holding her ring. Your cousins, Mandie and Zach, will be helping as well." He looked from Emilia to Rollie. "Think you both can help me?"

"But I don't have any flowers, Angel. They have all died. Now I don't have a job." Emilia's face wrinkled and she was near tears.

"Don't worry, Emilia. I will find some flowers if you will toss them for me."

Merina was listening. After the children ran off, she hugged her brother.

"I like Anna. I think I almost like her better than you sometimes." She laughed as she kissed her brother.

"And when is the wedding?"

"Monday at one o'clock. We already talked to Father Cummiskey."

Merina's eyes opened in surprise. "That is very soon. Anna agreed to this date?"

Angel grinned and winked at her. "Of course. How could she say no?" He shook Gabe's hand and sang his own version of *Red River Valley* as he led his horse to the barn.

CHAPTER 82

An Emotional Day

MARTHA HAD EVERYONE UP EARLY THE NEXT morning. The women wanted to help Anna prepare for her wedding.

Tillie arrived shortly after seven and the four of them hurried out to Anna's new home. They were soon joined by Molly, Beth, Merina, and Larry.

All their children except Rusty and Larry's nursing twins were left at Molly's. Rowdy's oldest daughter, Mari, was in charge of them. Lance and Rowdy would pick them up later in the day and bring them to Angel's.

Josie, Sadie, and Annie arrived just after seven-thirty. Annie was Tiny Small's wife. Angel had enlisted Tiny to help him build his furniture, and Annie insisted on helping prepare Anna's house.

Angel had done quite a bit of work on the house the month before. The women were surprised how clean everything was.

Four of them began to make fabric flowers from the fabric scraps Sadie provided. The variety of colors was beautiful.

Martha brought the quilt top her quilting group had just completed as well as some padding and a sheet to use on the bottom. The women quilted it while they all visited.

Cappy and Margaret Livingston arrived mid-morning. They brought Josie's and Sadie's children with them along with Zach and Amanda. They brought four cotton tick mattresses as well. Lance and Rowdy arrived shortly after that with the rest of the children. Before long, Angel, Rusty, and Gabe drove in with a wagon-full of food and kitchen supplies.

For once, Angel was quiet when he looked toward Anna. However, Gabe's grin was large as he jumped down from the wagon seat. He looked around at the group of people as he gestured toward the back of the wagon.

"It seems Angel here went and bought up half of Isaac Herman's provisions. Isaac had it all packed and ready for us to pick up this afternoon." His grin became bigger as he added, "At least we know we will be fed before we head back home since our wives neglected us today!"

The men began to unload the full wagon. Anna stared at the busy group. She hurried to grab some things as she whispered to Angel.

"Can we afford all this? I don't want to owe anyone."

Angel frowned and shrugged. "Gabe said it was a wedding gift. I did not pay for anything. Señor Herman had everything packaged. It was ready when we arrived."

Badger and Levi drove in with a large man sitting in the back of the wagon. Tiny Small jumped out and grabbed Angel's hand.

"Good thing we made all that there furniture last month. Looks like you's a goin' to need it now." Tiny's smile was wide. He hollered at the group of men.

"Ya fellers git on over here an' help me unload these here bookcases. Ol' Angel there ordered 'em fer his new wife, an' I 'most hurt myself tryin' to git 'em done.

"Angel said his gal loved books an' he was a goin' to make sure she had somethin' nice to keep 'em in."

The men soon unloaded two large bookcases and Anna started crying. Angel hugged his future wife as he smiled proudly. He pushed her toward the house.

"Tell the men where you want them, Anna. They are too heavy for a handsome vaquero such as myself to move once these men all leave."

Anna wiped her face and hurried into the house. She stood staring at them after the men left. Angel appeared beside her. He hugged her as he motioned toward the bookcases.

"Señor Tiny is a talented man. See how he put our brand on them? Beautiful bookcases for my new wife's treasured books. Perhaps she will read them to me at night while I lay my head on her lap."

Anna's eyes filled with tears as she looked up at Angel. "I love them," she whispered, "but one would have been enough. I don't even have enough books to fill them." She leaned over and took a deep breath. "I so love the smell of wood. Thank you, Angel. I can't think of a more wonderful gift."

Angel turned her toward him. "I love to give gifts to beautiful women." He added with a whisper, "Especially if she offers favors back to me." Once again, his eyes were twinkling. Anna pulled away as she turned a deep red.

"You are so bold. I think I will spend the rest of my years being embarrassed."

"Perhaps, and still you smile. I think you love me, Anna Whitman."

Just then Zach and Amanda rushed into the room. They grabbed Anna by her hands and drug her toward the stairs.

"Come and see! We have our own room! We have a soft bed and lots of blankets!" Amanda's voice was excited as she raced up the stairs.

Anna stopped in the doorway. She stared at the box Beth held in her hands. Molly held it out to Anna.

"This box arrived from Fort Laramie yesterday. It was addressed to Martha and Badger. Martha assumed it was a quilt you had left at the hotel there. She brought it out with her today.

"Beth and I put it on the children's bed. We didn't know there was a letter with it until just now." Molly handed Anna a crumpled letter. "This was in the bottom of the box."

Anna set the box on the bed. She put her hand over her heart as she read the letter. She sat down on the bed and patted a spot on either side of her.

"Come, children. I want to read you a letter from the Aults. Remember them? They are the couple who wanted you to live with them in Fort Laramie."

Molly and Beth slipped out of the room as Anna began to read.

Miss Whitman,

Please give this quilt to Zach and Amanda. Their mother started it before Amanda was born. She passed before she finished it. I thought about sending it with you when you left here. but I really wanted to complete it first. The colors and pattern Mary used were so beautiful. I just didn't know how to finish it without taking away from what she had done.

I told Lizzy Ford about the quilt. She brought Mary's quilting basket to me when she cleaned out Dan and Mary's house. Lizzy and her husband, Cletus, are the ones who bought Dan's ranch, you know.

After Lizzy gave me the basket, I was able to complete the quilt using scraps and pieces of fabric Mary had saved. I guess the Good Lord just provides.

Lizzy also sent some little clothes. I wrapped them up inside the quilt. Mary made them for Zach and Mandie when they were small. I hope you will be able to give them to the children when they are older. Perhaps one of those little ones will want their babies to wear those special clothes.

I don't know if you like to quilt but I plan to bring Mary's quilting basket down with me the next time I come to Cheyenne. I am afraid it will be destroyed if I try to send it by stage. There are so many little projects started in there. Perhaps you and Amanda will want to finish them someday.

We often think of you and those two precious young ones. We are so pleased they found a new home—one where they will be loved and treasured.

May God bless you someday with a wonderful husband and many more children.

Jasper and Anita Ault

Tears sparkled in Anna's eyes when she finished reading the note. She hugged both children and whispered, "You have many wonderful friends at Fort Laramie. Once we are settled, we will write to the Aults and the Fords. We will thank them for all they have done and we will tell them you have a new father."

Amanda looked up with bright eyes. "I will pray Mrs. Ault has a baby. I heard her crying the night before we left. She really wants to be a mommy."

Anna hugged her tighter and nodded. "That is a wonderful idea, Amanda. We will all pray. Now you run and play. And remember, don't ever put your shoes up on your Mama's pretty quilt. Shoes stay on the floor. Only clean feet can touch this quilt."

Anna sat on the bed for a time. She was wiping her eyes when Merina stepped into the room.

She touched the quilt.

"It is beautiful."

Anna nodded and choked back a sob. "I owe so much to Dan and Mary Morton. If it hadn't been for Mary's death and Dan's ad for a wife, I never would have come west. I would never have met Angel or Zach and Amanda. The Mortons' death brought me happiness."

Merina sat down on the bed. She hugged Anna.

"Sí, it is true, but now they are together with our Dios. They were not able to raise their children, but He saw to their care. You were chosen and were given a great gift." She hugged Anna tighter and whispered, "We will not always understand the ways of our Dios. Still, we must always be grateful."

She smiled at Anna and added softly, "You make my brother happy. Never has he loved a woman before. Many women have come into his life, but never did he try to make one stay." Merina looked away. There were tears in her eyes when she looked at Anna again.

"I found love with Gabe because another woman showed me his heart after she died. I too have found love because of someone's loss." She touched her stomach and smiled. "If this child is a girl, I hope to call her Grace. It was Grace who gave me my husband.

"Now come. Let us go downstairs and join your party. Many friends have come to help you today. I am new here as well, and sometimes their noise overwhelms me. Still, they have wonderful hearts. They have made you and me part of their family."

Anna nodded as she wiped her eyes. Both women were smiling when they walked down the stairs.

CHAPTER 83

A Nervous Bride

MONDAY MORNING BROKE BRIGHT AND SUNNY. THE two days before had been warmer as well. The men scrambled to pull the runners off their sleighs and put the wheels back on. The roads were a little muddy but they would dry quickly.

Anna was struggling to breathe as Flory pulled the ties on her corset tight.

"You should just leave this off, Anna. You are so nervous you can barely breathe now. If I get this too tight, you will pass out.

"Besides, your waist is small. This is smashing your rib cage and it's barely affecting your waist."

Flory's blue eyes danced as she added, "And how are you going to get it off? Angel will have to help you. He will probably just cut the ties rather than uncinching this thing!"

Anna gasped and slowly sat down. "Proper women always wear corsets. I hate it but I must wear it."

"Says who? It looks to me like most of these women do their own thing. I studied each of them and I didn't see any strings or corset bones showing through their clothes. I decided not to wear one myself. I am going to go free and easy today!

"Let's take it off and see if Tillie's suit still fits. I am sure it will. You didn't have a corset on when you tried it the first time."

Flory quickly loosened the ties and Anna let out a deep breath.

"That does feel much better. I am so nervous. I certainly don't want to faint."

Flory quickly helped Anna pull the corset off and slip back into the jacketed suit. It was a little tighter, but it still fit nicely. Flory studied her sister and giggled.

"I think you look more curvy without one. And softer. You will be much more fun for Angel to dance with."

"Flory! Don't be so brash. Goodness, you almost sound like Angel. He is so bold and unfettered. He whispers to me all the time and most of it is not proper. And sometimes I laugh. I am as bad as he is.

"Now hurry—we must get to the church. I don't want to be late to my own wedding."

Badger was smiling as the two sisters hurried out of the bedroom. Flory had twisted Anna's hair loosely on the back of her head. Red curls had fallen out and were trailing around her face and neck. Anna's face was flushed and she was having trouble catching her breath.

Just then, Merina hurried through the door. She took Anna's hand and smiled at her.

"I told Angel I would ride with my new sister to the church. He was afraid you would panic and run away."

Badger helped the three young women into the back seat. He lifted Martha in and hopped up beside her. He cracked his whip over the back of the black horses, and they moved smartly down the muddy street.

"Now ya git on up, horses. Ya ain't so quick as mules an' ya ain't so smart neither. Now move, ya flea bags."

Martha put her arm through Badger's and smiled at him.

"You love weddings, don't you? Every time we bring another woman into our little family, you just get prouder and happier."

Badger chuckled as he patted Martha's hand. "I reckon I do. This one had me wonderin' though. That little Anna is mighty skittish." He looked back behind him where the three young women were riding.

"You'ins all right back there? Ain't nobody a goin' ta git sick today, is ya?"

Flory giggled but Anna didn't answer. Merina leaned toward her.

"Here, Anna. Try some of this peppermint water." Merina uncorked the bottle. "Drink a little of this. It will help your nerves to settle and maybe clear your head as well."

Anna stared at Merina and then tipped the flask up. After three long drinks, Merina took it from her.

"That is better, yes? Your breath is not coming so quickly, Anna."

Anna nodded slowly. "Much better. My hands are still shaking though.

"Badger, did you bring your potion with you? Perhaps I can drink some of that."

Badger held out his flask, but Merina pushed it back toward him.

"No, Anna." She frowned at Badger before she looked again at Anna. "We don't want you tripping as you walk up the aisle."

Anna stared from one woman to the other before she answered.

"It is a very long aisle and I do not like people looking at me. I think I will not do this." She stood up and tried to climb over Merina to get out of the moving buggy. Badger hauled the buggy to a stop while Merina and Flory both pulled Anna down.

Flory was staring at her sister in shock when Anna shook her arm loose. Merina held onto her other arm.

"Anna, do you love Angel?"

Anna stared at Merina. She pulled at her shirt as she gasped for air.

"I can't breathe! Loosen the top button. I am suffocating!" She began to unbutton her blouse.

Merina laughed softly and nodded.

"I understand. I felt the same way.

"Now come. Let me button your blouse. You have unbuttoned it too far. Let us button the blouse and take off your jacket."

Anna pulled off her jacket and slowly began to breathe normally. She looked over at Merina.

"Were you afraid? Did you want to run away?"

Badger grinned and started the team again.

Merina laughed and sat back in her seat. "Sí. I was very afraid. I wanted to wait and marry Gabe another day. And then I saw him. He was waiting for me in front of the church, and he was so happy. I knew—I knew I loved him, and I wanted to be with him forever. I wasn't afraid anymore." She rolled her eyes. "Of course, after he fainted, I didn't know what to do. I just kept walking towards the front of the church. Finally, he was able to stand, and we were married."

Anna stared at Merina. She shook her head. "Angel would never faint. Nothing fazes him. He will whisper something to me just to make me blush. Then my face will turn all red and I will get hot again." She leaned toward Merina and whispered, "Your brother is very bold. He likes to embarrass me."

"Sí, but Father Cummiskey will not allow him to misbehave. He has told Angel already he expects proper behavior. After the wedding I cannot say, but in the church, he will behave."

Anna smiled at Merina. She whispered, "I think I love you almost as much as I love Angel. You are so like him, you know." She slipped her jacket back on and leaned back in her seat. "I am so happy to have both of my sisters beside me today."

CHAPTER 84

ANOTHER INTERESTING WEDDING

MERINA BREATHED A SIGH OF RELIEF WHEN ANNA walked up the aisle. Badger held her left arm and Tillie held her right. Anna's face was pale, and Angel fidgeted as he watched her. Gabe finally grabbed Angel's arm to hold him still and Miguel laughed.

When Angel stepped forward to take Anna's arm her eyes were wide, and she was almost gasping for air. She whispered, "I think I am going to pass out. I can't breathe and I can't unbutton my blouse because I left my corset at home."

Angel could feel the heat rush up his neck as he fought to keep his eyes on Anna's face.

Gabe began laughing and Father Cummiskey cleared his throat loudly.

Angel pressed Anna's arm to his side and kissed her hand before he turned around to face the priest. Miguel laughed again and Angel glared at his brother.

The rest of the wedding went smoothly. Anna finally relaxed although she barely smiled. When it was over, Emilia and Mandie rushed down the aisle as they threw the fabric flowers. The two little girls sang and smiled at everyone. Livvy crawled under her seat and joined them.

When they were almost to the door, Emilia turned around and hollered, "Hurry up, Angel! We get to eat as soon as we're done here. Walk faster!"

Once they were outside, Anna began pulling at the neckline of her blouse again as she gasped for air. Badger offered her his flask and she took five long drinks before Angel saw and took it from her.

"You should not drink that today, Anna. It will make you much relaxed and you will say things that maybe you shouldn't."

Anna started giggling and her foot slipped as she tried to put it up on the buggy. She took a shaky breath and Merina slipped her a cookie.

"Eat this, Anna."

Angel glared at his sister and barked at her in Spanish. Merina shook her head and answered softly, "She was panicking and wanted to run. I only gave her peppermint water before Mass. Now take her to the Rollins House and get her some food. She hasn't eaten today at all.

"Go! You can greet our friends there."

Angel wheeled the buggy around as he looked at Anna with concern on his face.

"You are all right? I think perhaps you took too many sips from Badger's flask."

Anna stared up at him and scooted closer.

"You are never afraid, are you, Angel? Nothing bothers you. Problems roll off you like water off a mink." She looked away and whispered softly, "I would have run today but Merina stopped me. She asked me if I loved you." Anna's eyes were bright when she looked at Angel.

"I do love you, Angel. I think I fell in love with you when you took me to the dance. Oh, I was interested before, but I didn't think I would see you again. After the dance, I knew there would be no other man for me but you.

"Then I met Dan Morton. He was wonderful and kind. He loved his children. He didn't make me tingle when I looked at him though. You unleash something in me that I try to keep hidden and it is terrifying.

That is why I ran the first time and why I almost ran again today." Anna's eyes were wide as she looked up at Angel.

"I asked Badger for some of his potion before Mass, but Merina wouldn't let him give me any. He gave it to me afterwards though, and now I am talking too much. But I am not afraid, and I don't want to run anymore. I just want you to kiss me."

Angel stared down at Anna. He lifted her onto his lap. "I don't think I have ever driven a buggy with my feet but perhaps I must do it today." The horses continued down the street, snorting from time to time at the unfamiliar hold on the lines.

Gabe rode up beside them with a grin on his face. Anna slid off Angel's lap and Gabe laughed.

"You best turn that team to the right, Brother. They are headed south toward home, and you have a wedding party to go to at the Rollins House!"

Anna's face was pink and Angel was laughing when he turned the horses north. "Miss Anna, you are a distracting woman. I think we might not stay so late at this party."

CHAPTER 85

OLD FRIENDS AND STRANGERS

A NGEL FROWNED AS HE LOOKED AROUND THE DANCE hall.

Three strangers were leaning against the wall as they passed a whiskey bottle back and forth. They watched the dancers, but they made no effort to talk to those around them. Angel nodded at them as he spoke softly to Gabe in Spanish.

"Those men over there with the whiskey. I do not know them. I do not think they are here to have fun. I think they are here to cause trouble."

Gabe looked hard at them and nodded. "I'll pass the word. We'll keep an eye on them. I hate to start a fight this early in the night. Maybe we can put it off for at least an hour or so." Gabe grinned at Angel and the smaller man laughed.

"I do not think you are the man to put in charge of keeping the peace. Your peace is why there are fights."

Gabe chuckled and the two men separated. They slowly wandered down by the food tables, glancing casually at the strangers as they walked by.

The three men didn't look up as Angel walked by. After he passed, one nodded his head toward Angel's back. He pulled a piece of paper from his pocket and stared at it.

"That there is one of the fellers we are looking for. There are two of them who look alike. We will most likely have to kill them to get to the woman." He stared at Angel's departing back. "Reckon they are brothers?"

"Most likely. Play it cool. We don't want to show our cards just yet. We don't know how many friends they have here."

"Can't be too many. Johnson said they was bringin' cattle north just this spring. Most of those drovers don't stick around. Not sure why they are still here but I doubt they know many folks."

Miguel appeared in the doorway and nodded at his brother.

Just then, Anna and Flory walked across the room. Angel offered each an arm and led them to a table along the side. He whispered something to Anna and slipped through the crowd as he headed for the door.

All three men stared at the two women and one muttered, "That's the gal we are looking for. Her sister is the blond. We don't have any orders for the short one, just the tall redhead.

"The second feller we are supposed to get just came through the door. We need to get this done tonight. Once the Whitman gal gets her hands on that mining deed, we will be too late."

One man grabbed the bottle and the three men sauntered across the room to take seats at a small table.

The dance was in full swing, and Gabe hurried up front. He pulled out his harmonica and joined the current song. When it was over, an announcement was made.

"The Hat Dance Contest is next! Grab your partner and head to the dance floor. If we have more than ten couples, we'll spit you into two groups."

Miguel leaned in the doorway and smiled as he looked around the room. His eyes scanned the groups of women. He leaned forward and looked closer.

"Ah, I see the little sister. Perhaps I will see if she likes to dance." He strolled up to the table where Flory was surrounded by cowboys. She was all dimples and smiles. She talked to each man as he introduced himself. When it was Miguel's turn, he bowed low and held his hat across his heart.

"Perhaps when this dance is over, you will do me the honor of a dance, Miss Whitman."

Flory cocked her head. "Because you don't know how to dance this one?"

Miguel stood a little straighter as surprise washed over his face. "I assure you, I do know how to dance the Hat Dance. Perhaps you would like to join me?"

Flory laughed and took his hand. He whispered to her as he led her to the dance floor. "Should I go slow, Miss Whitman? Are you sure you know how to dance the Hat Dance?"

Flory laughed at him again. "Give me your best, cowboy, and we'll see how good my dance lessons were."

The dance began and the music was fast. Angel and Merina were favorites from the beginning, but Miguel and Flory came in a proud second.

Miguel laughed down at Flory as he spun her away from him. He bowed deeply.

"You surprise me, Miss Whitman. Perhaps you would like to dance again or are your feet too tired?"

Flory's eyes sparkled as she looked up at the smiling cowboy.

"Cowboy, I dance all the time. Let's just see who gets winded first."

CHAPTER 86

My Bride is Missing!

ANGEL SCANNED THE ROOM. THE SMILE REMAINED on his face as he looked for Anna. When she didn't appear, he strolled across the room to where Tillie was sitting.

"Have you seen Anna? I have lost my bride."

Tillie looked around in surprise as she shook her head. "The last time I saw her was when you were dancing the Hat Dance. She was standing by the door clapping." Tillie stood. "I will check outside. Perhaps she went to relieve herself."

Angel looked around the room. The table where the three strangers had been sitting was empty. He waved at Gabe.

"Something is wrong. Anna is missing and so are the three men whom we spoke of."

Just then, Tillie came rushing in followed by Sam and Nate. Nate's hat was gone and he was holding his head.

"I tried to stop them, Angel. Three fellows grabbed Miss Anna and threw her on a horse. I tried to stop them, but one of them slugged me with his gun. They took off to the northwest. I wanted to follow them but I couldn't get up. Sam here found me." Nate's voice cracked as he added, "I'd give my life for Miss Anna, Angel. I'm sorry."

Angel waved to Doc as he yelled, "Look at Nate's head. Some fellow whacked him a good one with the butt of his gun." He ran toward the door and whistled loudly. His horse pulled the slipknot loose and raced toward him. Miguel's horse followed and the two brothers were soon on their way out of town.

Badger cursed. He dropped the plate he was carrying and followed them out the door. "Mule! Git over here, ya dad gum critter. We have us a gurl ta find." He pointed toward a cloak laying in a pile on the ground.

"That belong to Miss Anna?"

Tillie hurried to look at it and nodded. Badger mounted Mule and turned him toward the cloak. The mule picked it up with his teeth and Badger grabbed it.

"Find 'er, boy. Find our gurl."

Mule sniffed the ground in several places and snorted before he headed north out of town at a trot. He stopped from time to time to smell the ground before he continued on.

Gabe and Rusty rushed down to the livery. Rooster already had horses saddled and the men were soon racing north after Mule.

Lance stood there a moment and watched before he turned back inside. He stopped and looked back as he asked.

"How did Mule come to be here, all ready to go?"

Rowdy nodded toward the livery. "Rooster told me that sometimes Mule just shows up. If he lifts his bridle off the hook, he wants saddled. He said that is the only time he will mess with Mule—when Mule tells him to.

"That mule is uncanny. It's like he knows when trouble is coming. He wants to be ready."

"I'd say this dance is over. Let's get the women and kids over to Martha's. Once they are situated, maybe you and I should try to find Badger. Mule is a tracking animal in daylight or dark." Lance's voice was hard as he looked around the crowded room.

Levi moved up to stand beside Lance. "You and Rowdy go on. Doc and I will be in charge of the women. I know Nate wants to go but Doc said he shouldn't ride."

Rusty raced up. "Count me in. Larry's goin' home with Tiny and Annie."

Lance nodded. He called Sam over. "Nate isn't supposed to ride for a time. You stay with him and make sure he doesn't follow us. Help Levi get all the women and kids loaded up."

Sam's face broke into a scowl. Lance took his son by the shoulders as he spoke softly.

"We don't know who these men are, Sam. We know there are three but there could be more. Now I want you to help Levi. When you finish, you get down to the train station. You watch for any strangers to get off that train. The eastbound train is due around midnight and the westbound will be in tomorrow afternoon. I hope we are back by daylight, but if we aren't, I want you to meet those trains. If they are wearing guns, get the drop on them. Don't kill them but I want them stopped. Now go."

Sam studied his father's face. He was quiet when he nodded. He hurried to where Nate was trying to mount his horse. His friend shook his head several times as Sam spoke. He slid to the ground holding his head.

Doc stopped beside him. "Nate, I want you to come with me. I want to check you over a little more closely. Sam can come for you when he's done here, but I want to look at that gash in your skull."

Nate shook his head and then almost groaned as he looked up at Doc. "No, I need to go. It is my fault Miss Anna was taken."

Doc dropped down by the young man. "Nate, it wasn't your fault. Because of you, we know how many men there were and what direction they went. You are the reason the search party could act so quickly.

"Now you come with me. If you have a concussion, we need to know that. If you don't, I'll send you on your way. Either way, I need to check you over."

Nate scowled but finally agreed. Doc tied Nate's horse behind his buggy and hurried his team down the street.

Paul offered to ride with them. "I can take your rig back to the livery, Doc. No one needs me right now anyway."

Doc hurriedly agreed. He unloaded his family quickly and rushed Nate into a small room with a large gas light. He gently cleaned the wound. When he finished, he sat back on his chair.

"You need stitches, Nate. I'm going to wait for Josie to help me, but you aren't going anywhere this evening. You have a concussion, and you need to be still for a time. Paul said he would come back and sit with you until midnight. He can take your place with Sam. Now you stay quiet. I'll be back here in about five minutes."

Doc hurried out and Nate looked up at the ceiling. "Stay here while Miss Anna is missing? Not a chance. I'll let Doc put in those stitches but then I'm leaving. No way am I going to lie here while Sam and Paul watch for the trains by themselves."

Josie and Doc were back quickly. Nate was given chloroform. When he stopped moving and was breathing easily, Doc began to stitch him up.

"Twelve stitches. That was a large gash. Good thing he has a hard head like his brother. A blow like that could have killed him."

Josie looked down at the quiet young man and commented softly, "I believe it was meant to kill him. Those men couldn't afford to take a shot as it would have alerted the crowd, but they certainly didn't want any witnesses." She glanced up at her husband.

"I will sit by him until Paul gets back. I hope you gave him a heavy dose of chloroform. I doubt he has any intention of staying in this bed tonight."

Doc kissed her cheek and chuckled. "I did. That was my thought too. He's a stubborn Hawkins through and through.

"I'll check on him in a couple of hours, but he should be out until tomorrow morning sometime."

CHAPTER 87

WAITING ON THE TRAIN

SAM AND PAUL CROUCHED BY THE STATION OR HEAD house as the building was called. The train was about fifteen minutes late. Finally, they saw a dim light coming down the tracks. Sam wheeled when he heard a noise behind him. He grinned when Nate dropped down beside him.

"I think Doc gave me an extra-large dose of whatever it was that knocked me out. I could barely crawl out of that bed. Good thing it's cold out here. That is what brought me around."

Sam grinned at his friend. "That bandage glows in the dark. Better wrap your bandana around it since you can't get your durn hat on."

He looked over the station. "I think we need to spread out. Paul, you get over behind the outhouse and I'll climb around behind the platform. Nate, you stay here. We should have them surrounded."

As Paul hurried off, running low, Sam called softly, "Pa said to wing them if they put up a fight. We'll let Nate do the calling out. No shooting unless they make us."

The boys were quiet as the tired passengers disembarked. The last one to get off stretched before he clambered down. The rifle he held in his hands was easily visible. Nate started to call out when he noticed

405

a badge. He whistled and the other two young men stood. All three walked toward the train.

Sheriff Nathaniel Boswell greeted them in surprise. "Sam and Nate. Paul. What are you fellows doing here? Expecting someone besides me on this train?"

"Pa told us to meet the train. Miss Anna was taken this evening. We don't know why or who took her. Pa just said to watch for any armed men who might get off the train and to put them out of commission if they didn't drop their weapons."

Sheriff Boswell studied the three young men and slowly nodded. "Let's go up to my office and see if I have any wires or messages. There won't be another train in until tomorrow afternoon, so you boys just as well go on home after we check."

The three young men didn't talk as they followed the sheriff to his office. Boswell shuffled through some papers. He paused as he read a paper toward the bottom of the pile. He read it again and held it up.

"This wire says to be watching for three men. They were hired by a fellow back East to kill a woman who is the owner of a mine.

"You boys go on home. I'll get a posse together in the morning and see if we can track them down. We can't see to track anyone tonight."

The three young men stood on the street and discussed what to do. Sam pointed down the street. "Let's go over to Papa Samuel's place. He'll have more room than Martha and Badger. We can get up early and be ready to ride out with that posse."

Paul was quiet as he listened. He finally commented, "Ma won't be happy if she doesn't know where we are. You fellows go on. I'll go back to Badger's. Ma doesn't even know I'm gone. If I get back now, I might not have to explain anything."

Sam nodded and the brothers were soon headed their separate ways.

"How's yore head?"

"Doc said I have a concussion. He gave me twelve stitches. I woke up once and heard him talking to Josie, but I was too tired to stay awake."

"Good thing roundup is over. You cain't be doin' any rough work with a concussion. I've heard the men in the bunkhouse talk about that. Concussions ain't nothin' to mess with. I reckon ol' Gabe will stick you in the house an' make you stay there for three or four days. An' if he don't, Merina will climb all over him until he does."

Nate was quiet as he listened to his friend. He finally laughed. "I reckon that's right. She can get Gabe to do just about anything she wants him to.

"Did you know they have a little one coming?"

Sam looked at Nate in surprise as he shook his head.

"Sure do. I'll be an uncle come spring, right around calving season. Ain't never been around a little baby before. I reckon that will be different.

"Gabe's talking about adding onto the house. With Rollie and Emilia, there are five of us in two rooms. It's already crowded and a baby will make it more so."

"You like Merina bein' married to Gabe? She seems alright to me. I for sure like her as a teacher."

"Yeah, Gabe's not so cranky anymore. Merina makes him happy, and he smiles a lot. He acts more like my brother now and not my pa. I like that.

"She doesn't treat me like a kid either. She treats me like Gabe's brother and like one of the hands.

"Yeah, I do like her. She's a good cook too. We never go hungry anymore." Nate elbowed Sam. "Life is good now. Good friends, lots of fishing, and riding horses every day. Just about the best I have ever had it."

Sam looped Nate's arm over his shoulders and grinned at his friend. "You are walking crooked. We had better get you to bed. Doc said you were to wake up every three or four hours but I'm not sure I can stay awake to do that.

"Come on. Papa Samuel's house is just up ahead. Be quiet like and we'll sneak in."

CHAPTER 88

An Angry Groom

NGEL AND MIGUEL LOST ANNA'S TRAIL IN THE DARK. They had just made camp when they heard riders behind them. Badger called out and Mule gave his strange call. Rusty and Gabe were with him, and the brothers waved them in.

"Mount up, fellers. Mule don't need no daylight ta track those outlaws. Shoot, we might even come up on 'em yet tonight if'n we's ta keep a movin'."

Angel and Miguel were quickly mounted, and the little group moved out. Lance, Rowdy, and Rusty caught up just as they were leaving. The night was almost black, but Mule didn't slow down. He walked with his head down sniffing the ground for a time and moved to a trot. It was nearly three in the morning when they rode up on the outlaw's camp. Badger quietly pulled the saddle and bridle off Mule while the big jack stood silent.

Anna was tied and was leaning against a rock. Two of the men were asleep and the third was watching her as he talked.

"Durn shame to hurt a purty woman, but you have somethin' Wilbur Jackson wants. He intends to get it too.

"There's a feller comin' in on the train tomorrow with that deed. When we have both a ya, we'll have the deed an' the owner to that mine. Once ya sign it over, we cin let ya go. 'Course if ya don't want to sign, then we's to make ya, usin' whatever means we need."

Anna's voice was cold when she replied. "Don't be foolish. If your boss has his way, none of us will walk out of here. They can't let me go. I know all your faces. And you—you will have outlived your usefulness. Once the mine is signed over, you three will be a liability. You will need to be disposed of.

"Besides, I know Wilbur Jackson. I always knew he was a crook and a liar. I just didn't know he stole that mine from my father.

"He's a sly one though. I doubt he will ride the train all the way to Cheyenne. I am guessing he will ride under a false name and get off between stations so there is no accurate record of him." Anna's voice was quiet but hard when she spoke. "You men are dead either way. If my husband and his friends catch you, you will be killed. If they don't, Wilbur Jackson will make sure you die. I at least have a chance at life. You have no chance at all."

Angel growled low in his chest. He started forward but Badger pulled him back.

"Somebody's a comin' quiet like. Ol' Mule hears 'im too. I'm a guessin' that's the feller they's a been waitin' on. Let's hold off a bit an' see if'n we'uns cin git the whole passel of 'em at once." He grinned wickedly at Angel and added, "An' then, we'uns cin turn Mule loost an' let 'im do our killin' fer us."

A man with his hat pulled low rode into the clearing followed by a small man with pointed features. The smaller man smirked when he saw Anna. He slid to the ground.

"Well lookie here. Miss Smartie Britches School Teacher all tied up. I guess you aren't so sassy anymore, are you?"

"Wilbur Jackson, you despicable little worm of a man. How dare you steal that mine from my father! I'm guessing you had something to do with their buggy accident too.

"You made a mistake coming out here though. You aren't tough enough to survive one day let alone pull off this steal. By morning, half of Cheyenne will be looking for the five of you."

Wilbur Jackson laughed shrilly. "Three men. The good people of Cheyenne will be looking for three men. There is no record of me being part of this deal."

"So three thugs would just decide to kidnap me for no good reason? No, there will be an investigation and it will all lead back to you.

"You should have stayed in Altoona where you were a mean fish in a very small pond."

"And I would have if it hadn't been for that snoopy lawyer!" Wilbur Jackson's voice was shrill and the two men sleeping by the fire sat up. They rubbed their eyes and stared at the small man who was almost hopping in anger.

"Some lawyer in Kansas City sent inspectors to snoop around. They found some discrepancies in my deed. I never did find the original deed. Someone must have because that lawyer in Kansas City has it. He is sending it out here with one of his men for you to verify. Once your signature is on it, *my* mine will belong to you."

"It was never your mine. It was only a mine you stole. And stealing it wasn't enough. You had to cheat those who worked for you as well.

"Sampson always despised you and I'm glad he gave you a whipping before he left town." Anna's voice expressed the disdain she felt for Wilbur Jackson.

"Hanging would almost be too good for you."

Wilbur Jackson leaned over and slapped Anna hard.

"You always had a mouth on you. You were a nothing teacher and now you will be a nothing body. No one will miss you."

Angel pushed past Badger's outstretched hand.

"No, señor Jackson, you are very wrong. Anna is my wife. I will allow no man to treat her as you have and live." His knife was in his hand, and he held it up to the light.

"I think I will gut you like the pig you are. One cut for touching my Anna and more cuts because of how you treated her family."

Wilbur stared at the man in front of him. He laughed.

"One man with a knife before five men with guns? No, I believe you will be the one to die today."

The three men on the ground were ready to pull their guns when they heard guns cocking in the darkness behind the lone cowboy.

Only the quiet cowboy behind Jackson showed no surprise. He lifted his hands away from his body.

"Hello, Angel. When this fellow put the word out in Denver that he needed a guide in this country, I volunteered. I decided to take his money and ride along so I could keep an eye on him. I didn't think he was on the up and up with the story he told and I was right." He looked around the group of men and glared at Wilbur Jackson. "Jackson, you are not only a thief. You are just plain unlikeable." He looked down at Anna and smiled.

"Miss Anna, I think you are going to keep Angel very busy rescuing you. If I didn't have to head back to Texas, I would stick around just for the pure entertainment.

"Now if you fellows don't mind, I will turn my horse to the side and get out of your way—unless you want me to keep my guns and help you out some."

Miguel laughed from the darkness and Angel grinned. "You may keep your guns, señor Tex, but I think there are very few men. Not nearly enough for all of us." He smiled at the four men in front of him.

"Who would like to go first? Which of you is a brave man? Surely you know all of you must die."

Wilbur lunged for his gun and Mule charged. He hit the horse beside Jackson with his mouth open. The horse wheeled and almost

412

went down. Wilbur Jackson tripped trying to get out of the way and Mule caught him in his teeth.

The big mule threw Wilbur Jackson up in the air. The man screamed as he hit the ground but Mule didn't stop. He grabbed Jackson by the leg, running through the rocks and brambles as the screaming man bounced behind him.

The campsite was quiet as the other three men stared in shock from Angel to the direction of Wilbur's distant screams.

Angel dropped down beside Anna and cut the ropes that tied her. He lifted her up, looking closely at her face.

"Did these men hurt you?"

Anna shook her head as she trembled. Angel turned toward the three outlaws with his knife still in his hand. Gabe and Rusty pushed their horses into the campsite.

"Take Anna home, Angel. We will deal with these men."

Angel hesitated as he turned his knife from side to side.

"Take her home now." Gabe's voice was sharp.

Angel slipped his knife back inside his shirt and lifted Anna up. He set her on a horse and mounted, leading her horse into the darkness. When they were nearly a mile away, he stopped his horse and lifted her onto his lap.

"My beautiful Anna, I think I will spend the rest of my life rescuing you, yes?"

Anna clung to him. "I knew you would come. I could feel you before you spoke." She snuggled closer to him. "Take me home, Angel. Take me to our home."

Angel pulled his bed roll from behind his saddle and wrapped his blanket around his wife. They rode in silence. The night was cold and Anna shivered for nearly an hour before she fell asleep.

CHAPTER 89

Let's Stay a Little Longer

IT WAS ALMOST DAYLIGHT WHEN ANGEL REACHED Cheyenne. A tall young man rose from the steps of the Rollins House and Angel turned his horse toward him.

"Sam, let the women know we caught those men. I am taking Anna home. Please ask your mother to cancel school for the rest of the week. You celebrate Thanksgiving here, yes? If so, Miss Anna's students will only miss two days. And let Sheriff Boswell know as well if he's back in town.

"Gracias, Sam." Angel tipped his hat and rode on through town.

Tillie smiled as she watched from her window. "Anna is safe. I think I will change our tickets anyway. We can stay here one or two more days. That will give those sisters a little more time together too." Her smile was pensive as she quietly pulled the window shut. "Anna found a good man. I wasn't sure since it was so fast, but her heart knew."

Tillie tossed around in bed for nearly an hour before she finally gave up on sleeping. She dressed and walked toward Badger's. Sam and Nate were just coming out of Samuel Brewster's house and Tillie waited for them.

"How is your head this morning, Nate? Do you have a concussion?"

Nate gingerly touched his skull. "I have one and it hurts like a son of a gun. I might ask Badger for some of that mixture he makes up. It healed Gabe up fast and I'm thinking it might work for me too."

Tillie laughed in agreement. "Perhaps. Where are you from, Nate? Did you grow up on a ranch around here?"

"Naw. My folks had a little two by nothing ranch down by Bandera in Texas. My pa was—well, he wasn't much of a rancher. Gabe was working and sending money home, but Pa took it from Ma. He drank and gambled it away. He finally died and Ma passed away last year. Gabe hired on as a trail boss to move some cattle up here, and we decided to stay. Nothing in Texas for us to go back to.

"It's been a fine change though. Gabe married Angel's sister, Merina, and we bought Badger's spread. We plan to add land as we can." He grinned and bumped Sam's arm. "And now Sam and me get to ride and fish together. Sometimes we even work together. We are for sure pards."

Sam grinned and laughed.

"You are walking better this morning. Last night, you couldn't track in a straight line." His face became more serious as he added, "I reckon Gabe will make you go back to Doc's. Neither of them will be too happy about you cutting out of there last night."

Nate scowled. "Gabe's got nothin' to say. He wouldn't have stayed either if his pard was watching for gunmen in the middle of the night. I reckon Gabe won't be pleased but he won't say much neither."

Tillie listened quietly. She finally asked, "Do you have any sisters, Nate? Anyone besides Gabe and you?"

"Yeah, Merina has a little sister who lives with us. We have another brother too. Rollie showed up this past summer. He was livin' on the streets up in Blackfoot in the Idaho Territory. Gabe and I didn't know we had another brother.

"Clare and Rock Beckler picked him up on their way down here from the Montana Territory when they passed through there. Rock was coming down to buy black cattle to trail north, and he brought his family along.

"Rollie was looking for his pa and he found us. He's a good kid. He was mighty skinny when he first showed up, but Merina is working to fatten him up.

"He likes her too. She's tough and sassy but she hugs a lot. None of us Hawkins was ever hugged on much. I'm not so sure I like it, but Gabe and Rollie do."

Sam laughed and jabbed his friend. "Oh, you'd like it all right if Miss Anna's little sister hugged on you! I think you'd like that just fine."

Nate blushed and muttered something. Sam grinned but said nothing more.

Tillie laughed. "It is wonderful you two young men have each other. You know, life-long friends are hard to find."

Sam looked over at Tillie. "Pa said you lived out here for a time. Is that when you met Badger?"

"No, Badger and I met in Kansas City over twenty years ago. I met Martha about five years later when she still lived in Manhattan.

"She's a lovely woman with a very big heart. I liked her the first time I met her. I like her even more since I've gotten to know her better.

"I met my husband Oliver when I lived here though. Badger was a friend to both Oliver and me. He introduced us. We married over ten years ago and now we live in Kansas City. I moved around a lot before Oliver came along but we are settled now. He is a wonderful man. I cannot imagine my life without him."

Their conversation was interrupted when the door to Badger's house flew open and children poured outside. They were all talking at once and only a few of their questions could be understood.

"Is Miss Anna alright? Did Pa catch the bad guys?"

"Ma said we don't have to go to school today, so we are going to play at Papa Samuel's until breakfast." Livvy led the charge down the street, but the older kids soon passed her.

Molly called from the doorway, "Mari, you have them all back here in an hour. I don't want them eating Papa Samuel out of house and home!"

Mari turned around to wave at them. She smiled at Nate and he waved back.

Samuel came to the door. He laughed as he stepped aside to let his grandchildren rush into the house.

Molly pulled Tillie into Martha and Badger's house.

"Come in, Tillie. We have most of the food left over from the wedding since the party broke up so early. It won't be wasted though with all these mouths to feed.

"You are all smiling so they must have found Anna."

Tillie nodded. "Yes, the men should be back soon. Angel went through town before daylight with Anna. I saw him from my hotel window."

"We were so worried about her. My goodness, that girl has had a time of it since she left Pennsylvania." Molly smiled and added, "We are pleased she decided to marry Angel. She's a delightful person and a wonderful teacher.

"Are you going to leave this morning, or do you want to change your tickets? We can have one of the older boys do that for you if you'd like to stay longer."

Tillie laughed as she took the chair Molly offered her.

"I think we will stay a little longer. We were going to leave today but two more days would be nice. I'm sure Flory is worried about Anna. Staying will give them a little more time together.

"And if you want to have your boys do that, it would be wonderful." She took two tickets out of her bag and handed them to Molly. "The ticket booth should open around seven this morning.

"Let's change them to Thursday. I will send Oliver a wire this afternoon telling him I will be later."

Paul was leaning against the doorway with a smile on his face. He stepped forward and listened intently when Molly spoke to him. He gave Tillie a quick smile, pulled on his hat, and hurried up the street.

Molly watched him go with a smile on her face. She was still smiling when she turned around.

"Paul is my sweet boy. Sam is precious too, but he is more like his father." Molly laughed and added, "I love Lance but sweet doesn't really describe him.

"Here those men come now and I'm sure they are hungry. Let's get them fed before that army of children descends on us again."

CHAPTER 90

BLAME THE MULE

A KNOCK SOUNDED ON THE DOOR AND LANCE hollered," Come in!"

Sheriff Boswell appeared with his hat in his hand.

"I have a wire here for Mrs. Montero. Is she here or did Angel take her out to his place?"

"Angel took her home earlier this morning."

Lance's voice was hard when he asked, "Those fellows we brought in this morning—will they be tried here or over in Laramie."

"The kidnapping was here so they will be tried here. And kidnapping is not usually a hanging offence, so I'm pleased you brought them to town." The sheriff's voice was soft when he asked, "Where's the fourth man?"

Badger waved his hand toward the north. "He be out on the prairie somewhere. Last we saw a 'im, he be headed east mighty fast. He was alive 'cause he were a hollerin' like a banshee."

The sheriff studied the six men in front of him. Gabe and Rusty never looked up from their plates while Rowdy laughed around his food. Miguel sat back in his chair and smiled as he watched the sheriff.

"If I look, will I find him?"

Lance studied the chicken leg in his hand for a moment before he shrugged. "Might. Don't know. We didn't care enough to look. A fellow who comes all the way out here to kidnap a woman so he can steal her property just isn't enough of a man for his life to be a concern to us.

"If you find him before the wolves and the coyotes get him, why there might be enough to bury. If you don't..." Lance shrugged again. "Not a concern either way. Who's to care if he has a decent burying? He wasn't a decent man and he wasn't worth our time to try to find what was left of his body."

Sheriff Boswell's eyes narrowed down as he watched Lance. He moved his gaze over to Badger.

"Was that mule of yours involved in this deal?"

Badger grinned at the sheriff and scratched his head. "Could a been. 'Course, he could be out ta the ranch an' in his pen too. Mule is notional an' he fer sure don't take ta fellers hurtin' a woman."

"Where is he?"

"Don't rightly know. Mule kinda does what Mule wants. He ain't 'round here though or you'd a seen 'im." Badger's grin became bigger and he added, "He don't seem ta like you'ins much, Sheriff. Now most a the time, Mule gets riled up at the bad sorts. You'ins be a good man but ya jist plumb irritate ol' Mule. Yep, he be a notional feller."

"I've a notion to shoot him. I am tired of him prowling all over town scaring folks."

Gabe laid down his fork. His eyes were cold and hard when he spoke.

"That mule is important to every person in this house, Sheriff. He saved my wife and has helped with the bad element in this town more times than you care to admit.

"You leave him alone. Most of the time, he is on my ranch in his own corral. That makes him my property...I don't give you permission to go on my place unless I am around."

The two men stared at each other for a time. Gabe finally grinned.

"I told you before, Sheriff. Just make him a deputy. He might enjoy that job. Shoot, you could just sit back and tell ol' Mule what to do. He could take care of business and you could sit around and eat pie."

The men laughed and nodded. Most of them never stopped eating, but they didn't fool Sheriff Boswell. He knew some of the most dangerous men around Cheyenne were seated at that table. He was just thankful they spent the majority of their time solidly on the side of the law.

He looked around the table and slowly nodded.

"I am going to ride out and try to find that body so I'd sure appreciate it if one of you would deliver this wire to Mrs. Montero."

Tillie stepped forward. "I'll take it, Sheriff. I will be going out to spend the day with her. I'm Tillie Maynard. I came west from Kansas City with Anna's sister."

Recognition flickered through Sheriff Boswell's eyes. He hooded them quickly and nodded as he handed her the paper.

"I think there is a wire at the express office for you too so you might want to stop on your way out of town."

Molly handed the sheriff a packet of food and he smiled for the first time that morning.

"Thank you, Mrs. Rankin." He tipped his hat and backed toward the doorway.

"Ladies, you have a fine day." His eyes swung to the men who were eating quietly.

"You men, get on home. Every time a whole passel of you show up in this town, I have problems."

The women all bid him goodbye while the men said nothing.

Paul had slipped in behind the men. He asked quietly, "Should I take Mule to the South Pasture?"

Lance shook his head and Badger laughed evilly.

"Naw. It'll take Boswell all day ta find that camp. The sheriff be a good man but he ain't much on trackin'." He grinned around the room and chuckled before he continued. "The best trackers all be sittin' at this here table.

"An' even if he finds that camp, I doubt he'll find much a that Jackson feller. I'm a guessin' Mule ran till he be tired, an' that mule cin run a long way."

Tillie scanned the wire and looked up in surprise.

"Sampson Jones is coming here! He says he wants to see Anna as soon as he arrives. He has some information for her involving a mine her father bequeathed her upon his death." She looked around the room.

"I would like to take this out to her as soon as possible."

Paul was already moving toward the door. Sam and Nate joined him.

"We'll go get you a buggy, Miss Tillie." The three young men were headed toward the door when Gabe spoke up.

"Not you, Nate. Not until you have Doc look you over this morning."

Nate looked from his brother to Merina and back at his friends. He rushed toward the door.

"You fellows can pick me up at Doc's office. Thanks for the medicine, Badger!"

CHAPTER 91

SMILE OR CHANGE

T HE DOOR SLAMMED SHUT AND GABE STARED AT IT A moment before he muttered under his breath.

Soon all the men were laughing. Rusty slapped Gabe on the back and nodded his head toward the door.

"Reckon he did jist what his brother would a done. No point in a gittin' mad. He learned from y'all!"

Merina smiled and commented softly, "I think perhaps I will walk down to Doc's office. Nate took my horse, and I want to go home."

When Gabe glared at her, she shrugged. "I thought perhaps it would be better to ride a smooth horse at a walk than for him to run, yes?" She kissed Gabe's cheek and whispered, "He acts just like you. Smile or change." Her eyes were sparkling when she stood upright. She grabbed her shawl and hurried for the door. She could see Nate ahead of her on Bonita. The little filly was moving at a fast walk and Merina laughed.

"Sí, Nate is much like his brother. He is kind and generous, and oh, so stubborn. Yes, much like his brother."

Doc Williams frowned when Nate hurried into his clinic.

"I'm sorry, Doc, but I had to leave. Sam and Paul were waiting for the train, and they needed a third man."

Doc stared at the sincere young man for a moment and sighed.

"Sit down and let me look you over."

Doc checked the stitches and looked at Nate's eyes. They were much clearer and more focused than he expected them to be. He stepped back and looked hard at Nate as he asked, "What did you take for medicine? I didn't send anything with you."

Nate stood and grabbed his hat. "Badger gave me some of his medicine. I knew it helped Gabe along so I thought I would try it.

"Thanks, Doc. I promise to only ride at a walk for a day…"

"Five days."

"And I won't roughhouse with the fellows for—"

"Until a month after those stitches come out. This is no joke, Nate. Concussions can kill. Don't take this injury lightly."

Nate twisted his hat in his hands and finally nodded.

"Okay, Doc. Can I go now? I hear the fellows coming with Miss Tillie's surrey. We are taking Miss Flory out to see her sister."

Doc tried hard not to laugh but a chuckle leaked out. "You go on. I want to see you next week though to take those stitches out. And no running!"

He shook his head as Nate rushed out to the road to meet his buddies. Doc was turning back into his clinic when he saw Merina hurrying up the street.

"Do you need to see me, Merina?"

"No, I just loaned Nate my horse and I am here to pick her up."

Doc's eyes twinkled and he laughed. "So nothing you want to discuss with me? I do have a little time right now."

Merina's face colored just a little and she looked away. When she looked back, she was smiling. "Perhaps I do have a few questions if you have some time." Doc nodded and Merina followed him into his office.

CHAPTER 92

THE RIDE

NATE, SAM, AND PAUL WERE BACK IN TOWN SHORTLY after dinner. They were to wait until the train arrived and pick up Sampson.

Paul had read that folks in the larger cities sometimes made signs when they needed to meet someone they didn't know. The three decided to make one themselves. It said:

**SAMPSON JONES
WE ARE YOUR RIDE.**

Sampson spotted the sign as soon as he stepped off the train and he repressed a grin. He walked toward the young men with his hand outstretched.

"Thanks, fellows. You are my ride to see Anna Whitman?"

"Sure are except she is Anna Montero now. She married Angel yesterday." Sam's grin was big as he answered the stranger.

Sampson looked surprised.

"Well, I appreciate the ride." He shook each of their hands. "As you know, I am Sampson Jones. Is the other Miss Whitman here as well or did she marry too?"

Paul was quiet but Sam grinned. "She's here. She's a looker too. It was a durn shame Angel's weddin' party broke up early. We were all lookin' forward to dancin' with Miss Flora. Then Miss Anna was kidnapped an' things went south." When Sampson frowned, Sam added quickly, "Angel found her though an' she's fine.

"I'm Sam an' this is Paul. Nate is the one on the wagon. As soon as we get your bags loaded, we can go."

Sampson grinned and held up a valise. "I travel light so let's get going.

"So you fellows live around here? You all brothers?"

"Paul an' me are brothers. Nate is our friend. We are all pards though."

By the time they arrived at Angel's ranch, Sampson had heard the name of every rancher around Cheyenne. He also had the entire story of Anna's kidnapping.

"But Miss Flory wasn't taken? Where is she now?"

"Why, she's visiting Miss Anna. I reckon she'll be leaving soon though. Miss Tillie had me change their tickets to Thursday." It was the first time Paul had spoken and Sampson noticed what a contrast the two brothers were.

"We were all kind of hoping she would stay. Not all pretty gals are as nice as Miss Flory," Nate commented. "I think Miguel would like that too. He is Angel's brother, and he danced the Hat Dance with Miss Flory.

"Miss Flory laughed a lot when Miguel danced with her so she might like him a little more than the rest of the fellows."

"How about Wilbur Jackson? He's the man who orchestrated this entire deal. Do you know where he is?"

All three were quiet. Nate commented quietly, "We think he's dead. No one saw him die but the men aren't worried he's coming back. That means they think he's dead. And if they think he's dead, they have reason to believe that.

"Miss Anna doesn't know though, so we aren't to talk about it around her."

Sam was studying Sampson and he asked suddenly, "Are you sweet on Miss Flora? Is that why you're here?"

Sampson grinned and laughed. "I reckon I'm as sweet on Miss Flora as all the men are when they meet her—kind of like you fellows. Miss Flora kind of draws a man in.

"The reason I'm here though is to talk to Miss Anna on business. My brother-in-law is a lawyer, and he found some information Miss Anna didn't know about when she left Pennsylvania. He sent me out here to tell her."

CHAPTER 93

BECAUSE OF A BOOK

NNA CAME TO THE DOOR WHEN THE WAGON PULLED
in. She rushed outside to greet Sampson. He picked her up and
swung her around. After he set her down, he put out his hand to Angel.

"I hear congratulations are in order. These fellows told me you are
the lucky groom."

Angel stepped up beside Anna and grinned as he put his arm around
her.

"Sí, it was a difficult journey but I'm the winner. Welcome to our
casa, señor Jones.

"I believe you know señora Tillie and Miss Flory? Please have a chair.
These women have been fussing all day over what food to fix. It must
be for you because Anna didn't ask me what I liked."

Sampson's eyes rested a moment on Flory. She gave him a glorious
smile and then blushed. Sampson's smile became larger.

He handed Anna a book he pulled out of his bag. It was called,
Cowboys and Vaqueros of the Wild West.

"Remember this?"

Anna took the book from Sampson in surprise.

"Of course. It was one of my favorite books when I was a child. I gave it to Gerald Campbell when I left Kansas City this past summer. He was struggling to read, and this book was something he enjoyed." Anna touched the cover and smiled as she looked up.

"Father gave it to me for my eighth birthday. I was fascinated by all the stories of the West. He bought this on one of his trips. I'm not even sure where he purchased it, but it was one of my most treasured possessions." She laughed softly as she opened the book.

"I didn't want to give it away, but Gerald was a sweet boy and this book brought him joy. I thought perhaps it was time for me to share something I loved when I was young with another child. Perhaps it would give to him the love of reading it instilled in me." Anna stared at the book as she smiled.

"How did you come to have this?"

Sampson pulled a yellowed piece of paper from his bag. He smiled as he handed it to Anna.

"The deed to your father's mine was folded up inside the book along with this note. Gerald found it when he was reading the book and showed it to his father. That started the investigation into the mine—your mine—bequeathed to you by your father before he died. He knew you would share with Flory, so he only put your name on it. Besides, she was too young anyway.

"But here. You read his note." Sampson handed Anna the yellowed paper.

Anna's hands shook as she unfolded the note. When her eyes filled with tears, Flory reached over her shoulder.

"Let me read it, Anna. I can read it."

Anna and Flory,

My Darling Daughters, if you are reading this, Mother and I may no longer be alive. I put this note and the deed to the mine in this book because it was Anna's favorite. I believe this is the safest place to hide it where no one but she will find it. And I know Anna will never part with this book.

There are forces I don't wish to speak of who are trying to take over the mine. I am not sure how far they are willing to go, but I fear they are not above murder.

I put the mine in Anna's name because she is the eldest and it will be her responsibility to take care of you, Flory. It was also easier for me to make the transfer to Anna since she is now fourteen years old. I also know Anna would never try to cheat you of anything.

We never talked about money when you were growing up, Anna. Flory was too young, but I believe now I should have tried to include you more. I fear what I saw as protection was actually a mistake. Regardless, neither of you were raised with any knowledge of our finances, our mining investments, nor with any business management skills.

I realize I am dropping a lot of weight on you by giving you the mine now. However, it must be yours. It will provide you a living and a secure one so you will not be homeless should your mother and I die.

Old Mr. Murphy at the mercantile can give you advice should I pass on. However, I have not involved him in my finances in case someone wishes to do me harm. The less everyone knows, the safer they will be, including you.

Ask Mr. Murphy to go with you to Pittsburg. Go to the First National Bank of Pittsburg on Wood Street. Show the president of the bank this letter and ask for the key to my safety deposit box there. It will contain some money as well as deeds to other properties we own. It will also include the name of a lawyer you can trust. Do not talk to any lawyer in

Altoona as I don't know who all will be offering their services there by the time you find this. You must go far enough away from Altoona that the fingers of influence cannot touch whomever you ask for advice.

Perhaps someday, you will both choose to sell the mine and move west. Anna, remember how you used to tell me you were going to marry a vaquero? I think it was probably because you liked the way the word slid off your tongue. Still, you have always been my little adventurer. You were our explorer and Flora was our socialite.

Anna and Flora, take care of each other and always remember the love we shared in our family.

Love, Father and Mother
Charles and Philomena Whitman

Flory handed the paper back to Anna.

"Now what? What should we do? I don't want to move back to Altoona, and I know Anna doesn't. Sampson, what do you think?"

"I would suggest you sell the mine. You could try to find a manager, but it might be easier to sell it. I don't know what the value is, but a good lawyer could help you with that. In fact, John Campbell offered to help. If there is a lawyer here in town, he can write up a document to give John permission to handle your affairs. John can handle those sales in your presence or without you." Sampson paused as he watched Flory. He turned his eyes back to Anna as he waited.

Anna looked over at Angel and he shrugged.

"I do not think there is a need for handsome vaqueros in mines. I prefer to ride my caballo above the ground."

Anna smiled as she looked at Sampson.

"Perhaps we could hire you as our representative. You could go with John and make decisions on our part. You can wire me if there is something I should know. Otherwise, you can stay in communication with Flory."

Sampson stared at Anna for a moment. He caught the laughter that flitted through her eyes, and he laughed dryly. "I would be happy to help you with that.

"There is a possibility you may be entitled to some of Wilbur Jackson's assets as well. John is going after his estate. He said you deserve it because of how difficult he made things for you." Sampson paused as he looked from one sister to the other.

"I will be willing to work as your representative if Miss Flora will allow me to keep her updated. That will require us meeting one-on-one though."

Flory's blue eyes were wide as she agreed. She gave Sampson a smile full of dimples and Anna had to work hard not to laugh.

"If Wilbur Jackson does have assets, I don't want them. Please ask John to split them among the mining families. Wilbur was constantly cheating them—if not in wages, he shorted their hours. Let those families have what John can get." Anna's voice was firm and her chin was set. "I want nothing our father didn't leave us." She paused and looked over at Flory. "Unless Flory wants part of it."

Flory shook her head. They visited a while longer. Sampson finally stood with a smile.

"I will stop by that lawyer's office I saw on my way out here. I will see if he can meet with the three of us tomorrow. Four if you want to come, Angel."

"Sí, I think I need to stay close to my wife for a time. She requires much rescuing, and I am a tired vaquero."

Sampson chuckled and shook Angel's hand. He was just turning to leave when a knock sounded on the door. Miguel poked his head in with a smile on his face.

"Ah, I see the business is completed. Perhaps Miss Flory would like to go for a ride with me? I promise to have her home before it becomes too dark."

Flory stared from Miguel to Sampson. She almost looked panicked and Anna laughed.

"Our business is completed, Miguel. As far as the ride goes, that is up to Flory."

Tillie stood. "Flory, let's ride to town with those young men who are eating in the kitchen. They have been waiting some time. And I don't think you need to go riding today with Miguel. By the time we get back to town, it will be time to start supper. Of course, Miguel may ride with us if he wishes."

Miguel and Sampson followed Flory out the door.

Tillie winked at Anna. "Let's let her stew a little in her own juice," she whispered. "Miguel will never give up and Sampson knows she is going back on the train with him. Oh, what a fun ride this will be!"

Anna had to cover her mouth to keep from laughing, and for once, Flory seemed a little nervous over all the attention she was getting.

CHAPTER 94

Anna's Vaquero

ANGEL PUT HIS ARM AROUND ANNA AND WHISPERED to her as the surrey pulled away. "Even when you were small, you dreamed of me. Sí, I think my Anna has wished for me for many years."

Anna's sob caught in her throat. It turned to a laugh as she looked at Angel.

"Our father would have liked you. He would have given you permission to ask for my hand."

Anna turned to face Angel with a smile.

"Father was right. I always liked the way vaquero felt on my tongue when I said it. I just didn't know that I would fall in love with a real vaquero."

"Sí, and a handsome one as well. Come with me into the house. I think perhaps this conversation must be discussed in more detail. Perhaps with a little kissing. Maybe we will even see what a real vaquero feels like on your —"

"Shush, Angel! Someone will hear you!"

"No one is around to hear us, Anna. I can even howl like a wolf if you want. A call from a wolf to his mate. We spoke of that once before, that time when you showed me your legs."

"Angel! You are so bold!"

A low wolf howl sounded from inside the house followed by a woman's soft laugh. Then the little house was quiet and still in the winter evening.

Made in United States
Troutdale, OR
09/03/2023

12597039R00268